GHOST SHADOW

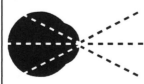 This Large Print Book carries the
Seal of Approval of N.A.V.H.

GHOST SHADOW

HEATHER GRAHAM

THORNDIKE PRESS
A part of Gale, Cengage Learning

Detroit • New York • San Francisco • New Haven, Conn • Waterville, Maine • London

GALE
CENGAGE Learning˚

Copyright © 2010 by Heather Graham Pozzessere.
The Bone Island Trilogy #1.
Thorndike Press, a part of Gale, Cengage Learning.

Thorndike Press® Large Print Basic.
The text of this Large Print edition is unabridged.
Other aspects of the book may vary from the original edition.
Set in 16 pt. Plantin.

LIBRARY OF CONGRESS CATALOGING-IN-PUBLICATION DATA

Graham, Heather.
  Ghost shadow / by Heather Graham.
    p. cm. — (Bone Island trilogy ; 1)
  Originally published: New York : Mira, 2010.
  ISBN-13: 978-1-4104-2765-6
  ISBN-10: 1-4104-2765-X
  1. Murder—Investigation—Fiction. 2. Large type books. I. Title.
PS3557.R198G45 2010
813'.54—dc22   2010017407

Published in 2010 by arrangement with Harlequin Books S. A.

Printed in the United States of America
1 2 3 4 5 6 7 14 13 12 11 10

With lots of love and thanks
to Jen Boise and "my cousin" Walt
Graham, Steve, Toni, Mike, and Lili

And for Boogie Man George
and Brian Penderleith

Bernie and Petey

Titanic Brewery, Waxy O'Connor's,
Red Koi, John Martin's, Mr. Moe's,
Sgt. Pepper's, and especially,
Jada Cole's

Two Friends Patio and Ric's

And the wonderful, crazy, historic,
wild, wicked, and sweet city of
Key West, Florida

KEY WEST HISTORY TIMELINE

1513–Ponce de León is thought to be the first European to discover Florida for Spain. His sailors, watching as they pass the southern islands (the Keys), decide that the mangrove roots look like tortured souls, and call them "Los Martires," the Martyrs.

Circa 1600–Key West begins to appear on European maps and charts. The first explorers came upon the bones of deceased native tribes, and thus the island was called the Island of Bones, or Cayo Hueso.

The Golden Age of Piracy begins as New World ships carry vast treasures through dangerous waters.

1763–The Treaty of Paris gives Florida and Key West to the British and gives Cuba to the Spanish. The Spanish and Native Americans are forced to leave the Keys and move to Havana. The Spanish, however, claim that the Keys are not part of mainland Florida and are really North Havana. The English say the Keys are a part of Florida. In reality, the dispute is merely a war of words. Hardy souls of many nationalities fish, cut timber, hunt turtles — and avoid pirates — with little restraint from any government.

1783–The Treaty of Versailles ends the American Revolution and returns Florida to Spain.

1815–Spain deeds the island of Key West to a loyal Spaniard, Juan Pablo Salas of St. Augustine, Florida.

1819–1822–Florida ceded to the United States. Pablo Salas sells the island to John Simonton, for $2,000. Simonton divides the island into four parts, three going to businessmen Whitehead, Fleming and Greene. Cayo Hueso becomes more generally known as Key West.

1822–Simonton convinces the U.S. Navy to come to Key West — the deepwater harbor, which had kept pirates, wreckers and others busy while the land was scarcely developed, would be an incredible asset to the United

States. Lieutenant Matthew C. Perry arrives to assess the situation. Perry reports favorably on the strategic military importance, but warns the government that the area is filled with unsavory characters — such as pirates.

1823–Captain David Porter is appointed commodore of the West Indies Anti-Pirate Squadron. He takes over ruthlessly, basically putting Key West under martial law. People do not like him. However, starting in 1823, he does begin to put a halt to piracy in the area.

The United States of America is in full control of Key West, part of the U.S. Territory of Florida, and colonizing begins in earnest by Americans, though, as always, those Americans come from many places.

Circa 1828–Wrecking becomes an important service in Key West, and much of the island becomes involved in the activity. It's such big business that over the next twenty years, the island becomes one of the richest areas per capita in the United States. In the minds of some, a new kind of piracy has replaced the old. Although wrecking and salvage were licensed and legal, many a ship was lured to its doom by less than scrupulous businessmen.

1845–Florida becomes a state. Construction begins on a fort to protect Key West.

1846–Construction is begun on Fort Jefferson in the Dry Tortugas.

1850–The fort on the island of Key West is named after President Zachary Taylor.

New lighthouses bring about the end of the golden age of wrecking.

1861–January 10, Florida secedes from the Union. Fort Zachary Taylor is staunchly held in Union hands and helps defeat the Confederate Navy and control the movement of blockade-runners during the war. Key West remains a divided city throughout the Great Conflict. Construction is begun on the East and West Martello Towers, which will serve as supply depots. The salt ponds of Key West supply both sides.

1865–The War of Northern Aggression comes to an end with the surrender of Lee at Appomattox Courthouse. Salvage of blockade-runners comes to an end.

1865–Dr. Samuel Mudd, deemed guilty of

conspiracy for setting John Booth's broken leg after Lincoln's assassination, is incarcerated at Fort Jefferson, the Dry Tortugas.

As salt and salvage industries come to an end, cigar-making becomes a major business. The Keys are filled with Cuban cigar makers following Cuba's war of independence, but the cigar makers eventually move to Ybor City. Sponging is also big business for a period, but the sponge divers head for waters near Tampa as disease riddles Key West's beds and the remote location makes industry difficult.

1890–The building that will become known as "the little White House" is built for use as an officer's quarters at the naval station. President Truman will spend at least 175 days here, and it will also be visited by Eisenhower, Kennedy and many other dignitaries.

1898–The USS *Maine* explodes in Havana Harbor, precipitating the Spanish-American War. Her loss is heavily felt in Key West, as she had been sent from Key West to Havana.

Circa 1900–Robert Eugene Otto is born. At the age of four, he receives the doll he will call Robert, and a legend is born, as well.

11

1912–Henry Flagler brings the Overseas Railroad to Key West, connecting the islands to the mainland for the first time.

1917–April 6, the United States enters World War I. Key West maintains a military presence.

1919–The Treaty of Versailles ends World War I.

1920s–Prohibition gives Key West a new industry — bootlegging.

1927–Pan American Airways is founded in Key West to fly visitors back and forth to Havana.

Carl Tanzler, Count von Cosel, arrives in Key West and takes a job at the Marine Hospital as a radiologist.

1928–Ernest Hemingway comes to Key West. It's rumored that while waiting for a roadster, he writes *A Farewell to Arms.*

1931–Hemingway and his wife, Pauline, are gifted with the house on Whitehead Street. Polydactyl cats descend from his pet Snowball.

Death of Elena Milagro de Hoyos.

1933–Count von Cosel removes Elena's body from the cemetery.

1935–The Labor Day Hurricane wipes out the Overseas Railroad and kills hundreds of people. The railroad will not be rebuilt. The Great Depression comes to Key West as well, and the island, once the richest in the country, struggles with severe unemployment.

1938–An Overseas Highway is completed, U.S. 1, connecting Key West and the Keys to the mainland.

1940–Hemingway and Pauline divorce; Key West loses her great writer, except as a visitor.

1940–Tanzler is found living with Elena's corpse. Her second viewing at the Dean-Lopez Funeral Home draws thousands of visitors.

1941–December 7, "A date that will live in infamy," occurs, and the United States enters World War II.

Tennessee Williams first comes to Key West.

1945–World War II ends with the Armistice of August 14 (Europe) and the surrender of Japan, September 2.

Key West struggles to regain a livable economy.

1947–It is believed that Tennessee Williams wrote his first draft of *A Streetcar Named Desire* while staying at La Concha Hotel on Duval Street.

1962–The Cuban Missile Crisis occurs. President John F. Kennedy warns the United States that Cuba is only ninety miles away.

1979–The first Fantasy Fest is celebrated.

1980–The Mariel Boatlift brings tens of thousands of Cuban refugees to Key West.

1982–The Conch Republic is born. In an effort to control illegal immigration and drugs, the United States sets up a blockade in Florida City, at the northern end of U.S. 1. Traffic is at a stop for seventeen miles, and the mayor of Key West retaliates on April 23, seceding from the U.S. Key West Mayor Dennis Wardlow secedes, declares war, surrenders and demands foreign aid. As the U.S. has never responded, under international law, the Conch Republic still exists. Its foreign policy is stated as, "The Mitigation of World Tension through the Exercise of Humor." Even though the U.S. never officially recognizes the action, it has the desired effect; the paralyzing blockade is lifted.

1985–Jimmy Buffett opens his first Margaritaville restaurant in Key West.

Fort Zachary Taylor becomes a Florida State Park (and a wonderful place for reenactments, picnics and beach-bumming).

Treasure hunter Mel Fisher at long last finds the *Atocha*.

1999–First Pirates in Paradise is celebrated.

2000 to present–Key West remains a unique paradise itself, garish, loud, charming, filled with history, water sports, family activities and down-and-dirty bars. "The Gibraltar of the East," she offers diving, shipwrecks and the spirit of adventure that makes her a fabulous destination, for a day, or forever.

PROLOGUE

Then

The blue light made the hallway dark and eerie, though just beyond the doors of the museum, the magic sunlight of the island glowed upon tourists and the few locals who considered early morning to be a time before noon. Traces of fog, designed for effect in the museum, lingered and created an atmosphere that was ghostly and suspenseful.

"Blood and gory guts! Murder, most foul!"

The teasing cry came from a man in the group of fifteen. He was dressed as a tourist, in shorts, T-shirt and baseball cap. His nose still bore traces of white zinc and, as typical of most tourists, he was sporting a sunburn that would soon hurt.

"No, death most absurd," David Beckett corrected. He had to admit — he loved filling in as a tour guide, and had been glad to

17

give Danny Zigler, the weekend tour host, time off.

"Ooh," murmured one of the teenaged girls.

David heard a small, aborted laugh. It came from Pete Dryer, Key West policeman, who happened to be on the tour with his sister, brother-in-law, niece and nephew, family down from Fort Lauderdale for a few weeks during summer break.

"This is going to be dramatic, folks," Pete teased.

"Our next exhibit is definitely one of our most bizarre stories — even in a place where the bizarre is quite customary," David said.

They had been moving at a steady but relaxed pace through the exhibits. The museum was a family business, and covered all of the colorful history of Florida's Key West. Each major event was shown in an incredibly detailed and authentic tableau. The tableaux were not wax. Once upon a time, the place had been a small wax museum, but David's grandfather, something of a mechanical and electrical genius, had avoided the constant loss of wax figurines when the heat soared in Key West, when storms came through, when air-conditioning ceased to work. The figures in the exhibit were brilliant mechanical masterpieces.

18

The group was heading to David's favorite historical exhibit. He grinned and said as an introduction, "A story of true love to some — true evil and wickedness to others."

A few of the young women in the crowd of tourists smiled, as well. David played the part of host well, he thought, and had the right appearance for it. He was tall, dark-haired and in damned decent shape at the moment, thanks to the navy. He wore a top hat and Victorian cape, though why that was the uniform, he wasn't sure. Many of the women and girls in the crowd were nervous — museums with tableaux often made people nervous, and many of the figures here were so realistic that it did seem they might come to life. David was enjoying himself. It was good to be home, and good to be dealing with the family business for a stint, giving employees time off here and there, even if he wouldn't be staying for long right now. Finished with the military, he was headed to the University of Florida — a bit old for a freshman, but he'd be going on the "uncle" he'd so recently served, Uncle Sam.

The blonde in the Hog's Breath Saloon T-shirt and short-shorts was really cute, he thought.

He felt a moment's guilt; he wasn't accustomed to feeling free to flirt when he met a lovely young woman. He'd been engaged. He'd had a fiancée he loved, that is until he'd returned home to find out that Tanya had decided that she was moving north with a football player who'd come down to Key West from Ohio State.

It hurt. It still hurt. But his time in the military had driven them apart. They had dated all through high school. It had seemed like real love. But it hadn't been. Not on Tanya's part, at least.

But he had been gone often, and for long periods, and maybe it was just natural that she had moved on. Now, he needed to do the same.

He stopped just before his favorite tableau and said, "Carl Tanzler was born in Dresden, Germany, and came to the United States via a circuitous route that took him to Cuba, Zephyrhills, Florida, and finally down to Key West. Here he worked as an X-ray technician at the U.S. Marine Hospital, while, for some reason, his wife remained in Zephyrhills with his family. Now, when he was young, so the story goes, he had visions, and his grandmother encouraged those visions. One was a beautiful dark-haired woman who would prove to be his true love."

"Typical — his true love wasn't his wife," the blonde woman said. David thought one of the college girls with her group had called her Genevieve. She looked like a Genevieve. Really pretty face, beautiful eyes.

"It wasn't his wife?" Pete's sister, Sally, said. "His true love wasn't his wife?"

Her husband, Gerry, laughed and gave her a hug.

"Nope, not his wife," David agreed. "One day, into the hospital walked a stunning young Cuban woman named Elena de Hoyos. Sadly, the young woman suffered from tuberculosis. Carl — who called himself Count von Cosel — fell instantly in love with her. Problems abounded. He had his wife, and Elena was married, as well. Ah, but that particular problem was quickly solved, because her husband left her as soon as the diagnosis was made. Carl swore to her and her family that he could cure her. At the time, though, there was nothing at all that he could do, even though he ingratiated himself to the family and was a constant guest in their home with his cures. When Elena died on October twenty-fifth in nineteen thirty-one, he offered to build her a beautiful mausoleum, which he did, and he visited it night after night, playing

21

music for her, speaking to her in her grave, giving her gifts."

"That's sad and tragic," an older woman offered. She had zinc on her nose, too. She seemed to be the wife of the fellow with the sunburn. Her shade almost matched his.

"Yes, well, one day, he quit visiting. Now, folks, this is Key West, Florida. For the next several years, Carl Tanzler, Count von Cosel, spent his days buying perfume, mortician's wax, wire and women's lingerie and clothing, and no one really seemed to notice. Then one day, Nana, Elena's sister, heard rumors that Tanzler was sleeping with her sister's corpse. She accosted Tanzler, and he was soon arrested. Now, legend has it that Nana let him have three days with the body before the police came in to take him, but I'm not sure I believe that bend in the story. Tanzler was taken into custody. He was examined by psychiatrists. Just to prove the rest of the country can be as crazy as folks in Key West, the story became romanticized in papers across America. Eventually, Tanzler was released — the statute of limitations for disturbing a grave had run out. An autopsy suggested that the man had been practicing necrophilia for years. Tanzler's own memoirs speak of his love for Elena and his belief that they would

22

fly to the stars together as man and wife, since he had married her in a secret and private ceremony. Elena was given a second viewing at the Dean-Lopez Funeral Home. Maybe five or six hundred people attended her first, thousands attended her second. Our next display is one that recalls the famous story of true love — Carl Tanzler stands by the bedside of his bride."

With those words, David strode into the next room, his arm sweeping out dramatically.

He frowned, startled by the sudden silence.

Then the blonde screamed. It was a tragic and horrible scream, and he was destined to hear that sound over and over again in the years to come.

David turned.

The robotic recreation of Carl Tanzler stood just as usual, a small, thin-faced man with a balding head at the rear of the bed, bending over Elena Milagro de Hoyos.

But the body on the bed was not Elena's.

He didn't scream. He felt as if ice washed over him and permeated him, blood and bone.

A woman lay on the bed.

But it was not the model of Elena!

She wasn't dark; she was blonde. Her hair,

long and lustrous, fell over the pillow and curled down the side of the bed. Her eyes, blue and open, stared at the ceiling in frozen horror. She was wearing a sundress, and while stretched out in a natural pose, she might have been getting her beauty sleep had it not been for her eyes, staring sightlessly in terror.

David felt his knees buckle. Only the ice in his veins kept him standing.

Blood and guts! Murder most foul!

There was no blood. But it was murder. Despite the pristine beauty of her body as she lay, dark gray bruises were apparent around her neck.

It was murder. The murder of a beautiful young woman.

Not a stranger. Not just any woman.

It was Tanya, his ex-fiancée.

1

Now

"Personally, I think you've taken on way too much," Clarinda said, voicing her opinion in a loud whisper next to Katie's ear. She had to come down to Katie's ear to be heard so close to the sound system. A drunken frat boy from Omaha was in the midst of a soulful Alice Cooper song, the bar was full and the noise level was high.

Katie shrugged and grinned, looking up at her friend. Maybe she was taking on too much, but an opportunity had come up, and she hadn't been able to resist.

"It will be wonderful, it will work out — and it will be good for Key West," Katie said in return.

Clarinda arched a doubtful brow, set down a glass of water with lime on the small table at Katie's side and shook her head. "I'll help you, of course," she said. "And, you know, Danny Zigler will be delighted to come and work for you. He was heartbroken when the place shut down years ago. People say that it's haunted, of course. You know that, right?"

"So I've heard," Katie said.

"Sweetie, can we get another round over here?" a man shouted above the din.

"Just don't call me sweetie," Clarinda said, exhaling a sigh of exasperation. "What is this tonight? We usually get the locals who actually know how to hold their liquor."

"Gee. We're in Key West and we've been discovered by tourists. Go figure," Katie said.

"Yeah, well, I wish I were the karaoke hostess and not the waitress," Clarinda said.

"Hey, I've told you that you can work for me —"

"And when the place is slow and the hostess is supposed to sing, I assure you that I'll clean out not just the bar, but the entire street. No — eventually, I'll make my fortune doing caricatures on Mallory Square, but until that day, I'll be your support by helping drunks get drunker and therefore hand out big tips. Okay, that helps both of us."

"Sweetie!" the man called again. "Another round!"

"He's going to get the round on top of his

head," Clarinda promised and strode toward the bar.

The Alice Cooper tune was winding down. Next up was a fellow who wanted to do Sinatra. Katie applauded both the man returning to his seat and the one walking up to the microphone.

Stumbling up to the microphone. What was it with tonight? It was true — the strange and totally inebriated seemed to be coming out of the woodwork. Well, it was Key West. Home to some, but mainly a tourist town where the primary activity was drinking too much.

Key West has much more to offer, she thought, defending her native territory. The fishing was excellent, diving was spectacular and many visitors came for the water sports. But it was true as well that young and old flocked from far and wide to Jimmy Buffett's Margaritaville for the sheer pleasure of a bachelor party, or just wild nights along Duval. Duval was the hub of nightlife, and it was the main place for cheap hotel rooms.

Her place — or her uncle Jamie's place, O'Hara's, where she ran Katie-oke — was off the southern end of Duval while most of the more popular watering holes were at the northern end. She did tend to draw a lot of the locals. Many of the entertainers who worked at the festivals — Fantasy Fest, Pirates in Paradise, art fests, music fests, Hemingway Days and more — came in to practice their newest songs with Katie. She operated Katie-oke four nights a week. She also worked at O'Hara's when she wasn't doing karaoke, helping set the sound and stage for performers working on their own music, or doing easy acoustic and vocal numbers on Monday and Tuesday nights.

She had received a degree from Juilliard and taken work with a prestigious theater company in New England, and she had loved New England, but it hadn't been home. She'd eventually discovered that she couldn't take snow and sleet, and wanted to make her living in Key West.

She realized that she was good at the heat, good at sweating. She just never learned to layer properly.

And the water! How she missed the water when she was away. Her own home, a small Victorian — one of more than three thousand houses in the area on the state's historic roster — wasn't on the water, but on Elizabeth Street. She was in Old Town, and surrounded by tourism. She got her fill of water, however, because one of her best friends, an old high-school mate, Jonas Weston, now dating Clarinda, owned and operated the Salvage Inn, a place on the Gulf side with its own little stretch of man-made beach. She was welcome there, whenever she wanted to go.

"Those fellows are being quite obnoxious. Want me to take one of them out?"

Katie heard the question, but she didn't even look over at the speaker. Bartholomew knew that he irritated her when he decided to converse in the company of others.

Unaware of Bartholomew casually and handsomely draped upon a bar stool near Katie, Marty Jenkins, local pirate entertainer, came to her side. "Will you play a sea-shanty disc for me, Katie?"

"Of course, Marty," she said.

He handed her his disc and she slid it into her system. "No words can come up on the screen, Marty. But you don't need them, right?"

He grinned. "Gearing up for the next pirate show, my sweet. No words needed. Thanks."

"I'm sure everyone will love it, Marty."

"Hey, I heard you bought the old wax museum, Katie," Marty said.

"Marty, it's not a wax museum. It's full of robotics."

"Isn't that supposed to mean that they all move?" Marty asked.

"I believe that they all can move. They're just not operating right now."

"Actually, none of them work, from what I understand." Marty wagged a finger at her. "That place has been closed down for five years now. Craig Beckett tried to keep it going after that girl's body was found, but he threw in the towel. If you can get your money back, young lady, you ought to do it."

"I want to open it, Marty. I loved the place when I was a little kid," she told him.

He shook his head. "They say it's haunted, and not haunted by good. You know what happened there. Murder!"

"It was very sad, and a long time ago, Marty. What happened was tragic — some idiot making use of someone else's dream for a dramatic effect, but it's all in the past now. I'll be all right, Marty."

"They never caught the killer, missy," he reminded her.

"And I'm thinking that the killer moved on, Marty. Nothing like it has happened again."

Still shaking his head, Marty left her.

"I think he must be right. It doesn't sound like a good place to be," Bartholomew informed her, leaning near and whispering, though why he whispered, she didn't know.

30

"Hey! That man is still behaving in a rude and disrespectful way toward Clarinda. Should I do something about it?"

Katie grated her teeth and looked toward the bar and the revenant of the man who stood next to her. She was sure that to the rest of the people present, there was nothing to be seen.

Or heard.

She lowered her head and spoke in an intense whisper. "Bartholomew, if you wish to maintain a mortal friend, I entreat you to cease and desist — shut up! You make me appear unbalanced, talking to myself all the time."

"That chap is an utter ass," Bartholomew protested. "Oh, and there *she* goes again, out on the street."

Katie looked up. She couldn't help herself.

It was true. A woman in white was walking along the sidewalk, staring straight ahead. She was in a Victorian white dress, and she knotted a handkerchief in her hands. She looked so sad that Katie felt a pang in her heart, and she bit her lower lip to remind herself that it was a curse seeing ghosts, that she couldn't become involved with all of them — there were simply too many in Key West — and that the woman was long dead and needed only to discover

31

some kind of inner peace to move on.

"She haunts me so," Bartholomew said. He grimaced. "No pun intended."

Katie looked around as Bartholomew chuckled. His long-dead state did not seem to dampen his good spirits. He'd been an adventurer in life — and a *privateer,* not a pirate! — and his sense of curiosity and longing for new experiences had not deserted him in death. He stared at Katie. "You really don't know who she is? And she won't talk to you?"

"She never has," Katie said.

"Watch it," Bartholomew warned.

She realized Clarinda was staring at her with concern in her eyes.

Katie knew that thus far in her life, only she seemed to be blessed by Bartholomew's presence.

He was quite the dandy. His shoes were buckled and bore heels, his hose didn't display a single knot and his breeches were impeccable. He wore a ruffled shirt, red vest and black jacket. His hair was jet-black and neatly queued beneath his tricornered hat. She knew he was especially fond of the Pirates in Paradise festival himself, and he insisted that they spend their time watching the musicians and joining in with the festivities because he loved to comment on the modern-day pirates roaming Key West.

"Are you all right?" Clarinda asked, coming back up to Katie's equipment stand and sidling around to stand next to her chair. "You're talking to yourself again," she warned. "One of the fellows over there wanted to buy you a drink. He thought you were already well on the way."

Katie looked over to the group where her would-be admirer was sitting. She frowned, recognizing the man, but not knowing why. "I don't want a drink — thank him for me. I was singing under my breath to the song, that's all. Clarinda, who is that guy?"

Clarinda turned and waved a hand. The fellow shrugged. He had tawny-blond hair, a neatly trimmed beard and mustache, and appeared to be in his midthirties. He was so familiar, and not anyone she saw on a daily basis.

"He does look — like we should know him, huh?"

"But I don't think he's a local," Katie said.

"Maybe he's on the news — or a fishing show, or something like that," Clarinda suggested.

"Well, let's not make enemies. Tell him thanks for me but no thanks, and that I don't drink when I work. I was just humming and halfway singing along with the music," Katie said.

"Of course. And don't worry. I already told him that you didn't drink while you were working. He said all karaoke hosts drank. I said you didn't."

"Thanks. Just be pleasant to him. I can always take care of myself, honestly," Katie assured her.

"Indeed! Because I'm at your side," Bartholomew said. "And I can take my cutlass to any rat bastard's throat."

Katie glared at him.

"All right, all right, so I can't master a sword anymore. I can trip the bastard," Bartholomew assured her. "I'm quite an accomplished trip artist for a ghost, if I do say so myself."

"Lovely," Katie said.

"What's lovely?" Clarinda asked.

"That it's finally near closing time. Marty is about to come up. Oh, and it's thinning out, so . . . ah! I know what we'll do."

"Katie, I do not sing —"

"It will be fine," Katie assured her. As she walked back to check on the state of her customers, Katie turned to Bartholomew. "Hush until I'm done here tonight, do you hear me? What fun will you have if they lock me up for insanity?"

"Here? In modern-day Key West? Oh,

posh. I've yet to see an even semisane person living in or visiting the place," Bartholomew protested.

"Shut up now, and I mean it!" Katie warned.

Of course, what she could possibly do to him — how to really threaten a ghost — she didn't know herself. She'd been plagued for years and years by . . . whatever it was that allowed her to see those who had "crossed the veil into the light," as many seemed to term it.

Bartholomew sniffed indignantly and went to lean against the bar, his sense of humor returning as he crossed his arms over his chest and indulged in eavesdropping on everyone around him.

Soon after, Marty went up to do his new song, the crowd, a mix of locals and tourists, went wild and he invited everyone down for Fantasy Fest. Someone asked him about Fantasy Fest and Marty explained that it was kind of like Mardi Gras — a king and queen were elected — and kind of like Halloween, and kind of like the biggest, wildest party anyone could think of. Costumes, parties and special events all around the city. There was a parade with dressed up pets — and *un*dressed people in body paint. It was fabulous, a feast and pure fantasy for the heart and the imagination.

He was proud of himself for his explanation. The next person asked about Pirates in Paradise, and Marty looked troubled. After thinking he said that it was kind of like Fantasy Fest but not — there were pirate parties, pirate encampments, historical demonstrations — and heck, a lot of swaggering and grog drinking, but people were welcome to wear costumes. They could see a mock trial of Anne Bonny, they could learn so much — and run around, saying *arrgh, avast* and *ahoy* all day if they liked.

When the crowd finally began to thin around 3:00 a.m., Katie and Clarinda did a song together from *Jekyll and Hyde,* despite Clarinda's objections. Her friend had a lovely, strong voice but didn't believe it; she would only go up late at night and when it was fairly quiet, and only with Katie.

The bar didn't close up until 4:00 a.m., but Katie ended her karaoke at three, giving folks time to finish up and pay their bar tabs. After she had secured her equipment for the night — she only had to see that the karaoke computer and all her amps were covered and that her good microphones were locked away — she was ready to head home and to sleep. Clarinda stopped her at the door. "Hey, Jonas is coming by for me in an hour or so. We'll walk you home. Hang around."

Katie shook her head. "I'm fine, honestly. I grew up here, remember? I know how to avoid drunks and —"

"We actually get gangs down here now, you know," Clarinda said firmly.

"I'm going straight home. I'll take Simonton, I won't walk on Duval. I'll be fine."

Clarinda remained unhappy, but Katie had no intention of being swayed. Her uncle was up in St. Augustine, and Jon Merrillo was managing the bar, so she intended to slip out without being stopped by anyone. On Saturday, she would officially take ownership of the Beckett family's myth-and-legends museum, and she was tense and wanted to be anywhere but at work. "You watch yourself with those drunks!" she warned.

"Oh, honey, if there's one thing I learned while you were away at school, it's how to handle drunks. Oh, wait! We both knew how to manage that before you left. Go. I'll be fine. And Jonas will be here soon."

Waving and clutching her carryall, Katie left the bar.

At 3:00 a.m., Duval Street was far from closed down. She wondered with a quirk of humor what DuVal — the first governor of territorial Florida — would have thought of the street named in his honor.

Certainly, it kept the name from being forgotten.

Key West was filled with history that shouldn't be forgotten. The name itself was a bastardization of Cayo Hueso, Island of Bones, and came from the fact that *hueso* had sounded like *west* to the English-speaking British who had claimed the state from the Spaniards. The name fit because it was the most western of the Islands of the Martyrs, which was what the chain of Florida "keys" had been known as to the Spanish. Actually, the Islands of the Dry Tortugas were farther west, but the name had been given, and it had stuck. Street names came from the early Americans — Simonton and his friends, colleagues and their families. Simonton had purchased Key West from a Spaniard named Salas when Florida had become an American territory. Salas had received the island as a gift — or back payment for a debt — from the Spanish governor who had ruled before the American governor. The island had seen British rule as well, and often, no matter who ruled, it wasn't ruled much at all.

The place was colorful, throughout history, and now.

"You do love this place," Bartholomew noted as he walked alongside her.

She shrugged. "It's home. If you're used to the beautiful fall colors in Massachusetts, that's home. Down here, it's the water, and the craziness. Yes, I do love it."

She stopped walking and stared across Simonton, frowning.

"What?" Bartholomew asked her. "I see nothing. Not even the beauty in white who frets so night after night."

"Lights."

"Lights? They're everywhere, and trust me, I can remember when they weren't," Bartholomew told her.

"No! There are lights on in the entry at the old Beckett museum. *My* museum."

"You don't officially own it until Saturday, or so you said."

"Right, I have a meeting at the bank on Saturday — Liam is going to come and help me — and I sign the final papers, but . . ."

There shouldn't have been anyone in the museum. Craig Beckett had passed away at eighty-eight almost a year ago, a dear man, one who might have lived forever. His health had been excellent. But his life had existed around a true love affair. When Leandra, his wife of sixty-plus years had passed away, he had never quite recovered. He hadn't taken a pistol to his head or an overdose of prescription medication, he had simply lost his love for life. Liam Beckett, a friend of Katie's since she had come back — they hadn't been friends before, since Liam had graduated high school before she had started — had been the assumed executor of the estate, and he'd planned to tear the museum down rather than invest in repairing it. The place hadn't been open in years; Katie had loved it as a child, and she had long dreamed of reopening it. She had talked Liam into agreeing. David Beckett, Liam's cousin and coexecutor of the estate, hadn't actually corresponded about the matter yet. He'd been working in Africa, Asia, Australia or somewhere far away for the past few years, and Liam was convinced that David wouldn't care one way or another what happened to the place. It was unlikely he would remain in the Keys if he actually returned at all. Since David had left, almost ten years ago, he had never wanted to come home.

His former fiancée, the great love of his life at the time, even though she had left him, had been murdered. Strangled. She was left there, in the family museum, posed in position as the legendary Elena Milagro

40

de Hoyos.

He'd been under suspicion. He'd had an alibi — his grandparents. That alibi had made some people suspicious. After all, what would his grandparents say? But he hadn't run; he had waited through the beginning of the investigation, he had stayed in town until the case had gone cold and then he had left, never to return.

Katie knew that some people thought that he should have been further investigated. She remembered him, but just vaguely. He'd been a big high-school sports star down here. Sean, her brother, had also loved sports. He was older and knew David Beckett better.

Curious, Katie crossed the street. It was quiet; street-lamps illuminated the road itself, but here on Simonton the revelry taking place still on Duval was muted and seemed far away. She stared up at the building that housed the Beckett family museum.

Originally, she knew, it hadn't been chosen for any historical reason. The house was built in the late eighteen-fifties by Perry Shane. Shane had deserted it to fight for the Federals back in his native New Jersey. For years afterward, the house had just been one of many old places that needed work. The Beckett family had purchased it in the twenties because it had been cheap, a seventy-year-old fixer-upper. Now it was one of the grand dames of the street, mid-Victorian, boasting wraparound porches on both the first and second floors, and around the attic garret, a widow's walk. Kate didn't think anyone had ever really been able to see the water and incoming ships from the walk, but it had been a fashionable addition to the house at the time it had been built.

Once, it had offered six bedrooms on the second floor and two in the attic. Down-stairs had been the parlor, library, dining room, office and pantry. The kitchen had been out back about twenty feet away. There was also a carriage house. Now, when you entered through the front door, the gate and turnstiles were positioned there. The tour began on the second floor and wound around through the rooms, brought visitors down the servants' stairway to the first floor and then around once again, back to the front.

"What are you doing?" Bartholomew demanded, following her.

"I want to know why there's a light on," Katie said.

"Because someone is in there. And you don't own it yet. It could be someone dangerous."

"It could be frat boys on a lark, and I'm getting them out of there before they do damage to the place. Craig Beckett might have closed it down a few years ago, but it still has all of the exhibits in place," Katie said.

"What if it's not a frat boy?" Bartholomew protested. "Katie, don't go in there."

"You're with me. I'll be fine."

"Katie! Awake and see the sunrise, lass! Me — ghost. I love to remember the days when I was strong and tough and could defend a girl with certainty and vigor. If you get into real trouble because the place is being pilfered or plundered by a criminal —"

"Bartholomew, what thief turns on the lights?" Katie demanded.

Bartholomew groaned. "A drunk one? Katie — !"

Bartholomew groaned. Katie had jumped the low white-picket gate that surrounded the place.

"Katie!"

"What?"

"Murder, murder most foul!" Bartholomew cried.

He'd always been fond of quoting and paraphrasing Shakespeare.

"Murderers do not turn the lights on!"

she tossed over her shoulder in return.

"How do you know?" he demanded

She ignored him and walked up the limestone path that led to broad steps to the porch and the door.

She felt him close behind her.

Was she crazy? No! This was about to be her place, and she could speed-dial the police in two seconds. She wasn't going in with lights blazing; she would see what was going on by lurking in the darkness. She knew the place.

At the door she paused. She reached for the knob and as she did so, the door opened, creaking a bit, as if it had been pushed by a sudden wind.

"I did not do that!" Bartholomew whispered.

She shook her head impatiently and stepped in.

The once beautiful hardwood floors did need work, she noticed. Workmen had been in and out through the years, and their boots had done some damage. The gate area still boasted an old-fashioned cash register, but the mahogany desk, where an attendant sold tickets, was beautiful. It had been bought from an auctioneer and had once been the captain's desk in an old sailing ship. The swivel chair behind it was equally old, handsome and still comfortable. Katie

44

was familiar with everything; she had walked through with Liam Beckett just a few days earlier.

The light that she had seen from the street had come from the entry. It was the muted light of the foyer's chandelier, and it cast a gentle glow over the place.

Katie opened her mouth, about to call out, but she didn't. She chose not to twist the turnstile — the noise here would be like an explosion. She sat atop the old mahogany desk and swung her legs around, then stepped to the other side.

Looking up was eerie. Figures of Papa Hemingway and his second wife, Pauline, were posed coming down the stairway. They had always been a big hit at the museum, with eighty percent of those going through the place having their pictures taken with the pair.

"Don't you dare go up those stairs," Bartholomew commanded sternly.

Katie almost smiled, grinning at him. "Bartholomew, you're scared. A ghost can't be scared. My God, Bartholomew. You were a pirate."

"Privateer. My boat was authorized by the government," Bartholomew corrected irritably. "And don't be ridiculous, I'm not frightened. Yes, wait, I am frightened for you, foolish girl. What is the matter with you? I know your family taught you better. Innocent young ladies do not wander into dark alleys."

"This isn't a dark alley."

"No, it's worse. You can get trapped in here."

"I'm not going upstairs," she assured him.

She walked to the side, realizing that she was going in the wrong historical order. She wasn't going up the stairs; she just wanted to see what was going on.

"Katie," Bartholomew warned, following her.

She turned and stared at him. "What? I'm going to be scared silly? I'm going to see ghosts?"

"Ghosts will seldom hurt you. Living people, bad people, criminals, rapists, murderers and thieves — they will hurt you," Bartholomew said sternly.

"Just one more minute . . . We'll check out the downstairs, and I'll call the cops. Or Liam. Liam is a cop. All right? I just don't want to cry wolf."

"What?"

"I don't want to create an alarm when there's no need. Maybe Liam was here earlier and left the light on."

"And the door open?" Bartholomew said

doubtfully.

Katie shrugged.

She walked to the left, where the tour began once visitors reached the first floor. The first room offered one of Key West's most dramatic tales — the doll story. As a little boy, Robert Eugene Otto had been given a very creepy doll, supposedly cursed by an angry family servant who knew something about voodoo. Robert Eugene Otto became obsessed with the doll, even naming it Robert, after himself. Robert the Doll moved about the house and played pranks. In later years he drove the real Robert's wife quite crazy.

From the somewhat psychotic, the history in the museum became sad and grimly real with a memorial to the sailors who had died aboard the battleship *Maine* when it had exploded in Havana Harbor in 1898. The museum's exhibit showed sailors working on the ship. From there, curtains segued into an area where dancers moved about at the Silver Slipper. World War I came and went. Prohibition arrived, and bootleg alcohol made its way in an easy flow from Havana to Key West.

A pathway through the pantry in back led around to the other side of the house. It was dark, with little light from the glow in

47

the foyer seeping through. Papa Hemingway made another appearance as 1931 rolled in and Pauline's uncle bought them the house on Whitehead Street as a wedding present.

Katie knew what she was coming up to — the exhibit on Count von Cosel and Elena de Hoyos. Just a small piece of the museum, really, in a curtained sector through an archway. It had always been a popular exhibit. Until, of course, the re-created figure of poor Elena had been replaced by the strangled body of a young Conch woman. The beginning of the end.

People liked the bizarre, the romance and even the tragedy of history, but with this event fear had suddenly come too close. It was one thing to be eccentric in the Keys.

Real violence was not welcome.

There was more, she thought, so much more, to the museum. It was sad, really, that the story got so much attention.

There was fun history. Sloppy Joe moving his entire bar across the street in the middle of the night, angry over a hike in his rent. Tennessee Williams, working away at La Concha Hotel, penning the words of his play *A Streetcar Named Desire*. Another war, soldiers and sailors, the roadblocks that caused Key West to secede and become, if only for hours, the Conch Republic.

The rest of history paled beside the story of von Cosel and Elena. So it had always been.

Morbid curiosity. Had he really slept with the corpse? Ooh, Lord, disgusting! How?

Katie knew the story, of course. She'd heard it all her life. She'd retold it at college a dozen times, with friends denying the truth of it until they looked it up on the Internet. It was tragic, it was sad, it was sick, but it always drew people.

As it had tonight. She put her hand out to draw back the curtain leading to the exhibit.

"Don't, Katie, don't!" Bartholomew whispered.

She closed her eyes for a moment.

She was suddenly terrified that she would draw back the curtain — and stumble upon a corpse herself.

And yet . . .

She had to draw back the curtain.

She did so, and screamed.

2

David nearly jumped, he was so startled by the sudden scream.

That irritated him. Greatly. He was thirty-two, a veteran of foreign action and a professional who trekked through the wilds and jungles of the world.

He was not supposed to jump at the sound of a silly girl's scream.

Of course, it had been stupid to come here. He had thought that he'd come back just to sign whatever papers he needed to settle his grandfather's estate. But he had come home. And no way out of it — the past had called to him. No matter how far he had gone, he had been haunted by that night. He'd had to come here.

He wasn't sure what he'd expected to find.

There were no fresh corpses in the old museum.

Elena Milagro de Hoyos rested in robotic finery — as sadly as she had, years ago, at the real funeral parlor.

But he could remember the night they had found Tanya. He could remember it as if it had been yesterday.

She hadn't been killed here, she had been brought here. She had been positioned for the shock value. It was something certain killers did. This fellow wanted to enjoy his sadistic exploits and wanted his handiwork to be discovered.

The killer had never been caught. No clues, no profile had ever led anyone anywhere, even when the local police had pulled in the FBI. There hadn't been a fiber, a speck of DNA, not a single skin cell to be analyzed. That meant that the killer had been organized. The Keys had even braced for a wave of such murders, because such killers usually kept killing. But it seemed that Tanya's murder had been a lone incident. Despite the fact that he had been cleared, he had been the only person ever actually under suspicion, no matter how they worded it.

The Keys hadn't been crime-free by any means. Accidents occurred far too frequently because people overimbibed and still thought they'd be fine on the highway — often two-lane only — that led back to the mainland. Crosses along the way warned travelers of places where others had died,

51

and the police could be fierce on speeders, but deaths still happened. Gangs were coming in, just as elsewhere, but they were seldom seen in the usual tourist mainstream on Duval Street. Domestic violence was always a problem, and now and then, as Liam seemed to believe, "outsiders" came into the state to commit their crimes.

But there was nothing like the strangulation death and bizarre display of Tanya Barnard. Not in the decade since David had been gone.

When it had happened, Craig Beckett had tried to hold his head high. He knew, of course, that his grandson was innocent because they had been together during the time it had happened — only a small window of opportunity. The museum had closed late on Friday night because there had been a festival in the city — and Craig Beckett had agreed with his fellows in the business association that his museum should remain open until midnight. David had come in with the first tour just after nine the next morning.

And Tanya's body had been discovered.

David understood that, to many, he might well appear guilty as all hell.

But he had an alibi.

He'd been at the museum the night before, filling in for Danny Zigler then, too. But it was a small museum. It was only open for tours. There had been times between tours, people reckoned, when he might have slipped out. Or, according to others, the coroner might have been wrong. He might have left the museum and gone to quickly kill Tanya before returning home.

Think about it. Just how long did it take for a tall, muscular man to strangle the life out of a small, trusting woman?

Luckily, the coroner wouldn't be called wrong. He insisted on the time of Tanya's death.

And there were enough tourists to swear that David couldn't have gone far in between the tours.

And after? David and his grandfather had stayed up until nearly four, engaged in a chess match. Then they'd even fallen asleep watching a movie in the den; his grandmother had come in to throw blankets over the two of them. By seven in the morning, the family had been engaged in breakfast. David knew many people believed that his grandparents had just been covering for him, but the one thing that gave David strength was the fact that he *had* been with his grandparents, and they did *know* that he was innocent.

Craig had tried to maintain the museum. But when everyone coming in had wanted to know about Tanya and little else about the history of the island, he had given it up at last. He had cared for the place, but he had closed its doors to the public. He had dreamed of the right time to reopen it.

Now his grandfather was gone. They would never reopen the museum. Tomorrow, he'd talk to Liam about selling off the characters. He knew many were made with fine craftsmanship and were valuable. Then work could be done to restore the house, and it would definitely be a valuable commodity.

So what the hell was he doing here himself?

He'd had to come. And he'd found himself staring at the exhibit, wishing he remembered more about Tanya and yet aware that the sight of her on Elena's bed was permanently embedded in his memory. Nothing of the girl herself. Everything about the horror of her death.

And now, this girl, standing there staring at him, her scream just an echo in their minds.

"Who the hell are you and what in hell are you doing here?" he demanded.

The girl flushed. She was an exceptionally

attractive young woman, early to mid-twenties, with deep auburn hair, long and loose down her back, and, even in the muted light, eyes so startlingly hazel they seemed to be gold. Her features were cleanly cut and beautiful, and her body, clad in jeans and a T-shirt that advertised a local bar, was lean and well formed. There was something familiar about her, but he wasn't sure what or why.

She stared at him, obviously recovering herself. Her cheeks were red at first, but then she appeared to be angry, as well.

"Who are you, and what the hell are you doing here?" she demanded in return.

"What?" he snapped.

"You heard me — I asked who you are, and what in hell you're doing here," she said, an edge of real anger in her voice.

He stared at her incredulously.

"Are you drunk?" he demanded.

"No! Are you?"

He walked around from the rear of the exhibit to accost her. She stepped back warily, as if ready to run out of the room.

Good. He was tempted to come closer and shout, "Boo!"

He didn't.

"I'm here because I own the place," he told her. "And you're trespassing. You have about two seconds to get out of here, and then I'm going to call the police."

"You are absolutely full of it," she told him. "I own this place."

Again, he was startled.

"You're wrong," he said harshly, "and I'm tired of the joke. This place is owned by the Beckett family, and it's not for sale — yet."

"Beckett!" she gasped.

"Beckett, yes. The name that you see on the marquis outside. *B-E-C-K-E-T-T.* This museum has been the property of my family for decades. I'm David Beckett. It is four in the morning and I'm wondering what *you* are doing here at this time. I actually belong here — at any hour. *Now,* if you please, get out." He spoke evenly, almost pleasantly. But he meant the *get out.*

It seemed now, after hearing his name, as if the young woman facing him had changed her attitude suddenly. She seemed to back away. *I'm a Beckett. Oh, yeah, David Beckett. Person of interest!* he almost shouted.

It had been ten years since he had left, determined that he wouldn't let the past follow him, not when he was innocent, not when someone else had taken his fiancée's life, long after she had taken leave of him.

"I'm so sorry; I should have known," she said. "Actually, we've met. It was years ago,

56

but I should have known, you do look a lot like Liam. I'm Katie —"

"I don't care who you are," he said, startled by his abrupt rudeness. He shook his head. "Just get out. It's private property."

"You don't understand. I believe that I do own this place. I just have a few last papers to sign on Saturday. Tomorrow. Liam is, after all, Craig's executor — okay, you both are, if I understand it right, and you'd told him to go ahead and act in his absence. Liam was ready to sell."

David frowned.

Sell? Never. Not the museum. The museum needed to be dismantled, taken apart. He wasn't superstitious, he didn't believe in curses. But this place held a miasma. There was something that appeared to be evil in the robotics. The faces were too lifelike. The ones that moved didn't jerk about — they looked like the real thing from a distance.

They invited idiots and drunks and psychotics to behave insanely. Commit murder, and leave the corpses behind, far more fragile than the imitations that might survive many decades.

David shook his head, feeling a twinge less hostile. He still couldn't really figure out who in hell the girl was, but, at least she wasn't a drunken tourist who had stumbled in. A Northerner, probably. Someone who had come to Key West convinced it was not only a sunny Eden, but a place to make a good few bucks off the spending habits of vacationers. But she'd said that they'd met?

"Whatever you might have thought, whatever you might have come to believe, the museum is not and will never be for sale. If it's the house you're interested in, it may come up on the market in a year or so," David said flatly.

She stared at him steadily. Now it seemed that she was the hostile one. "So, you're David Beckett, suddenly home and taking interest in the family — and the family property. How nice. Perhaps you should speak with the lawyers. I believe that the sale has gone through."

"Look, Miss —"

"Katherine O'Hara, and don't be superior with me, because my family has been down here as long as yours — or longer. I hope that you're wrong, and that this sale can go through. I love what your family created. This is a beautiful place, and your grandfather and great-grandfather did such a fabulous job showing history, the simple, true and the bizarre. I don't understand . . ."

Her voice had trailed as she stared at him. She looked nervous suddenly.

58

Was she thinking that no matter what the newspapers or police had said, he might be a murderer? A very sick one at that, setting a corpse into an historical tableau?

After all, she had said that her family had been here forever, and yes, he did know of O'Haras who were longtime residents, but. . . .

"Katie O'Hara?" he said sharply.

"Yes, I just introduced myself," she said with aggravation.

"Sean's little sister?"

"Sean's sister, yes," she said. She left out the "little," her aggravation apparently growing.

"Sean doesn't have any part of this, does he?" His tone was sharper than he had intended.

"My brother is working in the South China Sea right now, filming a documentary, and no, he has nothing to do with this. But I don't see what —"

"Nothing. Look, nothing has anything to do with anything. This place will never be a museum again, and I'm pretty damned sure you just looked at me and remembered why I feel that way."

She inhaled, as if steeling herself to speak patiently. "Something terrible happened. You were cleared. Your grandfather closed

59

the place, but he always wanted to reopen it. We will never rid the world of psychos. I intend to have security, and locks and make sure that nothing so terrible could ever happen again," she assured him.

He leaned back against the wall, arms crossed over his chest, and stared at her incredulously. "And a bunch of frat-boy idiots wouldn't try to put a blonde mannequin in here, ever, or suggest that you do a mock-up tableau of Elena with Tanya's body? Haven't you ever watched those horror movies with parts one, two, three, four, five and so on, where the same stupid people keep going to the same stupid, dark woods to wind up dead? What if the psycho who did it is still hanging in the Keys? What do you think of that kind of temptation?"

"I wouldn't let it happen. All people are not horrible, and it's a wonderful museum. I've worked really long and hard —"

"Right. You must be all of what now, twenty-two, twenty-three?"

"Twenty-four, and that's hardly relevant. I already have my own business —"

"Katie? Katie O'Hara?" He laughed suddenly. "Katie-oke! *That's* your business?"

She stiffened and her face became an ice mask. "For your information, Mr. Beckett, karaoke is big business these days."

"At your uncle's bar, of course."

"You really have matured into a rather insufferable ass, Mr. Beckett," she said, her tone pleasant. "I will leave. I'll see you with my attorneys tomorrow."

"As you choose. Good night, Miss O'Hara. And forgive me. I didn't mean to laugh at Sean's little sister."

She stared at him. "I really don't care, Mr. Beckett. And neither would Sean. We've both worked hard and been responsible, and we make our way quite fine, thank you. And by the way, I never knew you were friends with my brother. Is he aware of the fact?"

He laughed then. He had been an insufferable ass. It was this place. It was the possibility that it might be opened again.

It was him.

He had left here. He never hid his past. People knew about Tanya, about what had happened. But outside of this place, no one assumed that he had done it, that despite his honest and upright alibi, his entire family had lied to save him.

Being back here . . .

"I'm really sorry. I didn't mean to be offensive. To you, Miss O'Hara, and not to anyone's sister, younger or otherwise. However, the place is seriously not for sale. And my reasons are valid. I don't want to see

61

history repeating itself."

"We'll see tomorrow," she said.

She moved away, but then turned back to him. "I should have known you. Recognized you, I mean. Your grandfather talked about you all the time. Craig Beckett was a wonderful man."

He was surprised at how her remark seemed to sting. He had loved his grandfather — he didn't know anyone who hadn't liked and respected his grandfather. And he had seen him often over the years.

Just not in Key West.

"Thank you," he said, lowering his head.

"I'm glad you've managed to make it back now, since you couldn't be here for the funeral."

"If you knew my grandfather, Miss O'Hara, you know that he didn't believe much in funerals — or in massive monuments to the dead, caskets worth thousands and thousands of dollars or any other such thing. Memories exist in the mind, he always told me. And love was something distance could never quell. So I am fine with my memories, and in my conscience."

"I'm happy for you. Personally, I find a funeral a special time to remember and honor a loved one, but to each his own, of course. I'll get out of here, Mr. Beckett. I will see you tomorrow at the bank."

"My pleasure," he said with a shrug.

She was near the door. "I take it you're not planning on staying in town long?"

"No."

She hesitated again. "Then what do you care?" she asked quietly.

He didn't answer.

"I would keep it alive with the dignity it deserves," she told him.

"I apologize for being so rude. You seriously startled me, being here. I really do apologize for any offense given."

She nodded and turned to leave.

He watched her go. Sean's little sister. He and Sean had played high-school football together. She didn't remember, but he had been in her home. She'd sported a head of almost orange-red hair back then, a lot of skinned and bruised knees and freckles that seemed to have faded now. She was definitely a striking young woman. She had unnerved him. He wasn't customarily such an ass, and didn't make light of the endeavors of others.

And yet, seriously . . . *Katie-oke?*

He started. It was suddenly cold — ice-cold — where he stood in the museum. He thought about the many sayings people had, such as, "It was as if a ghost walked right through me." It was as if he had been . . . *shoved* by something very cold. Well, ghosts didn't go around shoving people. Oh, and he didn't believe in ghosts.

He went about turning off the lights and, when he left, he locked the place securely.

"I gave him a good comeuppance," Bartholomew announced. "A strong right hook, right on the fellow's jaw. And I could swear he felt it. All right, all right, so he didn't crash down on the floor in a knockout, but I'd swear he knew he'd been given a licking of one kind or another."

Katie waved a hand in the air, distracted. "I don't believe it. No one thought that he'd even come home. He was supposed to stay off in Africa, Asia or Australia, or wherever it was that he was working. Why? Why? He's got to be wrong on this. Liam was certain that he could go through with the sale, that David despised the place and never intended to come back."

"You're welcome. Yes, I would defend you to the death against such an oaf. Oh, wait. I am dead. And still, my dear, I did my best."

Katie had offended Bartholomew, she realized. "I'm sorry, I'm so sorry, Bartholomew. I'm sure you sprang instantly to my defense, and I deeply appreciate your efforts."

"I will keep trying. As long as that man is in the city, I swear, I will keep trying," Bartholomew promised.

"I don't understand. He doesn't want to be here. He plans on living elsewhere forever and ever," Katie said.

She realized that he was silent then.

"What?" she demanded. "He hasn't been here in ten years, Bartholomew. He doesn't care about the place, and I don't care what he said, he showed no respect, not making it home for his grandfather's funeral."

"I thought they couldn't locate him — since he was off somewhere," Bartholomew said.

"You're standing up for him?" she asked skeptically.

"No, no . . . his behavior to a lady was reprehensible, abominable!" Bartholomew said. "Completely unacceptable. Except . . ."

"Except what?"

Bartholomew looked at her, appeared to take a deep breath and said, "I think, in a way, I understand his feelings."

"I would never let anything horrible like that happen again," Katie protested.

"I don't think they expected it to happen the first time," Bartholomew told her.

"But they weren't aware of what might happen. I'd be way ahead. And please, we don't have murderers crawling through the city, visiting the museums on a daily basis."

"At the least, though, you should understand his feelings. If I know the story right, he was engaged to the girl. And she was found dead, right where you came upon him tonight."

"I don't think they were engaged anymore," Katie said.

"And there the point. Motive for murder."

"So you think that he did it."

"No, actually, I don't think so. But a ruined romance? That's a motive for murder."

"You're watching too much TV," Katie said.

"Hmm. TV. Such an amazing and wonderful invention. So vastly entertaining!" Bartholomew agreed. "But it's true. He was a spurned lover. That's a motive. She was leaving him. For a brute of a game-playing fellow. That is, by any reckoning, definitely a motive for murder."

"He was cleared," Katie said.

"He wasn't arrested or prosecuted. He had an alibi. His alibi, however, was his family."

She turned to him sharply. "I thought you

just said that you didn't think that he murdered her?"

"True. No. No, I don't think he killed her. He was rude, but I know many a fine fellow who can actually be rude. But murder, especially such a crime of passion — he doesn't look the type. He seems to be the type who easily attracts women, and therefore, he might have been heartbroken, but he would have moved on. I mean, that's the way I see it. The man is — appears to be, at least — a man's man. He could completely lose his temper and engage in a rowdy bar fight, maybe, but murder . . . Ah! But then again, what does the type look like? Now, in my day, many a man looked the part of a cutthroat and a thief — because he was one. But these days . . . ah, well. We did come upon him at the scene of the crime."

"It wasn't actually the scene of the crime. She was strangled, but the police believe she was killed elsewhere and brought to the museum. I was a child when it all happened. Well, a teenager, at any rate, and it was a scandal, and I know it disturbed Sean. . . . I vaguely remember that he and David Beckett were . . . friends. They both loved sports, football, swim team, diving, fishing . . . all that. But then David left. And never came back. And the talk died down. Mainly, I believe, because everyone loved Craig Beckett. But if David Beckett is innocent, I really don't understand his position — or yours. And he's deserted Key West. So?"

"I have to admit, I rather admire the fact that he's so determined, especially because he doesn't want to stay here. He doesn't want to see anything like it happen again, whether it affects him or not. I'll still do my best to take him down for you, though!" he vowed.

The streets here were quiet, with only the sound of distant, muted laughter coming to them now and again. Even that was infrequent now. The hour was growing late — or early.

They came to Katie's house. She'd left lights on in the kitchen, parlor area and porch. The two-seater swing on the porch rocked gently in the breeze. She had a small — very small — patch of ground before the steps to the porch, but her hibiscus bushes were in bloom and they made the entry pretty.

Set in stained glass from the Tiffany era on the double doors, a Victorian lady and her gentleman friend sat properly, immortalized in timeless ovals.

Katie unlocked the door and stepped in. Her world was familiar. Her parents were now boating around the world, her brother would always be off filming another documentary and the house was hers. Certainly, her folks had given her a bargain price. But she had purchased it through a bank, she had come up with the down payment and she had never missed a mortgage payment.

She loved the house. She was delighted that she owned it, that she had kept it in the family.

And yet, as she stood there, she wondered about the years David Beckett had spent away. He had gone to exotic places. He had discovered the entire globe.

She'd gone away, too, she reminded herself.

Right . . . all the way up the eastern seaboard!

"Katie?" Bartholomew said.

She looked at him.

"What's the matter now?" he asked.

"Nothing. I just realized that I've made an island my world."

"That's not a bad thing."

"But is it a good thing? Anyway, don't answer. I'm exhausted. I'm going to bed."

"We have to be at the bank bright and early."

She blew him a kiss. "Don't go watching more television, Bartholomew."

"It will stunt my growth? Make me die young?" he asked.

She groaned and walked up the stairs.

He had been restless that night, all through the night.

That was the only reason he had been out walking.

And when he had been walking, he had seen the lights on at the museum.

And so, he had looked up at the old mansion, and he had stared.

There could only be one person who would be there tonight, only one person who would have gone in, turned on the lights. Someone with a right to be there.

Someone who knew it well. Beckett.

Silently, he cursed Beckett. The man shouldn't have come back. The past was the past; settled, over, accepted. Some believed it had been David Beckett, but that he was long gone and despicably above the law. Others believed that a psycho had come and was also long gone. It was over. It was part of the myth and legend of Key West.

He shouldn't have come back.

But he had.

He had seen Katie O'Hara, seen her go in. He'd heard the squeak of her scream, but he hadn't been alarmed. He'd held his ground.

Watched. Waited.

Then, he'd seen her come out, and he'd stepped quickly back into the shadows. He hadn't intended to be seen that night.

Katie had left in what appeared to be a fury.

She'd thought she owned the place. But Beckett was back.

A few minutes later, Beckett had come out, and he'd headed in the same direction but then turned down the street to the Beckett estate.

When Beckett was gone, he'd followed Katie. He knew where she lived. He'd walked, and stood in the shadows, and he'd looked at her house.

He stayed, feeling time go by. No need to be here, staring up at the house in the darkness.

But he stayed, watching.

His fingers itched.

He felt a bizarre fury growing inside of him.

And then he understood.

He felt the sudden temptation to let history repeat itself.

3

There was no meeting at the bank.

Liam called her before eight.

Katie had set her alarm, but it wasn't set to go off for another thirty minutes. She was only a few blocks away from the bank, and she was capable of showering and dressing in less than fifteen minutes — a nice survival technique if you worked nights and wanted to maintain any kind of a daytime existence.

She groaned while she fumbled for her phone. She only kept a cell, but it was sitting on the bedside table and, naturally, she knocked it off as she went to answer it. She had to feel around on the floor to find it and answer it.

It was Liam.

"Liam! I saw your cousin last night. He was in the house. And he said that —"

"Katie, I am so sorry."

"What?"

"He won't sell."

"But — but — I thought you were the executor!"

"Coexecutor."

"But he was having you make decisions!"

"I was acting solely while we all made an attempt to reach David. He was deep in the jungle. When he wrote, he told me to move along as I saw fit. But as you've seen, he's back. Katie, this is all my fault. I thought that David would certainly be pleased to sell. I didn't know how he felt about the museum. I made a dozen decisions and he didn't have a problem with a thing, but . . . Katie . . . I'm sorry."

"But all we needed to do today was sign the last papers," she said with dismay.

"I know. I'm sorry, so very sorry."

"No, no, Liam, I know it's not your fault," she said.

"It is," he said. "I mean, it's not my fault David won't agree to sell, but I led you on. Katie, it's . . . go ahead. Please. Get mad at me."

She laughed. "Okay. I'm mad at you. But your cousin is a jerk and an ass."

Liam was silent. She had forgotten that it was a close-knit family, and she understood because she would defend her brother until the stars ceased to shine.

"Now I'm sorry, Liam," she said.

"No, Katie, no, it's all right. I know how disappointed you are. And I feel just terrible. Honestly. I can still try to persuade him, but I think I'm going to lay off for a while now. Give him some time to realize that you are never going to make a mockery of anything that happened, sensationalize or make profit off the murder. . . ."

"That's what he believes?" she asked, astonished.

"I think it's what he was afraid of at first. I know that he met you last night; he explained it this morning when he said we needed to stop the sale before we wasted everyone's time. Katie, I think he has a phobia that it could happen again."

"So he said," she murmured. "But — every museum down here has an exhibit that's dedicated to Elena and Count von Cosel. It could happen anywhere. How do we make him see that, and make him understand that . . . that what happened . . . Oh, I don't know. Ten years have gone by. The killer is dead, or living in another state, or in prison for another offense. I loved your grandfather, you know that. He fueled the dream in me, Liam. How do we make your cousin see that?"

"I don't know. But for now . . ."

"For now, it's off," she said flatly.

"Yes. Forgive me, please. I am unworthy, but forgive me."

She smiled, running her fingers through the tangle of her hair. She knew that Liam was really sorry, that he had wanted to see the museum opened. "I forgive you. On one condition. As long as he's here, you help me. Quietly. Maybe he'll see that I'm for real, and that . . . Oh, please! Why would the same thing happen again? Tanya was probably a random victim, and if someone had a grudge against the Becketts, well, David doesn't have an ex-fiancée here anymore. You have to help me. We wait. But you are on my side, right?"

"I am. I love the old museum. I just don't want to work it, manage it or maintain it. I thought you were perfect as a buyer. So we'll see, huh?"

He said goodbye and hung up.

David Beckett walked into the police station and was surprised to be hailed by a number of his old classmates and not just his cousin, Liam. They seemed honestly glad to see him, though he would surely be a topic of conversation at their evening meals. He was back.

He greeted old friends warmly, and

thanked those who commented on his camerawork for wildlife publications in the past few years. He was surprised that they knew what he did — still photographers rarely received much of the applause. He told friends who asked that there were safe places to photograph wild animals. You just had to develop a skill for knowing those places. "Just like anything," he said, heading off to find not Liam, but Pete Dryer, the man who had been a fledgling patrolman when he had taken the fateful tour all those years ago.

"David!" Pete was behind a desk now. A lieutenant in the criminal investigation unit, he delved into the streets when serious crime had been committed. Key West had a low murder rate, statistically two persons a year. But Key West was vulnerable to drug runners, and in the past few years, the department had made firm headway against the narcotics invasion. Most of what was really bad in the Keys was related to drugs; big money was at stake, and many of the deaths that had been reported were associated with gangs or drugs.

David had been away, but he'd kept up. Unconsciously, he'd waited to hear about another bizarre murder — or that someone had finally solved what happened to Tanya.

Pete had gained weight. He was stout now, and his blond hair was turning white. He had a smile for David, and a warm embrace, indicating the chair in front of his desk.

David took it.

"Wow. You're really back here," Pete said. "Any chance you're here to stay?"

David shook his head. "No, I'm afraid not. But I haven't accepted any projects for the immediate future, so I'll be around for a while."

"That's great. We're damned glad to have you here, for whatever time you stay. This is your home, you know."

"Yeah, it's my home. I haven't settled anywhere yet. Pete, I don't think I can settle anywhere. You know, my grandfather's death got me thinking about Tanya."

Pete shook his head sadly and looked down. "David, I wish to God I could give you some kind of closure. We pursued everything we could."

"Right. The police pursued me," David said.

"Not fair, David. Your alibi stood up. Craig Beckett was never any kind of a liar, so we all know you were with him —"

"After the museum closed," David said dryly.

"I believe the coroner — and the dozens

77

of people who said you would not have possibly had the time to leave the museum between your tours. We know Tanya wasn't killed at the museum, and we all know too that you just weren't capable of doing that to anyone. Thing is, we just had nowhere to go. I wasn't in charge, but I remember. We went house-to-house. No one saw anyone go in. There wasn't a break-in. There was no clue as to where he strangled that girl. Now, if there had been blood, we might have been able to trace something somewhere —" He paused, staring at David. "Well, hell, now I didn't mean that I wanted that poor girl cut up or tortured, but . . . strangulation. He left no clues."

"Pete, I want you to help me. I want to go back over everything."

Pete stared at him. He groaned. "It was all ten years ago, David."

"Look, Liam is a cop, a detective now — with the criminal investigation unit. Let him have the paperwork. Assign him to the murder as a cold-case file. Pete, give me something," David said. "Hell, I've made a name for myself in the world. I'm moving on fine. But this haunts me still, every damned day of my life, Pete."

David heard a noise behind him. He turned and Liam was there. His cousin was two years his junior, his hair was a lighter shade of brown but his eyes were the same color and he knew that most people realized quickly that they were related. David had never known his parents; they'd died together in an automobile accident when he was a year old. He'd lived with his grandparents, but Liam's mother and father had treated him like their own.

"I can handle it," Liam said. "Come on, Pete. You know I can take time to reopen the investigation. I can handle my cases, and I can handle an added-on cold case, as well. I'll keep it low profile."

"I don't . . . Ah, it's a waste of manpower!" Pete said.

"No. I won't fail in any way on anything else, and if I do, you pull it back. Pete, what the hell can it hurt?" Liam demanded.

"You may be causing a truckload of trouble down here, you know," he said.

"Why?" David asked flatly. "We're looking for truth. Why would the truth disturb anyone?"

"Thing is, this fellow is probably long gone," Pete said. "David, nothing else has happened. Nothing remotely similar has happened since."

"How can it hurt? Look, let Liam reopen it as a cold case, and he'll only use his spare time. We'll keep it quiet. No other officers need to be involved."

"Ah, hell, fellows, as long as it's your time you intend to waste." Pete wagged a finger at Liam. "Don't you dare neglect a thing, you hear me?"

"Loud and clear," Liam said.

"And you — don't you go doing anything illegal!" Pete charged David.

"Never," David said, and smiled.

"I'll see about the files," Liam said, and left.

"Thanks, Pete," David told him.

He rose and left the office. He'd intended on getting to the truth, one way or the other. But it was better having the blessing of the local cops.

Heading out, he ran into Liam. His cousin started to speak, but David shook his head slightly and indicated the door.

Outside the station, Liam frowned, handing David the files. "What was that all about?"

"I don't care to talk in front of anyone else," David told him.

"Why? If you're on a hunt to solve a murder from the past, you're going to need lots of help, and we'll be questioning lots of people."

"Liam, you're the cop, yeah, and I'm

grateful. I want to keep it low profile. No big announcements that we're opening up the case again."

"Okay . . . but actually reopening the case. Hell, you didn't even tell me that you were thinking of doing this — didn't warn me. I would have helped you talk to Pete. You're a civilian. You know he couldn't have given you any files."

"Yeah, I know, which makes it good that you're a cop — in the right division."

Liam nodded and looked away. "I know you. You want to investigate on your own. It's a wild-goose chase, and you're worried about bringing in our cops. Why?"

"Because someone from this city killed Tanya, I'm sure of it. Cops down here, they all think that they know everyone, and they'll be blinded to what they should be seeing. And I'm not sure that any of the members of the old-boy network will be happy to discover that I'm coming after one of their own."

Katie walked down the stairs, trying to swallow down her disappointment.

She'd dreamed about owning the place for years. She'd been sad for a while after talking to Liam but now she was ready to go to battle again.

As she came down the stairs, she was surprised to smell coffee. The timer hadn't been set to go off for another few minutes.

Bartholomew met her at the foot of the stairs. He looked grave, but as if he was trying not to smile, as well.

"I'm sorry, Katie. I heard you talking. And the bank is off — really, we both knew that it would be — and I'm sorry. But . . ."

"But what?"

"I did it!" he told her proudly. "I did it!"

"What did you do?"

"Can't you smell it? Coffee! I — *I* — managed to push the button on the coffeemaker. Katie, I moved something. Something tangible."

She wanted to be happy for him.

It was the start button on a coffeemaker!

But it was a start.

"That's wonderful. Truly wonderful. And thank you. Coffee is excellent right now, and —"

"I think a good grog would have suited me better, but for you — yes, coffee. And it's ready."

She continued to congratulate him as she walked to the large kitchen in back. Once it had been a bedroom and the kitchen had been the apartment in back. But now, it was all a kitchen, and a very nice one, state-of-the-art. Her mother had loved to cook.

She caught her reflection in the back of one of the pans hanging from an old ship's rack above the counter.

Ugh.

She was wearing an old Disney nightshirt tee and her abundant hair was in tangles all about her. Thank God Bartholomew never commented on her morning appearance.

"Next, we need to work on me stepping out for the newspaper," he said somberly. "Give the neighbors a terrible fright!"

"Hey! And I was just thinking how kind you were, and how much of a gentleman you were proving to be — for a pirate."

"Privateer!"

"Whatever," Katie said sweetly.

She opened the front door, coffee cup in hand, and stepped outside. She saw the paper on the little patch of ground to her right and headed to it.

But as she stooped down to retrieve it, she saw a hand ahead of hers.

"Allow me."

She looked up and stood quickly, staring at the man in her yard. The sudden bane of her existence.

David Beckett.

She stared at him, not sure if she was feeling ill, angry or simply surprised. He'd just ruined her life. Well, that was an exaggeration, but he had destroyed her future plans and the dream she'd harbored for years. And he was in her yard.

"Can I help you?" she said at last.

"Your paper," he told her.

"Yes, I see that."

"Don't worry. I was just walking. I got in last night, and I'm seeing what hasn't changed and what has. Your house is the same, exactly the same, as I remember it."

"I'm so glad to give you something familiar, and happy to make you feel right at home," she said flatly.

He grinned. By day, she was surprised to realize what a fine face he had. He had a look that was intense, as if the world around him was solemn. But when he smiled his grin broke the chiseled structure, and lightened his eyes. Without a smile, he was compelling — tall, well built, lithe, an outdoorsman with bronzed skin, honed muscles and the rugged appeal that went with it all. When he did pause to smile or laugh, there was an added dimension to him that was even more appealing; the man was sensual.

She wasn't admiring him, she decided. He'd ruined her life, and he remembered her as a little kid. Sean's much younger sister.

"I really wish you understood what I feel about the museum," he said. "I'm not out to destroy anyone's dream."

"Well, you managed anyway," she said. She remembered her apparel — and the fact that she looked like Simba on a very bad mane day.

They were both holding the newspaper. She tugged at it. "Thanks for my paper," she said. He released it immediately.

Behind her, she felt Bartholomew. "Hey, he's trying to be nice," Bartholomew said.

She forced a rigid smile.

"You think you can talk him into seeing it all your way, remember?" Bartholomew asked. "Invite him in. *I* just made coffee!"

"Don't be ridiculous," she snapped, not thinking.

David Beckett's dark brown brows arched high. "Pardon?"

"Sorry, I'm sorry," she murmured. She cleared her throat and looked around. It was going to be a beautiful day. Hot, but with a really nice breeze coming through. "I've just brewed a pot of coffee, if you'd like to come in."

He hesitated.

"Seriously, you're welcome to come in," she said. "If you don't mind helping yourself for a moment and letting me run up."

85

"You're going to try to convince me to sell the museum," he said.

"Well, I won't be able to if you're really determined, right?"

"I was actually headed to the Starbucks at La Concha. Sure, I'd love a cup of coffee," he told her.

"Then, please . . ." She indicated the steps.

She came in behind him but headed straight for the stairs. "Go ahead, help yourself. I'll be right down."

She showered, dressed and brushed her hair with the speed of light and came hurrying back down the stairs. Heading toward the kitchen, she stopped. David Beckett was sitting at the table in the breakfast nook, perusing the paper and sipping coffee.

Bartholomew was sitting across from him, one leg tossed casually over the other, his fingers laced around his knees as he observed David attentively.

David Beckett, of course, was oblivious to him.

"Thus far, he has perpetrated no evil deeds," Bartholomew said, immediately aware of Katie's presence and looking up at her.

She ignored him. She had gotten very good — most of the time — at ignoring his comments.

She poured herself a cup of coffee and came striding toward the table. Bartholomew instantly moved over to make room for her. She wasn't sure what ghosts felt when the living — or inanimate objects — went through them, but Bartholomew wasn't fond of being sat upon, she knew. A husky fellow at karaoke had sunk down upon his lap once, and Bartholomew's face had screwed into such an expression of distaste that Katie had quickly lowered her head to hide a laugh.

"So." She held her cup in both hands and sipped from it. "Lovely day."

"The kind I remember," he said.

"What are you doing while you're here?" she asked him. "You did say you weren't staying."

He shrugged. "I don't like to think of anything as permanent," he told her. "I don't have fixed plans at the moment. I'll spend some time with Liam, and with my great-aunts. Alice and Esther. I believe you know them — everyone always seemed to, anyway."

Katie nodded. "Of course. They don't spend much time in town, though."

"No, at the age of eighty, they still compete over their flowers. Oh, and they both enjoy volunteering at a few of the museums. But will you see them swigging down a pint or two at Sloppy Joe's? Probably not!"

"The man does seem to have a dry, pleasant and even self-deprecating sense of humor," Bartholomew commented.

Katie refused to glance his way.

"So, family time, eh?" she queried.

He nodded.

"And dismantling the museum?"

He set his cup down. "Actually, I will get to that. In a month or so."

"Okay, so, immediately on your agenda? Are you planning on swilling down a few pints at Sloppy Joe's?"

He laughed. "I may. But that's not my main intent or purpose."

"What is?" she asked.

"I want to find out who did kill Tanya," he told her.

She frowned, so surprised that she just stared at him for long seconds. "I . . . I don't see what you can discover now. It happened a decade ago. The police tried — very hard, I'm certain — to find her killer. It's now ten years after the fact. How could you possibly find out something now that they couldn't discover then. And why would the killer have hung around?"

"A random killer wasn't going to bring Tanya's corpse and leave it in our family museum," David said.

"Perhaps it had nothing to do with it being your family's museum. Maybe he had just seen the Elena/Carl Tanzler tableau and decided it was the right place to leave a corpse. God knows, maybe he even thought that the body wouldn't be discovered."

"I have the files. Liam is a detective now. He's been given leave to reopen the case. It's time that it's done."

"They never even had another suspect," Katie said. She bit her lip. She saw the slight tensing of his features. "I mean, they never had a suspect at all —"

"Other than me."

"You were never really a suspect, were you?" She flushed slightly, looking away. *Of course he'd been a suspect!*

"Just a 'person of interest,' " he told her. "And you're right — there was never another suspect. And there had to be a reason for that. Either the police continued to believe that I had done it, or they were protecting someone else."

"Like who?" Katie asked.

"I don't know. But I intend to find out. Tanya deserves justice."

"Her family is long gone, you know," Katie told him.

He nodded, looking away. "I know. Her

89

mother never recovered from what happened, but she came to see me, telling me that she knew I could have never done such a thing. I never saw her father, except at the funeral, and he took Tanya's mother away the next day. They moved up to St. Augustine, and he had a heart attack a month later and died. Her mother went into psychiatric care, and she died about five years later. Tanya had an older brother — Sam — and to the best of my knowledge, he's still doing charters out of Key Largo."

"Oh," Katie said, surprised. "I thought he had left the state."

"Just Key West."

For a moment, they were both silent. To her surprise, it wasn't an awkward silence, just a sad one. And she did understand why he hated to see the museum reopened.

She reached a hand out to touch his across the table. Sparks seemed to jump into her, and she realized that he was far more tense and vital than she had imagined. "I'm sorry, really sorry," she told him.

"Well, you see, their lives were destroyed. Our family was torn apart — I couldn't stay here. I really couldn't stay here. I might have been running away, but I honestly don't think so. I just couldn't stay. The destruction of lives and families was just too much. But now, I know that I will never really be fine with myself if I don't discover the truth, no matter what it takes."

"That's ominous," Katie told him.

"No, I don't intend to hold people up at gunpoint or anything of the like. But I'm going to delve until I find something. A young woman was murdered. She had to have fought — Tanya was fond of living, believe me."

Katie frowned. The case had been years ago. Of course, everyone had been talking about it at the time. It was a small community, especially as far as true conchs — those who were born and bred in Key West — went. Even fresh-water conchs — those who had been in Key West at least seven years — were often rare. Naturally, a scandal, a murder that involved one of the city's oldest families, was a cause for endless horror and gossip.

"I'm sorry, I don't remember much about the case. I mean, to be honest, we all whispered about it, but our parents would always hush us up. And my brother was upset, of course, and we went to the funeral — everyone in town went to the funeral. But I don't know a lot about what was discovered. The body was found in a fairly pristine condition. She hadn't decomposed much. . . . They should have been able to discover some facts regarding the case," Katie said. She flushed, realizing the things she was saying had to be painful, since he had known Tanya so well. Loved her, at least at some point in his life.

He stared at her a moment. She realized she was holding her breath. But he let out a soft sigh and she was grateful that he didn't seem angry, or that he hadn't taken her words as callous.

"Our relationship was over," David said. "I was sad, maybe enjoying being a bit heartbroken. I wasn't angry. I'd been gone a long time — military service had seemed like the right course. I know at the time my grandfather had been worried about finances and he was determined that we get to college, so . . . I figured that would make it easier on him. I had a partial scholarship and the government to back me up. But I was gone way too long for a young woman with little to do down here but bask in the sun. I wasn't that surprised that she left me. Tanya was a party girl. We'd parted ways — she had written me before I returned home to tell me that time and distance were too much, she felt that we should break off the engagement. We never even fought. I hadn't seen her since I'd come home — I'd been

92

avoiding her — though I heard she intended to talk to me that evening, to meet me face-to-face to apologize for what she had done. She didn't mention the other guy in the letter. I'd heard about that through others, but I was hardly surprised. She was supposed to leave in the next few days to live in Ohio but I'd heard from others that she may have decided to stay. Supposedly, she'd had a change of heart. That night. Or maybe it had been brewing. She was trying to get her courage up to come see me. Whether that's true or not, I don't know. I thought that we were over. I'd helped out at the museum while waiting to head up to school. I loved working in the museum. I'd always loved the Carl Tanzler story — I mean, it's just too bizarre, even for Key West! I was telling it with relish, I believe. And then, there she was. Tanya — where Elena de Hoyos should have rested."

"What — what about the fellow from Ohio she fell in love with?" Katie asked. "Did they ever question him?"

"Mike Sanderson. He was in Ohio, or on the road to Ohio," David said. "He'd left several days earlier. Tanya had actually stayed behind to get herself organized. She also told people that she'd wanted to see me again — without Mike around. She was a party girl, but a very decent human being. As far as I remember. And that's painful. I remember her dead far better than I remember her alive."

"So, the new guy was out of state . . ." Katie murmured.

"It's easy to see why I appeared to be the perfect suspect," David said. "Especially because, at times, I was alone in the museum that night. Between tours. We didn't find her until the following morning, and I thank God for the coroner. He insisted that she had been killed before nine the night before, and there were a number of people who swore that I couldn't possibly have left the museum with enough time to kill her."

"Because she wasn't killed at the museum?"

He nodded. "She had been killed and lain somewhere long enough for lividity to set in — and the way her blood had settled, she'd been on her side for a while after she was killed." He winced. "You're thinking that I shouldn't be able to talk about her this way?"

She looked at him. "No! Actually, I wasn't thinking that at all," she said. "I was just wondering how on earth you could begin to go back to find out what did happen."

He stood. "Well, it's quite a challenge. I

94

may fail. I have to try."

She stood, as well. It was obvious that he was leaving.

"What if you find out the truth?" she asked him.

He frowned. "What do you mean?"

"Say you manage to lay all your ghosts to rest. Will you leave again?"

"Probably."

"Then, if all was solved, you just might feel differently about the museum."

She shouldn't have spoken; she saw a spark of anger in his eyes. "I see where your sympathy for my plight lies, Miss O'Hara," he said, his words pleasant enough.

"I didn't mean —"

"Yes, actually, yes, you did."

"If that's how you wish to feel, fine. There's little I can do," she said with a shrug.

He started toward the door but stopped and turned back. "Thank you for the coffee." He hesitated. "Do you manage to suck everyone in like this — then irritate them beyond measure?"

"I — I, no! I wasn't *sucking you in.* I was listening. And I would dearly love to see the murder solved. It was an injustice all the way around. A killer got away with murder. Lives were ruined. I — and surely everyone else — would like to see that rectified. In fact, and seriously, with no side benefit, I'm more than willing to help you in any way. I just can't begin to see how."

He walked back to her. He loomed tall, and she felt a slight tremor touch her, but it wasn't fear. He was simply a charismatic man, whether talking thoughtfully, or staring at her the way he was now.

Even wagging a finger at her.

"Don't! No, I mean, don't! Don't help me, don't look into this, don't be involved in any way. Please, and I mean it. Do you understand me — don't help, don't ask questions — just don't!"

"Hey! All right!" Katie flared. "What — do you have this problem with everyone who attempts to be nice to you?"

He let out a breath. His eyes were an intense blue as he stared at her, and yet they seemed to spark with a different emotion, as well.

"No, I just don't want anyone involved in any way, all right?"

She lifted her hands. "Hey, you're on your own. I won't darken your door, I won't even speak on your behalf!"

He nodded, turned and headed to the door. Once more, he turned back. "Seriously, thanks for the coffee." He lingered for a moment. She was surprised to see something of a nostalgic smile on his face.

"What?"

"I don't know. Remembering times . . . before, I guess." He looked at her a long moment. "You don't remember. I came here one day to see your brother and you were mad at him. You opened the door for me, and then slammed it in my face."

"I did not!"

"You did."

She flushed. "Hey, he was quite a bit older, and very superior at times."

"It's all right. I knocked again, and Sean came down. He threatened to lock you in your dollhouse."

"I never had a dollhouse."

"Then he must not have been all that mad."

He stepped outside, the door closed and he was gone.

"Well," Bartholomew exclaimed. "Well, well — well. How touching."

"Don't be — a jerk," Katie said.

"Excuse me," Bartholomew said indignantly. "I wasn't being a jerk. I meant it. How touching. I think I do like this fellow after all."

Katie was thoughtful. "If he is able to find out the truth . . ."

97

"Stop right there," Bartholomew said.

"What do you mean?"

"Did you hear him? He doesn't want you involved. And, hey — it's never been proved that he was guilty, but it's never been proved that he was innocent."

Katie looked solidly at Bartholomew. "I don't intend to do anything, seriously. I'm going to hope for the best for him. But if he does find out the truth, he may change his mind, and I may get the museum."

Bartholomew appeared to shudder. "Katie, if he's right, the situation is dangerous. Oh, yes, there's so much more that can be discovered these days than when I was walking the shoreline. DNA, RNA, whichever is which and what. Skin cells, even fingerprints, footprints . . . genetic markers. Whatever. The thing is, the killer was never caught. David Beckett thinks that it wasn't a random act or the act of a psycho who moved on. If he's trying to discover the truth and it was someone from around here who *still lives here,* that person isn't going to want anyone knowing the truth."

"What we want isn't always what we get — it's time for a murderer to come to justice," Katie said.

"Right. Great sentiment," Bartholomew agreed. "But this person killed once, very cleverly, so it seems. If he's threatened, he'll certainly kill again. Katie, look at me — this guy will kill again. Like Beckett said, young woman, you stay the hell out of it. You wouldn't want to wind up being a tableau in the museum yourself now, would you, Miss Katherine O'Hara?"

4

Danny Zigler seemed the right place to start. He knew Key West like the back of his hand. He had been here then — and he'd remained to sometimes tell stories about the night, along with other bits and pieces of Key West myth and legend. He had been something of a friend. He was a legend in his own peculiar way.

At the moment, Danny worked part-time for one of the ghost-tour companies and part-time for an ice-cream parlor on Duval. He had always been a nice guy with an easygoing personality — and not a bit of ambition. Maybe that wasn't a bad thing, David didn't know. Sometimes Danny was unemployed, and that would be fine with Danny until he was dead broke, then he'd make the effort to become employed again. He was a fixture in Key West.

It was still early, and not much on or just off Duval Street opened early, except for the chain drugstore, coffee shops and an Internet café. But David knew that the ice-cream shop would be getting ready to open, and it might be the best time to talk to Danny.

When he reached the shop, David could see Danny inside, wiping down one of the milk-shake machines. He rapped on the glass. Danny looked up and over at him, and a broad smile lit up his face. He hurried to the door. David heard the locks being sprung, and then the door opened.

"David Beckett! I heard you were headed back into town. Man, how are you! It's so damned cool to see you!" Danny declared. His enthusiasm seemed real, and he gave David a hug and stepped back. "Damn, man, and you are looking good!"

Danny was eternally thin. His brown hair, long and worn in a queue at his nape, was now beginning to show threads of gray. His face was pockmarked from a now preventable childhood illness and his features were lean. His eyes, however, were a warm brown, and he did well with people. He excelled at telling stories, and he'd been a wonderful guide years ago, when he had worked at the museum. David wondered if Danny's life hadn't been altered by the events at the museum, as well.

"Thanks, Danny," David said. "So how are you doing?"

Danny shrugged, wiping his hands on the white apron he wore over his jeans and a Metallica tee. "I can't complain, can't complain. They're getting more and more letters on what a great 'ghost host' I am for the weekend tours and, hey — I can have all the free ice cream I want. I have a sunset every night, and saltwater and sand between my toes." He frowned. "Hey, there's a rumor that you're refusing to sell the museum to Katie O'Hara. Is that true?"

David nodded. "I'm sorry, Danny."

"Your museum, your call."

"It's not actually my museum. I do have the major interest, but my grandfather left Liam and me in charge of his estate. We have to agree on everything, and I just don't agree with reopening that place."

"I understand, man."

"I'm sorry, Danny. You were the best guide known to man."

"No skin off my nose, David. Seriously. I just live, and I get by, and that's what makes me happy," Danny assured him. "Katie would have done a good job, though. She's a great little go-getter, good business-woman. But you know her, right?"

"She was a kid when I left."

"Hey, we were all kids when you left. So, where have you been? They said you became some kind of a big-shot photographer. A photojournalist."

"I'm not sure if I'm a big shot. I make a decent living," David told him.

"I'm sorry you missed Craig's funeral," Danny said.

"I saw him when he was alive. He was always the mainstay of my life," David told him.

"You been to the grave site?"

"Not yet."

Danny obviously disapproved of that fact, but he didn't say so. He asked, "So how long do you plan on staying around?"

"I'm not sure yet. I haven't made any commitments for the near future. We'll see. Tell me how you've been, Danny."

"Me? I'm fine. I don't need a lot. Just enough to survive and enjoy myself."

"Still never married? Is there a special girl?"

Danny laughed. "Well, I know several girls who are special. Girls I like, and girls I see. But they're not the kind you bring home to Mom, you know what I mean? But, hey, I know the scoop around here. I'm just looking for fun, and they're just looking for a few bucks. It's cool, it's the way I want it."

"Sure."

"No commitments, and that's the way I like it. Don't be feeling sorry for me, I'm a happy man. Really."

"Glad to hear it."

Danny looked at him thoughtfully. "So, what are you up to?"

"Settling affairs."

"Of course. Hey, I have one of the ghost tours Saturday night. You should come. I'm in rare form, and I really do a good job."

"Maybe I will."

Danny hesitated again. He winced. "You know, they usually do mention Tanya now in the tours. They say that she's a ghost, and that she haunts the museum house."

"And you tell the story, too, right?" David asked.

"I'm sorry," Danny said.

"If you're doing a ghost tour, I'm assuming it makes a good story, and it's not your fault," David assured him.

Danny looked around awkwardly for a moment. "Hey, you want some ice cream?"

David shook his head. "No, thanks, Danny. You know, you said that you retell the story on your tours. What do you say?"

Danny looked pale suddenly. "I — I —"

"You say that I was under suspicion, right?"

"No, no, nothing like that." He was lying; he was lying out of kindness, so it seemed.

"Do you remember what really happened?" David asked.

"What do you mean, what really happened? I wasn't working either day. You were working for me, don't you remember?"

"Of course, I remember that. But what do you remember?"

"Not much, man."

"What did you do the night of her murder with your free time?"

Danny thought a minute. "I had a few drinks at one of the joints on Duval. And I was down at Mallory Square. Then I went home. I woke up the next morning when I heard all the sirens — I was living in an apartment on Elizabeth Street back then. I came outside and saw the cops and the M.E.'s car over at the museum and walked over."

"Did you see Tanya at all that night?" David asked.

"No . . . yes! Early. Well, it was late afternoon, I guess. Around five. I saw her down in one of the bars. I talked to her, I think. Yes, I did talk to her. I'd heard she was leaving town, and that things had kind of faded apart between you two. She said she had a few people to see that night, and that she'd be taking a rental up to Miami, and flying out from there the next day."

"So, five o'clock. Where?"

Danny shook his head. "I think . . . maybe, yeah! I was toward the south side of Duval. It might even have been Katie's uncle's place."

"Thanks, Danny," David told him. "Did you tell the cops that at the time?"

"I'm sure that I did," Danny told him. "Why?"

"Because her killer has never been caught," David said.

"Right," Danny said.

"Well, good to see you, and thanks again," David told him.

"Sure thing. Sure. And I really can't give you an ice cream?"

"No, but thanks," David told him.

He waved to Danny and left.

Five o'clock. If Danny was right, Tanya had been at O'Hara's at five o'clock on the Saturday night she had been murdered.

And Danny hadn't seen her again.

Important, if it was the truth. If he wasn't covering up.

For himself.

Or for someone else.

It was Danny's story then, and it was Danny's story now. He had seen Tanya at five.

Sometime in the next few hours, she'd been murdered, and sometime after that — certainly after midnight, after the museum had closed — she had been laid out in place of Elena de Hoyos.

David had returned for the first tour the following morning.

Had she been laid out just for him to find?

The answer to that question might be the answer to her murder.

"People aren't really to be found at the cemetery, you know," Bartholomew said. "Well, most people. The thing is, of course, that most of us move on. And we remain behind only in the memories of those who loved us. Or hated us. Well, usually, people move on. Okay, okay, well, sometimes you can find people wandering around a cemetery, but . . . Well, that's because they have to remain because . . . Wait, why am I remaining? Oh, hmm. I think it may be because of you. But I digress. You will not find Craig Beckett in this cemetery. He was a good man, and his conscience was clean. He's moved on."

"I know that he's not in the cemetery," Katie said.

"Then . . . why are we here?" Bartholomew asked.

"You don't have to be here," she said.

"No, I don't have to be here. But you do not behave with the intelligence you were granted at birth. Therefore, I feel it is my cross to bear in life to follow you around," Bartholomew told her.

"Hey! I am not your cross to bear, and I do behave intelligently," Katie said, shaking her head and praying for patience. "It's broad daylight. There are tourists all over the cemetery."

"But why are we here?"

"Whether the person is here or not — and, of course, I don't begin to assume that Craig Beckett's soul would be in his worn and embalmed body in his tomb — I just like to come. It's beautiful, and it's a place where I can think. When other people, alive or dead, are not driving me right up the wall."

"What is it you need to think about?" Bartholomew demanded.

"Craig. I just want to remember him. Could I have a bit of respectful silence?" she asked.

The Key West cemetery was on a high point in the center of the island. In 1846, a massive hurricane had washed up a number of earlier graves and sent bodies down Duval Street in a flood. After that, high ground was chosen. Now, many of the graves were in the ground, but many more were above-ground graves. Tombs, shelves and strange grave sites dotted the cemetery, along with more typical mausoleum-type graves.

It was estimated that there were one-hundred-thousand people interred at the Key West cemetery, in one way or another, triple the actual full-time population of the island.

Katie did love the cemetery. It was just like the island itself, historic and eccentric, full of the old and the new. There were Civil War soldiers buried here, there was a monument to those lost aboard the *Maine* and there were many graves with curious sentiments, her favorite being, "I told you I was sick!"

Craig Beckett was in a family mausoleum that had been there since the majority of the island's dead had been moved here. One of the most beautiful angel sculptures in the cemetery stood high atop the roof of the mausoleum, and tourists were frequently near, taking pictures of the sculpture. When the Beckett family had originally purchased their final resting place, the cost had been minimal. Now such a structure, along with the small spit of ground it stood upon, would cost in the mid-to-high hundreds of thousands of dollars.

"There she is!" Bartholomew said suddenly.

"Who? Where?" Katie asked.

"The woman in white," Bartholomew said. "There, where the oldest graves are."

Bartholomew was right. She was standing above one of the graves. Her head was lowered, and her hands were folded before her.

"I'm going to talk to her," Bartholomew said.

"I don't think she wants to talk," Katie said. "Bartholomew, you should wait."

He didn't want to wait. He left Katie and went striding quickly toward the beautiful ghost figure in long, flowing white. As he neared her, she turned. She saw him.

And then she was gone.

Katie shook her head. Sadly, the world of relationships was always hard. Even for ghosts. Maybe more so for ghosts.

She heard laughter and turned. A group of tourists was coming along; they had just been visiting the area of the monument to the survivors of the *Maine;* a wrought-iron fence encircled a single bronze sailor who looked out over the markers of his companions.

They were now coming to take pictures of

the Beckett tomb with its beautiful, high-rising angel. Katie decided to slip away.

She walked around to an area where graves were stacked mausoleum-style in several rows, and stood where she wouldn't be seen. The group was a happy one, and she knew that visiting the historic and unusual cemetery was something that people did. Since life was basically a circle and all men died, it seemed a good thing that people enjoyed a walk in the cemetery. But today, for some reason, the laughter irritated her.

Bartholomew remained around the oldest graves. He had gone down on one knee, and she assumed he was trying to read the etching on some of the gravestones.

As she waited and watched, she was surprised to see the woman in white appear again. She was behind Bartholomew. Bartholomew didn't see her. As Katie watched, the woman started to place a hand on his shoulder.

Again, the group of tourists seemed to issue, in unison, a loud stream of laughter. The woman turned to fog, and she was gone.

But there was someone else there. A girl. She was also in white, but she was wearing a more modern gown, one similar to the famous halter dress in which Marilyn Monroe had been immortalized in dozens of pictures.

She, too, watched Bartholomew.

She looked around, though, and saw Katie. She seemed to panic.

Then she, too, was gone.

Katie frowned; there had been something about that particular ghost — something that seemed to stir inside her. Katie should have recognized her.

But she didn't. Irritated, Katie dismissed the idea.

Ghosts everywhere! she thought.

Well, she was in a cemetery. But, as Bartholomew had said, ghosts didn't really linger that often in cemeteries. They haunted the areas where they had been happy, where they had faced trauma or where they searched for something they hadn't found in life.

"Hiding?"

The very real, solid and almost tangible sound of a deep male voice made her jump. Katie swung around.

David Beckett had come to the cemetery.

"Hiding? No. Just — waiting," she said.

"I guess it's a good thing that a cemetery, even an active cemetery, draws the laughter of the living," David said. He watched as

the loud group moved on.

"You came to see your grandfather?" she asked.

"My grandfather isn't here," he said.

She smiled. "No. When did you see him last?"

"Right before I headed out to Kenya," he said, looking toward the mausoleum.

"Oh," Katie said.

He looked at her with a tight smile. "I didn't desert my grandfather, Miss O'Hara, though that seems to be the consensus here. I didn't like my home anymore, and I can't help it. I like living a life where you don't stare into faces every day that are speculative — are you or are you not a murderer? I met Craig in Miami often enough, even Key Largo and sometimes Orlando. Imagine. Craig loved theme parks. Here's the thing of which I am certain — if there is a heaven, Craig is there, and he's with my grandmother. They had a beautiful love that was quite complete. They will not be misty ghouls running around a graveyard."

"You know, you sound defensive," Katie observed.

He shook his head. "Yep. I have a big chip on my shoulder." He lifted his hands and she saw that he carried a beautiful bouquet of lilacs. "Gram's favorites," he said.

The tourists were gone. Katie followed him back to the Beckett mausoleum. He set the bouquet right before the wrought-iron doors.

"Very nice — pretty flowers," Katie said.

"They seem forlorn," David said.

She shook her head. "No, that's forlorn," she told him, pointing to a family graveyard that was surrounded by an iron fence. Cemetery maintenance was kept up, but no one had been to see the graves in decades. The stones were broken, a stray weed was growing through here and there and all within the site were long forgotten, not even their names remaining legibly upon the stones.

"That's life," David said flatly. "Well, I'll leave you to whatever you were doing," he told her. But as he turned, he stopped suddenly.

Katie saw that he was looking at a man across from them, in another section of the cemetery, one that was bordered by Olivia Street.

She knew that Tanya Barnard was buried in that section; most people knew that she was buried there, even though her marker wasn't on her grave. Because of the Carl Tanzler/Elena de Hoyos story, the powers-that-be at the time of her death, along with

114

the family, had determined that no one but Tanya's parents would know exactly where she had been buried; there would be no grave robbing. In death, Tanya had become a celebrity.

Katie had never seen Tanya's astral self, soul or haunt.

She had seen Elena de Hoyos frequently. Then again, if anyone had the right to haunt a place, it was poor Elena. Ripped from her grave, her body adored and yet desecrated, she had missed out on the beauty of youth and the sweetness of aging in the midst of normal love.

She didn't weep when she walked. She did so with her head high. And sometimes, she danced, as if she could return to the dance halls of her day, as if she imagined herself young again, falling in love with her handsome husband — happy days before tuberculosis, desertion and the bizarre adoration of Carl Tanzler.

Would she know Tanya if she saw her? She had heard the story about the woman, of course. It had been Key West's scandal and horror. Her picture had certainly been in the newspapers. But Katie had never really seen Tanya.

"Damn," David murmured.

The man across the way seemed to know

115

exactly where he was, and what he was looking for.

Katie stared, squinting against the sun. He was the man who had been in O'Hara's last night, the man who had appeared to be familiar, who had tried to buy her a drink. He had flowers; he laid them at the foot of a grave.

"Who is it?" she asked.

He didn't glance her way. "Sam Barnard. Tanya's brother," he said.

Katie stared, looking at David, and then at the man again. David left her, striding across the cemetery. He passed the brick vaults and kept going, at last calling out. His voice carried on the breeze. She heard him calling out, "Sam!"

Sam turned slowly. He was clean shaven now, in Dockers and a polo shirt, and she wondered if he had been as drunk as she had thought last night, or if he had been playing the drunk, watching folks at the bar. He had to have been familiar with O'Hara's — her uncle's bar had been there for twenty-five years. But her uncle, Jamie O'Hara, had not been there. Jon Merrillo had been on as the manager, and Jon had only been in Key West for five years.

Katie felt her heart thundering. For a moment she thought that she should turn away, that none of this was any of her business. But then she felt a trigger of unease. No, fear. What if the two men were about to go after one another? Maybe Sam Barnard had vengeance on his mind. David Beckett had just returned, and suddenly Sam Barnard was back in the city, as well.

She dug into her handbag for her phone, ready to dial 911.

But she didn't.

The two men embraced like old friends. They began speaking to one another, and walked toward the grave together.

She felt a strange sensation — not cold, not heat, just a movement in the air. She turned her head slightly. Bartholomew had an arm draped around her. "That's touching," he said. "Seriously, you know, I like that fellow. He reminds me of someone I knew years and years ago. . . ." He shrugged. "Hey, it might have been one of his ancestors, come to think of it."

"I thought he was a jerk and you were going to protect me from him," Katie said dryly.

Bartholomew shook his head. "He's redeeming himself. That's what life is all about, eh? We make mistakes, we earn redemption. So, you want to join up with them?"

"No. No, I want to slip away."

"Wait."

"Wait — for what?" Katie asked.

"Maybe Tanya Barnard is hanging around the cemetery."

"Do you see anyone? I don't," Katie said.

"No," Bartholomew admitted. "Maybe she's gone on all the way. But she was murdered, and her murder was never solved. You'd think, with her brother and ex-fiancé together, she would make an appearance."

Katie looked around the cemetery. No ghosts were stirring. None at all.

They were probably unhappy with the laughing tourists.

Every man and woman born came to the end of their lives. Death was the only certainty in life.

But ghosts could be touchy.

"Let's go. I have to go to work tonight and I want to do some searching online," Katie said.

"You go on. I'm going to hang around a bit longer," Bartholomew said.

"Snooping — or looking for your lady in white?" Katie asked.

"A bit of both. I'm looking for my beauty . . . or waiting for you, my love. But you're awfully young, so I'd have a long wait."

"Well, thanks for that vote of encouragement," Katie said.

She walked quickly, exiting the cemetery from the main gate. Neither of the men, now involved in a deep conversation together, noticed that she left.

Sam Barnard was David's senior by four years. He'd been in college when David had been in the military, so they hadn't hung out, but they'd shared many a holiday dinner with one or the other's family.

"I heard about Craig's death, and I'd heard they were trying to reach you," Sam Barnard told David. "To be honest, though, I didn't come down to pay my respects to anyone. I'd heard a local was trying to buy the museum. It brought everything back. Not just the fact that my kid sister was murdered, but the way she was left . . . and the fact that her killer was never found. Hell, I didn't come down to start trouble. I've spent the past years not even a hundred miles away, and I haven't made the trip down here since my folks left. But now . . ."

"I'm not letting anyone reopen the museum," David told him.

They sat at a sidewalk bar on Front Street. Sam lifted his beer to David. "Glad to hear it. And I'm not here to hound or harass you, either. I know you didn't do it."

"Do you?" David asked.

Sam nodded. "I guess a lot of folks think I've followed you down here to pick a fight, beat you to a pulp, something like that."

"Probably."

"My folks knew you didn't do it. I knew you didn't do it."

"That means a lot."

"You know, I knew what was going on. She was my sister, but I never put her on a pedestal. I really loved her, but she was human, you know. Real. From the time she was a little kid, she wanted to live every second of the day. When you left for the military, I had a bad feeling. Tanya was never the kind to wait around. She was never going to find true love with that football jock — he had a roving eye. I told her so. She'd made all her arrangements for college in the north. But she wasn't leaving until she had talked to you. I'm pretty sure she was going to make a stab at getting back with you. That's why she was drinking. She needed courage."

"She never needed courage to see me."

"You didn't know — you really didn't know that she wanted to make up, did you?" Sam asked.

"No. And no matter what, we would have

stayed friends," David said. "I didn't hate her. Maybe I understood."

"She's just a cold, closed case now," Sam said.

"I hope not. I hope there's still a way to find the truth," David said.

"How, after all this time?" Sam demanded. "Hey, you didn't secretly go off and become some kind of investigator, or medium, eh? What the hell could anyone possibly find now?"

"Actually, cold cases do get solved. Not all of them, no. And no — I can't conjure up Tanya to find out what happened."

"So you are a photographer?" Sam said, frowning. "And you film stuff, too, for nature films? Underwater — like Sean."

"Yep. Oddly enough, yes, Sean and I wound up doing close to the same thing. I do more straight photography than Sean, though." He waited a minute, but Sam remained silent. "And you — you're still running charter fishing boats, right?"

Sam nodded, rubbing his thumb down his beer glass. "Yep, I do fishing charters."

"Is there a Mrs. Sam yet?"

"No. And you — you never married either, huh?"

"I'm all over the globe," David said.

Sam leaned toward him, his grin lopsided

and rueful. "Neither one of us has married because we're both fucked up. The murderer might as well have strangled my folks right alongside my sister. And let's see — the girl you thought you were going to marry winds up dead and replacing an automaton, and everyone thinks you did it. Hell, yeah, I can see where you're pretty screwed up in the head."

"Oddly enough, I've been fairly functional," David told him. "But I guess maybe I thought that my grandfather would live forever. And I sure as hell never thought anyone would want to open the place again. Hell, I had told Liam to do whatever he wanted with whatever. I got back here just in time to stop him from selling the place."

"So, what, are you just going to let it decay, crumble into itself like the House of Usher?" Sam asked.

"No, my plan with the place is to clear it all out, whitewash it and put it on the market. Liam's parents are living on their private island now so he's got a house — his mom and dad sold it to him for a dollar since he was their only child. I have my grandfather's house, so I don't need another one. And I'm not staying forever."

Sam laughed. "And you think folks will just forget about what happened here? The ghost tours will go by there, night after night. Tanya was killed and discovered in the museum, and the story will never die."

"Nor will the suggestion that I managed to kill her and carry her into the tableau," David said. "Unless —"

"Unless you discover who really did it," Sam interrupted. "Yeah, well, I can see that. And I'm here, if you need me. I've rented a house up at the end of Duval. And here's my cell." He scratched out a number on a cocktail napkin. "Call me if you need me."

"Yeah, I will. Actually, I do have some questions for you," David said.

"Like, where was I the night of the twelfth?" Sam asked.

"Sure. That would be good to know. Did you see your sister that night? I'm trying to trace her footsteps."

"Trace them until they walk you right up to a killer?" Sam asked.

David nodded. "So?"

"So?"

"So where were you that night?"

"That night? You found her in the morning. . . . Oh, right. The police said that she was killed sometime between seven and nine on the twelfth, the night before. The museum was open until midnight, so sometime after midnight, the killer brought her body into the museum for you to find during the first tour the next morning."

"Everyone thought she had left for Ohio," David said. "Your parents thought that she had left for Ohio, and I think they were just angry at first that she had gone without her final goodbye. I wasn't expecting to see her, so I wouldn't have looked for her. The killer held her — somewhere, and then brought her into the museum after closing."

"I was on Duval Street the night she was killed, drinking it up with a bunch of friends. Did I see my sister? Yes. I yelled at her for drinking."

"Drinking on Duval? How bizarre," David said dryly.

"Hey, those of us who live in paradise know that you can't drink yourself silly every night. You know what she told me?" Sam asked.

"What?"

"Just what I was trying to explain to you. She wanted some liquid courage. She wanted to be strong when she saw you. She wasn't sure anymore. She'd seen you from a distance, and she felt as if the years had all gone away. She needed courage, but not to tell you goodbye. She needed courage because she was afraid she wanted to ask if she could come back, instead of telling you

124

goodbye, and she was afraid of what you would have to say to her."

He'd heard it before. Somehow, that information, coming from Sam especially, still hurt.

He didn't know if it was true or not.

He just knew that it hurt.

5

Dying Love, Dead Loss was the name of the most popular book that had been written on the subject of Tanya Barnard's murder. Naturally, there had been dozens of newspaper reports and the sensationalism of the way she had been left had drawn coverage from across the country.

Katie had never purchased the book. She didn't feel that anyone should make a profit off such a contemporary tragedy.

That day, however, on her way back from the cemetery, she stopped by a store to purchase the book. She bought it in one of the tourist shops on Duval that sold sandals, clothing, souvenirs and about ten titles that were pertinent to the Keys. Two of the books held maps and histories, two were on water sports on the island, another was on housing styles. There was a book on Carl Tanzler, one on Key West ghost stories and one on the murder of Tanya Barnard. The shop was owned and operated by Eastern Europeans new to the area, but it was still a small world. It wouldn't be any secret that she had bought the book.

She picked up a tuna croissant sandwich from one of her favorite restaurants and headed home with her book. She had several hours before she had to return to work.

Saturday night.

It was going to be busy.

Friday nights started the craziness of weekend revelers, bachelor parties, bachelorette parties and general let's-drive-down-to-Key-West-and-get-plastered celebrations. Also, Fantasy Fest would be starting the next week, so many people who intended to enjoy that week of bacchanalia would start filtering in.

As she walked to her house, lunch and reading material in hand, she suddenly felt an odd sense of apprehension.

It was broad daylight. Tourists were everywhere, walking, on bikes, in rental minicars. Music was blaring from a dozen clubs. She wondered at first if she was being followed by a ghost who had suddenly discovered the need to talk.

Tanya. Maybe Tanya Barnard was walking around Key West, and she had seen her brother and her onetime fiancé again, and discovered the need to try to help them find the truth.

But looking around, she saw no one, not even the usual crowd she sometimes saw, all from their different eras, sometimes seeing one another and sometimes not. There were a few Spanish conquistadors who hung out near the wharf fairly frequently, and many of the seafarers seemed to see one another and gather near the docks, almost as if they could taste the beer and grog being served by the waterside restaurants now. An early-nineteenth-century pirate seemed to look around Captain Tony's now and then, and rumor had it that he'd been seen by a number of people.

But the dead were quiet this afternoon. She had no idea why she'd felt the chilling sensation, as if she had been watched.

She felt it again when she reached her house and turned the key in the lock, so much so that she turned around to assure herself that she hadn't been followed. "Bartholomew?" she muttered, turning one last time before releasing the knob. Her ethereal houseguest might be feeling that she needed to be more careful than she was. But, apparently, Bartholomew was still hanging around the cemetery. Every now and then, he got a kick out of trying to breathe down someone's neck and give them a chill or a scare. He could also make leaves rustle, and sometimes, tap on glass or some other hard surface. He loved seeing pretty young women squeal with fear.

Sometimes, he followed the ghost tours around. He'd stand next to the guides, and blow out their lanterns now and then. She didn't really blame him. Surely, after nearly two hundred years of hanging around, he needed a form of entertainment. But Bartholomew didn't seem to be playing jokes — not on her — at the moment.

She stepped inside and quickly closed the door behind her, locking it. Once inside, she felt somewhat silly, but she still checked the locks anyway. With her sandwich, a cold glass of tea and the book, she curled up on the sofa in the parlor and started to read.

The author first painted a picture of Key West at the time of the murder; then she told the Carl Tanzler story, and gave a history of the Beckett family. Their history was similar to that of her own family. David Beckett — the original David Beckett — had been a pirate who had claimed that he had actually been a privateer, attacking only Spanish ships in the name of Great Britain. The Becketts purchased lands, probably with ill-gotten gains, became wreckers and salvage divers, supported sponging and, by the eighteen hundreds, had become rich. They were able to shift with the winds of time, owning tourist businesses as the days of wrecking became bygone, investing in a number of different ventures. Into the mid-nineteen hundreds, the family was still hanging on, but with their worth more in property than bank accounts. Few families were more respected. Her own family was named along with the Barnards. They weren't the earliest, like the Whiteheads and Simontons, but they had family members who had remained through the decades.

Then — the murder.

Everyone involved with the museum had been questioned. Pete Dryer, a uniformed cop at the time, had been at the museum during the discovery, and he had perfectly preserved the crime scene — except that the murder hadn't taken place in the museum, according to the medical examiner's report. Where she met her fate, no one knew. No one had broken into the museum, and there were no security cameras at the time. Crime-scene units had not been able to find hairs, fibers or any other microcosm of evidence. David Beckett had naturally fallen under suspicion; Key West was a small place. Though extremely improbable, it was possible that he had slipped out — and come upon Tanya.

Katie scrambled over to the kitchen counter for a notepad. The police were convinced that the murderer was someone who had lived on the island and knew their way around. They also thought that the murderer was probably a very strong man. She listed the people who had been on the tour: four female college students; Molly and Turk Kenward from Portland, Oregon; Pete Dryer; his sister, Sally; her husband, Gerry Matthews; and the Matthewses' children, Suzie and Whelan.

She scratched out the names of the female college students, then the two Matthews children. She was about to scratch out the names of Pete Dryer and his sister and brother-in-law, but she didn't. Nor did she scratch out David Beckett's name. She did scratch out Molly and Turk. Not only were they not local, but they were also listed as "senior citizens." It was possible, of course, that they had been a pair of homicidal octogenarians. It simply wasn't probable.

She leafed through more pages, searching for the names of locals who had been questioned. Lily and Gunn Barnard, Tanya's parents, were dead; Sam Barnard, Tanya's brother, was alive and well and in Key West now. Danny Zigler had been questioned, and all the Becketts living in the Keys had been questioned, including Liam, who now worked investigation in Key West. Her own brother, Sean, had been questioned, along with many of those who had gone to high school with Tanya.

Katie frowned, seeing Sean's name. She had never realized that the police had questioned him.

Bartenders up and down Duval had been questioned. Once again, Katie was surprised when she saw where Tanya Barnard had last been seen.

O'Hara's Pub.

Her uncle Jamie had been questioned! Jamie, and Sean. She hesitated and wrote down their names.

She was still so stunned by what she read that she jumped a mile when her cell phone started to ring. She frowned, looking at all the numbers on the caller ID.

"Hello?" she said, feeling a strange sense of trepidation.

"Katie, it's Sean," her brother's voice said.

"I was home because it was summer," Sam Barnard said to David as they sat in the sidewalk bar. "I'd gone to college for a straight business degree, then decided I

132

wanted a minor in marine sciences. It was going to take me five years to get my degree. I never went back for the last year. Doesn't matter — I never wanted to breed trout anyway. I have a good business — I learned enough to keep up five charter boats and a Gulf-side house right on the water up in Key Largo. I was fishing with my dad during the day, and I saw Tanya around four when we came in. I think I told her she was a jerk. Because of the Ohio State guy. I was on your side, though, of course, now I know that none of us can ever tell anyone else what to do. But like I said, she didn't tell me to fly a kite, kiss my ass or any other such thing. She said she knew she had messed up, but that if you didn't want her, she was leaving. She asked me if I thought she was a bad person, not knowing until you were back — all in one piece — before thinking that she'd made a mistake. I told her, yeah, she'd kind of been a selfish bitch. She'd wanted everything — the parties, the good times and then the guy she'd cheated on. She didn't even get mad. I was a jerk, and it was the last time I ever saw my sister alive."

"So she left the house after four that afternoon?" David said after a moment.

Sam nodded.

"Danny Zigler saw her at five at O'Hara's Pub. In the police reports, Jamie O'Hara said that he served her a pint of Guinness, and that she was nervous. She smiled at him, and told him to wish her luck, stayed until around seven — and then she left, and no one saw her alive again," David said.

"You've seen the police reports?" Sam asked, curious and surprised.

"My cousin is working it as a cold case," David said.

Sam pointed a finger at him. "I remember something. Your cousin, Liam, was one of the people who saw her at O'Hara's."

"At least ten people saw her at O'Hara's that night," David pointed out.

"The question is, which of those ten people weren't seen in the bar after? Or, oh, hell, that would be the point here, huh? No one knows who saw her once she left that pub. Somewhere, in the next hour, someone found her and killed her. That's nothing new, not really. I'm sure the police must have narrowed down the timeline when it happened. And, of course, the problem around here isn't that there was no one on the streets. There were hundreds of people on the streets. And it was a long, long time ago now," Sam said. He hesitated. "She wasn't raped. So it's not as if they can suddenly find a miraculous match with honed DNA science."

"No," David agreed.

This time, Sam let out a long sigh. "They figured it was some kind of psycho who lived here and then moved on. Hell, he could have driven north that night, or taken a puddle jumper up the state. But you don't think that a whacko killed my sister?"

"I don't know anything. I just don't think it was a psycho. I think it was someone who knew the area and had an agenda."

"Like what?"

"That's what I need to find out."

"I still don't understand. I mean, obviously, I really wish we knew what happened — who killed my baby sister. But, what's different now? The cops swore they chased down every lead, no matter how small. *What's different now?* How do you think you can solve anything?"

David stared at him and smiled tightly. "I'm different now. I'm not a kid. And I don't intend to stop, or be stopped by anyone. I know that I had nothing to do with her death, and I know that someone did. Someone got away with murder, and I believe that we do know the person who killed her. The truth exists. And I want it."

"Hey! Where are you?" Katie asked her brother. "Far away still, I take it. It's great to hear from you."

"We talked a week ago on Skype," he reminded her.

"Skype is great — when you have a sibling halfway across the world."

"I'm in Hawaii now. I'm coming home for a while, kid."

"That's wonderful! It will be like old-home week."

"I know," Sean said.

She frowned. "How do you know?"

"David Beckett left me a message about going back."

"He left you a message?"

"E-mail," Sean explained.

"But I thought —"

"I didn't have access for a few days, but the filming project finished up. I'm in Hawaii, and I head back to California the day after tomorrow. Then Miami the following morning —"

"I'll come pick you up."

"No, no, I'm going to rent a car. I'll be there sometime on Tuesday or Wednesday."

"That's wonderful, Sean! Oh, watch the

traffic. The first events for Fantasy Fest are starting soon."

"Yeah, yeah, I know the traffic. It will just be aggravating. I could hop a puddle jumper in Miami, but I kind of want to drive down. Even with the tourists clogging the road."

"Okay. That's super, Sean!"

He was quiet. She thought that she had lost the connection. "Katie?" he said then.

"What?"

"Don't go telling anyone that . . . that you see things."

It was her turn to be quiet. Sean had been amused the first time she had seen a ghost. She had been six, in first grade, and they'd been playing at the church. The ghost she had seen had been a nun. Sean had taken it all as a joke. Her feelings had been terribly hurt, but she had quickly realized that he had been trying to defend her. The other kids meant to torment her and laugh at her — which they did, until Sean turned it all around, laughing at them for falling for the joke.

Later, Katie had been alone at the playground. The nun had come to her, and spoken gently, assuring her that she had a gift, and that she must guard it carefully.

But when her grandfather had died, her mother's tears had shaken her. She had seen her grandfather, trying to comfort her mother. She told her mother. Her mother believed she was just trying to comfort her — until she told her mother where Grandpa had left his old gold pocket watch, and that he wanted Katie's father to have it.

Her mother had been looking everywhere for the pocket watch.

Katie was careful then. She didn't tell anybody about the sailors, servicemen and pirates who roamed the docks.

She avoided eye contact with the ghosts. It hadn't worked with Bartholomew.

She had thought that her brother had forgotten about her ghosts, because she never mentioned a ghost again. Sometimes, though, she had information or could tell him things because a ghost had pointed something out. She would remain stubbornly silent when he asked her how she knew something.

"Katie?"

"What?"

"Don't go saying anything, anything at all — especially not to David. I know why he's in town. If God himself comes down to speak to you, don't say anything — do you understand?"

"I think God is busy, Sean. The world is a mess, if you haven't noticed. I don't think that he's coming down to talk to me," she said.

"Katie, please. I know you . . . think you see things," Sean said. "I'm just . . ."

"Sean, you think that whoever killed Tanya Barnard is still around? It's been ten years."

"David has come home to find the killer, Katie. I'm willing to bet that he's making that pretty clear. And if he's right, the killer is going to be afraid. Please, Katie . . . listen to me?"

"Love you to death, big brother," she said. "And I'm listening. I don't know what you're talking about. I don't see things."

"That's what I need to hear, kid," Sean said. He was quiet for a minute. "And be careful."

"Of what?"

He was silent, but it was as if she could hear a single name in the silence between them.

David.

"Big brother, you either believe he's guilty, or you don't."

"I don't."

"Then?" she asked.

"It's — sad, sometimes . . ."

"You believe in a person or you don't."

"I do," he said.

"Then?"

"All right, let's say I believe in him. Belief isn't all black-and-white. And not only that, but what if someone had been after him? What if that person is still around? Just watch out for yourself. Careful on getting too friendly."

"I'm thrilled I'm going to get to see you," she said, ignoring the warning.

"Yeah. See you soon! And behave until then, huh?"

"I'm just a regular angel, Sean."

His snort was loud and clear. "Love you, Katie. And behave, I mean it."

"Oh! We're going in circles here, dear boy! I thought David was your friend, Sean."

"He was. He is, I assume," Sean said. "But . . ."

"Oh, my God! You are such a liar. You suspected him, too!"

"No. I never did. All right, that's a lie. I don't want to believe that David could have been guilty. I mean, I don't think he could have been guilty. But the thing is, no matter how mature a man he might have been trying to be, Tanya did hurt him. I understand that people think that she might have found him that night, that he might have been angry. I don't believe it, it's just . . . she is dead. David was a big strong kid from the time he was ten. But he was always — sane.

140

Craig taught him to be respectful at all times. He didn't have a maniacal or crazy temper. So, I really believe he was innocent. Except, inside me somewhere, I suppose, I couldn't help but let some of the theories and rumors get to me."

"But now — you don't believe it was David? Or you don't want to believe it was David?"

Sean was quiet a moment. "Yes."

"To which?"

"To both."

"Okay, I'm saying that it wasn't David. Then who?"

"I don't know, Katie."

"The police questioned you. I read it in a book."

"They questioned everyone. I had been hanging at Uncle Jamie's place that night — O'Hara's. I saw Tanya there. I told them the truth."

"Do you remember who left the bar?" Katie asked.

"If I do, kid, I'm not telling you."

"What?"

"Stay out of it, do you hear me?"

"Love you, big bro. Losing the connection," Katie said. "See you when you get here."

She cut off the conversation before her

141

brother could give her more instructions.

She looked back to her paper. Her brother's name was the last thing she had written down. She scratched through his name. Sean certainly never hurt anyone. And neither did her uncle. She scratched through his name, as well. She looked at the list, shaking her head. It couldn't have been Liam, or Pete Dryer, or . . .

Lord! No wonder the police had never discovered the truth. No matter what they thought, the murderer had to have been a passerby in the Keys. Had to have been!

She heard a soft sound at the door and looked up. Bartholomew was back; he hadn't opened and closed the door, but he did make a strange noise as he came through it.

"Where have you been?" she asked him.

"Eavesdropping," he said.

"On who?"

He pulled out his pocket watch, which couldn't possibly work, but it seemed to, at least for Bartholomew. "You'd better get going. You're going to be late for work. Not to mention that your uncle owns the place and you should be keeping an eye on it."

She frowned and jumped up, realizing the time. She swore softly, gathered her purse and her keys and headed out. She closed the door; Bartholomew stepped through.

"Where were you eavesdropping?" she demanded.

"The police station," Bartholomew informed her.

"Oh?"

"Maybe I shouldn't tell you," Bartholomew said slowly.

"You wretched pirate —"

"Privateer!"

"I'm going to call for an exorcist and send you downward with your scalawag friends!" she threatened.

He laughed, but then saw her eyes. "All right, all right. I was at the police station, and the officers have been warned to keep an eye on David Beckett," he told her. "See, I shouldn't have said anything. They weren't sure what had happened because there was no evidence. There's some discussion about the fact that David is still obsessed with Tanya and her murder. Evidence! Like that mattered in my day. They just hanged us right and left, right and left!"

She paused, looking at him. "So you were hanged? You never told me that you were hanged!"

In his astral form, he puffed up, shoulders back, head high. "I was a victim of false arrest, Miss O'Hara. And my end was untimely and unjust!" He appeared to let out his breath. "But that doesn't matter now, Katie. What does matter is that you seem to be getting chummy with a murderer."

She shook her head, thinking she might be crazy. "He's not a murderer, Bartholomew. He's not."

"How do you know?"

"I just know. I just — know."

"You must keep your distance," Bartholomew said.

"Don't worry — my brother's on his way here. And, supposedly, Liam Beckett has the files now and they're working the murder as a cold case."

"I don't like it, not one bit," Bartholomew said.

"Well, I'm sorry. And please hush up and mind yourself. My uncle may own O'Hara's, but I'd just as soon his customers don't all insist to him that I'm crazy and talk to myself!"

What seemed to lurk in the human soul was odd, David decided. Being in Key West didn't bother him. Being in his grandparents' home didn't disturb him, either; it was actually good. The old place spoke of conch chowder on nights when the temperature dipped to forty, lemonade and good seafood. Some aspects of the house needed updating, and some remained cozy and warm. His grandmother had knitted throws for the furniture, and they were as neat and tidy as the day she had died. Her tea service remained on a small Duncan Fife table by the kitchen. His room had changed little — his rock band and *Sports Illustrated* posters were still on the wall. Okay, so that needed updating.

Being here, however, was not painful.

The museum was painful.

And when he walked into O'Hara's Pub with Liam, it was painful, as well.

It was the last place anyone admitted to seeing Tanya alive.

O'Hara's hadn't changed. The bar was well-crafted mahogany, and there were a number of booths with deep cushions and high wooden backs. Wooden double doors opened to the sidewalk. Air-conditioning slipped out, but that happened with most establishments on Duval Street. O'Hara's served typical Irish fare, fish and chips, shepherd's pie and a choice of corned beef or Canadian bacon and cabbage. "Leprechauns" were thin-sliced beef rolled in pastry and "banshees" were drink concoctions that seemed to mix every alcohol known to man.

The stage offered Irish music during the week, and now, karaoke some nights. It was apparently a popular notion because the place was packed when he entered with Liam. It seemed, however, that unlike many places on Duval, the music was kept at a nondeafening level, and at the back tables, it would actually be possible to carry on a conversation. Closer to the stage, it was louder, but not so painful that your head pounded or you felt the need to escape.

Katie was at her computer, listening to a group of girls, smiling and suggesting something, as they seemed perplexed over their choices. They all smiled and stepped back. Katie looked up at him suddenly, almost as if someone had tapped her on the shoulder and pointed out that he was there. She didn't smile, she just stared at him. Then again, he told himself, at least she didn't appear to be angry.

He noticed that a lot of locals still came to O'Hara's. It was a little closer to the southern side of the island than some of the other popular and must-see haunts, such as Sloppy Joe's or Captain Tony's. Many of the bars didn't sell food, either, especially after a certain time. O'Hara's served until 1:00 a.m., and when Jamie O'Hara was home, it might serve as late as 5:00 a.m., depending on Jamie's mood and who was in the place. That wasn't written on any of the brochures given out by the Chamber of Commerce.

"What would you like?"

He turned. Liam was smiling at the waitress, calling her by name. Obviously, he knew her. Clarinda.

"Shepherd's pie and a Guinness," he said. "Thank you."

At first, it appeared that the girl was trying not to look at him, then she stared him in the eyes and cleared her throat. "Welcome back, David," she said.

"Thank you."

"I'm Clarinda. I'm a conch, too," she said.

"Nice to meet you, Clarinda," he said.

She blushed. "You spoke to my class when I was in grade school. You talked to us about being a soldier."

"I hope I said all the right things," he said.

She smiled. "You did. Well, um. Well. Welcome back."

She went off to get their order. A group of young people in Florida State T-shirts were singing a Kiss song. They weren't bad.

"You know, I don't mind being here — but what are we doing here?" Liam asked him.

"Having dinner?"

"There are lots of restaurants here," Liam said.

"Retracing the past," David said.

"The last place she was seen," Liam said. "God, David, you know I want to help you. I just don't see what being here is going to do for us."

David lifted his hands. "I don't know, but doesn't it seem odd that the principals are reappearing?"

"What do you mean?"

"Liam, you're the detective," David said. "All right — so I can't help but see things that may not be here on this. But look who just got a job busing the place."

Liam turned around as David suggested, and saw that Danny Zigler was cleaning tables in the back.

"He wasn't working here when I talked to him this morning," David pointed out. "And let's see if I'm right. . . . Yes, yes, I am. There's Sam Barnard at the bar."

The FSU kids left the stage; a group of balding businessmen went up to butcher Billy Joel, but they seemed to have a good time doing it.

"Sam is here because you're here," Liam said flatly. "David, I pulled the files, I supported you in there today, I'm on it. I intend to give it my all. But locals have been coming to O'Hara's forever. It's a hot spot for those who live on the island."

"All right, Sam is in town because I'm in town — I spent some time with him today. And I'm sure Sam is in O'Hara's tonight for the same reason I am — it was the last place Tanya was seen. But what about Danny Zigler?"

"Zigler is always looking for work. He lost out when the museum closed," Liam pointed out.

Clarinda came with their stouts. "Food will be right up, gentlemen," she said.

"Thanks," Liam told her. "How's Jonas?"

"Doing well, thanks. He's still doing dive tours. He'll be by later."

"Great, we'll see him then. Hey, Clarinda, there's something I've been meaning to ask you. You're not walking home alone after your shift ends are you?" Liam said.

"I never do. Yell at Katie, though. She's terrible. I'll be right back," she said, and hurried over to another table to take an order.

A man David vaguely remembered as being Marty . . . *Something* went up to sing. He was good. He had a deep baritone and did a sea ditty.

Katie announced that they were gearing up in Key West for Fantasy Fest, and then

Pirates in Paradise. Any folks who returned for the party days would see Marty *Jenkins* performing.

People started clanging beer mugs on the tables. They were chanting something. Katie stood up and beckoned to Clarinda.

The girls did a Broadway number. It was actually very funny, and David discovered that it wasn't exactly Broadway, but rather Off-Broadway. The language was fast and furious, and both girls, though laughing, excelled with it. The audience went wild with clapping, but Katie quickly moved on, announcing an Elvis number by a fellow who would also be performing at Fantasy Fest.

Elvis announced that during Fantasy Fest, he painted on his show duds. He sang, and again, he was someone who did a really nice rendition of "Blue Suede Shoes."

Their meals arrived. David had his fork halfway to his mouth when he noted that Katie was staring out the door. When Elvis finished, the place clapped enthusiastically. Katie didn't seem to notice. She seemed unaware of anything; she stared at the open doors as if the bright lights of heaven had suddenly exploded there.

As if she had seen a ghost.

To his incredulity, she stood, totally heedless of Elvis leaving and her empty stage. She raced to the doors and straight through them.

He leapt to his feet, and followed.

6

He was stunned to see Katie O'Hara suddenly on the street. She was staring after someone — as if she had just seen a long-dead relative.

And she was making her way down Duval. The crowd had thinned, but she was oblivious of the people who remained out.

She was chasing someone.

David Beckett was on the street, too, searching for Katie, then following her.

She seemed to be in some kind of a daze, intent on nothing but her purpose.

"Katie!" Beckett called, seeing her, racing after her. He reached Katie. Caught her by her shoulders and spun her around with surprise.

He couldn't have known her, couldn't have really known her, she'd been a kid back then.

But he'd known her brother, of course. Sean. Who had gotten out of town when it all broke, as well.

Beckett shook her gently, saying her name again, and then once again.

It was bizarre. She snapped out of whatever spell had gripped her. She seemed surprised to be in the street, there, with him. He was touching her. And her eyes met his. There was no hostility in them, just curiosity.

She shook her head then. Beckett was still concerned. Katie seemed to be determined to assure him that everything was all right. What was she saying to him?

He could tell . . .

There was just something about the two.

There was tenderness in Beckett's eyes. It wasn't the same kind of tenderness a man might show the younger sibling of an old friend.

And his hands. The way that he touched her . . .

The way that they stood. Why not? She was a stunning young woman. And Beckett . . . ah, Beckett. He played the part. The sterling son of a sterling family. Tall and handsome, a vet, an educated man, a famed photographer . . .

He felt his fists tensing into knots at his side.

Yes, there was something there.

Regrettable. Katie was a good kid. She didn't sleep around, she didn't drink herself silly. But it looked as if Katie was going to be the one. Maybe not first . . . maybe that would be too obvious far too quickly. But Katie would be the one who mattered.

Katie wasn't as alarmed by what had happened as she was by the fact that David Beckett had followed her, that he had seen her.

And she couldn't even try to explain.

I finally saw a ghost who might be Tanya. No, she probably is Tanya. She was in the cemetery today. I think she's trying to reach me. I thought there was something familiar about her, and, of course, there was. I've seen her picture, I saw it years ago.

"I could have sworn I saw an old friend," she lied. "I mean, I could have sworn it, but . . . I guess I was wrong. I thought it was . . . Janis Seacloud," she said. She'd had to search her mind swiftly for the name of anyone she had gone to school with whom she was certain had left town years ago and not returned. He wouldn't know her friends, of course. Still, a lie had to be as close to the truth as possible.

Bartholomew was beside her, as well.

"Oh, good save, young lady," he told her. "I mean, seriously, what was that? I thought you'd lost your mind. And you say I'm going to make you look crazy! You're doing just fine on that all by yourself."

"Stop!" she murmured.

"Pardon?" David asked, frowning. He still had his hands on her shoulders. She liked the feel of them.

But they were still standing in the street, and she was looking more unbalanced every second.

"Oh, God, I ran out in the middle of a song!" she said. She turned, escaping his hold, and hurried back.

She paused at the door, looking back at David. "Um, thank you. I'm sorry, didn't mean to alarm anyone . . . I'm . . . Thanks!"

She hurried back to the microphone at her station, and called up the group of partying girls she'd helped choose a song. It was an old Madonna song, and the group had a lot of fun doing it. She felt unnerved, and prayed for the business of the place and the music to calm her sense of unease.

For God's sake, she'd seen ghosts forever. Sometimes they approached her — most often they didn't. Only Bartholomew had ever decided that he needed a best friend among the living!

"Steady, kid, steady," Bartholomew whispered to her.

"Did you see her?" Katie asked.

"Yes."

"Who is she?"

"I don't know."

"You're a ghost."

"Right! And do you know every tourist walking down the street? Tourists are living, you're living. Does it mean that you know everyone? No! Just hold it together, Katie O'Hara. And stay away from this whole thing. I know you're thinking that girl was Tanya. Maybe she was, maybe she wasn't. Doesn't matter — you need to stay out of it and away from David."

Katie ignored him. She needed to get through the night.

"Katie?" he persisted.

"Bartholomew, you need to make up your mind. You said that you liked David, but you keep suggesting that he might be a murderer."

"I do like him."

"Okay, so?"

"He still may be a murderer."

She groaned and turned her attention to her computer.

"What the hell happened?" Liam asked David as he took his chair next to his cousin.

"Beats me. I've never seen anyone with a look like that. . . . She said she saw an old friend."

"It's still bizarre," Liam noted. "I guess I'll hang around and walk her home. I've never seen Katie behave so oddly. And it looks like she's talking to herself."

Clarinda swept over to the table; she had heard Liam. "Anything else for the moment, fellows? Oh, and she isn't talking to herself — she sings along with the music."

"Of course," Liam said.

"How late does she keep the music going?" David asked.

"It's Saturday night; she'll go to three," Clarinda said. "Jamie O'Hara says that three is just right. By then, folks are in, and the place stays open, so people will stay. And hard-core karaoke folks can go down the street to Rick's. Share the wealth, so he says."

She smiled, arched a brow, saw they wanted nothing else at the moment and moved on to check on other tables.

"Don't worry about hanging around," David told Liam. "I'll stay."

"No, I've known Katie a long time now. And . . . there's an interesting, rowdy crew in here tonight."

"Liam, I don't work in the morning. You do."

"All right. You stay. But don't decide she's all right, okay? Make sure you see her all the way home."

"I will," David promised.

Soon after Liam left, Sam walked over to his table. "How's it going?"

"Slowly."

Sam nodded and lifted his beer, indicating Danny Zigler, who was busing a table nearby. "There's a suspicious character for you," he said.

"Danny?"

"Scrawny little fellow just making his way."

"Right. Which makes you wonder if such a scrawny little fellow just making his way would have the capability of planning out such a murder," David said.

"I wouldn't count him out," Sam said morosely.

Katie announced the last singer of the evening and Marty went up to do a Jimmy Buffett song. When he was done, Katie started closing down the equipment. She announced that if anyone wanted to keep on singing, they could head down Duval to Rick's.

A few moments later, Katie joined them at the table. She seemed pleased to meet Sam, told him that it was good to see him. "You were in the other night, weren't you?" she asked him. "But you've shaved since then."

"Observant girl!" Sam noted.

"Well, it was quite a beard!"

Sam seemed to like Katie, which seemed equally natural. She spoke softly with a sweet voice, her eyes were like crystal and her scent was definitely compelling. She was a beautiful young woman.

If a little strange! She had almost appeared to be in some kind of a trance when she had walked out so suddenly.

Katie frowned, listening, and turned toward the doors. David realized there was some kind of disturbance going on in the street.

David didn't say anything — he gave her a glance that told her he would check it out. He walked to the door. There was a bar fight going on. Pete Dryer was there, a big man, holding the battling drunks apart from one another. He saw David. "Get the little one, running down the street, David!"

David went after the man. He looked to be about twenty-one or twenty-two, and it wasn't any problem getting him — he ducked and shrank, putting his hands up. "Hey, you got me, you got me, don't hurt me!"

"I'm not going to hurt you. The cop down the street wants to talk to you, that's all,"

David said. "Turn around, and head on back."

The kid did so. He looked younger, and terrified.

Two bigger fellows had been cowed. They stood on either side of Pete. "All right, what the hell is going on here?" Pete demanded.

"That little shit robbed me!" one fellow said.

"That's my brother. He didn't rob you," the other big guy said.

Pete looked at the kid. "Did you rob him?"

"Hell, no! That stripper came out and started busing him all up — I didn't take anything from him. Check my pockets!" the younger kid said.

Pete arched a brow. The kid pulled out his pockets. He had only his own wallet, which contained his ID. He was Lewis Agaro, age twenty-one, and he had ten bucks, an ATM card and one credit card, in his name.

"What are you three doing together?" Pete asked.

"We're not together. That thug just suddenly started going after my little brother!" one man said explosively.

"Hey, sorry, man! So, now, come on, let's go after the stripper!" the other man said.

"What stripper?" Pete asked.

"Well, what the hell, she's gone now, what

do you think?" the apparent robbery victim asked.

"All right, we'll take a report from the robbery victim — the two of you need to get to your rooms for tonight, cause no more trouble, or I'll see that you're locked up for your vacation, and you're not going to find any margaritas or hurricanes or any other such concoction when you're in my custody!"

Pete looked at David. "Hell, I'm not even on duty!" he moaned. "I was going to join you guys for a drink. I got a car coming. I think I know which lovely little stripper is at her pocket-picking again. I'll have to find her."

David grinned. "Tomorrow, Pete," he said. He had come halfway down the street. When he turned around and went back into the bar, Katie was gone.

He caught Clarinda by the arm, his touch far more forceful than he had intended. "Where's Katie?"

"Gone, she went on home."

There must have been a look of alarm on his face.

"I tell her all the time not to go alone!" Clarinda said.

"It's all right, it's all right," David said. "Which way does she go?"

"Down Simonton," Clarinda said. "Make her call me!"

David turned and headed out, running around the corner to the back. Almost two blocks ahead, he could see Katie.

Between them, he could see Sam Barnard. His heart leapt to his throat. Sam had to be watching out for her.

Why was Sam following her late at night, though?

"Katie!" He shouted her name.

Both Katie and Sam stopped, and turned back. Katie seemed surprised to see him; so did Sam.

"Sam, where are you heading?" he asked, moving up.

"My B and B is down the street," Sam said. He blushed. "I'm staying at Artist House. We don't have a place anymore."

"Oh, well, it's a beautiful place," David said. They walked together on down to Katie where she waited.

"A couple of drunks got rowdy?" she asked.

"Yeah, Pete was there."

She laughed. "Pete doesn't have to deal with the drunks much these days. He must have been ticked that they acted up right in front of him."

"Yep," David said.

"Hey, a cop is a cop," Sam said. He stood awkwardly for a moment. "Well, good night. See you all. Tomorrow, I imagine. Hey, Katie, you got your act up tomorrow night, too, right?"

"Sunday, yes," she said. "Good night, Sam."

Sam walked on. The streets were quiet. Katie waited, looking at David. "I was trying to walk you home," he told her.

She smiled. "That's nice."

"Let me see you in."

"Okay."

They walked in silence for a minute. They reached her house and she opened the door. She seemed to hesitate, as if she was about to ask him in, but wasn't sure.

He waited.

She didn't.

"Thank you," she said.

He nodded. "Well, keep your door locked, all right?" he asked.

Her smile deepened. In the muted light her eyes were truly a crystal that seemed hypnotic. He reminded himself that she was Sean's little sister.

But Sean's little sister had grown up.

"Well, good night," he told her.

"Good night."

She closed the door; he heard her lock it.

He turned and walked slowly back to the Beckett house.

He paused on the street. He loved the house but tonight, it seemed cold, empty and forlorn.

And down the street, he could see the museum. He wasn't given to anything illogical, but it seemed that night that the museum had a life of its own. It looked large in the shadows, dark and evil.

Irritated, he let himself into the house he now owned. He went to bed, and lay awake a long time, staring up at the ceiling.

Katie was exhausted, but the events of the past few days seemed to rush through her mind. She was restless, jumping at sounds. But then she grew angry with herself; she wasn't easily scared. For God's sake, it wasn't as if she thought there was a ghost in her closet.

There might be a ghost in her closet, but if there was, she wasn't afraid of it! Ghosts reached out. They needed help. They weren't evil puffs of air or mist or . . . whatever. They were lost, and frequently, in pain.

She wondered then if there were *evil* ghosts. In her experience, no. For her, they were a part of life — just like allergies were

164

to some people. Sometimes startling and annoying, and sometimes, like Bartholomew, they just seemed to hang around endlessly.

She was fond of Bartholomew. And he actually made her feel safe. In his odd, ghostly way, he was a very good friend. He was fond of her, as well.

She thought about David, and what he believed — that *surely* there was nothing in the world beyond the obvious. David wouldn't be a big believer in ghosts.

She tried counting sheep. That was ridiculous. She looked at the clock. It was 4:00 a.m. She prayed for sleep.

At last, she drifted off, and then fell deeply asleep. She woke slowly in the morning, feeling the coolness of her sheets, hearing the hum of the air conditioner. Her drapes were closed, but the sun was filtering into her room. It was day; she had rested. And she felt good.

She stretched, and then rolled over, cuddling her pillow, wanting just a few more minutes in bed.

She froze.

Despite herself, she screamed.

She wasn't alone in bed. The woman she had seen on Duval was there, lying next to her, staring into her eyes.

The woman was dead.
Her eyes were wide open, huge and blue,
and staring sightlessly.
She was a ghost, of course. . . .
The ghost of Tanya Barnard.

No matter where he went, no matter the project, David preferred staying close to the sea.

Actually, one thing that he had missed about home was the guarantee that the water was going to be temperate and beautiful. Sure, in the middle of winter even the Atlantic and the Gulf could be cold. But usually, nine months out of the year at least, the water was beautiful.

Today he felt the need for the water. He thought best when he was in the water, and he wasn't feeling close enough to anyone else from his past to ask for company — *not true, he'd have asked Katie O'Hara, except that she had kept her distance the night before* — and though he knew damned well he shouldn't plan on going out by himself, he was going to do so. He'd had good friends, expert divers, who had actually died by believing that they were so good they didn't need company. He preached diving with a buddy.

But today, he was going to live recklessly.

He was going out alone.

He knew that his grandfather had kept the *Lucky Life* in good repair at the dock; he knew that Liam took the boat out often enough, as well. He walked the distance to the boat, knowing that Liam kept dive equipment on her. The dive shop right at the docks rented tanks, and he could also buy sandwiches, water and beer.

Lainie Regent still worked at the dive shop; she greeted him and rented him four tanks with thirty minutes each. These would work as long as he controlled his breathing and kept his dives around sixty feet. He assured her he wasn't doing any of the deep wrecks, and that he'd be fine.

"Welcome back, David," Lainie told him. "Be nice if you stuck around a bit. Hey! I saw some of your work in that national earth-thingy magazine. David, what great pictures!"

"Thanks, Lainie." He bid her goodbye without making any commitments and headed on down to the *Lucky Life*. Craig had never really been much of a fisherman; in his younger days, he'd been an avid diver. The boat was designed to that end with eight tank holds, a freshwater hose and bucket, a small cabin with a very small working galley and a head. Since David had been gone, sonar equipment and global positioning had been added.

Nice.

He checked his gas, then started to slip the ties that tethered the boat to the dock.

"David!"

He looked up, startled by the sense of pleasure that seemed to wash over him.

Warmly.

Hotly.

Katie O'Hara was hurrying down the dock toward him. She was wearing deck shoes, shorts, a bikini top with an open long-sleeved shirt over it and a huge, floppy sun hat. She was all long legs and flowing hair, and she seemed to make his heart beat too hard, his libido to flip about. He kept his features rigid, thinking of the years he had been gone, the women who had come and gone from his life, many nice, kind, cute, beautiful, intelligent — and some not. They had all been friends, but all like ships at sea, passing in high and low waters, in storm and in calm.

None had made him feel this way, and he had to wonder why.

He barely knew her.

And she was Sean's little sister.

"Hey, Katie," he said, pausing. He frowned. "How did you know where I was?"

"I don't exactly have a phone number for you," she apologized. "I called Liam. Then I did try you, but you're not answering."

"Sorry, my stuff is thrown in the cabin."

She nodded. She looked like she had the night before.

"Why were you looking for me? Is something wrong, has something happened?"

"No, no, nothing is wrong and nothing has happened. I guess I wanted to talk to you, mull things over more. Now that I'm here, I think you need company. It's dangerous to dive alone, you know."

He smiled. She sounded like one of the very serious and professional instructors they might have had when they'd been young, just old enough for certification.

"Climb aboard," he told her.

"Where are you heading?"

"Sand Key — nothing deep. I'm looking for something peaceful, protected . . . lots of fish, clear water."

"Sounds good to me. Do I need more tanks?"

"We can make two dives — and I imagine you have to be back for work."

"Great. Food?"

"We're good. Climb aboard."

She hopped on, releasing the last loop as she did so and winding the lines. She knew the boats; she knew diving.

They were conchs.

He kept his speed slow while exiting the no-wake zone, then picked up as they headed out in a southwesterly direction. The sound of the motor kept them from talking much, nothing more than, "Want a water?" And, "Sure!" And then his thank-you to her as she produced the plastic bottles from the ice chest.

At last he slowed the boat; there were charters out in the area and a number of smaller craft, as well. He set their dive flag out, and went for his equipment.

She slipped into a skin, telling him that she hated running into jellyfish, and they helped one another with their tanks, rinsed their masks, held them and back-dove into the water. He had taken one of his underwater digital cameras for the day, not planning to do any professional work, but seldom without a camera.

It was good to have Katie with him.

It was good to be down.

The deepest the area went was seventy-five feet or so, but most of the reefs and the fish were found at depths shallow enough for snorkelers to enjoy the water, too.

They kept a distance of about five feet apart, and the dive was everything he'd wanted. Crystal clear water, just cool enough to be pleasant, warm enough to be comfortable. Tangs in a variety of colors shot around the reef, anemones flared and larger fish appeared as well, one giant grouper, a curious barracuda that politely kept its distance and, beneath them, a number of little nurse sharks.

Katie, in her light dive skin, hair flaring out around her, eyes large and beautiful behind her mask, made a perfect subject for quick takes with his camera. She frowned when he first started snapping, but he shrugged, and he saw her smile around her regulator.

It's what I do, he reminded her silently.

Especially where there was such an abundance of colors. And since they weren't deep, the sunlight penetrated beautifully. He had shot and filmed in so many exotic places. And yet, his own backyard offered some of the most enchanting underwater locations around.

He saw something in the sand and headed down, touching the granules to find a little ray nestled there, happy to move, even sit in his hand and puff as Katie joined him. He shot the little ray, and Katie's finger just brushed a wing. But then her attention was diverted.

And it was while they were there, kneeling in the sand at about forty feet, that Katie suddenly made one of her startling and frightening changes again.

She was touching the little ray. . . .

Then she was frozen.

Staring wide-eyed.

And she wasn't breathing. No bubbles were escaping from her regulator.

He dropped his camera and the ray and gripped her shoulder. Her eyes met his. He couldn't begin to understand what he was seeing in them. And those eyes of hers, framed and huge behind the lenses of her mask. . . .

She didn't appear to be afraid of *him.*

In fact . . .

She wasn't afraid at all.

She suddenly looked as if she were about to cry.

He tapped her chest. She inhaled; her bubbles began again.

He signaled that they go topside. She shook her head, but he was firm. She lowered her head, and then she nodded.

He crawled up the stern ladder first, doffing his flippers and then, once up, his tank. She removed her flippers and threw them over and he reached to help her up with the weight of her tank. She stripped off her dive skin and accepted the bottle of water he gave her. He studied her, and waited for her to speak.

She sat in the cushioned seat behind the helm and said nothing.

"Katie."

"Hmm?" She looked at him and smiled.

"Katie, what the hell is going on with you?" he asked.

She looked out at the water. She started to speak, hesitated, then didn't. Then she looked at him. "Do you . . . do you believe in dreams, or hunches, or . . . I don't know, the mind trying to tell us things that maybe we just can't really understand logically?"

Like seeing an image in the sea of Tanya trying to communicate?

He shook his head. "Katie . . . no. Not really."

"Experts know that our dreams reflect our lives," she said defensively.

"I'm lost, Katie. What are you talking about?"

He didn't want to be lost. Her hair was tousled and soaked and flying around her head, and she was just curled on the cushion, staring off. She was still beautiful. He wanted to reach out, touch her, tell her that whatever it was, it was okay.

Her legs were endless, muscled and lean,

173

her breasts were full against the bathing-suit top. She had a belly-button ring, a little dangling silver dolphin, and it made her belly seem like the most desirable stretch of bronzed flesh ever imagined. . . .

"I just had a dream last night, that's all," she said.

"Good dream, bad dream?" he asked her.

"Good dream."

"Are you going to tell me about it?" he asked. It wouldn't explain what had happened in the water, but it might lead to an explanation.

"I don't want you to laugh at me — or hate me," she turned her gaze from the sea to stare at him.

"All right. I swear, I won't laugh at you. And," he added, hearing his own voice grow huskier, "I won't hate you."

She spoke quickly, suddenly. "I dreamed about Tanya."

He started to move; the words made him want to bolt, no matter what he had said.

"It was a good dream," Katie said. Her hand fell on his knee.

His knee had never felt so naked. Nor had he ever known that a kneecap could suddenly be such an erogenous zone.

"Tell me," he said. His voice was tight.

"She didn't know who had killed her in

the dream. She did know that you didn't do it."

"Great. We can put that in the news-paper."

She flushed. She looked as if she would have walked away from him — if she could have walked away.

"Look, I'm sorry," he said. "I just don't really believe in that kind of thing. I mean, maybe dreams are a reflection of our lives. You don't want me to be guilty, and since I swear to God I'm not, I'm grateful that you feel that way. But . . ." He leaned toward her. A mistake. She still smelled faintly of her intoxicating cologne, even though she was drenched in salt water. She seemed to emit an aura of warmth that lured him closer, or made him want to drown in touching her.

He eased back. "Katie, last night was scary. And freezing like that when you're diving, well, that's damned scary. Why did you freeze in the water?"

She looked away again and chewed on a thumbnail. She shook her head. "It won't happen again," she told him.

"Katie —"

"Sorry. I believe in dreams. And it's nice. She loved you — in my dream. She knows that you're innocent — in my dream."

"She's dead," he said bluntly.

"Yes, she is. But I dreamed about her." She inhaled. "And then I saw her in the water. Not in a bad way. She's trying to help."

"What?" David said sharply. *What was this? Was she taunting him somehow? Torturing him. Foolish, it was long ago. His heart had hardened.*

Not enough, maybe.

She wasn't taunting him. Maybe it was worse. Maybe she was just crazy. He didn't want her to be crazy. He cared about her . . . far too quickly, and far too deeply. He needed to remain rational.

"Katie, I am a big believer in the power of suggestion. And with everything going on . . ."

He let his voice trail with its own logical suggestion.

"Yes, that's it, of course. It's nice, though, that this kind of power of suggestion is a good one — the images I'm seeing in my crazy little suggestible mind seem fond of you, hurt for you."

"Katie, look, I didn't mean anything by what I said."

She looked at her watch, all business all of a sudden. "Oh, Lord, I'm so sorry. It's gotten so late. We need to head back — I have to get to work. I ruined your diving day. I'm so, so sorry." She was sincere and contrite. And she didn't seem to be really angry with him.

"Don't be sorry. I'm not," he told her softly. And he did touch her. He touched her cheek, and he met her eyes, and he realized that whatever it was that made a man attracted to one woman and not another, he had just found it in Katie. He wasn't just attracted. He was entwined.

He stood. "Grab a few of the sandwiches. We'll eat while we motor back in."

She nodded; he pulled in the flag and the anchor while she went about pulling food from the ice chest. He chewed on a ham-and-cheese-on-wheat while she stood next to him, facing the wind and the spray while they motored back in to the dock. He slowed his speed and followed the markers until they reached the dock. Katie jumped out with the ties.

"Hey, I'll start rinsing equipment," she called to him.

"No, go on. It's nothing — I've got it. Get cleaned up for work," he told her.

She stood on the dock, looking down at him. Now, she was just in her bikini. It wasn't a super-string thing or anything like that, just hip-hugging bottoms and a bra top.

Lord, but she was beautifully built. Athletic, curved, lean . . .

"It's all right, Katie. You're working. I'm not. Get going."

She still stared.

"I'll see you at O'Hara's later," he told her.

She smiled.

It seemed a fire started in his chest. Or his loins. He couldn't really tell. It was just burning everywhere.

He handed up the rest of her belongings, watched her slide into her oversize shirt and shorts and then turn and start home.

He plowed into the ice chest for a beer, and sat on the chest then for a moment, puzzled, staring after her.

It was still fairly early, afternoon. Daylight. Sun was streaming down on the island.

But he was worried. About Katie.

He forgot the equipment and the boat. Or, they were there, in the back of his mind. But they would wait.

He slid into his deck shoes and leapt to the dock and went racing after her.

The streets were crowded today. Sunday. People were shopping, taking dive-and-snorkel and party boats, Jet Skis and more. They were eating and drinking, and buzzing slowly around on scooters.

178

He raced from the wharf to Front Street. He could see Katie turning off, right before Two Friends bar and restaurant. He followed.

He reached her in time to see her enter her house and close the door behind her.

He stood still on the street, wondering about her earlier words.

He could see no one who seemed to be paying the least attention to him.

He looked up to the windows in the old Victorian and Deco houses around him. No one seemed to be peeking down from behind shutters or curtains.

And yet, he could swear that he was being watched. He was being watched because . . .

Katie had been followed.

7

Stella Martin woke in the late afternoon. It was late, and she was startled to have slept so long. She bolted up, looked around and smiled.

The night hadn't started out well. She'd not been able to resist the temptation to pick a jerk's pocket up on Duval. She'd seen the commotion that had followed. She'd felt bad for the kid who was accused — so she'd followed him.

She'd seen his brother leave him, taking off with a pathetically sluttish rich girl who'd sauntered out of the Irish bar. So much for heading back to their rooms as they'd been told!

She'd managed to snare the kid — who knew that she'd ripped off the other guy. It was a great joke between them. She laughed with him, got to know him and arranged to meet him back at his hotel room after her shift. The kid had been to the ATM machine and was rich. If not rich, Mommy and Daddy were very well off. The two brothers weren't even sharing a room.

They'd had a number of drinks. Now he was still sleeping. Snoring. Usually, she hated men who snored. But this kid probably was barely twenty-one. He had long dark hair that fell over his forehead and eyes now as he slept, and he was kind of cute. He'd actually been fun, too. No finesse, but he could fuck like the proverbial bunny. She hadn't even been tempted to charge him more for going at it again and again. It had been fantastic. Most of the time she was exhausted in an hour, trying to coax a middle-aged drunk asshole into getting it up.

Ah, the kid was cute. Thanks to him and his room, she'd eluded all the cops.

A smile curved into her features. A few of them, she was certain, would always let her go on purpose. They really wouldn't want to have her talking to them down at the station.

She slipped out of bed and gathered her clothing quickly — she was just as good at dressing quickly as she was at undressing slowly. His wallet was sitting on the dresser, and she had to pause. She wouldn't take all his money. Just fifty — the kid would still have over a hundred bucks on him. He probably had no idea of how much money he had left anyway. She also took his credit card. She saw his ID. She smiled. Touching. He was an art major at U of M. Silly kids. They came from other states, and they couldn't wait to get down to the decadence of Duval Street. It was such a bizarre place. She worked one of the strip clubs. Eighteen-year-olds could walk into any strip club. They couldn't drink, which meant they couldn't go into a few of the bars that offered karaoke. Stella found that ironic. Kids could watch strippers, but they couldn't sing. Well, it worked for her.

She counted the money she'd stuffed into her pocket from the night before. It had been so easy to lift the wallet off that big bruiser — and funny, too, to see the idiot attack the guys walking behind him. What an oaf.

But, thanks to the oaf and the kid, she'd had one hell of a good night. She counted her hundreds, smiled and slipped out the door.

Luckily, he'd been staying at one of the inns right off Duval that had a back entrance. There was a stone wall, but it was low, and she scrambled over it quickly. Coming along the sidewalk, she turned onto

Duval Street.

There were a couple of mounted cops down the street, so she slid into a bar. She ordered a beer quickly, and turned her back to the street.

The mounted cops went by.

Stella finished her beer, paid and tipped — she always tipped well — and started out on Duval again.

She swore when she walked right into *him.*

"Stella," he said.

He was one of her few johns who wasn't married. He was a creep. She knew it. Maybe other people didn't.

"Hey."

"You smell like stale sex, Stella. Bad booze, bad money and stinky, old sex."

"Fuck you," she said, and pushed by him.

Her heart thundered for a minute. He could do bad things if he wanted. But it was broad daylight. Hell, it didn't matter what the light was.

She quickened her pace, but when she turned around, he wasn't there. She kept on moving, and passed the church.

She heard the sound of a siren. Damn, the cops!

The ice-cream parlor was right ahead.

She ran inside it, her back to the street.

She winced. *Danny, yeah, Danny was sup-*

posed to be here!

It didn't matter; she just needed to stand here for a minute. She set her hands on the counter. It was sticky. She shoved her hands into her pockets, making a face.

The cop car was passing.

Then Danny was back. With that way that he looked at her.

"Ice cream? Really, Stella?"

The way that he looked at her . . .

He was sad, he was angry.

"Danny —"

The cop car was gone.

"Danny — oh, whatever!" she said.

She turned away, and decided that she really had to get off the main streets. She hurried outside and around the church. She could hear a car, and she started running, paranoid now.

She cut through one of the yards. Damn it — she knew too many men in this town. Knew them too intimately.

Maybe *he* was in a car. He might have gotten his car, and he could be following her in it now.

No. Why on earth would he do that?

To harass her.

He was a creep.

She cut into a yard and crawled through palms and crotons that grew heavily there.

She looked at the street. No car.

She started to turn around, aware of a sound behind her.

She wasn't able to turn. Something came over her head. A plastic bag. She grabbed at it, incredulous. Hands wound around her neck. The world began to grow black.

It couldn't be happening. . . .

She was vaguely aware of sirens. She tried to fight; to live. Help was coming. The sirens came closer, closer. . . .

And the sound moved away. Help might be coming for someone, but not for her.

And the blackness swamped over her.

"You're falling apart — you are simply falling apart," Bartholomew said. "I'd slap you across the cheek to wake you up and make you see clearly — if I could," he added sternly.

They were just inside the house, and he was clearly agitated.

"All this time, I keep asking you about the lady in white. She ignores you, you ignore her. Now you have this new ghost appearing and disappearing, and you've gone straight to pieces."

"She's not just any ghost," Katie said. "And you saw her last night."

"I didn't see her today."

185

"You weren't with me down there when I was diving with David. You're afraid of the water!" Katie accused him.

"I'm not afraid of it. I can swim," he argued indignantly. "I can't see why I should go down getting soaked and wet when there's no reason for it."

"Would you really get wet?" she asked. "I mean, do ghosts get wet?"

"It's the thought and the memory," he said, and shuddered. "You swim when your boat sinks, when you're under attack, when it's your only recourse. Not for the pleasure of it!"

"Wow. How dirty and icky were you?" Katie asked.

"I bathed!" he protested. "When possible. I wasn't repulsive in the least. I had amazing hygiene habits for my day and you are getting completely off the subject here. Katie, you must stop being so hypnotized by this ghost!"

"You don't understand. It's a true pity that you don't go into water for the pleasure of it, and you didn't follow David and me down on that dive. Then you'd understand. The ghost is Tanya. She's trying to communicate with me — she just doesn't know how. It's very bizarre, really. She's trying so hard to reach out. But . . . I understand her a bit because . . . there's something in her eyes. She can materialize, but she fades so quickly. I can see her try to whisper, but she's so hard to hear. Maybe she hasn't been a ghost long enough —"

"Ten years," Bartholomew noted.

"And the lady in white, the one who fascinates you? She doesn't know how to communicate and she's been a ghost for nearly two hundred years, I'd reckon."

Bartholomew plopped down on the sofa in the parlor. "You be careful, or they will lock you up. I don't enjoy jails — modern or otherwise — and I know that I wouldn't at all enjoy a mental hospital."

"Oh, that's just great — coming from you. Bartholomew, Tanya was in my bed this morning."

"Very rude," he said. "I would never dream of disturbing the sanctity of your private quarters!"

Katie ignored his words. She hurried on. "And then in the water. Bartholomew, I told you, you had to have been there. She appeared slowly in the sea dust, as if she gained her image from the particles of plankton and microscopic debris. . . . She formed right behind him, and she looked so, so sad, and she touched his shoulder and his cheek. I could have sworn that there were tears in her eyes."

"In the water?" Bartholomew mocked.

"She looked sad, as if she was crying — yes, in the water! She wants me to know, even if she can't tell me who *did* do it, that he didn't."

"That's ridiculous. She was murdered. If she knows who did do it, she needs to tell you."

"Maybe she doesn't know. Her attacker might have struck from the back."

"Then if she doesn't know who did do it, how does she know that it wasn't David Beckett?" Bartholomew demanded.

"She might have known where he was at the time of her death — and if he was nowhere near her, it couldn't have been him."

"Well, you do need to stop running about in a trance. He will think that you're as daft as a loon!"

"I will. I have it under control. Now."

"I certainly hope so," he said. He looked at his pocket watch. "Time's a-wasting, my dear."

She spun on him and started up the stairs.

David washed down his equipment, rinsed himself off and headed back to the house for a real shower. After that, he went out to

188

find Danny Zigler.

He was serving ice cream. He grinned at David. "Hey."

"Hey."

"Ice cream?"

"You know what, I'll take a shake. Vanilla."

"Cool."

David paid him, adding a handsome tip.

"Hey, thanks, David, you don't have to go overboard. I'm not a charity case, you know. I keep working."

"Yeah, I see that. I was so surprised to see you at O'Hara's last night. I thought you were doing the ghost tours. And, hell, the crowds on weekends are huge. Didn't think you could take time off like that."

"Yeah, I miss doing the weekend tours. Thing is, all the companies out there have hired on too many people. Most can work weekends, around their other jobs, you know? I can work weeknights, and to be honest, I don't like an overcrowded tour. I like to be able to tell the stories good, you know? And when there are too many people, half of 'em don't hear you, and when you repeat all kinds of stuff, you lose the whole effect," Danny said.

"I know what you mean. Too many in a group, and you just don't get the effect," David agreed. "Well, thanks. See ya, Danny.

Oh — you working at O'Hara's tonight?"

"I start at ten there. I am taking out an eight-o'clock tour tonight."

"Cool."

David waved, and headed down the street. He walked toward La Concha Hotel, and around to the stand where ghost-tour tickets were sold. A young girl was selling tickets. He asked her about Danny Zigler. "Oh, yeah, he's working tonight. Eight o'clock. He's a good guide."

"Yeah. It surprises me that you all don't use him all the time," David said.

She shrugged. "Hey, I'm not management. But I think that Danny likes his other jobs, too. Strange fellow, but a good story-teller!"

David bought a ticket and moved out of the way for the couple who waited behind him. He glanced at his watch, and headed back home. He had left the police files on his grandfather's desk. He set an alarm to warn him when it would be nearing eight.

A long, hot shower and shampoo felt won-derful, rinsing away the cakey salt and ef-fects of the sun and the sea. Katie lingered under the flow of water, then emerged regretfully at last, aware that she should be conserving water — and that she was pruning.

She slipped into a terry robe and towel-dried her hair, then studied her reflection in the mirror. Wet, she decided, was really not her look. But too bad — she loved the water too much.

She looked over at the bathroom cabinet, choosing a moisturizer.

When she looked back at the mirror, there was someone behind her.

It wasn't Tanya. It was a different entity. She had dark hair, too much makeup and her eyes were red and slightly bulging.

A tear slipped down her astral cheek.

"No!" Katie whispered. "Please!"

The girl remained, that tear sliding down her face.

"Please!" Katie whispered again. "I'm not nine-one-one for ghosts. I don't know how to help you. I don't know who you are!" she whispered vehemently.

She closed her eyes, praying for the image to go away. She opened her eyes. It did.

Her hands were shaking when she reached for her cosmetic base and looked back to the mirror.

The image was back.

The girl was no longer crying. She was just standing there, staring at Katie, as if she were in shock. Her face was starkly white. Her features seemed to have shriveled. Her eyes were clouded with red dots.

"I wish I could help you!" Katie whispered. "Please . . ."

The image faded.

Katie collected her makeup and went running down the stairs.

Bartholomew was perched at the kitchen counter. He stared at her, frowning. "What now?"

"Another ghost," she said.

He looked annoyed. "What is this — spirit central?" he demanded. "This is my house."

"It's my house," she corrected.

He sighed. "Actually, Katie, once upon a time, I lived in the upstairs bedroom. Well, I didn't live there, I spent a great deal of time there. Eighteen twenty-six, to be exact."

"But this house —"

"Oh, the house has been rebuilt. It was just a tiny wooden structure at the time. The place was a shantytown, really, except for some of the places built by big money. Simontons and Whiteheads . . . Anyway, I had a girl for a while. She wasn't the kind you brought home to mother. But she was one hell of a woman. Never mind, that's not the point. This is my haunt. You're my mortal."

"You're being selfish," Katie said, feeling a new strength. "They need help."

"Everyone needs help."

"She was murdered," Katie said suddenly.

"Most ghosts were murdered."

"No, Hemingway killed himself, and he's haunting this country, Spain and Cuba, so I understand," Katie argued.

Bartholomew sighed. "Katie, don't let them in. I'm afraid for you."

"Bartholomew, I'm not saying she was murdered this minute. It might have been years ago. Like . . . Tanya. Maybe it was the same person."

He swung off the bar stool and came before her, planting his hands on his hips. "Katie, I am very afraid for you."

"Sean will be here in another day or two and then I won't be living alone. I'll be fine. And I know the cops — I know everyone on the street. I'm from here, Bartholomew. I'll be fine."

"I'm sure that's what Tanya Barnard thought!" he said dourly. "Well, I won't be leaving you alone for a moment," he assured her. He looked her up and down in her terry robe, her makeup clustered in her hands. "And you are afraid."

"I was startled, that's all."

"Well, that robe is going to make a lovely

193

outfit when you go to work."

"I was startled. I'm not afraid."

"I'll follow you and guard the hallway, if you'd like to return to your bathroom and further prepare for the evening," he told her.

She lowered her head, smiling. He could trip people; he could now press the on button to start the coffee brewing. She still wasn't sure he could actually *guard* her. But he was quite the gentleman ghost.

"Thanks," she told him.

But when she returned upstairs, no matter how many times she looked into the mirror and then away from it, no ghosts appeared.

The first ghost, she knew, was Tanya.

But who the hell was the dark-haired woman with the tear glistening on her cheek?

As David had expected, evenly dividing the crowd that night left about forty people in each tour group. He was tall, and he stayed toward the back.

Key West was full of ghosts. Naturally. Since it was a walking ghost-tour, it didn't take in the cemetery, the Hemingway House, or many other spots reputed to be harboring ghosts. That was all right. There were many haunted places to still go to on the tour. Captain Tony's was haunted by

those who had died at the hanging tree — and those sixteen souls whose remains were found when work was done on the place.

Another favorite stop was an abandoned theater near Duval that was supposedly haunted by the souls of sixteen children who had burned to death there in the midst of a marital scandal — a spurned husband had meant to kill his wife, so people suspected. Instead, he had killed the children. Some of their little bones remained in St. Paul's Church yard, where the children were still heard to sigh with the breeze on a quiet night. Visitors standing beneath the theater overhang heard the soft cries as well — and the scent of smoke was still on the air, all these long years later.

Artist House was on every tour. The Victorian mansion was stunning, of course, but the real draw was what happened in that house years ago. The story went that a servant of the owners of the house, the Otto family, had given their young son, Robert, a doll. The servant had come from the islands and practiced some kind of magic or voodoo.

Of course, since it was a hideous doll, many people had been convinced that the servant really hated the family. Robert stood about three feet tall, stuffed with straw, and wore a white sailor suit and hat. He had beady little eyes, and the kind of fabric face that was just creepy from the get-go. Having grown up with the story, David was truly amazed that someone in young Robert Eugene Otto's life hadn't gotten rid of the damned thing. Instead, the doll had stayed, Robert and his wife had been given the house and they had moved in. The doll spent years playing evil pranks.

But Robert loved the doll throughout his life. When his wife thought that he was preparing a nursery, it was really just a special room for Robert. Robert the Doll tormented Robert's wife — slowly driving her crazy. Although many believed that it was Robert who abused her and blamed the attacks on Robert the Doll. She outlived her husband and left Artist House, but allowed it to be rented — with the stipulation that Robert the Doll's room be kept and that he remain closed away in his special place.

Robert the Doll supposedly moved. He looked down at people on the sidewalk. He went from window to window.

Eventually, new owners took over — the doll was given to the East Martello Museum, and was still known, according to popular legend, to escape from his chamber.

He was supposed to wreck film, or replace rolls of family film with pictures of himself.

Danny Zigler was an excellent guide and told all of these stories well. David could see the fear and awe he evoked in his listeners.

They walked toward the Beckett museum.

David thought that Danny told this particular story with relish, describing the dead Tanya with amazing detail. And though Danny never used his name, he suggested that someone prestigious had gotten away with murder, and that it had been a case of unrequited love.

Tanya, of course, according to Danny, roamed the now-defunct museum, crying out night after night, shrieking for justice.

David slipped away from the tour. He realized that his hands were clenched into fists at his side.

He'd be damned sure to stay away from Danny until he'd cooled down.

O'Hara's was quieter than usual that night. Katie did a duet with Marty Jenkins to get it all started — a song from *South Pacific,* as Marty didn't seem to care much for any song that didn't have something to do with ships or the water — and then a soprano down from her job as a character in an

Orlando theme-park musical came on and awed them all with a number from *Chicago*.

There weren't nearly as many inebriated people as on a Saturday night, but there was a group of ten students with the soprano who didn't have classes again until Tuesday, so Katie was kept busy. At eleven she decided that she needed a break, and she set the students up to do a six-minute version of "Bohemian Rhapsody."

David seemed to have chosen his table at O'Hara's; he was there with Liam, Sam Barnard and Pete Dryer.

"Katie, girl, lovely night, you keep it moving," Pete applauded.

"It's a nice crowd," she said. "So how about you, Pete? Sunday a better day?"

"Sunday is usually a better day — except folks are moving in big-time now. Fantasy Fest is in the works," he reminded her. "It officially starts next Friday."

"Oh, right. It will be super-busy," she said. She noted that David was barely listening to her; he was watching Danny Zigler.

He didn't look happy.

"Anyway, I'm going to have a busy week no matter what," Pete said. "I think I have a runaway stripper, and I'm pretty sure she's the one who took off with that man's wallet last night."

Liam laughed. "A runaway stripper? Is there such a thing? I mean, a stripper is free to come and go as she chooses, right?"

"Unless she's wanted by the law for being a pickpocket," Pete said grimly.

"But did you see her?" Liam asked, frowning.

"No, I didn't see her. But lately, we've only had one girl in trouble for helping herself to gents' wallets, instead of waiting for the bills in the garter — or whatever," Pete said.

"How do you know she's missing?" David asked, suddenly turning his attention to Pete.

"She works at the Top-O-The-Top, and when I went to try to talk to her — warn her that I'm on to her at the least — she hadn't shown up for work. One of the other girls told me that it was unusual. She likes money," Pete said.

"Well, it is a Sunday night," Sam commented. "Who knows? Maybe she heard about some better pickings up the islands."

"If I don't find her by tomorrow, I'll put out an APB," Pete said.

"Pete, can we prove anything?" Liam asked.

"I've got the kid's report — hell, yes, I can put out an APB. Anyway, good night, all. I'm heading out," Pete told them.

The college kids were having a good time, and they did so without being smashed or obnoxious. Katie kept the music going longer than she had intended.

Even so, David waited for her.

"You know," she told him, "I've been walking myself home for a very long time."

"Alone?" Bartholomew said.

She didn't look his way, but she added, "Physically walking my mortal self."

David seemed bemused by the comment. "But it is late and I am here. Do you mind?" he asked her.

"No. I'm glad." She waved good-night to Clarinda.

"Zigler is gone," David noted.

"I guess he took off early."

"Started late, and took off early. Interesting," David said.

"You've been looking at him with daggers in your eyes all night," Katie commented.

"I followed his tour around tonight," David said grimly.

"Oh."

"After what I heard on his tour, I'd be scared of me," he said.

"Danny is a good guy, though," she said. "And I guess there's no way to keep the tour guides from telling a story, especially if they

200

can conjure a good ghost."

"I wonder what he does with all his money," David said.

"Well, he isn't working jobs that set you in the upper stratosphere of income," Katie pointed out.

"Still, he eats where he works, lives frugally . . . He must have some kind of a pastime."

"Maybe he hides all his money in his mattress. Wasn't there a crazy person who did that once?" Katie asked.

"Crazy. Umm. There have been a lot of crazies down here. It must be the sun," David said.

They reached her house. He stood on the porch while she found her keys and fit one into the lock. The key turned and she looked at him. It seemed that she had no voice. She wanted to speak; she wanted to sound casual.

"Would you like to come in?" she asked. *Oh, God, she sounded as if she was applying for a job as phone-sex girl.*

He smiled and leaned against the door frame, not touching her, and yet looking at her in a way that made her feel as if he could send out rays of static heat.

"If I come in . . . well, it might be dangerous, you know."

"I don't think you're dangerous," she said.

"No, I meant it really might be dangerous. I'm torn — I want to be with you, but I'm not so sure you should be seen with me."

"Oh. Oh," she murmured and blushed, feeling incredibly awkward. She started to step past him but he blocked the way and she met his eyes again. They were deep royal-blue, a navy color that could be so dark it appeared black in the shadows. "I would love to come in, if the offer still stands."

She paused, feeling as if the night could change everything, and then feeling foolish, as well. Sex. So many people fell into it so easily. She'd never been able to play that game, she'd never wanted something that didn't mean something. This felt like more. It was sex . . . it was intimate. Natural. Biology, something that happened between people. But she meant something to him; she knew it. She cared about him, equally.

"I . . . I want you to come in." Ah, there she was, sounding like the phone-sex applicant again.

But he reached out, stroking a finger along her cheek and smoothing her hair back. "I didn't want to want you, but I do," he told her.

"I think . . . well, they do say there's just something that attracts certain people."

"Think we should make love and experiment?" he asked.

She shook her head slowly. "No."

"Well, we are still on the porch."

She smiled, suddenly feeling sure of herself, and at ease. "I like the idea best of us both knowing that we wanted . . . one another from the start."

"Actually, I really disliked you."

"Come to think of it, I loathed you."

"Let's get in," he said huskily.

They stepped inside. Katie closed and locked the door and wound up pinned against it. David leaned into her, and their lips met in their first kiss, something that seemed to ignite into an instant passion. It was a kiss, just a kiss, but hungry, wet, all over, openmouthed and so sensual that Katie heard a sound and realized that it was herself, it was a moan, but it was aggressive, and her hands were cradling his jaw, feeling the structure, holding him to her.

They broke breathlessly, staring at one another.

He kissed her again with a whisper, a brush of restraint and tenderness, and his eyes met hers and his lips formed hard and seeking over hers once again and their tongues filled one another's mouths.

She heard a groan. It wasn't him and it wasn't her.

"Oh, good God, woman, you've got a room, go to it!" Bartholomew said.

She started and jerked back. Bartholomew was leaning against the counter, appearing irritated and disturbed by the entire scene.

"Room!" he said, waving a hand at her. "Go, go!"

"What?" David said. "You can pull back at any time, Katie. I swear, I'll leave at any time. Now, if that's what you want. You've got to be sure."

She glared around his head at Bartholomew and pulled David back to her. But she practiced restraint. She kissed him, running her fingers over his shoulders up to his nape, and into his hair. It was so thick and rich. Touching his hair was arousing. She was in sad shape.

"Katie, go!" Bartholomew said.

"You go!" she whispered over his shoulder.

David backed away. "All right. I'll see you tomorrow."

"No, no!" She caught his hand and headed up the stairs. She ran, pulling him behind her, then stopped suddenly.

Ghosts. Ghosts kept interrupting her life. Victims who wanted to speak to her . . .

Ghosts who needed her.
But not tonight!

"Katie," David began.

She stopped him. "I'm sorry. I'm scared. But don't leave. I want you, I want this. It's just . . . the last time was Carl Waverly and I dated him all through college but then he wanted to get married and move to Seattle and I knew that I had to come home and that was . . . that was it and a long time ago, but don't worry, I won't make more out of it than it is . . . oh, God, way more detail than you needed, right?"

He smiled and laughed with a husky sound, and his eyes were dark and yet alive with a brilliance that seemed to be warmth or tenderness. "It was great detail," he assured her, and he pulled her against him and lifted her from her feet, sweeping her off them. Soft light came in gentle streaks where the drapes weren't completely closed and dust motes seemed to dance in a fantasy world. He laid her on the bed, and he came down beside her, kissing her as he began with the buttons of her blouse. For a second she was still, then it seemed the whole of her was on fire, and his movements weren't nearly fast enough. She writhed against him, finding buttons herself. She pressed her lips against his throat and his collarbone, working at his tailored shirt. Hers was slipping away at last, her breasts were free and her flesh was against his. Shadows made it easy, the glow of light made it beautiful. She felt his lips against her breast while his fingers found the belt buckle of her jeans, snap and zipper, and his fingers played erotically over the silk of her underwear while she shimmied from her jeans, tugging at his while she did so. She felt his muscles tense and ripple where she touched him, felt the crush of his mouth against hers, again the thrust and plunge of his tongue, deep and evocative. Somehow their clothing was gone, shed, a part of the tangle of coverlet and sheets on the bed and their hands and lips were everywhere. His mouth slid down the length of her, teased and tasted, while his fingers stroked up her inner thighs. There was a wonderful sense of power and strength about him, he was gentle and vital and vibrant. He seemed to know exactly where to touch and then kiss and caress, a slow burn started that seemed to flare out of control.

She felt herself explode within, and the feeling was growing again. He was over her, his eyes touching hers, and he moved into her, thrusting in a way that seemed to fill her completely and then stroked, moving with greater power and speed, reaching higher and higher, slowly, beginning again, leading her once again to a point where she exploded cataclysmically, shuddering and shaking in his arms, so sated that she felt she could die. She seemed to fall down in a field of clouds, except the clouds were sweaty and sleek, and it was amazing to be held against him with such a contrast of sensations filling her flesh and mind.

Sex. Just sex. First sex. Awkward when the clothing was strewn and the pinnacle reached . . .

But it wasn't. He came up on an elbow, and his smile was deep. His features were really masculine and beautiful, rugged, never pretty, and yet . . . beautiful.

"Umm. You were well worth waiting for," she whispered.

"We didn't wait that long," he said, smiling at her.

"Seems like forever," she said softly.

"Thank you. And . . . obviously, the point now is not to instantly jump your bones, so I suppose it will be all right if I tell you you are really amazingly beautiful and certainly, anyone could wait a lifetime for you."

She laughed. It was easy being with him. Naked and panting, it was still easy. "Did you get to Ireland in your travels?" She teased. "Kiss the Blarney stone?"

He stroked her hair, looked into her eyes. "Never," he assured her. He held her against him, still studying her face. "Sean's little sister. You did grow up well."

"You've really got to quit referring to me as Sean's little sister."

"I do, absolutely. I don't intend to feel guilty a moment when I see Sean. You are, beyond a doubt, very grown-up. And out. In all the right places."

"Thank you, again." She laughed, and then her breath caught, and suddenly they were clinging to one another again, and rolling on the bed, passionately touching and teasing, and once again, making love wildly, desperately reaching at moments, smiling at others, laughing . . . and then climaxing again. The world seemed to have no end. They talked about music and coming home from school and finding a way to make it all work. He talked about lighting and photography, getting into underwater film, loving the world beneath the sea, and she reminded him that Key West had some of the most fantastic sunsets in the world.

When she slept that night, it was deeply.

When she woke, the woman was back.

Not Tanya, the other woman. The dark-haired woman. She was seated across the room in the dressing-room chair, and she was looking at Katie forlornly.

Katie bit her lip and turned her head slightly, glad to see that she and David were both decently covered beneath the coolness of the air-conditioning.

She stared at the girl in her room, and she moved her lips without a whisper. "Not here! Never in my room."

The ghost frowned, blinked and then nodded. She stood, and glided sadly toward the door, and disappeared through it.

8

Katie woke up early. Lazy, smiling, she'd turned to David, and it seemed the most natural thing in the world that he was there with her. They made love again, slowly, leisurely, feeling the heat of the day grow and glow upon them as the sun rose.

When she drifted off again, David left her a note, telling her that he'd be at his grandfather's house.

He still couldn't call the place his own.

He wanted to spend more of his time with the files Liam had left for him. The police reports were filled with sheets on the detectives' door-to-door questioning of neighbors. No one had seen anyone enter the museum other than the Becketts and tourists.

Many neighbors saw him.

There were the statements, sworn by his grandfather and others, that he had worked at the museum until midnight, and then been at home and with his family until the next morning, when he had left to go to the museum once again.

Danny Zigler had been questioned; he was one of the few people with a key to the museum. But a set of keys had hung just inside the kitchen door of the Beckett house, and many people knew that they were there. It had been determined that there hadn't been a break-in, so someone had come in with a key. There hadn't been an alarm system, despite the expense that had been poured into the place over the years.

Forensics had yielded little other than the fact that Tanya had been strangled; an injury to her knee was at least a week old. She had apparently skinned it. The autopsy report noted that Tanya Barnard had not been tortured — a small blessing.

David dragged his fingers through his hair, and began drawing a chart of the timeline. First, time of death. Second, time in which to get into the museum. It had been open until midnight the night before. That meant her body had been elsewhere for several hours, then moved into the museum. Whoever had put her in the museum either had a key, or knew where the keys were kept. Many people knew about the key. But the

Becketts had all been home and together after midnight on the night of the murder. Which meant, David thought, that it had been planned. Meticulously planned. Days before, someone had to have taken the key and had it reproduced. He had a key, there was a key they kept in the house, Danny Zigler had a key and Liam had a key.

David drummed his fingers on the table.

It hadn't been a random killing. Tanya had been targeted, and the display of her body had been planned ahead of time. Likely, it was someone who had come and gone from the Beckett house. Himself, Liam. Danny Zigler, any member of Tanya's family, his friends at the time, his grandfather's friends . . .

He was going over the names, trying to think of anyone else. Craig Beckett had been smart, but he'd also had an open heart. They'd welcomed underprivileged kids in for tea, supported the police, the firefighters and every poor wretch who stumbled upon their family. The house had been an open highway.

Sam Barnard thought that Danny was shady. David had a hard time accepting the fact that he might be guilty of murder.

Who then? Who had been around? Himself, Liam, Sam, Jamie O'Hara . . . no, they said that he hadn't left his bar that night, not until the wee hours of the morning. Still, he could have hidden the body — but he hadn't been gone between the hours of seven and nine.

She had last been seen at O'Hara's.

There had to be something in the files.

There were pictures. Bizarre pictures, still barely real. He rubbed his finger over one of the photographs, touching Tanya's cheek. Had she been targeted and killed because someone wanted to punish her?

For being free and loose, for finding a new lover while she'd still been engaged?

He read more of the interview notes and realized that there was a small notation next to the name Mike Sanderson. *Itvw b p; subject oos.* What the hell did that mean?

He frowned. They were a policeman's notes to himself. Guy Levy. He was still a cop; he'd gotten transferred over to investigation from being a beat cop. Guy had at least ten years with the force now.

Interview by phone; subject out of state?

David pulled out his cell phone and called the station, asking for Guy. To his surprise, he reached him immediately.

"David! Saw you at the station the other day but you were gone before I could say hello. How are you doing? Dumb question.

We hear about — and see — your success all the time. It's good that you're back."

"Thanks. Hey, Guy, I wanted to ask you a question about Tanya's case."

There was silence, and then a groan. "Hey, you know, I wasn't really in on the case. I wasn't an official investigator. I was just doing interviews."

"I know, I was just curious. Did you go up and see Mike Sanderson, Tanya's new boyfriend?"

"No, no. I interviewed him by phone. He was gone, you know."

"Right. So I heard. Where was he when you spoke to him?"

"Uh — home?"

"You sure?"

"Well, he'd left Key West, you know. Like a day or two before the murder. I didn't talk to him until the following Monday. I'm sure he could have reached Ohio by then."

"Did you speak to him on a landline?"

"I spoke to him on the only number I had. He was all broken up. Said he wasn't surprised when he didn't hear from her right away — he'd been afraid that once she'd seen you, she'd change her mind."

Sloppy work, David thought. *Well, they'd dragged in patrolmen. Men who did what they were told, and didn't think to hunt down the man and talk to him in person.*

He didn't tell Guy that someone should have really traced Mike Sanderson's movements; he could have been hiding out somewhere in the Keys. He could have surprised Tanya. She wouldn't have fought him. She would have never suspected that he wanted to do her harm.

He thanked Guy and clicked the end button on his phone. He needed to get Liam going through official channels to draw credit-card receipts and find out if Mike Sanderson had really left the island.

The crime-scene photos were not good. The murder had been just ten years ago; the photos should have been better, more extensive. He turned on a high-powered light and ruffled through the desk for a magnifying glass.

There was something he hadn't noticed before. Spots. He tried to rub them off the photos. They didn't rub off. Was it poor photography? No, he thought. There was something there. Something that looked like light blue bruising on her nose and her lips.

He pulled out the autopsy photos and report. There was no mention of the bruising on the face.

Maybe it had been so light at the time that

the coroner hadn't seen it?

Impossible to tell at this late date, and it wasn't evident until now, until he took out the magnifying glass.

Death was officially suffocation by strangling. The bruises on the neck were evident. There had been nothing beneath her nails. Tanya hadn't fought her attacker. She had been taken completely by surprise.

That suggested someone strong, and, probably, an assault from behind.

He closed his eyes and tried to imagine someone coming up behind her, someone with the strength to encircle her neck with his hands and choke the life out of her before she could put her hands up to resist. It would have been natural for her hands to dig into the hands that were on her, for her nails to have curled into flesh.

Not if her attacker was wearing gloves, and not if he stole her air so quickly she couldn't scream or do more than lift her hands.

His phone started ringing and vibrating on the desk. He picked it up and checked his caller ID before answering it.

Pete. Lieutenant Pete Dryer.

"I thought I'd call you right away," Pete said.

"What's happened?" Was he calling because Guy had told him about his questioning?

"Oh, God," Pete said.

David felt a quickening of dread; he'd made sure that the museum was locked, but he still had a sinking feeling.

"What's happened?"

"I'm down off Front Street at the new oddities museum," Pete said.

Thank God, a different museum, thank God. . . .

But he knew, he knew something terrible had happened, and he had a feeling that it didn't matter much where the body had been discovered, just that one had been.

"I found my missing stripper," Pete said. "And God knows, maybe something is going on again, maybe your mumbo jumbo about an agenda is right. So I'm trying to unofficially let you in on this. Come on down, and I'll do what I can."

David was frankly surprised that he was permitted to pass by the yellow tape with Liam.

There was already a good crowd on the sidewalk as they made their way through the outer doors to the tourist attractions. People were whispering, pointing, speculating.

217

The museum was a medium-size place, much as the Beckett family had operated, but it was new since he'd been gone. One-storied, it occupied an old warehouse building that was just about ten thousand feet square. It was called the Eccentricities Museum, a good enough name for the exhibits it boasted on the posters flanking the doorway.

See Carl Tanzler and his Elena! Get to know Robert the Doll! Become a member of the Conch Republic — yes, it was real, for just a few hours. Find out about the secession! Meet Samuel Mudd, take a virtual tour out to the Dry Tortugas and learn what it was like when yellow fever struck.

Just as in most other museums, other exhibits came first.

There was a young woman talking to an officer at the entry, sobbing as she did so. She had been the cashier, he realized. There weren't tours here — visitors walked through at their own pace, he saw.

Liam was moving quickly, and David followed at the same speed. He almost bumped into a model of Hemingway — in death, the man was everywhere.

Pete was already at the crime scene. He was hunkered down by the body, speaking with the M.E., who had already been working on the corpse.

The exhibit displayed Elena in wedding gown, with Carl Tanzler standing by her side. A plaque announced that they were Tanzler and his bride — he had married her in a private ceremony officiated by himself, in his airplane on the beach. One day, he had believed, he and his bride would sail away to the heavens in his airplane.

David's muscles seemed to knot and contort; no model of Elena lay on the bed.

This time, the girl had dark hair. Long, dark, slightly kinky hair.

There was a photographer on hand, but Pete seemed to be impatient with him. "Angles — I need the angles. Come on, you should have a couple dozen shots by now."

David shot wildlife. Nature. He wasn't experienced with crime-scene photography. Luckily, there had been a few classes at college on the techniques. But they weren't much to help him as he tried to use his small digital camera discreetly to get a few snaps.

The woman's eyes were open wide. She stared in distorted horror into the air.

Déjà vu.

Pete, the M.E. and the police photographer — who mumbled something about the real guy being on vacation — stepped back.

Flash, flash, flash, flash, flash. The bruises on her neck. Flash, flash, flash . . . the way her body was situated on the bed. Flash, flash, flash, her eyes, her eyes, her eyes, just like Tanya's.

"This one has been dead for twenty-four hours," the M.E. told Pete, pointing his gloved hands at the body. "She was held somewhere else while lividity set in . . . note the blood and the coloration on her arms."

"The museum had just opened. Liam, you might go and interview the first group through here today, the ones who found her." He gave directions to other officers and techs, staring at the body and shaking his head. "Hell. I wanted to throw her in jail for a night or two, but this . . ."

"She was strangled?" David asked the M.E. It seemed obvious, but nothing could be taken for granted.

The man looked up at him curiously. "Same as before."

Flash, flash, flash. A sheet had been pulled up, but it seemed to have been done hastily. She wasn't pretty, as Pete had said. In life, she'd had a hard look about her, David thought. There was none of the innocence and youth that had made Tanya so stunning, even as a corpse in a tableau. The woman wasn't unattractive; she just wasn't

220

beautiful. Nor had she been laid out with care. There was something off about the scene, something discordant with the last.

And the last he could remember as if it had been yesterday.

Pete looked over at him. "This one isn't as pretty, maybe it's a copycat. Or maybe . . ."

"Maybe what?"

"Maybe, just maybe, you're right. Someone has an agenda. And . . ."

Pete's voice failed. David knew what he meant to say.

And look who is back on the island after ten years?

It was Pete. Because of Pete, he could be here, he was sure Pete's superiors would see that he was ejected from the scene soon.

David stared at the dead girl, trying to take in every detail that he could. Bruises rounded her throat. The petechia in her eyes was pronounced. She wore lipstick, but it was smudged. Her blouse had been buttoned out of whack.

Had she done it herself?

There was the sheet that had been tossed over her — it almost looked as if the murderer had been forced to hurry. Where Tanya had been laid out to appear perfectly beautiful, it seemed that this girl had been quickly dumped.

"Lieutenant!"

One of Dryer's top men came in and whispered to him. Pete glanced at David, sighed and nodded. He came to David and whispered, "Well, my men are beginning to comment on the fact that I've got a civilian in here. This is it — time for you to go."

David lifted a hand. "Thanks for calling me, Pete," he said.

Pete inhaled. "You were so adamant about not reopening the Beckett museum. But . . . hell, where there's a psycho . . . I'm afraid that it's not just you, David, who needs to worry about their displays. Now we know that. Any museum is up for grabs, so it seems. And Fantasy Fest is nearly here. Good God. We've got a murderer, and the streets are about to become wall-to-wall people. Heaven help us."

"People may start canceling."

"Hell, no. Okay, maybe. Some will. But a little thing like the murder of a prostitute isn't going to stop anyone from partying. Lord, I hope the crime-scene folk can get something!" Pete said with disgust. "Why can't we have a few more normal bar fights?"

"What about security cameras here?" David asked.

Pete gave him a dry look. "Ah, come on, David. This is your home — we're not the damned backwoods. We checked that out first. Tape is gone. They're dusting all over for prints, but . . ."

One of the techs finished for him. "The guy wore gloves. Seems like he knew just what we'd be looking for."

"Footprints?" David asked.

The man shook his head. "He might even have worn some kind of bootie. Umm, not that we know if we're dealing with a *he,*" he added, and looked away, busying himself with his work. He was a tech — the detectives were supposed to be doing the thinking.

David thanked Pete again.

He took shots as he left, shots of the entry, shots of ground. Shots of the locks, which seemed to have been undisturbed. He did so carefully, and still, he was surprised that none of the officers seemed to notice or stop him; maybe they were all in a bit of shock.

David left then, afraid that he'd be shown out soon. Just outside, he saw Liam questioning the people who had been the first through. They were two young girls and an elderly couple. He nodded to his cousin, who realized why he was leaving. Liam nodded in acknowledgment.

The crowd was growing. News stations were setting up, and several reporters were already on air.

As he walked out, he thought about Katie. He called her quickly to tell her about what had happened.

"I already saw the news," she said.

Katie stared at the television.

The dead woman was Stella Martin. She had worked at a strip club on Duval, and most of the locals on the street who didn't know her well still knew her. The club owner denied that any of his girls engaged in any illicit activity. Stella had been a good girl.

But the next person the reporter talked to was a pretty young girl from the Czech Republic. She worked in the bikini shop downstairs and next door.

"Stella . . . well, it is sad, so sad. But Stella . . . left with men often. She — she could not come in my shop anymore, the manager said. She propositioned men here, and my manager, he would not have it hap-pening in here. A stripper is one thing . . . well, it is illegal here to charge for sex."

A stripper.

A minute later, Lieutenant Pete Dryer was introduced by an anchor. "Lieutenant! Isn't

this a copy of one of the last unsolved murders to take place in Key West?" the reporter asked.

"A copy, just that," Pete said.

"How do you know? The previous killer was never arrested, or known," the reporter said.

"There are differences." A barrage of questions started coming his way and he lifted his hand. "Naturally, we don't want to give out details. We need to keep some information quiet so that we can investigate this killing and solve it. We have a lot more scientific investigative techniques now, and we'll find out the truth this time, I swear."

"But isn't it true that the last murder involved the Beckett family — and isn't it true that David Beckett has just returned home?" a reporter asked.

Pete was silent a second. Just a second too long.

"No further comment," he said.

"Hey, what about Beckett? Supposedly, all those years ago, he had an airtight alibi, didn't he?" someone else asked. "Airtight — through Grandpa!"

Liam must have been nearby. She heard an explosive sound, and the camera angle jiggled for a moment before it settled on Liam Beckett. "Trust me — David had an

airtight alibi, and he'll have one now. Watch it, unless you want to find yourself in court!" Liam said angrily.

The doorbell rang and she nearly jumped out of her chair. Bartholomew was watching her. "I'd get it for you if I could," he said.

She ran to the door and looked through the peephole. It was David. She threw the door open.

"This isn't something I was expecting," he said.

"Come in. Come on in," she said.

"You sure?"

She frowned. "Of course."

He stepped in. "All the old crap is being thrown back up," he told her.

"I know."

"You still believe in me?"

"Unconditionally," Katie said.

He smiled, closed the door and drew her close to him.

"Pete's trying to help — I mean me, specifically. He managed to get me in to see the crime scene. And I managed to get a few of my own pictures."

"Oh?" she seemed worried.

"Hey, I went to school for this. I took a couple of courses in crime-scene work."

"So — you think that this will help you

find out what happened in the past?" She stared at him frankly. She stepped back and put her hands on her hips as if she were indignant for him. In no way did it seem to occur to her that it was just too odd that this had happened right after he had returned.

"It's either the same killer or a copycat," he said. "Thanks to Pete, I won't have to rely on the memory of what I just saw."

"Shall I send out for some food?" she asked. "I can cook something —"

"No," he said. "Let's head out."

"On the streets?" she asked, surprised.

"Duval Street, as a matter of fact. I'm not hiding. I didn't do anything then, and I sure as hell didn't kill a stripper I've never seen before. Hell, if they're going to come at me, I'm going right out where they can do it!"

"He doesn't look overly agitated," Bartholomew commented. He was perched on a stool next to her at an open-air bar on Duval; David had just been cornered by the press again.

He could have gone into public speaking, Katie thought. He managed the press well. He spoke about leaving Key West after Tanya's death because his home memories were far too painful. He managed to make the Becketts sound like the typical American family, and when he spoke about Craig and his grandmother, affection was apparent in his tone. He admitted that he didn't understand how such bizarre murders could have occurred so far apart; yes, there might be a copycat at work, especially since some aspects of the crime seemed to be different. He had every confidence that the police would find the killer. Someone wanted to know how they thought they would find a killer now — when they hadn't done so years ago. Someone else suggested that they wouldn't try as hard. Stella Martin had been a stripper and probably a prostitute.

David clearly stated that he was sure the police would work every bit as hard; a human life was a human life, none less valuable than others.

Katie sipped a rum and Coke, listening to him. Bartholomew watched him, and turned back to her. "Ah, if I could but taste that grog," he moaned. "Hey!" He straightened in his seat. "Look. There."

Katie looked down the bar. There was a woman with huge breasts and tight shorts sitting at the end of the counter, shaded by some of the palms that covered the bar.

"I'm looking," she said.

"I don't know her name, but she works at

228

the strip club."

"And you know this because . . . ?" Katie asked.

"Well, I may be dead, but I can watch!" Bartholomew said.

Katie stood up and came around the bar slowly. She didn't recognize the woman. Strippers, however, had a tendency to be very transient. She might not have been in Key West long.

"Hi," Katie said, sliding up on the stool beside her. "Are you all right?"

"I'm fine, fine," the woman said, trying to act as if she hadn't been crying. She seemed defensive. And scared.

"I'm sorry, I didn't mean to disturb you. You just appear to be very sad, as if you'd lost a friend, and I just wanted to say that I'm so, so sorry."

The woman had been twirling her swizzle stick in her pink drink; she looked over at Katie. She nodded slowly. "Yes, we were friends. Stella had a few bad habits, but . . . she liked money. She wanted to travel one day — far, far from Florida. She was born in a trailer up in Palatka, and she always wanted to get out of the state."

"Well, we can imagine heaven as a place far away, and maybe as wonderful as any-place she might have wanted to see."

The woman stared at her. "You — you're Katie-oke, right?"

Katie nodded.

"Stella liked to stand outside and listen. She had a nice voice."

"She should have come in to sing," Katie said. "Do you know who . . . was she fighting with anyone? Do you know where she'd been?"

"She picked up a kid the night before. . . . Well, they say she died Sunday afternoon sometime. Yeah, she was with a kid. I might recognize him if I saw him again. But . . . he was young. He didn't look like a killer. Then again, that's what they always tell us — God alone knows what a killer looks like. Oh, Lord — she was murdered!" the woman said, and huge tears formed in her eyes again.

"Hey, hey," Katie murmured. She didn't try to tell the woman that everything was all right — murder wasn't all right. "What's your name?" she asked.

"Morgana," the woman said.

"Um — is that your real name?" Katie asked.

The woman managed a smile. "Yeah, it's my real name, not my stripper's pseudonym. My mom was a big fan of the King Arthur tales and fantasy."

"It's a pretty name," Katie told her. "Just unusual, even today. Umm, did Stella see anyone regularly?" Katie asked.

"Anyone?" Morgana asked. She blushed and looked away. "Lots of anyones. Stella said that these days, people came to bars — men and women — just to hook up for the night. She was smarter. You could get paid for sex, and why the hell not?"

"I meant like . . . like, almost a boyfriend, maybe?"

The woman sat up and stared across the street. "Yes," she said slowly. "Yes."

"Yes — who?"

The girl pointed.

Katie followed her line of vision.

She was pointing at Danny Zigler.

The museum was closed for the day, but as the afternoon rolled in, reporters announced on radio and television that it would be reopened the following day.

Fantasy Fest was coming.

Key West might have once been one of the wealthiest cities in the United States, but the days of privateers, wreckers and sponge divers were long gone.

The city survived on tourism, cruise ships and snowbirds longing for the sun. Fantasy Fest drew people from around the globe, and it was one of the many local festivals that kept the local shopkeepers, innkeepers and restaurant owners and workers in business. The fest went beyond just the obvious; the business surging down the Keys kept construction workers, charter captains, meter readers, housekeepers, antiques dealers and jacks-of-all-trades surviving, as well.

David made a point of staying on Duval Street during the day. He spoke with any reporter who approached him.

Katie was glad to see that he intended to keep himself in the public eye.

She was somewhat annoyed because she couldn't seem to get a minute to talk to him alone.

It was late when the news of the spectacular murder gave way at last to interviews about the upcoming festival days. David had made himself so available that by nightfall, he had spoken to just about every reporter who had rushed down to the city.

Morgana had disappeared by then. But as David slipped his arm through hers, suggesting that they pick up food somewhere and head back to her house or the Beckett home to eat in peace, Katie managed to tell him that she had talked to the woman, and that Morgana had told her that Stella Martin had carried on a somewhat long-term relationship with Danny Zigler.

He listened to her gravely, and then said that they should head to her place. Along the way, they picked up a few to-go meals from the Hog's Breath Saloon. They headed to Katie's.

Bartholomew was nowhere to be seen. In fact, Katie hadn't seen him all afternoon.

They set up their meal on Katie's dining-room table. "I know you've already been talking to Danny," Katie said. She shook her head while chewing a piece of chicken. "But . . . I . . . Danny is kind of a skinny little guy. And we've known him forever."

"Hey, women have lived with serial killers for years and not known what their husbands or boyfriends did at night," David reminded her.

"Okay — but you seem to think that whoever killed Tanya had an agenda. So maybe he's not your usual serial killer," Katie pointed out. She shook her head. "But Danny! I can't believe it, and yet . . . Morgana did say that Stella Martin saw him . . . regularly."

"As a customer?"

"More like a boyfriend. That's what I asked her — if Stella saw anybody more like a boyfriend," Katie told him.

"That doesn't necessarily make him a

killer," David said.

"Do you think that they'll get anything from forensics?" Katie asked.

"I don't know," David said. He finished off his last bite of chicken and stood, slipping his hand into the pocket of his short-sleeved tailored shirt. "You have a computer here?"

"Sure — what's that?"

"I'm going to study the photographs I have of the murder scene."

"In the back," Katie said, rising, as well. "In the family room."

David nodded and walked on through. He hit the power button and waited for the computer to boot up, then slid in the small memory stick he held.

He looked at Katie. "You may not want to see these."

"Don't be ridiculous. This is the age of media — soldiers dead on the battlefield, et cetera. I'm fine."

He studied her, then nodded and hit the key to open his photos. Despite her words of assurance, Katie wasn't really ready for what she saw.

The scene. The scene of Tanzler and Elena she knew so well from being a kid growing up in Key West was familiar and yet horrible.

But there was Tanzler.

And there was a woman in Elena's place on her bed who had lived and breathed at a different time. Elena had died of tuberculosis, the woman had been murdered.

And though Katie had never *known* her, she *knew* her.

She had seen her reflection in the bathroom mirror. She had seen the huge tear form in her eye, and trail down her cheek.

Stella Martin had not been a great beauty. In death, she was like a caricature of Elena.

"Just like Tanya, and yet . . ." David murmured.

"What do you mean? It's a copycat killing?"

He shook his head. "I think the same person killed Tanya and this woman," he said. "She is not laid out as carefully as Tanya had been. There's something rushed about the display. And Stella was older and not as beautiful as Tanya. There's something almost garish about Stella. I think she was a handy victim. I think the killer wanted her displayed because I'm here, because Sam is here. Why else would the killer wait all of this time to kill again? Nothing else makes sense."

"What else makes you think it's not a copycat?" Katie asked.

235

David enlarged the picture, showing her the face. "Petechia," he said. "It's a hemorrhage in the eyes . . . caused by strangling. Look, you can see the bruises on the neck. But there's more — more like the crime-scene photos in Tanya's file. See the slight bruises . . . not even bruises, really. But the blue-and-gray smudges on the nose . . . and there, on the chin."

Katie narrowed her eyes. She saw the little marks.

"What do you think they are?" she asked him.

"I think they're from some form of plastic. I think the killer is putting some kind of plastic bag over their heads. They don't see him until the last minute. He comes from behind, puts the plastic over their heads. While they're desperately gasping for breath already, he strangles them."

"So they really don't know who their killer is," Katie murmured.

"He steals their breath away so quickly, they can't even fight," David said thoughtfully.

Katie looked away. She didn't want to see her ghost, the woman who had been a stripper and a prostitute but strong and gutsy in her own way, dead in a tableau.

David left the memory stick in the computer and stood, looking at his watch. He frowned. "You don't work tonight?"

"Not tonight, though Uncle Jamie said something about doing karaoke all week next week for Fantasy Fest," Katie told him. "I'm looking forward to my days off here."

He was a few feet away. He nodded, and she was hoping, without being overt, that he meant to keep her with him, spend their time together, from now until then.

But that wasn't the case.

"I have to go," he told her.

"Where are you going?" she asked.

"The strip club."

"I'll go with you," she said.

"No, it's — it's a strip club."

She offered him a dry smile. "This is Key West, if you've forgotten. Men and women are more than welcome together."

He shook his head. "Katie, trust me. This is something I really need to do alone."

"David — Stella was discovered today. People in there . . ."

"They might be cruel to me? Treat me like a murderer?" he asked. He shook his head. "That's why I made a point of staying on the street today. I'm old hat, and sadly, she was a prostitute, and half the people out there assume that it's some kind of a copycat deal."

He walked over to her, caught her shoulders and looked into her eyes. She stared back at him, her heart beating hard, and she wondered how she could possibly feel so strongly about him when just days ago she had barely known him.

"Katie, I need to speak with Morgana. You're the one who told me about her, remember?"

She nodded. Great, she had told him about a stripper.

"Wait for me, please?" he asked huskily.

"Sure," she told him.

He kissed her. On the mouth. But it was a quick kiss. A goodbye-for-now kiss.

But his hands lingered on her shoulders. "Katie, I . . ."

"Yes?"

"Thank you," he said. "Thank you for believing me."

"You can't really thank me for that," she told him. "It's the way I feel, it's . . . intuition. Whatever, it's not something we really choose. We believe or we don't."

He smiled. The man had fabulous eyes. She felt tension ripping through her, and she wanted to hold on to him, beg him to stay with her.

He touched her cheek. "Still, thank you," he said.

She didn't grab him; she didn't hold him, speak to him or try to stop him.

She nodded, and his lips brushed hers once again.

She walked him to the door. When he was outside, she locked the bolt.

She looked through the peephole and saw him walking down the street, toward Duval. When he disappeared, she turned and leaned against the door.

"Bartholomew?" she said.

There was no answer. Her ghost was off for the day and night, so it seemed.

She waited, listening. But there was nothing to be heard, and she felt as if she were truly alone.

With a sigh she headed into the kitchen, and turned on the small television on the counter. She switched around on the news stations, but although Stella had barely been dead for twenty-four hours, the nation had moved on. There had been a bus accident in New Hampshire, killing five, and Cleveland police believed that they had caught a spree killer who was shooting the elderly in the streets. Nanny Nice, a nurse who had killed handicapped children in a California hospital, was planning on a psychiatric defense.

Finally, the bizarre murder of a prostitute

in Key West, Florida, came on the local news. Stella's name wasn't even mentioned at first.

But, as the story wound down, Katie felt as if a chill was settling over her. The tiny hairs at her nape seemed to be rising.

In the television screen she saw a reflection.

She turned, and Stella Martin was back, standing in her kitchen, watching the television screen. She looked at Katie, her features twisted in torment.

"Help me," she whispered.

"Who did this to you?" Katie asked.

But Stella shook her head, tears forming in her eyes again.

She lifted her hand, beckoning to Katie.

"Come with me," seemed to hover on the air.

The ghost of Stella Martin walked to Katie's front door, and beckoned again.

I'm an idiot! Katie thought.

And yet she followed.

9

Strippers came in all sizes, shapes and varieties — even ages. Once, in college, David and a friend had done a piece on the strippers of north Florida. A lot of their other friends had ribbed them about the project, but it had earned them both superior marks for a photojournalism class.

A lot of young and very attractive women went into the work for the money. And the story was usually the same. It was good money with little effort. Prostitution and stripping were not the same, though the latter sometimes led to the first. One girl they had interviewed told them that drugs were readily available, so stripping sometimes led to drug or alcohol addiction. The addiction meant that more money needed to be earned, and stripping allowed a girl to find out who had money and who didn't, and who would pay, what they would pay for and how much.

Some strippers remained, even when not addicted to drugs, alcohol or sex, because they liked the thrill of being sexy on a pole. To some, it was empowering.

Others did love sex.

Some just loved money.

When Morgana appeared on the floor, David at first felt sorry for her. The woman was not young, nor did she have a perfect body.

But she could move. He imagined, watching her, that as a young girl, she had wanted to be a dancer — a dancer, not a stripper. When she moved, there was something special about her.

Some of the customers in the establishment were talking and didn't even notice her. Some of the clientele hooted and hollered.

She seemed oblivious to all of them.

And yet, when her music ended, she was back playing the game. David thought it was all by rote. There was a look of abject sadness in her eyes, even when she smiled. She was far away, even when she bent down to squeeze a bill between her breasts or accept an offering in the thong bikini she wore that was just strings.

When she walked from the stage, David rose to meet her, reaching out a hundred-dollar bill. She looked at him, and her eyes grew wider. Fear registered in them. He was afraid she was going to press the bill back into his hands and run.

"My friend Katie told me about you today," he said quickly. "I'm so sorry. I just want to talk to you. I was hoping you could tell me more about Stella Martin."

She hesitated. She stared at him. "The place downstairs has a quiet patio in back. But the bartender is a big, old bruiser, and he's a good friend of mine," she said.

He smiled. "I swear, I have no intention of hurting you," he said gently.

"And don't go getting the police on me!" she warned.

"No," he said.

"Five minutes," she told him.

She left, and as she did so, David turned to see that someone was leaving from the far back of the room.

Someone who had been sitting in the shadows, and was now just about hugging the wall and the darkness to hurry out.

Danny Zigler.

There she was. Katie O'Hara. She was leaving her house behind, as she had surely done thousands of times before.

Katie O'Hara. Such a pretty thing. Sweet

kid. She always had been. No doormat, she could handle a drunk out of control, speak with a cool authority that seemed to demand attention and hold her own with the best of them. Actually, she might be called beautiful now. All the rough edges of the child and the teen were gone; she was a woman. She had a magical speaking voice, and as far as Katie-oke went, ah, she was great.

Katie O'Hara . . .

She was there, she was alone, she was vulnerable.

Tonight . . .

Ah, tonight . . .

Tonight was too soon.

Too soon; the death of the stripper had to be noted, puzzled and plastered all over the news. A stripper might be forgotten quickly. That was the way of the world. But Stella Martin, pathetic user that she had been, had now taken her place in importance. Now she was history; she was legend.

And, of course, that would be it with Katie, too.

For a moment, he frowned, regretting the fact that he had chosen such a whore to be his victim. Stella hadn't really deserved to be remembered in any way.

Then again, Tanya Barnard hadn't been pristine, either.

Katie . . . well, Katie was a good girl. She deserved the best. She truly deserved to be legend.

Something very, very special would have to be done for her. Nothing quick, nothing spur-of-the-moment. It must be thought out carefully.

Fantasy Fest was coming. . . .

Ah, yes. Something truly magnificent could be done with Fantasy Fest.

On a Monday night, the streets were quiet. Comparatively.

There were still people out and about. The bars were open on Duval, and scattered venues around the city. It was an odd Monday — still Monday, but a Monday with the city beginning to fill. Many people planned vacations around Fantasy Fest, and some had already trickled in. More would arrive on Friday night, when the city went into high gear.

Katie wondered if there would be an air of nervousness, or if tourists would simply need the diversion for their own lives.

Usually, people could rationalize away something wrong, heinous or even evil.

I'm not a prostitute. I can't be affected.

I am always with my friends . . . husband . . . lover. . . .

I will be safe.

Of course it was true.

The ghost walked ahead of Katie.

She thought that the ghost of Stella Martin was going to turn down the block before Duval, but she didn't. She seemed to hesitate, as if thinking out her move. She looked at Katie, and then she moved on to Duval.

Katie followed. There was no reason for her to be afraid. Duval was as familiar to her as her own front walk.

Rick's was open, as was the Irish bar across the street, and both seemed to be busy. Up ahead, more bars were still issuing the sounds of music out to the road and all those who still prowled the town. They passed the smallest bar, and a few old friends were hanging around; they waved to Katie. She waved back and hurried on.

They were near one of the inns on Duval Street that many people might pass on a daily basis — and barely notice. They were wonderful places for the city. Small, on top of storefronts, they often had the kind of rooms where spring-breakers might find an affordable stay. Her brother had rented one with a group of friends once. "Katie, there's one bed. There's a bed under the bed, and when you open the closet, there's a mattress standing up! It's just great. Of course,

246

you have a ton of folks and one bathroom, but it means that kids can afford to come!"

The ghost stopped. She stared at Katie, frowned, looked worried, then sighed.

And walked around back.

Katie hesitated, then followed her.

A narrow alley led to the back of the building and stairs that allowed guests at the place to depart through the rear of the establishment. Another alley ran between the shops, bars and restaurants on the main street and the shops, bars, restaurants, B and Bs and homes that were on the other side.

Katie could hear all the sounds from the street. The laughter. The music. The cars and small motorcycles going by. She could hear the light toot of a horn.

Laughter again.

The ghost looked anxiously about and ran along the back alley, then stood in the midst of bushes and the dripping branches of a large sea grape tree.

Katie walked over to her. The ghost seemed very afraid; she looked around constantly.

She opened her mouth. She couldn't really make sound. She wasn't anywhere near as comfortable in her death as Bartholomew had come to be. Katie could barely hear her.

I was here, it's all I remember, but the plastic, the darkness and the fact that I couldn't breathe. Then the hands, I can't forget the hands around my neck.

A car backfired away on the streets; the ghost of Stella Martin actually seemed to jump.

Get to the light, get to the light and the people, it's the darkness . . . he knows the streets. He was following me . . . I didn't realize. . . .

"Stella," Katie said aloud, "was it Danny? Danny Zigler?"

Stella frowned. *I . . . no. I don't know. I don't know! But go . . . please. It's dark. Go now, and help me, please help me. Go, and don't get yourself killed, or how the hell will you help me?*

The ghost was finding her personality. Brash in life, she would be so in death.

Katie turned.

She knew the city so well. Knew the streets, the legends, even where trees grew and bushes were thick, where foliage had been cut back, where locals gathered, and where they did not.

She knew her city.

But she felt as if she was being watched.

As if she had been followed.

And while just a block away the city was alive and bursting with music and colorful revelers, those who had come from near and from far, she felt alone.

But she knew it; she had been seen.

She had been seen talking to thin air, right at the place where Stella had been killed.

Something seemed to creep along her nape. Something more frightening than she had ever experienced. Not of another world, but of this world.

She sensed evil. Living, breathing evil.

He was hidden, watching. Her senses seemed acutely attuned, and it was as if she could hear him standing still, and yet causing a slight rustling. Watching her. Stalking her. Waiting, his breath coming fast, his hands clenched at his sides. Strong hands, the kind that could quickly cause suffocation, and then squeeze the life from the living.

The ghost was agitated, too.

She began to fade.

"Run!" she said.

And Katie did.

Cleaned up, dressed in jeans and T-shirt, her face scrubbed, her hair in a ponytail, Stella's friend Morgana Willams seemed like a woman in her late thirties — in fact, she looked like the girl next door.

"I know who you are," she told David wearily.

He had offered to buy her a drink. She hadn't wanted alcohol; just a cup of coffee. It was still readily available.

They sat at a little open-air table in the far back of the establishment, within sight of many who were escaping the music and yet still partying. Some looked as if they were already preparing for hellacious hangovers the next day.

Some had been moderate, and were watching out for their friends.

"I didn't kill your friend," he said.

She smiled, a dampness about her eyes. "I believe you. Of course, I wasn't here ten years ago. I came down from the farmlands of Indiana. I didn't want a boring life, you know. I'm not sure I exactly planned on this life, but . . . hey. Maybe I'll find Mr. Right somewhere."

"You never know," he told her.

"The police already questioned me," she told him.

"Well, it makes sense," he told her.

"They questioned everyone in the club. One of the guys is your relative, isn't he? A cop named Liam Beckett."

"He's my cousin."

"Yeah, you can tell."

"He's a good guy," David told her.

She nodded. "He was real respectful. He didn't treat us like we were all whores — or the underbelly of society."

David smiled. "Well, you are gainfully employed. And, by the way, I thought you might have been a dancer — as in musicals — at some time. Were you?"

Her face lit up. She was almost pretty. "You could tell that? Really?"

He nodded.

"I started off in the Big Apple — New York City," she said. "I even worked Off Broadway. But then I met Joe, and Joe introduced me to . . . a few friends who weren't friends at all. Cocaine and heroin, and before I knew it . . . Never mind. You're not here to listen to my story, are you?"

"You can dance," he assured her simply.

She sipped her coffee. "I can't tell you anything I haven't already told the cops. Stella did have a thing with Danny Zigler — on again, off again. And she had some regulars, but she didn't even tell me about them. She said that she was sworn to silence, 'cause big muckety-mucks never wanted anyone to know that they hung around with folks like us. I told her that the muckety-mucks were ashamed that they needed help

to get it up, you know what I mean? But —
you think that Danny might have killed her?
Danny always seems like a nice guy. He's
not ambitious, but . . . lots of guys down
here aren't exactly balls of fire, you know
what I mean?"

"So you can't name anyone else she might
have had a regular relationship with?"

Morgana sniffed. "You got a cigarette?"
she asked him.

He shook his head. "No, but I'll get you
one."

The bar itself was still open. The fellow
running it seemed to be Eastern European,
possibly Russian. When David asked for a
pack of cigarettes, the fellow's accent con-
firmed his thought. Russian or Ukrainian.

The bartender didn't know him, and he
accepted the money for the cigarettes with
no comment on his past or the day's events.

David brought the cigarettes to Morgana.
She lit up and inhaled greedily, looking at
David. "Yeah, yeah, they're going to kill me
one day. But they keep me off the hard
stuff."

"I'm not a judge, I promise," David told
her.

She managed a laugh. "No, no you're not,
are you. All right, what else can I tell you?
Whoever local she was seeing who was in

the higher echelon or whatever, I don't know. She did care about Danny, and they did see each other."

"Thank you for helping me, for telling me that. What I need to know now is what happened that night. When did you last see Stella?" David asked.

Morgana inhaled deeply and was silent for a few seconds. When she spoke at last, it was thoughtfully. "We worked that night, but she took off early. No, no, wait, that wasn't right. She took a break and went down the street. Then she came running back in. I tried to ask her what was going on — but she wouldn't tell me." Morgana hesitated a minute. She grimaced weakly and shrugged. "She — she could be a bit of a pickpocket, but she told me she figured she was actually helping the youth of America. If she stole their money and their cards, they couldn't get plastered and kill themselves on their way back up the island."

David smiled. "I guess there's some logic to that."

Morgana's smile deepened, and then faded.

"She really wasn't a bad person," she said. "She just — well, you know. She just didn't get the real opportunities in life. Both her folks are dead, at least that's what she told people. Whatever, she went from foster home to foster home and I guess she kind of learned how to survive. You understand?"

David nodded. He set a hand on Morgana's. "Morgana, you certainly don't have to excuse your friend to me. She didn't deserve what happened to her. She had her quirks, she might have been a petty thief and even a prostitute. But I understand. She'd never physically hurt anyone."

Morgana nodded vehemently. "That's it, exactly. I've seen the news. Some of those reporters are making it sound like she almost deserved what happened because of the life she led." Tears formed in Morgana's eyes again. "Oh, God, it must have been horrible. I can just imagine . . . I hope she didn't suffer long."

David said, "Morgana, I saw her. I think it was very quick. She might not have known anything at all — until it happened. And she probably lost consciousness very quickly, and died after she had passed out."

"You think?" she asked. "I mean, we're all going to die, aren't we? I just pray that she didn't suffer."

He waited for her to go on, but she seemed lost in thought.

"Morgana, please, help me," he said softly.

She stared at him and nodded. "Right.

She came back in, and she worked until late. Three or four in the morning. But she was all excited. She'd met a college kid. He'd been in here earlier with friends. I think she was seeing him after. She didn't tell me, she wouldn't — because I don't turn tricks. I won't. Okay, maybe I'm a fairly naked dancer and I do posture in front of old, hairy men, but I don't turn tricks!"

"So she wouldn't tell you about it — but you think she went back out to find some-one. Was it a real date, do you think? Or was she out looking, hoping to make it a real date?"

Morgana was thoughtful. "I'm trying so hard to remember what she said. . . . All right, I think she had a run-in with the police. No! Wait, not a run-in. I think she escaped because someone else got nabbed, but let go."

"Why do you think that?"

"She said something about the 'poor kid' being a cutie and she sure hoped that she could make it up to him."

"All right. She was out — picking a pocket. She returned, and she went back out again. But you think the kid — or young man — she went out to find had been in the club?"

"I think so, yes."

"Would you recognize the men who had been in?"

"Probably. Maybe," she said softly.

David leaned back. "You've been helpful, Morgana. You've been great." College kids. He was sure they were the kids he'd helped Pete with on the street the other night. He was already making a mental note of the local places that he'd need to go to find them again. Liam was already on the case, of course, and he'd already done a lot of the questioning that might be pertinent to this new information. "Let me walk you home," he told her.

"I'm way down on the south end. Off the really far south end of Duval."

"It's all right. I'll walk you," David assured her.

She smiled. Just as she did so, someone suddenly burst out from the bushes behind them, streaking into the light of the bar's patio area. She was running so fast she plowed directly into their table.

David stared in amazement while Morgana said, "What the fu— ?"

David jumped up to steady the whirlwind, already confused and angry.

Even before she looked at him with wide, green eyes, he knew who it was.

Katie O'Hara.

■ ■ ■ ■

"When I said wait for me, I didn't mean in a dark alley. There's a murderer on the loose."

David was seriously aggravated with her. Even before they had dropped Morgana at her apartment, his jaw had seemed locked, his words had been stilted and, when he touched her, it certainly wasn't with affection.

And what in God's name did she say?

You'll never believe this, but I see ghosts. And yes, they can startle me at times, but I'm not afraid of them — they're just looking for something. They're here because they need help.

Her brother had already warned her. She didn't want to be known as the crazy woman who lived in Key West.

She didn't know what to say. She decided that she had to be on the offensive.

She shook her head. "David, look. I like you. I really like you. But I grew up here. I work here. This is my home. I have walked these streets thousands of times. I can't lock myself in and forget about my life just because you've suddenly come home, determined to catch a murderer, certain tha

257

what went on in the past is relevant to today."

"Gee. What a concept," he said, his tone grating. She looked at his face. If his features became any more tense, she thought that they might crack and then shatter, like glass.

He stopped dead. They were alone; the street was deserted.

He spun around to stare at her, not touching her, his hands at his sides and far too knotted to do so. "What the hell were you doing?" he demanded. "That was the most ridiculous excuse I've ever heard! I just decided to go the quiet way," he mimicked. "And there was a rustle in the grass, and silly me, I just panicked. My God, is that a crock!"

Staring back at him, fighting for both composure and the right words, she felt ridiculously like crying herself.

It was really so hard. So hard to find someone in life who could make her feel the way that David made her feel. She'd spent so little time with him, and yet, when bizarre things hadn't been happening, he hadn't been just sensually and sexually amazing, he'd been someone who really knew her world, loved her world, diving, boats, the water, island life. . . .

She lifted her hands. It hadn't gone that

far, and by the look of him, it wasn't going any further. Stop it all right now before she was in deep, before it all hurt more than it already did.

"Look, I don't know what to tell you. I felt that I needed to be out. I'd intended to stay on Duval with a zillion other people. Then I idiotically cut off and — this should please you — managed to scare myself half to death. Nothing happened. Nothing happened at all. I heard a leaf rustle, and in my present mood, I crashed back into light and noise as quickly as I could. How the hell did I know you were going to be there? Okay, sorry, I did know you were going to the strip club, but I didn't know that you'd be out on the patio. I mean, they strip inside. Except at Fantasy Fest, and that's not really stripping, that's just folks who like to show off their body paint."

He just stared at her incredulously. Then he shook his head.

"Why are you lying?"

"I'm not lying!" But she was.

He stared at her awhile longer. She realized that she had caught her breath.

"Please, I'm sorry, and yet I'm not. I live here, this is my life," she told him. "You left, and now you're back, but that doesn't change the island and I — I can't let it change me. Please understand."

He let out a sigh of impatience.

He took her by the crook of her arm.

"All right. I'm not getting anything else out of you, not tonight anyway. Let's get you home."

At least he wasn't going to walk off, just leave her in the street.

They started walking, almost ten blocks down Duval. Again, music grew loud.

They turned off and came to her house. She opened the door, and looked at him.

"Am I invited in?" he asked flatly.

"Yes, of course. To stay," she added softly.

They walked in.

And there was truth to tension, passion and emotion creating something wild and turbulent. In the hallway, they were in one another's arms.

As they moved up the stairs, they were already removing one another's clothing and their own.

In her room, they didn't touch a light or even the bedspread.

They just crashed down, naked and hot, seeking one another's lips and flesh, and making love as if they had known one another forever. . . .

And as if there would never be another tomorrow.

David talked to Liam first thing in the morning, asking him if anyone had reported a burglary — other than the pickpocket the night before Stella Martin had been found. Liam brought up the reports for the night and the next day and told him no.

"Why are you asking?"

"I talked to Stella's friend Morgana."

"So did I," Liam told him.

"I know. She said that you were a gentleman."

"Well, gee, shucks. Glad to hear it," Liam said. "I've been checking out the angle you're talking about. I'm assuming that the guy you and Pete met up with Saturday night — the guy who filed a pickpocket report — is the guy who Stella worked over. Maybe those college guys involved in the fight are the guys Morgana is talking about."

"Morgana said she thought that Stella met up with a college student," David said.

"But the thing is, I don't think she was killed by a college student. Not that a psycho can't be that age — just that I doubt one of the kids down for the weekend would have the what-have-you to get into that museum, steal the tape and disappear

261

without leaving behind a fingerprint, hair or single skin cell."

"Do you know that there was no physical evidence?" David asked.

"If there is, the crime-scene folk don't have it so far."

"Still, I'm going around to see if I can find out who was with Stella," David said.

"I'll give you a list of where I, or other officers, have already been," Liam told him.

"Thanks," David said.

"You're going to double-check anyway, aren't you?" Liam asked.

"Wouldn't you?"

"I'm doing my best on this, you know that," Liam told him.

"I know. I know you've got my back, and I'm grateful," David assured him.

He was just closing his phone when Katie came down the stairs. She was freshly showered, her hair wet and back, wearing a terry robe.

"Good morning," he said a little huskily.

She came up to him. He was perched on one of the bar stools at the kitchen pass-through and she sat on the one beside him, setting her hands on his knees.

"I think I know where Stella might have been murdered," she told him.

He frowned and asked carefully, "Oh?"

She nodded, her gaze meeting his steadily. But she didn't speak again; she stood and walked around to help herself to coffee.

"Walk with me, and I'll tell you what I think."

She sipped her coffee black, staring at him over the rim of the cup.

"Why do you think you know?" he asked her.

"Logic," she told him flatly.

"Maybe you want to explain that logic?" he said.

"Come with me. Give me a minute — I just have to hop into some clothes, and I'll show you what I'm talking about."

"All right," he said gravely.

She smiled, and he realized that she had been waiting for him to believe in her.

"I'd like to get home, though. I need to shower and change," he told her.

"Go to Sean's room, just grab something of his for this time," she said.

"Isn't Sean on his way home? I feel a little strange, helping myself to his belongings."

She shrugged. "He told me ages ago that if he hadn't taken things, they didn't matter that much. And you two were friends. His room is down the hall from mine."

"Okay, thanks. But I still have to get home for a bit."

"Of course. But let's do this first. I may really be able to help you."

"All right."

She still stared at him for a moment. Smiling.

He should know the feeling. She looked at him the way people had once looked at him. He remembered his grandparents, his aunts and his cousin. Remembered what it was like to know that they didn't look at him with suspicion, but complete belief.

She turned and headed for the stairs. He followed her a second later. Sean and he were about the same size. He felt like an intruder, but he also hated putting on the same clothing after a shower. He figured Sean wouldn't mind a friend borrowing a pair of button-fly jeans and polo shirt.

He came downstairs, perched on the bar stool again and waited for Katie.

As he sat there, the newspaper sitting on the table, with a headline reading Murder in Paradise, suddenly rustled — and moved.

He frowned. He walked over to the table, thinking that the air-conditioning system must have a vent over the table.

But there was no vent.

He moved the paper. Nothing happened; there was no erstwhile bug hiding under the paper.

His imagination?

No, he'd seen it move.

Even as he still pondered the strange rustling, Katie came running back down the stairs, now wearing a pin-striped sundress.

He found himself watching her.

She was . . .

Katie. Stunning, perfect and with that smile and those eyes that seemed to offer so much honesty, and yet . . .

Not really. She was keeping something from him. He hoped that she'd trust him soon, and tell him what it was.

"Are you ready?" she asked.

He nodded.

They left the house together. He was silent, waiting for her to talk as they came around Duval.

She pointed. "There — the museum where Stella was posed."

"Right."

"I'm thinking that the person she was with stayed just on Duval — one of the cheaper places. But he didn't stay in a massive room with a bunch of other people. So, I was thinking there —" She paused and pointed across the street. There was a little inn above a swimsuit shop. "Or there." She pointed on the same side of the street, just down from the bar and the strip club.

"Possibly," he agreed.

"Now, if they were on this side of the street, she might have come through the back, trying to avoid the cops. Assuming that Stella did rip someone off. The cops tend to be on Duval. So if she ran around in back . . . Come on. I'll show you what I mean."

During the day, especially this early, the patio was quiet. There were people walking around, sipping coffee here and there, but not that many. The place really began to come alive in the afternoon.

Katie took his hand and led him across the bar's patio and to the alley. There were private homes and B and Bs lining that side of the street, with a Vespa rental place at the end of the corner.

"Here. Right here," Katie said.

She stood beneath the shade of a beautiful, old sea grape tree. The branches were overgrown, and it could certainly offer cover. If she had come here, though, and been murdered, she had to have been followed.

By her mark — or her john for the night?

Or by someone else. Someone else who may have known her lifestyle and her hours, and who might have followed her. If all the timing was right, she had been taken in the early or even late afternoon, before the real nightlife and music started.

Frowning, he came to stand beneath the sea grape tree. There were a lot of wild crotons in the area as well, making it a place where there was cover — where people might be hidden.

As he did so, he looked around, studying the patches of overgrown grass and weeds around them.

The wind rustled the leaves on the tree.

The sun glinted through.

David frowned and walked a few feet. He bent down. Something had caught the sun for just a moment.

It was a charge card, a "gold" card.

"You have a tissue?" he asked Katie.

She produced one. He carefully picked the card up by an edge. It bore the name Lewis Agaro.

Lewis Agaro. He was the kid he had chased down in the street for Pete Dryer. The kid who had been accused of being a pickpocket, when it was probably Stella Martin who had done the picking.

"You know the name?"

"Yes. I know who the kid is, but I sure don't see him murdering anyone. He was terrified when the cops looked at him for maybe being a thief. I'm pretty sure Pete will remember him, too. I think the kid was innocent, Pete just let him go. I think a few guys had been rolled by Stella, and they'd complained, and Pete was ready to call her out for her extracurricular activities."

"So, you think —"

"No, but I want to talk to the kid myself before the cops do. And I want to find Danny first." He frowned pensively. "Look. There's something sticky on the card."

Katie studied the card, as well. "What does it mean — anything?"

"Maybe. If Stella rolled her last john, she might have lost something along the way — this guy's stolen credit card. If you're right about her being killed here, it might help us. If you're right, it might lead us to the kid Stella spent her last night with — Lewis Agaro," he said. "But what the hell is on the card?"

She started to touch the card, but stopped, aware they might need to find prints on it. She looked him in the eyes. "If I'm not mistaken," she said, "I think it's the remnants of drying chocolate ice cream."

"Danny Zigler," he said.

10

"I just don't see it, I really don't see it," Katie said. "I can't believe Danny could be a murderer. He worked for your grandfather. I'd have had him work for me. Seriously, if we had to arrest everyone down here who didn't make a fortune and was happy just to be, we'd be arresting a lot of people. And he's responsible — he's not living off anyone else. He does work. He just doesn't need to own the world."

"Katie, I came back, Sam Barnard came back — and Danny Zigler was suddenly busing tables at O'Hara's. Don't you think that's a little suspicious?"

"No," she said stubbornly. "Everyone is grabbing extra help with Fantasy Fest on the way. Hey — I don't manage O'Hara's, and I don't want to," she said. "Jon Merrillo hires on extra help when Uncle Jamie is away. Danny Zigler has worked there before."

"Look, I don't want Danny to be a bad guy, either," David said. "But he was at O'Hara's the night Tanya died, and he's hanging around there now — and he was seeing Stella Martin. That makes him suspicious."

"I don't think that's politically correct anymore," Katie said. "He's a person of interest."

"Right. And I'm interested. And I want to talk to him before they get him down at the station, but I don't want to hang on to evidence too long." He looked at her. "Katie, I'm going to talk to Danny Zigler. I have to find him, of course, but he should be at the ice-cream parlor. I . . ."

"You don't want me around," she said.

"It will be easier for me to speak with him alone. And . . ."

"David, look, I appreciate the fact that you're afraid for me, I really do. But it's broad daylight. I'll hang in clear sight, all right?" Katie said. He was still staring at her. "David, this is my home. A home I love. I intend to stay here, live here and be part of whatever the future brings. I cannot become afraid of my own home." She inhaled, meeting his eyes. "I know how badly you want the truth, and I understand completely. But Tanya's death went unsolved for more than a decade. Let's face it, sometimes, things are never solved. I can't become paranoid, but we should always know how to be very careful."

"Do you ever carry Mace or pepper spray or anything like that?" he asked her.

"No. And I'm afraid I never took karate classes, either."

"I'll talk to Liam about getting you something," David said.

"David, really —" She broke off, seeing his eyes. "Pepper spray sounds like something good to keep in my bag," she agreed.

"All right. Listen for me to call, please," he told her.

She nodded. "I'll just get a bite to eat," she said.

He went his way.

David didn't know the man he found working at the ice-cream parlor.

When he asked about Danny Zigler, the man exploded, issuing a barrage of Spanish that David didn't really follow. But he knew enough to understand that Danny Zigler was being cursed.

"I'm sorry — he didn't show up for work?" David asked.

"The little rat bastard just disappeared," the man said. "He was due in to open up at eight this morning, clean the machines, get it all going. At ten Mrs. Clasky calls me to tell me that the place is not open, and here I am myself, working, when I gave that good-for-nothing a job!" the man said.

"Did you try calling him?" David asked.

The man glared at him as if he was an idiot. "Of course, I call him! His phone is turned off."

"Have you been to his house?" David asked.

The fellow, a tall, beefy man, leaned on the counter. "Do you see me here? If I'm here, I'm not going by his house!"

"Do you have an address for him?" David asked.

The man looked angry and exasperated. "You the cops or something?" he demanded.

"I'm the 'something,' " David told him.

The man stared another moment, muttered, then reached under the counter for a memo pad. He wrote down an address off Union Street. David thanked him.

David's cell rang as he started toward Union. It was Liam.

"Hey," David said. "Have they brought anyone in for questioning yet?"

"No. Uniforms are out looking for Danny Zigler, I guess he and Stella were an item, and Pete is trying to track down the crowd that was outside O'Hara's the other night. He thinks one of those college kids has to know something."

"Zigler didn't show up for work."

"We don't have anything for a search warrant, and he didn't answer at his place," Liam told him.

"So — do you have anything?" David asked.

"Yeah. You'd asked me before about tracing down Mike Sanderson — Tanya's new boyfriend, the guy she was supposed to meet up at Ohio State."

"And?"

"We know this much about Mike Sanderson — he used one of his credit cards for gas in St. Augustine on the thirteenth — the day *after* Tanya was killed," Liam said.

Katie felt Bartholomew striding along at her side. She cast a sideways glance his way. "Where have you been?" she asked.

"Naturally, I have been using my charm and persuasion to discover the truth," he told her.

"Oh? So — where have you been seeking this truth?" she asked him.

"I hung around the museum for a long time, just watching the crime-scene folks," he said.

"And what did you learn there?"

"That they're not going to get much of anything. Oh, well, I guess everyone knows this — there was no sign of a break-in. They had the owners and managers all gathered in an area, and that lieutenant fellow — Dryer — was pretty hard on them all, demanding to know how many keys were out and around. Two fellows — snowbirds — own the place, but there are three managers, and they're all local. Dryer wasn't getting anywhere, but Liam Beckett tried a bit more of an understanding approach, and it turns out that one of the managers left one of the employees to lock the place up a few nights ago, and she managed to lose the keys. They didn't rekey the place, they just had another set of keys made. Whoever broke into the place used the keys, apparently knew the alarm code and didn't disturb a thing — other than the Carl Tanzler/Elena de Hoyos exhibit. Oh — they found Elena. The mannequin of Elena, that is. She was just behind one of the other exhibits. So, this is what I know — whoever did it was bright enough to grab the security tapes, use gloves — and find out the alarm code before bringing in Stella Martin's body."

"So we are thinking local," Katie murmured. "Because I'd say whoever did it had to have followed people around. When the employee lost the keys, he had to have found them — and he had to have known what they opened."

Bartholomew grinned. "That, my dear, was not difficult. There was a medallion on the key chain that advertised the museum."

"That opens it up, I guess. Hey, did the police hold anyone from the museum?"

"As far as I know, they have a task force going over everything that they have and they'll be bringing folks in for questioning by this afternoon," Bartholomew said.

"You were gone overnight," Katie reminded Bartholomew.

"Ah, yes. I came back to the house, but you were — occupied. I turned on the coffeemaker again this morning. You didn't even realize it!" He was hurt.

"I'm sorry, Bartholomew," Katie said. "I really am. I didn't see you and David had gone down first."

"David!" Bartholomew said, and sniffed. "You have rushed headfirst into this!" he said.

"I keep telling you, make up your mind. You like him or you don't like him," Katie said.

"Since he was with you, he definitely

didn't kill the prostitute," Bartholomew said. "All right, I like the fellow enough. He reminds me of someone I knew a very long time ago."

"Really?"

Bartholomew swept aside, as if he were physically there, as a group carrying fresh margaritas came down the street, laughing.

They could have walked through him.

Bartholomew liked to think that there was substance to him.

"Sea captain," Bartholomew said. "Decent fellow."

"Maybe he was one of David's ancestors," Katie said. "The family dates back to the early years."

"That's what I figure," Bartholomew said.

She didn't reply; a woman standing with a beer just outside Sloppy Joe's was staring at her. It was evident that the woman was wondering if Katie was a crazy person talking to herself, or if she had started drinking too early.

Katie turned down Greene Street. Captain Tony's had been the original Sloppy Joe's. Sloppy Joe, however, had been a real Key West character. Angry over a hike in his rent, he had simply moved his establishment in the middle of the night, lock, stock and barrel. Now, Sloppy Joe's was right on Du-

276

val, and the space on Greene Street was Captain Tony's.

She stepped on into the bar.

A large, open doorway led to a setting with the feel of rustic outdoors, but air-conditioning still coursed through the place. The "hanging tree" was in the center of a sitting area, and it had become vogue for visitors to leave behind their bras, elegant and old-fashioned, whatever someone might be wearing.

Katie took a table near the tree. It was impossible to know, through the years, what was authentic and what was legend about the place. Fact or fiction, the stories behind the bar and the building were true Key West legend.

As she took her seat at the table, she closed her eyes and thought about all of the history behind this very spot.

Sloppy Joe, Joe Russell, had become friends with Hemingway when he had cashed a check for him that the banks wouldn't. He had been larger than life, just like Hemingway, and the two had been good friends. But, before that, the building had been a telegraph station that had first received the news about the *Maine,* an icehouse doubling as the city morgue, a cigar factory and a bordello.

The hanging tree in the middle of the room was now covered in undergarments. Throughout many years, it had been the place of execution for Key West and its environs. A woman had died here, accused of killing her husband and child, and she supposedly haunted the ladies' room.

"What can I get you?"

Katie opened her eyes. A perky and very young waitress smiled as she asked the question.

"A giant iced tea and a menu, please," Katie told her.

She seemed disappointed that Katie hadn't come in to drown her sorrows with some form of expensive alcohol, but her smile barely cracked. "Coming right up!" she said.

Bartholomew had seated himself next to Katie, extending a booted leg from one chair to another and doffing his hat. He looked disgusted.

"Is there a reason we're here?" he asked.

"I like the place."

"You're hoping that it's teeming with ghosts who will give you all the answers you want. Well, don't count on it. They're all still whining over the past, and they're not going to help you with anything in the present," he said.

"You're wrong," she said. "Stella Martin's ghost helped me tremendously."

"So, she should have told you who killed her, flat out!" Bartholomew said.

"But she doesn't know. Still, she led me to a clue."

"Yeah?"

"A credit card — and it was smudged with ice cream."

Bartholomew let out a chortle. A few tables up, Katie saw a woman frown and look around. Then she shivered. She had felt that a ghost was near, apparently.

"Behave," Katie murmured.

"Me? You're the one who appears to be talking to herself!"

She grimaced and waited for her tea. She thanked the young girl, sipped it and half-way closed her eyes. She tried to open up to anything that might be going on.

"Can you hear the rope swing against the branches?" Bartholomew asked softly. "You can hear it, back and forth, back and forth . . . swinging with the weight of a man."

She kept her glass in front of her lips. "You died here."

"Yes, I died here. I was snatched out of bed and dragged down to the hanging tree — for an act of piracy I did not commit. A bastard pirate named Eli Smith attacked an unarmed American vessel out in the straits, but when he was confronted by the authorities, he swore I was the guilty party, and I was hanged before the truth could be known. I was dead by the time a friend — the original Craig Beckett — came around to decry the act and tell them that I had truly turned merchant when my privateering days were over, and it was Eli Smith who attacked the vessel in the eight-gun sloop *Bessie Blue.* The true tragedy is that I, of all men, would have never attacked that ship. I was madly in love with Victoria Wyeth, and she died in the attack. Her father became a madman because of her death."

"Why did they believe Eli Smith and assume you had attacked the ship?" Katie asked.

"Because Victoria had been the love of my life, and we were going to run away together. Her father sent her out ahead, planning to make her live with relatives in Virginia until she forgot about me. I knew that I didn't have a chance of living with her, happily ever after, if I didn't convince her family that I was the man she should have, and Craig Beckett was highly respected. I'd been on a simple fishing expedition with him when the attack had taken place, and he had promised that — after dealing with a smuggling problem up the islands — he'd see to it that the old bastard Wyeth learned that I had been a *privateer,* and that I had never been a cutthroat pirate. All right, in some instance, there might have been little difference. But I had never, ever attacked an American ship. But that night, I was down toward the south of the island, sound asleep, and a lynch mob broke in on me. I managed a bit of a defense — slashed the nose off one hairy, old bastard! — but there were two dozen of them, and me. And so I was hanged from the neck until dead, and when I come in here now, I can still hear the rope scrape against the tree."

She forgot where they were, forgot that people might be watching, and set her hand over his. "Bartholomew, I am so sorry."

He nodded. "Well, there were interesting years, and dreary years. I wanted to get to know Hemingway, he was an odd and interesting fellow — and that Carl Tanzler, he was certainly a curiosity. I wondered what I was doing here. My Victoria seemed to be long gone. Then I came across you, and well, if nothing else, Katie-oke is entertaining, and I think I've decided that I'm hanging around because you so obviously need help and guidance!"

"Bartholomew, that's very sweet, but seriously, I'm all right."

"I'd not be leaving you now, dear girl, for all the tea in China!"

"That's kind, Bartholomew, but if the time comes when there's a better place for you, I want you to go," Katie told him earnestly.

He shook his head. "There's the strange thing. Maybe I have waited all these years for you."

"Really?"

"Well, you see, I was avenged," Bartholomew told her.

"You were?"

"Oh, yes, and that's probably why I like your boy David — even if I remain skeptical, wary and watchful. You see, his ancestor — Craig Beckett from many, many years ago — came back into town and saw that Eli Smith was hanged for his part in the attack and Victoria's death. Maybe that's what I hear!" Bartholomew said with a touch of bitterness. "Smith, eyes bulging, organs giving out, as he swung from the tree!"

As Katie glanced across the room, she saw a woman leaning against the wall near the ladies' room. Her hair was loose, hanging down her back, and her clothing wasn't the elegant apparel of a nineteenth-century lady, but more like that of a woman who worked hard in her home throughout the day. Her blouse was white cotton, open at her throat, which bore angry, red marks. She seemed very sad. Katie had seen her before, but the woman never spoke to her.

The ghost saw a table where a group of young children sat with a mother and father. The kids were drinking Shirley Temples and munching on fries.

The ghost drifted over to the table. She took an empty chair.

She looked longingly at the children.

The mother perked up, looking around. She nudged her husband, uncomfortable and not knowing why.

The husband asked for the check, and the family left.

The ghost faded away, still sad.

"I don't believe that Danny Zigler was capable of either of the murders," Katie said.

"You're back to the same question," Bartholomew told her. "Were they both committed by the same person? Or was this a copycat killing?"

Katie stood, deciding not to order any food. She left the girl bills that were double the price of the iced tea.

"Let's go. I want to see if Liam is at the

police station."

"What? Why?" Bartholomew asked her.

"I don't know — you said something that made me start thinking that somehow we're missing something."

"Like what?"

"Motive."

"The killer is crazy in the head, that's a motive!" Bartholomew said. "I'd hate to tell you a few of the things I saw in my day — just because someone could get away with it."

But Katie was already moving. She heard Bartholomew sigh — and follow her.

It took a few minutes to get through to Liam on the phone, but David knew his cousin would find the time to talk to him. Eventually, Liam came on.

"Sorry, David, this place is insane today. Procedure. We're bringing in everyone who worked at the strip club, and we're trying to track down anyone who was at the strip club that night."

"Understandable. What about Mike Sanderson? Has anyone pursued that angle?"

"We've put through some calls. Apparently, he became a salesman, and he isn't working by computer. We've reached his wife, and she said he was traveling. She gave us all his numbers, but we haven't reached him yet. We've contacted the Cleveland police to let them know that we need their help in a cold-case investigation."

"So no one knows where he is right now, right?"

"No. But to go assuming he might be in the Keys or Key West again is a long shot, David."

"I know. But it's not the time to ignore any suspicion, however thin."

"We're not ignoring it, I promise. I don't have much time. I have to get back to questioning folks. No one is under arrest — everyone is coming in willingly, so we have to make it all quick and cordial."

"No word yet on Danny Zigler?"

"Nothing. There's an APB out on him, and the black-and-whites have gone by his place to try to find him several times. We're getting a search warrant."

"Thanks."

"So," Liam said carefully, "what are you doing?"

"Following hunches."

"Nothing illegal, please."

"Liam, if I do anything illegal, I sure as hell don't intend to tell you and compromise your position."

"David —"

"Liam, I have the police reports and all the old crime-scene photos and info to study. Don't worry, all right?"

"Keep me posted," Liam said with a groan.

"I will," David said.

And he would. After his next stop, he'd go by the station and turn in the credit card. The police might have already questioned the kid who had been with Stella.

He was glad to have the card; he wanted to talk to the kid. But he was pretty sure that Stella hadn't been murdered by a chance john. Whoever had killed her had premeditated the murder. She'd been an easy mark. The display of her body had been far more important than her life.

He reached the house where Danny Zigler had his apartment.

It was on the second floor. He climbed up the stairs, came to the door and rapped on it loudly.

There was no answer.

He hesitated, looked around guiltily, then pulled out his key chain and looked for a small tool that had helped him a dozen times in his travels in third-world nations when his belongings had wound up behind locked doors. He jimmied the little tool in the lock and it gave easily. This was the kind of thing that Liam didn't need to know.

The house had been built sometime in the eighteen nineties, divided into four apartments in the nineteen seventies and had had little done to it since. If there was one thing David knew well, it was Key West architecture. Two nice old features remained — open beams held up the ceiling, and the original marble fireplace stood across from the entry.

He stepped into the room. "Danny?"

But there was no reply. A quick look through all the rooms — kitchen, parlor, dining room, bedroom and bath — assured him that Danny wasn't here. Frustrated, he stood in the parlor. Danny wasn't particularly neat and clean, but it seemed that he picked up his clothing and washed his dishes.

A pile of books on the dining-room table drew David's attention and he walked over to see what they were. He hadn't thought of Danny as being a big reader.

They were all on Key West. One was on the New World discovery and Spanish settlement of the island, one was on David Porter, military rule and the end of piracy, and another was on the age of wrecking and salvage.

As he looked at the last, something fell out.

Money.

Ten thousand dollars.

Curiouser and curiouser, he thought.

Had Danny been bribing someone? Did he know something, and was he taking blackmail?

David wasn't supposed to be in Danny's apartment. Technically, he was guilty of breaking and entering. He really needed to get moving.

He laid the bills out on the table along with the books and reached into his pocket for the small digital camera he carried as naturally as his wallet. He took photographs of the bills and then the books, then returned the bills where they had been and stacked the books in their original position. He quickly walked around the apartment, taking shots of each room.

At last, he left.

As he did so, he had the feeling that Danny hadn't been back to his apartment in a while. He wasn't at home, and he wasn't at work.

Somehow, that didn't seem to bode well for Danny.

Sergeant Andy McCluskey was at the recep-

tion desk when Katie reached the station. He greeted her warmly. Andy had been a few years older than she in high school, and had been with the police department for the past four years.

"Liam is pretty busy right now," Andy told her. He leaned across the counter, his voice low. "Nasty business going on. He's interviewing folks one by one."

"Of course. Well, I suppose there are a lot of people he needs to interview," Katie said.

"I can tell him that you're here," Andy offered.

"No, no, that's all right, thank you," Katie said.

"I really don't know what you thought you were going to do here, anyway," Bartholomew said.

She ignored him, thanked Andy again and headed back out into the sunshine.

"What are you trying to do?" Bartholomew demanded.

"I don't know. But when we were by the hanging tree, I felt that we needed to be looking into more than we're looking into. Let's say that these murders were carried out by the same person. That's kind of crazy in itself. Bizarre murders, or bizarre display of the victims. Over ten years apart. And both when people were suddenly reappear

ing in town. Sam Barnard is suddenly back. David is suddenly back."

"That's two people," Bartholomew pointed out.

"My brother is due in soon."

"Three people. What a horde."

"Don't be sarcastic. It's not at all gentle-manly," Katie told him.

"Hmm. Forgive me. You're young. I de-cided that my function in death was to keep you alive, and if it takes sarcasm . . ."

His voice drifted. She saw that he wasn't paying the least attention to her. He was looking down the street. "There she goes."

"Who?"

"My lady in white."

"From the story you just told me, you were in love with Victoria."

He nodded.

"Is she Victoria?"

He shook his head. "I don't know who she is." He gave Katie his attention again. "Okay, so, you wanted old police records — that's why we were visiting Liam. But I don't think you were going to get anything. David might be able to get information from Liam, but they don't hand out evi-dence to everyone on the street. We're not going to get any further on this today so maybe we should look into something else.

290

Maybe we can find out who the lady in white is through old records. Let's go to the library."

"Okay, but aren't you a bit fickle? What about Victoria?" Katie asked.

"I know, in my bones — or lack thereof — that Victoria has moved on, and is happy. The woman in white needs help." Bartholomew smiled. "She needs me. So . . . let's go do some research at the library!"

After spending some time reading the history of Key West, Katie looked up at Bartholomew. She glanced at the book he was reading, and was surprised to note that he had managed to turn a page.

She looked around quickly, but they were the only two seated in that section of the library. Leaning across the table, she saw that he was studying wreckers.

"Anything?" she asked him.

"Yes!"

"What?" Katie asked.

Bartholomew looked at her. "I found my lady in white. Look — look at the picture. That's her! You can see the picture has her in the same white dress we've seen her in. She's Lucinda — Lucy — Wellington. Her parents died of a fever, and she and her brother were left in penury. The brother earned command of a ship. She watched every day for him to return from a voyage to Boston. Captain Wellington was caught in a storm just off the south side of the island. Lucy's house was near O'Hara's, and she spent the storm atop the widow's walk, praying the ship would come home safely. The wreckers discovered the ship, but not the body of Captain Wellington. Some say that Lucy cast herself to her death from the same widow's walk she had paced, and others say that she fell, trying to get a better view down to the shore when they were bringing in the flotsam and jetsam — and the bodies that washed up."

"You were here then," Katie reminded him.

He nodded. "Yes, I wasn't hanged until a few years later."

"But you didn't know Lucy?"

He shook his head. "She might have been broke, but she was descended from . . . a better quality of people. I was a gentleman — surely you know that! But back then, social strata were strict. No matter what my demeanor, manners and riches, I wasn't easily accepted." He stared hard at Katie. "You have to talk to her for me."

"Bartholomew, I will try," she said firmly.

He smiled. "Look, Katie, I've turned

another page."

"That's great. Can we keep reading then?"

"Aha! I just found a reference to your house, Katie. It was sold to Shamus O'Hara in eighteen twenty-nine. He purchased it from a John Moreland, who had bought it from John Whitehead. Am I ever glad I was named Bartholomew! They were all John in those days. Thank the Lord." He looked up at her suddenly. "Imagine that, Katie. Your ancestors would have watched me on the day that I was hanged. And they certainly didn't lift a finger to stop the injustice of my execution."

11

It wasn't difficult in the least to find Lewis Agaro.

David simply went from bar to bar, and found him in a small but rustic place near Mallory Square.

He sat down on a bar stool next to the slim young man. Lewis Agaro turned, took one look at him and started to bolt.

David set a hand on the kid's on the bar.

"I'm not here to take you down," he said.

Lewis looked around. He was looking for his older brother, David thought. But the brother didn't appear to be here.

Lewis sat. A barmaid came up, and David ordered a beer.

"You'd be a blind and deaf man not to know about the murder," David said, his tone conversational. "And I'm wondering how it feels. You were the last one with her. She might have been a prostitute and a stripper, but she was a human being and you'd definitely been attracted to her. Even though the cops were trying to bust you for something that she did."

The kid let out a breath, picked up his drink and swallowed down the remainder. A pulse was ticking at his throat. "She was cool," he said. "She — she had balls. She ripped me off, and I knew that when I woke up, but she didn't take all my money — she left me enough to get around. I would have gone back to the club. I would have called her out on it, but I swear, I wouldn't have hurt her." He turned to David then, and he did look tortured.

"I don't think that you killed her, kid," David said.

Lewis Agaro let out a long breath. "I didn't. I swear I didn't. I had a night with her like no other. I woke up and my wallet had been rifled and she was gone. I went back to the club, but she wasn't there. Then — they found her body."

"Did you see anyone that night? Did she talk to you about anyone?"

Agaro frowned, shaking his head. He was thoughtful. "She — well, we talked about the fact that I had almost been arrested for a pocket she had picked! She thought it was funny, and she wasn't afraid — even when I told her the cops thought it was her. She said she knew her way around town, and she knew her away around the law, real well. You — you don't understand. She wasn't a bad person. She was cool. She was like one of those folks on that TV show — *Survivor!* She wasn't like all-sex. She was affectionate, she had feelings."

"I'm sure she did."

"The cops are going to arrest me, aren't they? They're going to think that I did it. Billy — my brother — he's all disgusted with me. He wanted to get the hell off the island. Billy —" He paused, wincing. "Billy didn't even know that I'd hired her for the night. He wound up hanging out with some of his friends from FSU. He thinks I'll be called in — along with him — cause we were stopped in the street by that Neanderthal the other night and accused of robbing him."

"You're not going to be arrested, Lewis, but they will bring you in for questioning. Just tell them the truth. You're a kid from out of town, you couldn't possibly have staged the death scene at the museum. The cops aren't stupid. They know that." He pulled a cocktail napkin toward him and reached in his pocket for a pen. He scribbled down a name and handed the paper to the young man. "There's a name for a good attorney down here — a criminal attorney. If you need help, call him. He's a good guy."

"I can't afford an attorney."

"Tell him I referred you. He's older than hell, better than anyone else you'll ever meet. I know — he stood by me once. He's an old family friend. You'll be all right. That's over with, so . . . Think. Please, think. Is there anything else you can tell me?"

He perked up suddenly. "There was one thing. There was this guy. He'd been upstairs — during the show. He tried to get Stella to talk to him, but she ripped her arm away from him and hissed something at him. And he told her he was working a whole lot. He was going to get money — she should quit what she was doing. I think that he knew that she had promised to come home with me."

"What did the guy look like?" David asked, though he was sure he knew the answer.

"Skinny, kind of thin face, about your age. Ah, hell, I'd seen him before around here. My brother's friends were heckling one of the ghost tours, and he was the guy leading it. He made everybody yell at the hecklers, something like, 'You're cursed!' "

David nodded. "Thanks."

He set a hand on the kid's shoulder and rose.

Danny Zigler.

But where the hell was he now? David was afraid that he wasn't going to find Danny. He still didn't believe that Danny Zigler was capable of murder. But neither was Danny capable of holding down the kind of job that could account for the money he had at his apartment. Danny had known or suspected something — maybe he even knew why and how Stella had died. The police would find the money in Danny's apartment eventually. Until then, it was something he was going to keep to himself.

He still had to find Danny. He was just afraid that he wasn't going to find him alive.

Katie's phone rang in the quiet of the library, making her jump. She answered it quickly, wondering if her heart was thumping because her caller ID read David Beckett, or just because she had been so startled.

"Hey," she said. "How's it going?"

"Interesting. Danny Zigler is nowhere to be found."

"Well, he'll turn up, I'm certain."

David didn't reply to her statement. "Where are you?" he asked instead.

"The library."

"That's not on Duval Street."

"It's a happening place."

He laughed softly. "Maybe, but . . . while you're there, want to do me a favor?"

"Sure."

"I need these books," he said, and rattled off three titles. She scrounged in her purse for a pen.

"All right, I'll get them — if they have them."

"I have a feeling that they do. Want to meet me at Craig's place?"

He didn't call it "my" house. He called it Craig's place.

He didn't intend to stay.

"Sure," she said. "I'll get the books and be right there."

She hung up. Bartholomew was watching her. "Well?"

"I'm meeting him at his house. Or — the Beckett house."

"The museum?" Bartholomew asked, frowning.

"No, no. The old Beckett homestead. Are you — coming with me?"

"Good God, no. The Lord alone knows where the two of you might start madly coupling once you're there! Far more than I want to know or see or . . ."

Katie groaned. "That's not all that . . . it's

certainly not all that we do."

"I'm going to hang around the street. Watch the Fantasy Fest preparations. See if I can find the regular habits of my lady in white. But I'll walk you over, and I'll not be gone too long. God knows, that fellow is so determined to find the truth, he keeps leaving you alone."

Katie planted her hands on her hips. "Chill. He's going to get me some pepper spray. And I'm not the karate kid, but I'm not a ninety-pound weakling, either."

Bartholomew leaned toward her, his face set seriously. "Katie, this killer is strong. It seems that he snuck up on Stella Martin, surprised her and killed her with his bare hands. You're not a weakling, but this isn't someone you want to tackle."

"Which makes it almost impossible for Danny to be guilty of anything," Katie said. "He is just about a ninety-pound weakling."

"Come, my dear, let me escort you," Bartholomew said.

"I just have to get these books," she said.

At home, David cleared off the formal dining-room table, removing his grandmother's silver candlesticks and the lace doilies she had used to protect the beautiful old, carved mahogany.

300

He laid out the photos from the original crime scene.

He also laid out his photos of the second crime scene.

He set out the files with pertinent crime-scene information and witness reports, but the latter revealed nothing. No one had seen anyone at the museum. No one had seen anyone on the street. No one had seen anything. In Tanya's case, she had been at O'Hara's bar. She had left. She had never been seen again by anyone — except the killer — until she had appeared in the tableau.

Stella Martin. The police were still questioning people, but he knew more than the police did. She had slept with Lewis Agaro. She had rifled through his wallet, left his small lodging house through the rear and been killed beneath the branches of a large sea grape tree.

Someone had seen her leave the lodging house. She had been staying off Duval to avoid the cops, probably. She had gone around back. She had argued with Danny Zigler, and he was missing.

The crime-scene pictures were different. Tanya had been laid out like Sleeping Beauty; in death, she had been gorgeous, heart-wrenching.

Stella Martin had been dumped.

Two different killers?

The doorbell rang. He left the table and went to the door, letting Katie in. She seemed to enter hesitantly. He had a feeling that it was the first time she had been in the house since his grandfather had died.

And he hadn't changed anything within it.

"Come on in," he told her huskily. He reached out, taking her hand, pulling her in. Then he pulled her against him and she looked up and he stroked her cheek and kissed her. Instant fire. Anticipation increased by the fact that he knew her, and knew what could come.

He stepped back, smiling. "Sorry."

"Not at all." She cleared her throat, looking down the hallway. "I got the books. What about these books do you think will help?"

"They were the books Danny Zigler was reading."

"And you know this because . . . ?"

"I broke into his house."

"Lord, David —"

"No one will know. I know what I'm doing."

"Great. You're a practiced lock pick."

"It was important that I see his place."

"Oh?"

"I think Danny was somehow in over his head. He was looking up all kinds of information on the area, too. Which makes me more curious about the past."

"The past? You mean, the past as in ten years ago?" she asked.

"No, I mean the past. Something happened in the past, that is, history, that somehow has to do with all of this. I don't really understand yet. I'm fishing. I think that Danny knows — or knew — something, and that it got him to thinking and . . . he was a carefree-Keys kind of guy, but we're mistaken if we take him for stupid. Anyway . . . I don't really know what we're looking for. I'm hoping we'll know when we find it."

She was frowning. "You have no idea where Danny is? You made it sound like something might have happened to him!"

"I don't know that at all," he said. "Let's just say that I'm concerned."

He took the library books from her and set a hand on her back, guiding her into the dining room. She stepped away from him, frowning as she saw the display on the table. She whitened, looking at the full array of photos of the dead women, but she didn't turn away.

"It's almost as if Tanya was treated with respect, and Stella was . . . well, treated as if she were lower class."

"Which makes me think that our killer may believe in a social stratum."

"Possibly. But none of this seems to jive. You'd need someone like a good old boy to have such a feeling of superiority, and someone smart to carry off planting the corpse in the museum, even if she was rather — dumped."

David pulled out a chair for Katie and then sat down, watching her. "Ah, Katie, it's rather nice and totally naive that you feel that way. Trust me. I've seen it around the world. White supremacy groups — east, west, north and south — are not all peopled by the stupid or illiterate. And someone doesn't have to be that rabid or prejudiced to feel superior to a woman they might see as white trash."

"I suppose that's true. David, what are the blue smudges — they're on the faces of both women. It's not something with the film, is it?" Katie asked.

He stood, rifled in a buffet drawer and produced a magnifying glass. He had noted the smudges before. They were on the tips of both noses, on the foreheads and the chins.

"They look like bruises. Pressure bruises, premortem," David said. "And, I believe, it means that we are looking for one killer — a man who attacks from behind with a plastic bag or some such other item, smothering his victims before strangling them when they haven't the breath left to struggle. He wears gloves, and that's why his victims can't get their nails into him."

He sat back. "I've got to give Liam a call and then talk to Pete. He let me reopen the old case through Liam, just so long as I report to him. I really want to let them both know that they need to be taking a look at what I think are bruises. It really shows, in my opinion, that the victims were ambushed from behind."

"Then what?" she asked.

"Then — let's go barhopping."

Dusk was coming. In another hour, the sun would fall. Then night, with the sound of music and laughter. It became distant, like whispers from the past. Darkness was a lovely time, a time when the old trees tipped down protective branches, when streets were shadowed, when all manner of evil might exist and never be seen.

She was with him again.

Soon, the sun would set again. A magnificent

305

sunset, the kind that had made Key West famous. On Mallory Square the entertainers would begin their night's work, hoping for tips. Cat trainers, magicians, acrobats, robotic people, all would begin in earnest. . . .

Katie O'Hara was with David Beckett.

Ah, yes, once again, David Beckett on top, carrying with him all the pompous righteousness of decades of Becketts, Becketts who shouldn't have survived to populate the island.

She couldn't be with him all the time.

No, she couldn't be with him all the time. There were times when she would have to be alone.

He stared at the house, and he smiled, because he felt powerful. They all thought they were such great detectives, and they were such fools.

It was all moving along so smoothly. The island was agog with the murder of a whore, but hell, it was a capitalist's world. Fantasy Fest was on the way.

Oh, Lord, that would be so much fun.

It would make everything so easy.

And it would set the scene for one final and beautiful curtain call. He would finish it all, taking down the family.

Katie would have to die, and be immortalized.

The main thorn was David Beckett, so

beloved of Craig!

And, at long last, David would go down.

He had seen his mistakes of the past; he knew better now. He had learned. David would go down.

Bless the state of Florida, and the death penalty.

The next time Katie's phone rang, it was Clarinda. David was still on his own phone, pacing around the table in the dining room as he put through two calls, one to his cousin Liam and another to Lieutenant Dryer.

"Hey, hey, you there?" Clarinda asked.

"Yes, hey, what's up?"

"Jonas and I are going to go down to Mallory Square. Want to join us?"

"You're going to Mallory Square?" It was a huge destination for tourists, and, actually, beautiful and a lot of fun. The sunsets were spectacular. Jugglers, musicians, all kinds of entertainers came from all over the world to perform on the square.

"We thought it would be nice. I take it you're still hanging with David Beckett?"

"Yes."

"And, of course, you're both obsessed with the death of that poor Stella Martin?"

"As you imagine," Katie agreed.

"Well, no one can solve something like that, and if you two become too obsessed, you'll be worthless because you won't see straight. Come on out, we'll have drinks and dinner."

David had hung up. Katie looked over at him. "It's Clarinda. She wants us to meet with her and Jonas and walk around Mallory Square, have drinks and dinner."

She thought that he would turn down the idea, because he was — obsessed.

"That sounds fine. What time are we meeting them, where?"

"What time, where?" Katie repeated to Clarinda.

"Half an hour — sunset is coming soon. The bar behind the Westin, how's that?"

David had turned and was starting for the stairs. "Hey, where are you going?"

"Just to freshen up."

"Well, then, I have to freshen up, too!"

"Ten minutes!" he said. "We'll run by your place, and you have twelve minutes."

He was good to his word, but he came down having stepped into the shower, and with freshly shaven cheeks and damp hair. He was devastating, she thought. It wasn't the simple fact of his good looks, it was more. There was something that seemed hard and chiseled about his features, strong about his stature and compelling when he smiled. She took one look at him and nearly ran for the door, eager to get out before she longed to do something rather than leave and make their appointment.

They walked to her house, and he seemed light, taking her hand, swinging it as they hurried along.

Once in the door, he was all business. "You have twelve to fourteen minutes," he told her.

"I can be faster than a speeding bullet," she promised.

And she was. She managed a sixty-second shower and chose a halter dress and sandals with one-inch heels, ran a brush through her hair, splashed water on her face and ran on back down.

"I'm impressed — you have two minutes to spare."

She smiled, walked to him, leaned against him and kissed him. He smelled divine. He felt rock-hard, and yet warm and vital. His tongue moved in her mouth, and she forgot all about the sunset.

He moved back, smiling, smoothing her hair. She quickly opened the door and stepped into the night, locking the door behind her.

"Sunset on Mallory Square. I can't remember the last time I was there," he said.

"I haven't been in a while myself," she said.

The city seemed to be teeming with people, even though it was a weekday. The air was already a hint cooler, and the sun was low in the western sky. Shadows seemed to darken doorways, as lights came on in the streets and streamed from shops and bars.

They crossed Front Street and continued to the square. The bar was crowded. There were advertisements everywhere for Fantasy Fest.

Body painting here. Whatever body part you want — painted!

Costumes of the absurd!

Beer for a buck!

Live your Fantasy — clothes optional up in the Garden!

"Hmm. I guess we are pretty decadent here," David said.

"Grown-ups still like to dress up, that's all," Katie said.

"Or dress down. I've seen lots of costumes that consisted of nothing but body paint," he said, grinning.

They'd reached the bar. Clarinda, dressed casually in a white pinstripe dress — one that made Katie glad that she had changed

— came running out to meet them. "Can you believe it? It's crowded as hell in there, and we haven't gotten to the first of the activities. But we've got a table up top, so we can see the sunset and some of the performers." Clarinda smiled broadly, looping her arm through David's. "Come on up and meet Jonas. He's a conch, too, but younger than you — he was in our class in high school."

"Sounds great," David said pleasantly.

It might have been a normal night, Katie thought. *Two couples out to enjoy time together.*

Jonas was tall, on the thin side, with a shy smile, but a pleasant manner. He seemed honestly pleased to meet David, and greeted him without any mention of the past — or the present.

"The city is insane!" he said, beckoning to their waiter. Katie and David ordered the draft-beer special for the night. David had his camera in his pocket, and though it looked like the usual slim digital camera that many people carried, Katie noticed that the lens was larger than most, and that it seemed to extend farther. Jonas asked him about the camera and David showed it to him, giving him the technical specifications. As he did so, Clarinda turned to Katie.

311

"You doing okay?" she asked.

"I'm fine. Why?"

"Well, that poor girl . . . it's a similar murder."

"Yes."

"It means a killer is loose," Clarinda said, and shivered. "I'm not making a move by myself, not a single move. I've moved right in with Jonas, and you know that I always liked keeping my independence. You — you're hanging with David, right?" she asked.

Katie opened her mouth to answer, but Clarinda kept going. "I mean, all you have to do is know him to know that he didn't kill anyone, but it is so bizarre that he's back here, and that girl . . . you know?"

"I have complete trust in David," Katie assured her.

As she spoke, David, who had been showing the camera to Jonas with the lens extended, suddenly stood.

He stared through the camera for a long moment.

She tried to see what had so captured his attention.

Below them, one of the local entertainers — originally from France — was performing with his multitude of cats. Cats that walked on wires and hopped over one

312

another, and cats who jumped through burning hoops. Katie had always liked the man — he adopted strays to train, or saved animals from the local pound. A group was around him, laughing and chatting, and he had just chosen two youngsters to come up and help with the act. Beyond him were a pair of comedians who worked with balloon animals, and they had the group around them laughing, as well.

Beyond the entertainers was the sea, darkening like the sky. It was a calm night. Sea and sky together were picture-perfect.

The lights in the square suddenly seemed to brighten.

The sun had taken another plunge downward into the night. Orange, mauve and crimson streaks were streaming across the sky, with a deep purple on top, promising that night was nearly here.

David suddenly moved. He dropped the camera on the table, and he was gone, streaking down the stairs to the ground level below.

"David!"

Katie strained again to see what had attracted his attention before grabbing the camera and bolting down to follow him.

Just past the balloon men, there was a lone figure gathering his own fair share of the audience. The actor was dressed up as Robert the Doll. His mask must have been off; as Katie watched him, frowning, she saw that he was adjusting it, retying the bow at the back of his head that held the mask in place.

Katie had always considered the doll to be an ugly thing — and she was stunned that any parents would have allowed anyone to give their child such a present. Maybe the parents had been afraid of the servant who had given their child the doll, and it was easy to believe that whoever had made the doll was well versed in voodoo. Though the real doll was about three feet tall, the man wearing the costume was at least six feet, his size seeming to make the "doll" even uglier. The man's mask was well made, and he seemed to have a bizarre and creepy face, just like the doll. Most of the time, Robert sat at the East Martello Museum, but he had recently been at a paranormal convention where he had been reputed to show an aura with special photography. The doll was good for the museum and for tourism.

But it was creepy.

The actor was standing on a little plastic platform, holding a stuffed dog toy just like the real doll's and looking around the crowd in straw-stuffed silence with threaten-

314

ing moves.

Katie saw that David was making his way through the crowds, watching the cat man and the balloon artists, and heading for the doll.

She raced down the stairs in his wake, doing her best to weave through the crowd without plowing anyone down.

But as she reached the area where Robert the Doll was working, David burst in on him.

The actor forgot that he was working in silence. He let out a startled scream, jumped off his pedestal and started running.

David took off after him, and Katie took off after David.

David caught up with Robert the Doll on the grass behind the aquarium. He tackled him, as if he were sacking a quarterback, and the two plowed to the earth together.

People around them jumped back. Some gasped. One lady screamed. Another laughed and said it was part of the entertainment.

Katie rushed up to David, grabbing him by the arm. "David! Stop it, stop! You're going to be nabbed for assault. What the hell are you doing?"

The man beneath him wasn't fighting. A crowd was gathering. David let her drag him

315

up, but he stared down at the man below him, then extended his hand. The actor took it slowly. He rose. David reached out, ripping the straw mask from the actor's face.

"Katie, I don't think you ever met Mike Sanderson. Mike was the fellow Tanya fell in love with while I was gone. He was supposedly in Ohio when she was murdered. But he wasn't. He was in St. Augustine, we know, the day after, which means he could have easily been down here when the deed was done. And how very, very odd. Here he is — back again. Playing with history, dressed up like Robert the Doll. Maybe he likes to play at being Carl Tanzler, Count von Cosel, too. Maybe he needs a new dead bride every decade."

The man was big; as big as David, and even bulkier. The sailor suit had hidden some of his muscle.

But it didn't look as if he wanted to fight anyone.

It looked as if he suddenly wanted to do anything but entertain the crowd.

There was a sudden spurt of applause. Katie turned around to see that they had garnered a loud crowd — and they seemed to think it was all being done for entertainment.

"Oh, good Lord! Go watch the cats,"

Katie cried out.

Mike Sanderson hadn't uttered a word. David was staring at him as if he could manifest daggers and press them into the man's heart.

"Let's get out of here!" she said.

She grabbed both men by the elbows, hating the fact that to get out of the crowd, she was going to have to get through the busy streets.

Walking arm in arm with Robert the Doll.

But Clarinda had reached them by then, and Jonas was right behind her. Neither of them had the least idea of what was going on, but Clarinda was always intuitive in any situation. "We can go right down Front Street, past the Old Customs House and the Westin, and then duck into Jonas's place. Follow me."

Katie felt absurdly like a college professor, struggling with fighting young adults. But after the first few seconds, there was no resistance from either man. When Mike Sanderson did stop suddenly, he explained himself quickly. "I have a boxful of money back there — I need it." He blushed. "I'm supposed to be on a sales trip."

"I'll get it," Jonas told them.

"You pretend to be on a sales trip — and you come here to pretend to be Robert the

317

Doll?" David demanded.

"Fantasy Fest, every year," Mike Sanderson admitted sheepishly.

"How long have you been doing this?" David asked.

"Since I left. Well, not exactly. I finished college, and then, since then . . ."

"Why?" Katie asked.

"I love it. I love Fantasy Fest. I always have. My wife hates it. So I pretend I'm on a sales trip."

"How can you love this place — when Tanya died here?" David demanded.

Mike Sanderson stopped walking. He was rock-solid; Katie almost tripped when as she had been leading him along, he then pulled her back.

"I didn't kill Tanya!" Sanderson said angrily. "And don't kid yourself — I know exactly who you are, and I know that she stayed here just because she wanted to talk to you. I don't think she was ever coming with me. Not once you had come back. But I didn't kill her."

"I really think we should get inside for this discussion," Clarinda said. "That's Jonas's place, there."

"It's an inn," David said.

"Yes, yes, but go up the stairs, he keeps the whole second floor of the main house for himself."

As she spoke, Jonas came running back up to them, Mike's donation hat in his hands. "Amazing, isn't it? Crowd like that — not a soul touched his money. Sometimes, human beings are decent."

No one answered him. He cleared his throat. "Okay, let's get upstairs," he said.

The outer door was open; it led to hallways with signs that indicated room numbers and pointed to cottages outside. They hurried up the stairs; the door in the hallway was locked and Jonas quickly opened it for them. They piled in.

Mike Sanderson moved first, striding across the room, tearing off the Velcro that held his Robert the Doll sailor outfit together in the back. He was wearing the costume over a pair of cutoff jeans and a simple white T-shirt. He folded it and put it at his feet. Katie realized that David was still holding the man's cloth mask and sailor hat when Sanderson reached out to him. "Do you mind? I don't intend to press charges, but I do make good money at this gig."

"You make good money, standing in Mallory Square, pretending to be Robert the Doll?" Clarinda said incredulously.

"Four hundred bucks already tonight,"

Sanderson said. "Beats selling vacuums, which I do to keep the family going."

"But — you were supposed to be a big-shot football player at Ohio State!" Katie said.

"Knee injury. They loved me before it — I was yesterday's news afterward," Sanderson said.

She studied him. He was a big fellow with sandy-blond hair, light brown eyes and a pretty-boy face that seemed to be getting just a little fleshy at the edges now, as if he were a man who liked his booze.

"The police down here want to talk to you," David told him.

"Yeah, I know, my wife called me," he said.

"So why didn't you come into the police station?" David asked him.

"I'm not supposed to be here," Sanderson said with a sigh of impatience. "Don't you get it? No one knows I do this. Hell, what, everyone's life turns out to be what they want? I come down here. I see all the naked painted boobs for Fantasy Fest. I don't go with any lowlifes, I don't pick up any sexual diseases, I just do a lot of looking and drinking, and I make money to bring home by putting on a Robert the Doll costume and scaring people in the square. It's a personal thing. What the hell is wrong with you, and what the hell business is it of yours that I do this?"

"It's police business because you lied when they questioned you a decade ago," David said. "And it's police business because another woman was murdered."

"Look — I do this for the money! I'm not hung up on Key West legend," Sanderson said. "I loved Tanya! I wouldn't have hurt her for the world. I was young. I waited for her — then I figured that she'd chosen you over me. When I heard about the murder, I panicked, and I got the hell out!"

"You will have to tell that story to the police," David said.

Sanderson straightened where he sat. "Sure. I'll be happy to do so."

"When did you get here?" he asked.

Sanderson shook his head and winced. "Last Friday," he said.

"Before Stella Martin was murdered," David pointed out.

Sanderson stood, pointing hard at David. "Look, you bastard, you were the jilted lover. You owned the damned museum. You're a fucking conch, for God's sake — you're the one all into the history and legend of Key West. They would have locked your ass up if you weren't David Beckett!"

To David's credit, he completely controlled his temper. He stood dead still without speaking for long seconds.

Sanderson took a step back from him. "Look, maybe you didn't do it. But I know this much — I didn't do it and you can haul me down to the station anytime you want."

David looked over at Jonas. "Want to take a ride?"

"I — uh — sure," Jonas said.

"What the hell? The sun has been down a long time now," Clarinda said. "What a lovely evening out with friends!"

12

The night sergeant on duty was ready to bring them in. David had called Liam, and Liam, who had just left for the evening, called Pete Dryer, who had left just a bit earlier, and the result was that both men would be returning to the station.

Clarinda sat in the waiting area, shaking her head at Katie. "I feel as if I've just been brought in on some kind of a sting. Look around, will you?"

There was an odd assortment of people in the station that night. There was a drunk who was crying in the arms of another drunk.

A junkie.

A belligerent fellow being held on a drunk-driving charge.

It was hopping.

Fantasy Fest was all but here.

Liam Beckett came back through the door first. His white polo shirt bore a police insignia and he was in neat work khakis. He was totally professional, shaking hands with Mike Sanderson and thanking him for coming in on a voluntary basis. Pete came through the doorway just a minute later, looking worn — as he should. One of the city's most important and biggest festivals was on the way, and a murderer was loose in the city.

Pete nodded at David. "Thanks. Thanks for talking this fellow into coming in. We can take this from here, David."

For a moment, David looked as if he didn't want to move. Then he nodded. "Of course," he said.

But as they started out, he held back for a minute. "Hang on, I just have to catch Liam quickly."

He went back in before Katie could try to stop him.

"Oh, Lord — is he coming back out, do you think?" Clarinda asked.

"I think," Katie said.

"Umm, maybe not," Jonas said after a minute.

Just when Katie was about to give up, David came out. He was smiling. He slipped an arm around her shoulders and one around Clarinda's shoulders. "Where shall we go for dinner?" he asked.

"Umm — anywhere," Jonas said.

"I'm not so sure we can get in anywhere," Clarinda said. "The city is teeming."

"O'Hara's," Katie said dryly. "I can always get in there."

Clarinda laughed. "My night off! But that's all right — I do know they have good food."

"And we can park in back there, too. I know the owner," Katie pointed out.

The evening ended, oddly enough, on a good note. Jonas was fascinated with photography, and David talked about different places he had been. Jonas pointed out that with all that David did, now was the time for him to go back and do some shots and film work in his own backyard. "My God, think about it. We've got more wildlife and shipwrecks than a dog has fleas," Jonas pointed out.

"You know, that's odd," Clarinda noted. "David, you and Sean wound up going into just about the same thing. You've been very successful with your still work and Sean's usually doing video or film or whatever. Do you ever work with video?"

David nodded. "I love both. Still life is capturing a single moment with the subject, light and characters just right. But film is great — it's life in motion, or dust motes moving through the air. Last year, I did some work in Australia, filming oceanographers searching for one of the really well-preserved wrecks recently discovered there."

"But have you and Sean worked together?" Jonas asked.

David shook his head. "I haven't seen Sean in ten years," he said. "We keep up with e-mail now and then, but we've never worked on the same project."

Jon Merrillo, Jamie O'Hara's main manager in his absence, stopped by the table. He was about forty, and hadn't been in the Keys very long. He had taken to the area like a native; he loved it, and never wanted to go back North.

"You guys can't get enough of this place, huh?" he teased.

"I just love a night when the drunks aren't pestering me!" Clarinda told him.

"Hey, we don't let drunks pester folks here, Clarinda, and you know I'd never let that happen," Jon said.

"I do know, Jon."

Jon nodded. "Hey, Katie, have you talked with your uncle Jamie?" he asked her.

She felt guilty. She shook her head. "No, but I have spoken with Sean. Sean is coming home — I expect by tomorrow."

"Well, it will be good to see Sean. I'll give

Jamie a call myself tomorrow. I figured he'd want to be back by the end of the week. It's already getting insane."

He left them. Clarinda sighed. "Ah, well, so much for my plans for a lovely sunset and dinner on the water."

"We'll try again later in the week," Katie said.

Clarinda sniffed. "I get next Monday off and that's it — we're heading straight into ten days of events and pure mayhem."

"So, we'll go next Monday," David assured her.

They finished with their coffee and the Key lime pie — really homemade — that Katie had talked them all into ordering. In the car, Jonas asked, "Should I drop Katie, we'll see her in safely, and then drop you, David?"

Clarinda smacked him on the arm. "Don't be ridiculous. Just go to Katie's place. David is staying there. This is not a time for pretense of any kind. Katie should not be alone, and that's that."

"Aha," Jonas said. He looked at David and David nodded.

Jonas left them at Katie's house, and they waved goodbye. They could still hear the loud sounds of revelry coming from Duval Street. "Kind of like Christmas, huh?" David asked. "Fantasy Fest starts just a little bit earlier every year."

"We need to be glad. We do survive off tourism," Katie pointed out.

"Yep. I guess I have been gone a long time," David noted.

They walked into the house. Katie moved ahead, into the kitchen. "You know, it's interesting that Danny Zigler was reading about the history of Key West. I mean, he grew up down here, we all heard it all the time."

"We heard the history — but Danny must have had a reason to want to learn more about it."

Bartholomew thought so, too. So did she.

Katie made a mental note to pursue that theory the following day. "Do you think that something happened in the far past that might have had something to do with Tanya's murder? Is that why her body was left in the museum?"

"I don't know. Oh, by the way, I gave the credit card we found to Liam and told him that I was pretty sure that the stuff on the card was ice cream. I don't know what is going on, but sure, maybe something from the past can explain it all. Tanya was from the area, and her family went way back — I don't know. I just don't know. But, I intend to find out. I'll start reading the books tomorrow," David said.

She had started to pick up the kettle. "Want some tea or something?" she asked.

He took the kettle from her hands and set it back on the range top. He pulled her into his arms. "Yes . . . I want to bury myself in you, and forget the world, and even my own obsessions for the night," he told her. "I mean, of course, if you don't mind."

She smiled. She stared up at him, wondering how she could feel so mesmerized by the sound of his voice and the feel of his arms.

She threaded her fingers through his dark hair and met his eyes. "You're good, you know," she teased. "Very good."

"Oh?"

"Eloquent."

"With words?"

"Oh, very."

"Really? It gets worse. I was thinking that I could die in the radiant sunset of your hair, drown in the sea of your eyes."

"My eyes are kind of hazel-green."

"I've seen our waters blue and green, every shade between, and even dark and wild and wicked when storms are coming through."

"Very eloquent."

"And strong, too," he assured her.

"Really?"

He swept her up into his arms.

Her world was in turmoil; he was still, she was certain, to others, a person of interest in a murder case — or cases. He was obsessed with the truth.

But at that moment, it didn't matter. The world was holding still, and the world was pure magic. Wonderful, carnal, hot, wet magic.

"Strong, too," she agreed.

They fell into her bed so easily. So quickly, naturally. Clothing only half off, they were kissing and removing tangles of clothes. She was aware of him as she had never been before, the sound of his breathing, every movement of his muscles, twist and turn, the beating of his heart. He was an experienced lover, and she didn't want to think of anything that had come before in his life, or in her own. She just wanted to feel. And it was so easy. He knew where to touch, and where to kiss, and where to tease most sensuously with his tongue and teeth. Movements could be so tempestuous and passionate, and then just a breath or a whisper against her skin could send her spinning into a new spiral of arousal.

He kissed along her breasts. Ribs and abdomen. Teased beneath her thighs.

Moved ever more erotically.

And when she nearly reached a pinnacle, he would pause, just to lead her upward again, until she was frantic, returning every whispered breath, every touch, seeking to crawl into his very flesh, writhe and arch in absolute unison and abandon.

Eventually they lay together sated, exhausted and replete, and still touching while the cool air moved over their flesh.

She curled more closely to him.

"Ever so eloquent, in so many ways!" she whispered to him.

"Aye, but you make it so very easy to speak ever so ardently!" he assured her.

Smiling, she lay against him, and slept.

An hour later, she opened her eyes.

A breeze was blowing.

A breeze shouldn't have been blowing. The windows were all closed.

But . . .

She thought that her drapes were billowing, blowing inward.

A bolt of lightning flashed across the sky.

And for a moment, it seemed that Danny Zigler was standing there. Standing there — just outside her window. He couldn't have been; her bedroom was on the second floor. There was no balcony beyond it. There was just . . . air.

She gasped, blinking.

She bolted up, and next to her, David bolted up, as well.

"What is it?"

"The window!" she said.

He jumped out of bed and went over to the window. The drapes were flat; there was no breeze. He moved the drapes.

The window was closed. And bolted.

He turned back to her in the shadows of night.

"David . . . I'm sorry. I must have had a nightmare," she said. "I'm truly sorry to have wakened you."

"That's all right. It's all right, perfectly all right," he assured her, climbing back in bed with her and taking her into his arms. "I'm probably the reason you're having nightmares," he said, smoothing her hair back.

She felt cold, chilled, and yet he was warming her.

She didn't speak, she just curled against him.

He wasn't the reason for her nightmares, she might have said. He was far more a dream of something real and wonderful.

But time here and now was suspended; she didn't know where it could take him, and pride was a wonderful thing. Something that was great to cling to — when the warmth went away. If it went away. She just didn't know what the future would bring.

She lay silent.

She drifted off, and it wasn't until morning that she opened her eyes and really wondered about what had happened the night before. What she had seen in her mind's eye, or in her soul, or with the strange gift/curse that was just part of who she was.

A sense of dread and pain filled her.

Danny Zigler was dead.

Coffee had already brewed when David came down the stairs. He was surprised; he'd never seen her set a timer the previous night, but the coffee was good.

He had come down quietly, trying not to wake Katie after slipping into Sean's room for a shower. He didn't dress, just put on a towel, but swept up his clothing, needing his cell phone, which was in the back pocket of his jeans.

It had seemed that Katie had tossed and turned much of the night. He didn't want to awaken her until she was ready; she might want to sleep late. He didn't want to leave the door unlocked, but he was also anxious to get to his house — they'd left the books there.

But he could at least make phone calls.

After he poured himself coffee, he called Liam.

"So?" he asked his cousin.

"So, we spent a couple of hours with Mike Sanderson. I have a bunch of computer geeks following all the information he gave me. He said that he wasn't in Key West when Tanya was killed, that he had gone up to Miami, and he can surely find the charge-card slips to prove that he'd taken a room — and if he can't find them, we can get them from the credit-card company. We found the one for St. Augustine, but not Miami, and he claims he had a bunch of student cards."

"Even if he was in Miami, it's a three- or three-and-a-half-hour drive down. You could easily book a room in Miami and come back down here."

"It's possible. But I'm not taking Mike Sanderson to be a boy genius. I just don't see him renting a room, getting down here, killing Tanya and getting her into the museum."

"Do you see Danny Zigler managing such a feat?" David demanded.

"Don't know. We still can't find hide nor hair of Danny Zigler," Liam told him. "He didn't show up for work as a tour guide last night. We're getting a search warrant to go through his house."

"Did you pick up the kid? Lewis Agaro?"

"Picked him up and questioned him. And I had the lab analyze the substance on the credit card. It was sticky, and might have given us a clue as to where Stella had gone once she took the card. Of course, the kid might have gotten the stuff on the card himself, but we can't leave anything to chance. Have to follow up on everything."

"It was chocolate ice cream," David said.

"How did you know?"

"I just do. I think Stella was pretty tight with Danny Zigler, which, of course, doesn't mean anything. She might have seen Danny, and she might not have," David said. "But I believe Danny knows something."

"Like what?"

"I went into his place. He was researching Key West, and had thousands of dollars in one of the books he was using. Liam, for now, let's not let this get out to others, or to the press."

Liam laughed. "I can't! I'd have to admit my cousin was guilty of breaking and entering."

"I didn't break anything," David assured him.

"Pete has called the D.A. about getting a

warrant to get in there, but if Danny has been guilty of . . . something, he wants it all by the book. I'm assuming a warrant is coming soon," Liam said. "But — you didn't leave fingerprints anywhere, did you?"

"No. Don't worry — I watch TV."

"Great."

"So how did it go with the kid? Was he able to give you anything?"

"No — I don't believe he's guilty of anything other than a wild crush on a wicked older woman," Liam said. "Now that you've told me about Danny Zigler's apartment and the money . . . what the hell do you think is going on?"

"I think that Danny is dead. He knew something. He was blackmailing someone, or someone was paying him off for his silence in some way, shape or form."

"Then why would he be dead now?"

"I believe that he suspected or knew something before — and that he might have pieced whatever it was together — and knew who killed Stella. Liam, I know you're a cop, a detective, and that you have to carry on an active investigation. But you only know about that because I'm guilty of a crime, so until you get that search warrant, can you keep what I've told you to yourself for your own investigation?"

"You're asking me to . . . Ah, hell. I'll follow whatever angles I can on that in confidence — for now."

"Thanks. Do you know anything else? What about forensics?"

"I'm pretty sure you know what I do. She wasn't violated — she'd had sex with condoms, don't know how much, but there was no evidence of sexual force or violence of any kind. She had chicken nuggets and fries for dinner. Oh — this is new. We had known, of course, that the killer wore gloves and took the women by surprise. But the lab found bits of cells that might help us eventually — amara."

"Amara? It's a synthetic leather, used in making warm-water dive gloves," David said.

"Right. Our killer wears dive gloves."

"Half of Key West might own dive gloves with amara," David said.

"True." Liam sighed. "Look, at this point, it eliminates half of Key West, so that's good. Oh, yeah, the gloves have silicone on the fingertips. That might narrow down the brand. Look, I'm grabbing at every straw out there, and so is the entire force."

"Are you holding anyone?"

"We still have Sanderson, but we can only

keep him until tonight. He hasn't called an attorney, because we aren't going to call his wife — unless we find something on him. I let the kid, Lewis Agaro, go. I don't think he's staying for Fantasy Fest anymore. It was his first year down here as a twenty-one-year-old. Guess he's going to be looking back at being underaged as the good old days."

"Maybe. All right. Keep me posted. I'll do the same."

"You're keeping an eye on Katie, I take it?" Liam asked.

"Absolutely," David said.

His cousin was silent.

"What, you disapprove?" David asked.

"She deserves more."

"Thanks."

"No, I mean she deserves more than someone who is just using her while trying to chase away the ghosts of his past. Sorry, you might want to belt me for that, but it's the truth."

David hesitated. "Did I move in on anything?" he asked.

"No, she and I are friends, good friends. She'd deserve a lot better than me, too — all I seem to do these days is work. You're leaving, David. You know you're leaving. So keep it honest, huh?"

"I am honest," David assured him. He hung up, reflecting.

He was honest, wasn't he? Or was anything about him really honest? What he felt was. The need to leave this place had been just as basic. What did he feel now? He didn't know. He'd been a lot of places — he'd hit every continent, every ocean.

And now?

He tensed, hearing something at the door. He tightened his towel and looked around instinctively for a weapon.

As he did so, Katie came tearing down the stairs from her room — heading straight for the door. "Katie!" he warned.

He grabbed the coffeepot; he wasn't going to be able to stop her.

She was already throwing the door open.

Sean O'Hara stood there.

It had been ten years, but Sean had changed little. He was tall, well built, redheaded, lithe and muscular. He'd made an amazing running back during their high-school days.

He had a backpack on, and two huge duffel bags sat by his feet.

"Sean!" Katie said, and threw herself in her brother's arms.

Awkward as hell! David thought. He hadn't ever intended to lie, he'd never meant any harm to anyone, nor did he feel any need to apologize. He and Katie were definitely adults now, and they had chosen to be together.

He just hadn't planned on wearing a towel when he first saw Sean.

"Katie O'Hara!" Sean said, sweeping her up and spinning her around as he came into the room. He let out a fake groan. "Wait, give it a minute, I'm getting old now, and you and the backpack at the same time . . . Nope, nope don't think so!"

"I'm so glad you're home!" she told him, standing, righting herself and stepping back. "I thought you'd call me, though, and tell me you were in the state."

"Hey, you have a cell phone, too."

"Yeah, but it never works when I try to call you!"

"All right, well, I'm here, and —" Sean's voice broke off sharply. He stared at David. David realized that he was still holding the coffeepot. He set it on the range and stepped forward, his arm extended.

"Sean. Good to see you."

He didn't think that Sean was going to accept this situation easily; he was just stunned. He shook David's hand.

But then he stepped back. He looked from Katie to David, and back to Katie. Then

David again.

"What the hell? What the hell is going on here?" he demanded. He lifted a hand. "No, no, no, wait. I don't want gory details, I can see what the hell is going on. The question is . . . what the hell is the matter with you? David, hell, this is my baby sister! Katie — the man could be a murderer. Sorry, David, no real offense meant, but by statistics . . . You idiots!" he finished.

"Sean, your 'baby' sister is in her mid-twenties, and capable of making choices and decisions," David said. "And I'm not a murderer, and frankly, no offense, our sleeping arrangements aren't any of your business."

"The hell they're not!" Sean exploded. He wasn't a redhead of Irish lineage for nothing, David decided. "Katie is — my sister!"

"Sean, this is my choice," Katie pleaded. "And David was one of your friends — a good friend, until you more or less deserted him and turned against him like everyone else."

"Katie," David said, grating his teeth, "thanks, but don't defend me. Look, Sean, I care about your sister a great deal. I believe she feels the same way about me."

Sean didn't answer him. He turned on

341

Katie. "I did not turn my back on David," he protested. "I never deserted anyone." He looked at David. "We've been in contact through the years, off and on. I have never turned on a friend."

"Sean, I never suggested that you turned on me," David said. "Look, Sean, honest to God, I mean no offense, and certainly no disrespect here. I care about your sister, a great deal."

"And there's a murderer loose in the city again," Katie said quietly.

"You're sleeping with him for protection?" Sean said.

"No!" Katie said, horrified. "No, oh, Lord, Sean, will you please . . . chill! Let's get your stuff. Have some coffee — give me a minute to take a shower and get dressed. You and David talk — you haven't actually seen each other in a decade. Talk. Don't either of you go defending me or my honor in any way, do you understand?" she demanded.

"He's wearing a towel!" Sean said. "And we're not in the high-school gym anymore."

"I have clothing," David assured him. With dignity, he swept up his shirt and jeans — desperately glad that he had needed his phone and so taken his clothing from Katie's room — and headed into the downstairs half bath. When he emerged, Sean had brought his bags in. They were dumped in the hall. Sean was sitting on one of the bar stools, a cup of coffee gripped in his hand.

Sean glowered at David. "So. Now a prostitute named Stella Martin has been found dead at a different museum in a similar pose. Fill me in," Sean said.

David told him what he could. There wasn't much.

"Danny Zigler?" Sean said. "He's weird enough — but he's a runt. And not the sharpest knife in the drawer."

"Danny didn't do it," David said.

"And you know that because?"

"I don't think that Danny had the strength to kill with his bare hands."

"Even if he suffocated his victims first?"

"Suffocating, you still fight. I think the killer had to be big."

"Our size," Sean said dryly.

"Yeah. Our size."

Sean shook his head. "And . . . Katie is the one who showed you the area where she thought that Stella had been killed."

"Yes."

"She didn't say . . . or do . . . anything weird, did she?" Sean asked.

"What do you mean by that?" David asked.

"Nothing, nothing." Sean stared at David. He was still frowning.

"Sean, I have never felt about anyone the way that I feel about Katie," he said flatly.

"That was fast," Sean said, his tone dubious.

"You're her brother."

"Remember that fact."

"Fast, slow, whatever, it's the truth."

"So, you suddenly love her and you're going to give up a life of fame and fortune to come home and live the easy life of an islander and raise a passel of little conchs?" Sean mocked.

"I don't know what will happen in the future," David said. "I'm telling you that I take nothing about your sister lightly, and that we are emotionally entangled and not just opting for something like a best-friends-with-benefits deal."

Sean looked away and nodded. "Sorry. She is my sister. And I did walk in to find a man who had been a good friend — and a suspect in a murder — in a towel in my house."

"I know. I'm sorry."

Katie came hurrying down the stairs. "So, do you know everything that's happened on the island since you've been gone?" she asked him.

Sean glanced over at David. "I haven't been gone for a decade — I was here at Christmas," he reminded her.

"I'm talking about — well, I guess I'm talking about Stella Martin," Katie said lamely. "And the past," she admitted.

Sean let out a sigh of aggravation. "Katie, I told you to stay out of it all."

"Sean, you're not my keeper. And thank God — you're never here. So don't go all protective on me now!"

"Why are you letting her get into danger?" Sean asked David.

"I'm not letting her into danger — I'm trying to stay with her as much as I can to make sure that she's not alone," David said.

"Well, I'm home now," Sean said.

"Hey!" Katie protested. "Hey, I did fine on my own without either of you, so don't you two go getting the testosterone thing going and try to manage me, either of you!"

She stared at the two of them.

Sean looked at David.

"I'll make sure I'm with her when you're not," he said.

"She shouldn't be alone. And there will be times . . . when I might be worried about her," David admitted.

"Hey!" Katie protested.

David's phone started to ring again. He

snapped it open. "David?"

The voice was sweet and feminine. And old.

"Aunt Alice!" he said, his heart sinking.

"David, you are here. And you haven't been by."

Alice and Esther were actually his great-aunts. They had never been anything but patient and kind, and he knew that they loved him, that his leaving had hurt them and that he had been a selfish ass not to have taken the time yet to see them. They were both octogenarians now, with Esther closing in on ninety.

He loved them both.

They were incredible storytellers; they knew the island far better than any teacher he had ever had in high school.

"David?"

"I know. I know. I'm so sorry," he said.

"Well," Alice told him, "we've heard all about that dreadful business with another poor woman murdered. Your cousin Liam has been terribly busy, and he's said you've helped out with talking to folks, but . . . we were hoping you could stop by for some lunch."

Katie and Sean were staring at him, curious. As he looked at them, they looked away, embarrassed at inadvertently eavesdropping.

"May I bring a few old friends?" he asked.

"Well, of course, David! When haven't we welcomed your friends?" Alice asked.

Katie had thought that Sean was going to refuse the invitation to David's aunts' house, but he was determined at the moment to stay close to her, she realized. It was good that her brother cared, she thought.

And irritating.

He had rented a two-seater convertible in Miami.

"I didn't know I could possibly need more than two seats," he said.

"My car is in the drive — just move your rental, mine is the obvious choice," Katie told him.

"We can walk," David said.

"They're past the cemetery — it's almost a mile. Let's just drive," Sean said. He was coming with them, but it was obvious that he was tired.

So they drove, Katie at the wheel. She slowed down as they passed the cemetery, trying to drive and see what spirits might be about in the bright light.

As ever, the beautiful, spectral figure of Elena de Hoyos moved among the graves.

She saw no one else.

"What are you doing?" Sean asked her sharply.

"Driving," she replied.

She pressed harder on the gas pedal. Past the cemetery two blocks, she turned the corner and came to the beautiful old Victorian where Alice and Esther Beckett, spinster sisters, had lived most of their lives. As she pulled into the drive, the two came hurrying out the door and down the porch steps.

She recognized them; they were known throughout Key West and the islands. They had been born rich, and they had used their money wisely and well all their lives, helping with every cause in the world. They gave money to several churches — Alice was quite certain that God didn't discriminate between minor differences in worship — as well as animal-rescue leagues and all the medical charities for every organ in the human body. They were truly loved.

They both rushed to David as he exited the car, fawning over him with hugs and kisses. They knew Sean as well, chiding him for not coming by when he was in town. Sean, perhaps feeling a bit of guilt, flushed and told them that he was seldom in town — he and David did similar work.

At last it was Katie's turn, and she received an abundance of love as well, even if she had never visited the house at all.

"My Lord! Sean's sister! Oh, my goodness, well, Jamie O'Hara's niece, of course. What a beauty!" Alice gushed. "Even more so than your mother, and oh, my, Esther, remember how lovely and sweet she was. I understand your parents have moved from the house, but when they're home, you must beg them to stop by, too. Sadly, we tend to be such hermits these days."

"We're just horrible," Esther said. "And, oh, how I miss your grandfather, David. The world is a far sadder place with Craig gone."

"He was certainly the best and finest man," David agreed.

"Well, well, we're standing around here outside when lunch is waiting!" Alice chastised.

"Come along in," Esther urged Katie, taking her by the arm.

They were all introduced to a woman named Betsy, an attractive thirty-something Bahamian who tended to the elderly sisters' needs. She had already set up lunch on what the sisters referred to as their spring porch, a back porch with a tiled floor and screened windows that caught the sea breezes.

Lunch was a feast. Salad with berries and

nuts, blackened grouper, vegetarian pasta — just in case — and all manner of fresh-baked breads.

The conversation was light at first as David and Sean talked about a few of their foreign exploits with photography and film, and Katie explained how she had wanted to come home to live, and thus formed her corporation, Katie-oke.

They were delighted.

"I used to carry quite a melody in my day!" Alice assured her.

"Ever hear a honking swan?" Esther asked.

"Esther!" Alice chastised.

"I'm teasing you, dear, of course!" Esther said. "My sister still has a lovely voice for a torch song."

"I'll have to get you in there," Katie told her.

"Well, certainly, but not until Fantasy Fest is over," Alice said.

Later, when pecan pie had been served, they moved out to the parlor for "a touch of sherry," as Alice phrased it.

"Excellent for the constitution," Esther assured them.

"What is that, Aunt Alice?" David asked, pointing to a large ledgerlike book that sat atop the mantel.

"That?" Alice replied. "That is our family

history, young man. It's always been there. You've never asked before."

"May I?" he asked.

"Certainly. We've been here forever — but then your family has, too, Katie, Sean."

David stood and brought the large, embossed book back to the sofa. "How old is this thing?" he asked.

"Oh, it was started in the eighteen twenties," Aunt Esther said. "The first fellow to write in it was Craig Beckett — not your grandfather, David, of course."

"He was quite a man, from all accounts," Alice said proudly.

"Craig Beckett?" Katie said. She wanted to see the book herself. Actually, she wanted to take it right out of David's hand. "He was a sea captain, right?"

"Yes, dear, he was. He sailed for Commodore Perry, and then for David Porter. In fact, the name David came into our family because of David Porter. Craig was admired far and wide. He could take down pirates — but he wasn't a cruel man. I mean, many a pirate was hanged here, of course, but if a man could prove himself a privateer, Craig Beckett always showed mercy. He was strong, and he was fair."

David was turning pages carefully. The ledger was nearly two hundred years old. It hadn't been kept under glass — it was part of the family's heritage, and Katie was certain that both aunts had read it through and through.

"Ah, well, look — he writes it himself. He had a fellow named Smith hanged. Seems like Smith was a bit of a bastard. Attacked a ship and killed all aboard — then saw another man hanged for the deed." David closed the book, carefully set it back on the mantel, and turned to his aunts. "That was wonderful. I'll be in town for a while, at least. Next time, I'll take you out."

Sean rose and Katie followed suit. The aunts stood as well, ready to walk their guests to the door.

"David, darling, you must come here again, too — anytime. You're family, and we do love you so!" Esther told him.

"Of course. But I want to take you out."

"I'm afraid it will have to be somewhere quiet these days," Esther said. "We'll talk!"

They both stood on tiptoe to kiss David then Sean goodbye. When they came to hug Katie, she asked, "Would you two trust me to take your ledger for a few days? I would absolutely love to read it. I'll be very careful with it."

"Well, of course!" Ester said. "We'll be delighted for you to read it."

"And we know you'll take care with it," Alice said.

She thanked them. Sean looked at her and rolled his eyes, shaking his head. "I'm going to be careful!" she whispered to him.

"It's a bit frightening, borrowing a family treasure," Sean said, aware that the others were looking at the two of them.

"Katie, I know you'll take it home and take good care of it," Alice said. "We're not worried in the least."

"I'll defend it with my life," Katie promised.

"Good Lord, don't do that, child," Alice said, smiling. "Your life is worth far more."

A minute later, they were in the car, heading back. One of the streets was blocked for construction; Katie hadn't intended on coming down Duval with its throngs of tourists, but she did so.

"Good God, what is that?" Sean demanded from the backseat.

"What?" she asked. Her eyes were on the road. Tourists didn't have the sense to look before they stepped off the sidewalk.

A red light allowed her the chance to look. One of the shops had a Robert the Doll mannequin out in front, except it was over-size.

"A balloon?" Sean asked, puzzled.

David was looking out the window, as well. "No, I think it might be canvas, but it's got some kind of an inner structure, wood or metal. Damn, that's ugly."

Katie kept driving. She could see that there was a line to get into the museum where Stella Martin had been killed and laid out.

Stella was still at the morgue.

And people would be thronging in to see where she had lain.

"Capitalism at its best," Sean murmured.

"We do need to survive as a city," Katie said.

She drove on, turning down her street and bringing the car into the drive. "Sean, should I back out and park in the street so that you can reach your car?"

"No. I'm going to bed. I could sleep for a week. If I go to sleep now, I may feel human again by tomorrow."

She parked the car and they all got out. Sean headed toward the house and then looked back. He strode over to them with purpose. "All right, someone has been killed, and Fantasy Fest may be starting off with a bang, but there is a killer on the loose. Katie, if you two don't come here for the night, you make sure that I know you're staying out."

He stared at David.

"Of course," David told him.

"All right, all right, it's a little bit weird, but I actually prefer it if you stay here at night," he said.

Neither of them moved.

Sean waved a hand in the air and walked on into the house.

"I'm going to take a run down to the police station. Will you go in for a while and promise me that you'll stay there?" David asked her.

She lifted the journal. "Sure. But you know, I work tomorrow night again."

"Hey, I'm getting to just love karaoke," he assured her.

She kissed his cheek and headed into the house. "Lock it!" he called to her, and then started walking.

Katie went on in and set the ledger on the dining-room table. She wished that she had the books from the library as well, but they were at David's house.

She couldn't read more than one at a time anyway, she told herself.

It had been hot outside. She ran upstairs, jumped into the shower and afterward slid into the coolest cotton dress she could find. The shower refreshed her, and she went back downstairs. She set the kettle on the range top to boil. Now that she was cooled down, she was in the mood for a cup of hot tea.

She turned away from the stove and went dead still.

Her heart thudded against her chest, and seemed to stop.

Danny Zigler was here.

She looked to the door, and saw that it remained locked.

She had seen him last night; it might have been a dream, or something like a dream, but she had already seen Danny, and she had thought that he was dead.

But now she knew.

How she had ever imagined that he might be flesh and blood, that he might have broken into the house, she didn't know.

He began to fade even as she stared at him. He had his old baseball cap in his hands, and his hair seemed unkempt. His clothes looked mussed and dirty.

"Danny," she said softly.

He faded away completely.

Then he reappeared. He pointed to the table.

She frowned, looking down.

He was pointing at the journal she had taken from the Beckett house.

"Danny, what is it? What am I looking

356

for?" she asked.

He faded away again, his arm, hand and then fingers disappearing last.

Then, there was no one there at all.

13

Craig Beckett wrote a wonderful log. It was personal, but she assumed that he had gotten accustomed to keeping such a diary because he'd been a ship's captain.

He had lived a long life, dying at the age of ninety-six in eighteen ninety-five. He painted a vivid picture of when Key West had been little more than a trading post with a hardy group of settlers working to turn it into a place that would boast, in the Victorian era, the highest per capita income in the United States.

It was the early pages she turned to first. He wrote about being a young sea captain in the navy and his decision to leave the navy and work for David Porter as a civilian.

He described the events she had learned about from Bartholomew in detail. Of course, he hadn't seen the attack that had taken Victoria's life — the attack that Eli

Smith had blamed on Bartholomew — but described it from imagination and experience. The canons firing and fire streaking through the sails of the ship, men and women screaming as smoke, fire or the tempestuous sea threatened their lives. Pirates killing everyone in their path with their broadswords. It was an unprovoked attack, and one that shocked the town, because David Porter had all but eliminated piracy a few years before it had taken place.

Craig Beckett wrote about his friendship with Bartholomew. "A man of my heart; a man who loved the sea, and his country. He might have remained a brigand, but he knew that I spoke to him truly, that I understood how he had taken enemy ships and no others. In the city, he was a model citizen, but also a man, who came to love too deeply if not with sense. I sincerely doubt that the rascal Smith could have ever started such a rumor, one so vile as to take a life, if Bartholomew had not so deeply loved Victoria. It was with the heaviest of hearts that I learned of the crowd that formed, a lynch mob, one with no more sense than that of a school of fish, darting here and there at the whim of one, that burst in upon that good fellow and dragged him to the hanging tree. They say that he died with dignity, claiming his innocence and showing no fear."

Katie was surprised to feel her eyes stinging, and then she realized that tears were dampening her cheeks.

She wished that she could hug Bartholomew.

Not that she knew where he was!

Ah, well, she would do her best when she did see him next.

When he had seemed so taken with the woman in white — the one he now knew to be Lucinda, whose brother had died in a storm — he had told her with a certain wistfulness that Victoria had moved on. She was not among those walking the streets of Key West in any spectral way. She must have been a very strong woman — killed so ruthlessly, and yet able to move on to the higher plain of heaven, or wherever it was that the souls of the dead finally found peace.

Katie turned a page in the book, careful to dry her hands so as not to smear the ink or hurt the delicate pages.

Bartholomew's story was a sad one. She could certainly understand it if he was to walk around near the hanging tree, still crying out his innocence.

She started reading again. The days of the bold wreckers came into play. Sponge divers, builders, settlers . . .

After a while, she felt a presence near her. She looked up, thinking that Sean might have awakened, even if he had said that he could sleep for a week. But it wasn't her brother.

Bartholomew was back. He was perched on the edge of the table.

"I was reading about you," she told him. "I'm so sorry."

He waved a hand in the air. "Yes, it was quite unjust, but a very long time ago."

"Where have you been this time?" she asked.

"Police headquarters. Apparently, Lieutenant Dryer has been combing the streets, and he's quite irritated by all the shenanigans for Fantasy Fest. Seems he can't get in the questioning he wants at various bars because there are so many people in the streets. Anyway, that's left most of everything at the station in the hands of Mr. Liam Beckett, who is dealing with all competently, even if his frustration level is quite high."

"Did you learn anything new?" she asked him.

"Not at the station," Bartholomew said.

"Then?"

"Well, I can tell you this — Danny Zigler

is dead."

"I know."

"You've seen him, too?" Bartholomew asked.

"He was here — for a split second. He pointed at the book," Katie said.

"And the book is?"

"Captain Craig Beckett started it, and other Becketts over the years have kept it up. It's not exactly a family bible, but it's history as the Becketts saw it over the years," Katie explained.

"There we are — back to the past," Bartholomew said, deep in thought.

"Where did you see him?" Katie asked.

"Down on Duval. He was looking up at the strip club. He faded to nothing the minute he saw me."

"I think that, unlike our other ghosts, Danny may know who killed him," Katie said.

"Have you told anyone that he's dead?" Bartholomew asked.

She shook her head.

"Why not?"

Katie sighed deeply. "Who is going to believe me? What am I going to say?"

"Well, that is a problem. You might suggest to someone that you believe that he's dead."

"Yes. But I don't think they need me for such a suggestion. No one has been able to find him."

Bartholomew waved a hand in the air. "They might believe that he killed Stella Martin, and that he's in hiding. I'm pretty sure that's what the lieutenant believes. When he left the station, he told Liam Beckett that he was sorry, but that he was going to damned well take care of the whole Danny Zigler disappearing act."

"Katie!"

The sharp sound of her name startled her. She glanced up the stairway.

Sean was awake. He hurried down the stairs, his hair tousled, a worried frown twisting his features. He came to her at the table, looking around.

"What are you doing?" he asked her.

"I'm reading the Beckett family book," she told him.

"Who were you talking to?" he demanded.

"I wasn't talking."

"Katie, I heard you — loud and clear."

"No one, Sean."

"Katie?"

She was suddenly weary of the doubt from her own brother. "Isn't that what you taught me to say, Sean? People will think that you're crazy, don't ever tell them that you

363

speak to ghosts?"

Sean groaned. "Oh, God, Katie, please!"

"Sean, I'm telling you the truth!"

He walked away from her, slamming his palm against his forehead. "I should never leave you. Screw the whole career thing. My only sister is going to wind up locked away in a nuthouse."

"Thank you. Thank you so much for the vote of confidence!"

"Katie, the dead are — dead."

"Fine. As you say. Therefore, I wasn't talking to anyone."

He stared at her and walked to the end of the table.

Right where Bartholomew was sitting.

He walked by Bartholomew, pacing. "All right, Katie, you talk to the dead. If you talk to the dead, why don't you mumbo jumbo up one of the murdered girls and ask her who killed them?" Sean demanded.

"They don't know who killed them."

"Right."

"The killer walked up behind them with some kind of plastic bag, slipped it over their heads and then strangled them."

"How convenient. They never saw his face."

"Well, it's true," she said stubbornly.

He reached for the chair at the end of the

table. "Call one of them. Let me ask a few questions through you."

He started to sit. She gasped as Bartholomew stood and angrily tugged at the chair. To Katie's amazement, it moved.

And Sean plunked down on the floor.

"What the hell?" he muttered.

Katie cast Bartholomew a glance and hurried to help her brother to his feet, but Sean was already up.

And confused. He gripped the chair hard before sitting in it again.

He stared at Katie, folding his hands slowly before him. "Katie, you're beautiful. And brilliant. And you have the voice of a lark. You love it here, you want to live and work here, and that's all great. But maybe you shouldn't be here. Maybe you're just too steeped in the history — and water sports," he added dryly.

"Sean, I talked to ghosts when I was in school, in New York, and in Boston," Katie said.

"Is there a ghost in here now?" Sean asked.

"Yes."

"One of the dead women?"

"No." Sean was waiting. "A pira— a privateer named Bartholomew," she said. "He moved the chair because you were mocking me."

"Bartholomew. Bartholomew, can you hear me?" Sean called out loudly in a deep voice.

"Will you tell him that I'm dead — not deaf?" Bartholomew demanded.

"He said that he's dead, not deaf," Katie said.

Her brother shook his head. "Katie, I want to believe you. If he's here, why can't I see him?"

"Why can't he see you?" Katie asked Bartholomew. "By the way, you can ask the questions yourself. I don't need to repeat them."

"He can't see me the way some people can't hear a tempo, the same way some people have no empathy for others, the same . . . He doesn't have the right sense for it, and he just isn't willing to try," Bartholomew said. "No insult — most people don't."

"He says that you don't have a sixth sense," Katie said.

"Why is he here?"

"To protect you, of course!" Bartholomew said.

"He wants to protect me," Katie said.

"Tell him that I'm home now."

"He can see that."

"So why won't he leave?"

"Because he's got the sense and intuition of a peg leg!" Bartholomew said.

"You've got the sense and intuition of a peg leg," Katie told her brother.

"Lord help us all!" Sean muttered.

"All right, Katie, he's your brother, but he's just about daft," Bartholomew said. He walked to the book. She saw him concentrate.

Then he picked it up; it floated in the air.

He let it fall with a heavy thud.

Sean leapt out of his chair, staring. He looked at Katie, then at the book. Naturally, he picked up the book, searching it for wires.

"I told you," Katie said, "I am good friends with this fine fellow, Bartholomew."

Sean set down the book. "Katie . . . Look, whatever this was, whatever you see . . . hear, you still have to keep it quiet. Do you understand? A man like David will think you're crazy."

"I didn't think that you were happy about David to begin with," Katie said.

"David was my friend. An all-right guy. But he's bitter, tainted. Life hit him hard, and now he's back, and there's been another murder. It's almost like someone is trying to frame him — or he is a murderer and brilliant and I'll have to shoot myself when

I haven't saved you from him."

"He's not a murderer."

"And how do you know that for a fact?"

"Because he was sleeping with me when the last murder was committed."

Sean groaned. "Oh, good God, I don't want details."

"You asked!"

"All right, then. Here's the truth of it. He's gone off and gotten rich on his own, and pretty damned famous and respected in his field, as well. He isn't going to stay here. He hates Key West. He's going to care for you — and leave you."

"When he leaves, I'll be glad of the time we shared," Katie said stubbornly.

Sean looked around the room. "Bartholomew, talk some sense into her."

Sean started for the stairs.

"Sean," Katie said.

"What?" he turned to look at her, a hand on the banister.

"Danny Zigler is dead."

Sean let out a long, low groan. "Do you happen to know who killed him? I mean, does he happen to know who killed him? Or where he is, for that matter?"

She shook her head. "He — he doesn't really know how to be a ghost yet."

Sean just continued up the stairs.

Katie sat back down at the table. Bartholomew perched on the edge of the table again, grinning. "Actually, your brother is not wretched. After all, he's an O'Hara. They usually knew how to drink, and how to fight — and all in all, remain honest men!"

David was glad of the phone call when it came. He'd been reading computer screens for so long, his eyes were blurring. He was going to find the truth. Where Mike Sanderson had been and when.

Thanks to Liam — and the fact that everyone knew Pete tolerated him, and he'd gone to school with half the force — he was able to hang around the station and make use of it.

"David, it's Sean."

"Is everything all right?"

"Yeah, everything is fine." Sean hesitated a minute. "I just wanted to check in. Any word on Danny? Katie is really worried about him. She thinks he might be dead."

David was quiet a minute. "I think he might be dead, too. I don't think he could have been the killer. I think Pete does, though. He's been out most of the day, hunting for Danny. I'm not sure if he thinks Danny was guilty, or if he's angry that he's disappeared. Or if he's worried. He's getting a search warrant for Danny's place, and he's going to serve it himself."

"All right, well . . . I've known Danny a long time and I was just thinking about him."

"Thanks."

When he hung up, David stood and stretched. He closed the files and glanced at his watch. It was eight o'clock, and he was getting hungry. He thought about stopping for takeout, but decided that though he could call, he'd just walk back to Katie's house and find out what she wanted to do for dinner.

What *they* wanted to do. Her brother was home now. Sean would be included.

He stuck his head into Pete's office, where Liam was still working. "Do you ever go home?" he asked his cousin.

Liam looked at him bleakly. "I want to be on the street. Can't — not with Pete out. Sure, I get to go home. I usually have it pretty easy. But, sweet Mother Mary, this is just not good. Fantasy Fest — in the midst of all this." He sat back and tapped a pencil on the desk. "Mike Sanderson is back out there now, and Tanya's brother is out on the street, as well. No one seems to care too much about Stella Martin, other than her friend Morgana. She'll wind up in a pauper's grave."

"Did you follow through on the location where I found the charge card?"

"I did. Couldn't find anything else. Here's what's sad, really sad. This guy is good. He doesn't leave evidence. He leaves the bodies in an exposed place — seriously exposed. They're posed almost as if he's fooling around, as if he's using the most bizarre local story. I talked to one of our police behavioral profilers today. He's convinced that the killer has to be local and uses the scenarios to prove that he's local, that this is his place."

"Great."

"I'm hoping we find something soon. Before he strikes again."

"Me, too," David said. "Well, thanks for letting me pry. I'll see you tomorrow."

"Katie goes back to work," Liam said.

"I'll be there. Oh, and Sean got home today."

"He did?" Liam seemed surprised.

"Yeah. Katie knew he was coming. She didn't know exactly when," he said dryly, remembering how Sean O'Hara had come upon them.

"I didn't think he was expected for another few weeks," Liam said.

"What's wrong with him being home?" David asked.

"Nothing. I was just thinking that it is all so odd. You're back. Sam Barnard is here. Mike Sanderson has apparently been coming back for years, and now . . . Sean O'Hara, too."

"Maybe it's the tides," David said.

"It's odd. That's all — it's odd. Hey," Liam said, changing the subject. "If I don't hear from you during the day, I'll see you at O'Hara's tomorrow night."

"It's Fantasy Fest starting up," David said.

Liam nodded, and let his head fall to the desk.

David left then, deciding to walk home and see what was going on. There were throngs on the sidewalks everywhere. Music blared from the clubs. He passed the giant effigy of Robert the Doll. It appeared to be anchored at the feet by a large weight, covered by plastic.

A woman walked by him, snorting. "It smells almost as bad as Bourbon Street!" she told her companions.

It did smell, David thought. He paused for a moment. It wasn't bad booze, it wasn't vomit. There was something dead somewhere. The Keys weren't immune to rats, and Lord knew, there were roosters everywhere. He couldn't pinpoint the odor; there was too much perfume in the air, too much smoke from the fellows hanging outside with cigars, and too much alcohol. Someone had just broken a bottle of bourbon somewhere nearby.

He kept walking. He was outside O'Hara's when he suddenly heard shouting. Frowning, even though he knew Katie wasn't working, he felt his heart pound. He rushed in. Clarinda was there; she had just jumped back from a table because the two men who had been seated at it were now standing.

"Fellows, you're going to have to sit, calm down or take it outside or I will call the police!" Clarinda said.

They didn't hear her.

One of the men was Mike Sanderson.

The other was Sam Barnard.

"Hey!" David said with deep authority.

The busboys were backing up. Jon Merrillo was coming around the bar nervously.

"Hey, you heard Clarinda," David said.

Sam looked at him, and shook his head sadly. "I'm sorry, but screw this!" he said. And he turned on Mike Sanderson with a wicked right hook.

David dove in, shouting for Clarinda to call the police. He tackled Sam Barnard down while Mike Sanderson made it back to his feet. Sanderson then tried to punch Barnard, but all he managed to do was fall on the man's abdomen.

They were both drunk as skunks.

David dragged Sam from beneath Mike, and by then, uniformed cops were spilling in. They dragged up both men, and assured them both they could discuss it all at the station. Clarinda turned to David, thanking him.

"That might have gotten really ugly," she said.

Jon had joined her by then. "Oh, man, they're both huge. They could have really torn this place to pieces."

"I don't think so — they're drunk. They'd have passed out before they'd gotten too many hits in."

"Well, thanks. Can I get you anything on the house?" Jon asked him.

"Sure. Actually, doesn't need to be on the house. What didn't we eat last night? I'll take three of anything different to go," David said.

"You got it," Jon told him.

Jon headed to the kitchen. He helped Clarinda right the chairs that had fallen. The other customers seemed disappointed that the show was over. They had turned back to their own conversations.

"Well, I guess it's good in a way," Clarinda said.

"What's good?"

"That those two got into a fight. That means that they'll be locked up for the night, and no one will have to be afraid of them."

"Afraid — of Mike Sanderson or Sam Barnard?"

"Let's face it, Mike Sanderson seems a little whacko. He's spent years — with no one knowing it — dressing up like Robert the Doll. And Barnard . . . well, he was Tanya's brother. He might be out for some kind of revenge, or God knows, he's here, and there's another murder . . . who knows? Maybe he secretly hated his sister. Maybe he strangled her in a rage. Stranger, more bizarre things have happened in Key West."

She gave him a kiss on the cheek. "I've got to get back to work. Thank you, David."

Then she made a face. "Fantasy Fest."

"Hey, it can be great."

"So you say — that's because guys love to see women with nothing but paint on their breasts."

"Ouch!" He grinned at her. "Okay, so women see male chests all the time. Sadly, that means the thrill is gone."

Clarinda laughed. "I repeat —" She made

a face. "Fantasy Fest!"

He went to the bar to pay for the food, but Jon wouldn't let him. He thanked him, took his to-go bags and headed back out.

He paused. So many sounds and scents in the air.

And yet . . .

Underlying it all . . .

There was the scent of death.

The knock on the door startled Katie.

She had left the kitchen to curl up on the sofa, the Beckett family book in her hands. Bartholomew was seated on the curve at her back.

"It's just Beckett," Bartholomew said.

She didn't have to get up to answer the door; Sean got it.

"Cool. Dinner. I was thinking I'd have to start cooking, since Katie has had her nose in that book all day."

Katie rose slowly, stretching. She saw David and smiled. "It's shepherd's pie from O'Hara's, right?"

"Good nose," he said.

"Oh, Katie has amazing senses," Sean said dryly. "Set her all down in the dining room. I'll get plates and utensils."

Sean did so. Katie met David in the hallway. He reached for her, pulling her close, and kissed her lightly on the lips.

Sean made a point of clearing his throat. "If you two don't mind? I'm not quite accustomed to this yet, if you could show a little restraint."

"Sean, I hardly attacked the man," Katie said.

Sean ignored her, as David opened the bags on the table.

"Anything at the station?" Sean asked.

"I told Liam that Katie thinks Danny is dead. He agrees. But Pete is on a tangent, looking for him, convinced that he's going to find him, and that he either killed the women, or had something to do with it."

They sat and passed around the tossed salad and entrées that David had brought. Sean went to the kitchen for beer, while Katie opted for a bottle of wine.

David wound up with a beer and a glass of wine.

"So, what's up here?" David asked.

"I slept most of the day. I'm figuring that by tomorrow, I'll be functioning again," Sean said. "And, naturally, tomorrow night, I'll be hanging out at the old family bar."

"I read that book all day. David, your family was fascinating. You know, your aunts have kept records in it since the nineteen forties. They were children here during the

Elena de Hoyos death and reburial. They remember the Otto family — they're really fascinating."

"You read the book all day?" David asked.

She nodded. "I'm convinced that . . . Oh, I don't even know why. But museums preserve the past. That's why a murderer might leave a body in a museum, right?" she asked.

Sean stared at her. "They have to find the guy this time," he said.

"They will," David said. "Someone will. So what else was in the book?"

"A lot was written by Craig Beckett, sea captain, a fellow who arrived in the area along with the first American settlers," Katie said.

"Your family showed up around the same time, right?" he asked.

She laughed. "Yes, so we've always heard. But we don't have anything like that great book your aunts have preserved so well."

" 'The truth is out there,' " Sean quoted wearily.

"So what is going on tomorrow, do you know?" David asked Katie.

"Tomorrow, for us, it's business as usual, with three extra servers. The first of the big pirate parties is happening tomorrow, and one of the bars is also throwing something

378

it's calling the Vampire Bite. I know that Mallory Square is supposed to be crazy, and that a lot of acts from elsewhere have already been out staking their ground."

"It will be a long day," David said thoughtfully.

"I agree."

When they finished, Sean yawned. Katie told him to go back to bed. He gave her a kiss, bid David good-night and went up the stairs.

Katie was going to pick up, but David stopped her. "I'll take care of it. You were yawning, too, and you have a really long day tomorrow. Go on up."

"But —"

"I insist."

She had left the book on the sofa in the parlor. She went back in to make sure that she had closed it, so that the delicate pages wouldn't be damaged. She thought that Bartholomew might have kept reading it, but he was nowhere to be seen.

She sat, reading the page that had been left open.

It was about the legal execution of Eli Smith, brought about by Craig Beckett, and the witnesses he had dragged into court.

As she was looking at the page, David came behind her. He moved aside her hair with a gentle brush and kissed the back of her neck.

"Tomorrow will be a long day for you. You need your sleep."

She turned in his arms. "Are you really thinking about sleep?"

"No. Yes. Eventually. I mean, if we get started early enough . . ."

"I do believe it's early."

"Great."

She went up the stairs quickly, letting him follow her. That night, she closed her door carefully, and had to turn on the lights to keep from tripping when they went in. With the lights still on, she saw him lying like a lion awaiting his due on the bed, and she started to laugh, and jumped down on him.

And once again, it was the most natural thing in the world to become naked and intimate. They made love with laughter, and then with passion, and then with tenderness.

It was late when she rose at last to turn out the lights, and they finally fell asleep.

The city was like something that breathed, as real and vital as any man or woman who had ever lived. It was the tempest of the past, the craziness of the present, the promise of the future.

It was his city.

He loved it as a parent loved a child.

And his people had borne the injustice of others, when they should have had free run. What was fair, and what was not? Beckett had fired many a cannon, he had set many a ship afire, he had killed time and time again. . . .

And yet he had been so self-righteous!

Ah, well . . .

The bitterness assailed him as he watched the house, and yet he continued to do so, despite the torture it brought him. His muscles were clamped tight, his jawline hurt, his teeth hurt, he was grating on them so hard. And still he stood, covered by the shadow of the trees, and he watched.

He saw her silhouette.

Saw as she disrobed.

The drapes were drawn, but she was there, curved and lean and glorious.

And he saw Beckett. Saw him rise to take the naked woman into his arms.

Saw them fall down together.

Saw them rise . . .

In his blood, he could feel them writhing, feel the thunder of their hearts.

Hatred burned through him.

It was his city.

It had been his city throughout time. Some fools didn't see it; they didn't realize that

381

things never really changed, nor did people. Beckett had been self-righteous and superior years ago, and he was the same now. But time came round and round, and the evils done in the past could and would be rectified now.

Beckett had brought death and destruction to his people. But he knew that it was all one. He knew that it was his duty to bring real justice to his city.

And the time was coming.

He was suddenly filled with pride; subterfuge was a game he played perfectly. There was simply not the least suggestion that he was anything but completely mentally fit; his calm, cool action and meticulous machinations proved that. That he could wait, that he could play the game of life so easily, and others never saw . . .

He nearly laughed aloud. There were those who might think him insane, when, in truth, he was simply a genius — a man with an agenda as deep and important as the spirit and the universe itself, and the brilliance to move about as if he were invisible. He knew more about life and death and time and pride than anyone, and he was so damned good that it was almost — criminal.

Katie O'Hara was so beautiful.

She rose, and he could see the perfection

of her silhouette on the drapes, the curve of her breasts, the lean length of her torso, the exquisite stretch of her legs. . . .

He imagined her, as she would be.

And his fingers itched to touch her.

Her death would be spectacular. She deserved the true immortality.

The light went off at last, and he turned away.

14

They'd barely woken up before the phone rang.

In fact, it was quite a jolt. Katie's eyes had just opened, and David's had just opened, and she was thinking that it could be a lovely morning.

Then the startling sound of her phone, and when she saw the caller ID, she answered.

For a moment, Katie had a strange sensation of, "Hail, hail, the gang's all here!"

Her uncle Jamie was back in town, just in time for the festivities.

"Pirates!" he said.

"Uncle Jamie? What are you talking about?"

"Pirates. Here, there, everywhere. Oh, and with a vampire or two thrown in. Katie, my girl, bless you, wonderful! I need you — desperately! I was afraid I wouldn't get you. Ah, and I heard that your brother is here in town, too, eh?" Jamie said. "Tell him to get his rich, famous, sorry ass down here with you. Jesus, Mary and Joseph! I thought we'd have a small breakfast crowd and the good Lord help me, I told Merrillo to open her up, and it's a deluge! A deluge of pirates. And, oh, Lord have mercy. You should see the hottie who just walked by with a wench's costume painted on."

"Uncle Jamie, if she's twenty, behave yourself."

He chucked. "I need you, my girl."

Katie covered her phone and looked at David.

"I need to go into O'Hara's," she told him.

"Now?" he asked, his hand on her midriff as he pulled her closer.

"I'll be there in just a bit, Uncle Jamie. And I'll get my brother's sorry ass out of bed, too."

She hung up. It was good hearing from Jamie. Business as usual.

No worry about corpses taking the places of mannequins.

"Hey."

"Hey."

She started to get out of bed, but the hand on her midriff didn't let go. David's eyes were alight and a subtle smile was curved into his features.

He rolled over, pinning her. "Now?" he repeated.

She laughed. Something seemed beautifully normal about the day. She ran her fingers through the thick richness of his hair. "Well, now, yes . . ."

She felt his fingers stroke down the length of her body.

"Well, almost now," she amended. "I mean, really, almost now. . . ."

"Time schedule, yes," he said, and they locked in one another's arms.

Fifteen minutes later, breathless and laughing, she leapt out of bed while he rolled over and groaned. She flew into the shower, raced out in a towel and banged on her brother's door while David took his turn in her shower.

"I've a message for you to get your sorry ass up!" she called to him.

"What? I'm still supposed to be filming in the China Sea!" he called back.

"You were seen. Get your —"

"Sorry ass up, yeah, yeah, all right. What the hell?"

"Uncle Jamie is back and we're being deluged by pirates," she called. "Ten minutes, downstairs!"

Jamie hadn't lied. Pirates were once again walking the streets of Key West. The street was already packed with people, but it helped everyone, and everyone knew — this was one of the big chances to make money. Shopkeepers and bars weren't stingy; they didn't try to grab customers and hang on to them all night. They depended on one another. O'Hara's was filled with flyers for another Irish bar, just as they advertised O'Hara's bands and Katie-oke nights.

Katie parked in back. Sean and David were with her.

"See, here's the point," Sean pointed out. "You go off, and the world respects you as a filmmaker. You come back, and you're a busboy," Sean said, shaking his head sadly.

"Hey, big shots," Katie said, "you have both forgotten what's in your own back-yards. You should get together and do a documentary right here. I know where you can find cheap divers. Then again, what would make a better film than Fantasy Fest?"

"Busboy by day, the Spielberg of documentaries by night! Like it — has a ring," Sean said. "Let's get in, and dig into the mayhem, huh? David, you're not obliged in any way."

"I can help out for a while," David assured them.

He did. They walked into pure insanity.

There was a mile-long line for the advertised breakfast.

Fantasy Fest Special! O'Hara's opens for ye olde Irish breakfast.

Clarinda was working the floor, and she'd gotten Jonas to come in. One bartender held down the liquor angle, even though it was ridiculously early. "Hair O the Dog that Bit ye!" was a Bloody Mary, while "Sunrise Screamer" was an O'Hara's concoction of rum and various juices.

Her uncle was a good-looking man, the family baby, sixteen years younger than her father and only nine years older than Sean. He was definitely harried when they walked in. He didn't seem disturbed in any way to see David Beckett arrive with his niece and nephew. He studied David and grinned. "Heard you came in last night and saved the place, Beckett. Thanks. I owe you."

Katie looked at Jamie and then at David, but they were still studying one another. "What went on?" Katie asked.

Clarinda came hurrying by with a tray carrying four of the house specialty — bangers and grits. She'd heard the question. "It was almost a heavyweight bout," she said. "Sanderson and Barnard — Mike versus Sam. But David set them straight."

"You beat them up?" Katie demanded.

388

"They beat themselves up. They were about to break into a mammoth fight, after, it appeared, drinking together in commiseration," David said.

"And then —"

"They went to lockup for the night to sober up," David said.

"Hey, hey, times a-wasting!" Jamie said. "We'll get onto all this later. Katie, you, in the kitchen. You still know the menu, eh? Gloria is still back there. She'll call the shots."

"Aye, aye, captain!" Katie said.

"David, the bar, if you will. Sean —"

"Yeah, yeah, I know. Bus tables," Sean said, rolling his eyes. "I'm on it."

"That damned Danny Zigler comes in, wanting work, and where is he now?" Jamie said, shaking his head with disgust.

Dead, Katie wanted to say, but she didn't. She hurried back to the kitchen.

The breakfast rush lasted into lunch, but by then, Jamie had managed to gather all his part-time employees and the operation was running smoothly again. At two o'clock, the regular employees had the dining stragglers under control. Katie, emerging from the kitchen, saw that her uncle, her brother and David were seated at one of the tables near the bar and the band stage where her karaoke equipment was set up. They seemed to be eased back, and talking.

Like old friends who hadn't seen each other in a very long time.

She saw that Clarinda had stepped outside and went to join her on the sidewalk. "The air! Ah, the air, the air!" Clarinda said.

"So, what was going on with Mike Sanderson and Sam Barnard last night?" Katie asked. "Did they come in together?"

"No. Sam came in — he's been coming in here pretty regularly since he got into town. Strange, huh? He's been living up in Key Largo all this time, never came here, as far as I know, and now, this week, here he is."

"And, wow, really go figure! Mike Sanderson, dressing up like Robert the Doll," Katie said.

Clarinda shuddered and grimaced. "Now, that is frigging creepy — Oh, look!"

Katie looked down the street. She didn't see anything unusual — not for Key West in the midst of Fantasy Fest. A pirate with a peg leg was escorting a vampire down Duval. The pirate was fairly customary — and good. He had an eye patch, a real peg leg and looked as if he might have stepped off the pages of *Treasure Island.*

The vampire wore a sweeping black skirt with stripes of blood that continued from the bodice of the gown, a tight-fitting corset. She was wearing the typical long black wig and white makeup, along with ruby-red lips.

"Cool costume — she looks good," Katie said.

"Look harder!" Clarinda said, laughing.

Katie did. She gasped. "That corset is body paint! Oh, my God, that is amazing!"

"Yes, it is!" Sean announced, stepping up behind them.

"You're a lech!" Clarinda accused.

"I am not. I'm commenting on a great paint job," Sean assured her. He yawned. "Ladies, it's been a thrill. Such a thrill. I'm going home and back to bed. Katie, be good, be careful. I'll be at the house if you need me. All right, well, I'll be at the house whether you need me or not, but I'll have my cell. And don't worry, I'll be here for the Katieoke, even if Jamie guilts me into busing tables again."

He gave her and Clarinda a kiss on the cheek and started walking.

"Hey, the car's in back!" Katie called.

"Leave it there — by the time tonight is over, we may be too tired to walk!"

Sean left, and David replaced him. "Hey, are you going to hang around here for a while?" he asked Katie.

"Maybe an hour," Katie said. "I'll just stay

long enough to see that Jamie really has things under control."

"I'll be back then."

He gave both girls a kiss on the cheek, and was gone.

"It's amazing, isn't it?" Clarinda said. "Think about it — all our lives! Except for college, of course. All of our lives, and this place is still just crazy."

"Yes, but that's why I love it," Katie said. "Black, white, gay, straight, Hispanic, Russian, Israeli, you name it. Somewhere along the line, someone made a rule that we'd all accept one another, and it seems to have stuck. I do. I love it here."

"And I've never even seen you in body paint!" Clarinda teased. "Hey — Jamie was just saying he wanted us in the pirate costumes tonight. Want to walk down to Front Street and the pirate-costume-slash-sex shop with me?"

"Sure. Let me tell Jamie what I'm doing."

"You need one, too, you know."

"Me?"

"Hey, he wants to help celebrate the Fantasy Fest pirate party," Clarinda said. "He's open to vampires, too."

"Great," Katie said. She hurried back in to tell Jamie what she was doing, then joined Clarinda on the street.

"That thing is just creepy," Clarinda commented as they passed by giant Robert the Doll.

"And it stinks around here," Katie commented.

Clarinda frowned. "Old booze. Sweat. Maybe someone was sick."

They walked down to Front Street, turned right and went the few blocks to the store. It was one of Katie's favorite places. Half of the store sold sexy lingerie, sex toys and naughty Halloween costumes. The other half carried an amazing array for the pirates of Key West. Vests, period coats, shirts, skirts and more. It was possible to be a wench, an aristocrat, an elegant buccaneer or a scurvy mate. The morning had been so busy, she'd been able to set aside everything that had been happening.

Certainly, the city did not seem to be mourning the passing of one of its strippers.

Clarinda tried on a variety of costumes, and decided on a wench. Katie was musing between a corset, blouse and skirt, and a recreation of an Elizabeth Swann costume when Bartholomew appeared at her elbow. "The corset," he said. "Very real. Miss Swann wasn't a true pirate wench in any way — she was forced aboard, a kidnap victim. I did love that movie," he said.

"Where have you been this time?" Katie asked him.

"Home," he said. She arched a brow, but the ghost had claimed her house as his own, and didn't appear to notice the way she looked at him. Bartholomew was deep in thought.

"I'm right here, Katie," Clarinda said, frowning.

"I'm going to go with the shirt, corset thing and skirt," Katie said.

"Can you sing in that thing?"

"The ties are fake — there's a zipper in back and it's stretchy. I'll be fine," Katie said.

"I've been reading the book," Bartholomew said. "Nice piece of nostalgia for me. Beckett was a damned decent man."

"That's good to hear," Katie said.

"Pardon?" Clarinda said.

"They'll be able to hear me fine," Katie said. She glared tight-lipped at Bartholomew, who shrugged.

"I know that the key to all this is in the past. Did you see the part where Beckett mentions that Smith cursed him from the noose?"

Katie lowered her head. "I can't talk to you now, Bartholomew," she said.

"Katie?" Clarinda said.

"Sorry, arguing with myself," Katie said. "Come on, let's pay for this stuff."

At the counter, she produced her credit card, assuring Clarinda that they were giving the bill to Jamie. As she waited to sign the slip, Katie gazed out the window.

The sun was filtering in. For a moment, it seemed to blind her.

Then, she saw that Tanya was standing there. Standing there, beautiful and sad in white, as if waiting for her company.

"Sign that for me, will you?" Katie said to Clarinda. "Please."

"Where are you going? Katie, are you all right? Hey, wait!" Clarinda said.

But Katie was already on her way out.

Tanya waited, caught in that glimmer of sunlight, until Katie was nearly upon her. Then she started to walk.

Katie made her way through buxom lasses and strapping pirates, and a U.S. Navy sea captain here and there. Vampires and zombies were crowding the streets, as well. The season was changing — it was just hot instead of dead hot — but all manner of costumes were being worn — naked and in paint, almost naked, to period frock coats and heavy fabric skirts.

Music was emitting from restaurants and

bars already; a fire-eater was working a corner of Front Street.

Tanya managed to stay just ahead of Katie.

Bartholomew was following close behind her.

"She's headed for the hanging tree," he said.

"Why?" Katie murmured.

Bartholomew said, "I keep telling you, it has to have something to do with the past. It has something to do with *me*," he said.

She turned to stare at him, crashed into a wolfman, righted herself, apologized and hurried on. "Wolfman — the guy is crazy! He'll be sweating to death before tonight," she murmured.

They reached the saloon. It was busy. Katie saw Tanya slip in and she followed. There were no tables. There was one seat at the bar and she grabbed it, ordered a drink from a harried bartender and looked around.

"Imagine back," Bartholomew said, standing right behind her and whispering in her ear. "When I died, the building wasn't here. The area where you're sitting was built in eighteen fifty-one. Morgue. Quite convenient. After one of the hurricanes, folks came back and found that the bodies weren't in great shape. They ripped up the

396

floorboards and buried them right here."

"I know. There's still a tombstone here," Katie said.

"And bones in the ground," Bartholomew said sadly.

"And the woman who haunts the bathroom," Katie said. "But, Bartholomew —"

"You've got to go back before that. Military law — and no law. Evidence? What was evidence in a buccaneer town like Key West?" he asked bitterly.

"Did you see Smith hang?" Katie asked him.

He shook his head. "I had friends. I was buried on the beach. After the same hurricane, they dug me up with the others — and what pieces they discovered were transferred to the new cemetery — the Key West cemetery."

She actually felt his hands on her shoulders. "Katie, it's all attached, I just know it, somehow. You have to go through that book again."

"Danny Zigler had checked out several books. They're at David's house. We'll get them first thing in the morning, how's that? Or, I'll call David. I'll ask him to get them before tonight, and then I'll have them to read."

"Is something wrong?" the bartender

asked Katie, concerned despite the insanity of the bar. She had large brown eyes and a Romanian accent.

"I'm sorry, muttering to myself, practicing for tonight," Katie told her.

Her cell phone was ringing. She saw that it was Clarinda. She answered quickly. "Sorry, I saw an old friend — from school," she said quickly.

"Anyone I know?" Clarinda asked.

"College," Katie lied, and winced. "Meet me on Duval and Front, okay?"

"I'm there, looking for you."

"I'm there!" Katie promised.

Katie offered the bartender a bill and slipped off the bar stool.

She turned, and Tanya was there, staring straight at her. Her lips were moving. Katie froze, staring, and then inhaled, watching Tanya's lips.

Then she could hear. Barely.

"Revenge. He whispered the word when he was behind me. Revenge."

Tanya then stared at Bartholomew; her lips moved again, and she seemed distressed.

She faded, and was gone.

"See, she wants you to listen to me," Bartholomew said. "That's why she brought you here. Revenge! And she must somehow know or sense that it has to do with the past."

Katie nodded. "Right. She's gaining strength as a ghost."

"And she just used it all, bringing you here, whispering."

"I got it, I got it!" Katie assured him.

Her cell started ringing again. Clarinda!

She waved a thanks to the bartender and hurried out. It was all crazy. Two women were dead, dressed up and laid out like a twentieth-century corpse. And yet Tanya had come here, and Bartholomew insisted that it all went back to something that had occurred before the buildings here even existed.

She saw Clarinda on the street, waved and blocked her mouth with her hand as she told Bartholomew, "Please, please, please! Don't make me keep talking, okay?"

He didn't reply. He was silent as they met Clarinda.

"Let's head back to O'Hara's, and I'll get the car and we'll bring it back later. We've only got an hour or so, but I'd like to take a shower before tonight. I feel like I'm covered in bangers and grits," Katie said.

"Ah, and I have a fine sheen of maple syrup," Clarinda said. "Sounds like a plan to me."

As they walked along, Katie thought that she might tease and mock, but she loved Fantasy Fest. So many of the costumes were amazing. They passed by a fellow dressed up as a parrot; he had magnificent feathers, body paint — and the subtle decency to wear a brilliantly fashioned loincloth. It was a beautiful costume — fitting right in with the fellow's Mohawk — and both Katie and Clarinda gave him quick compliments as they passed.

As they neared O'Hara's, Katie wrinkled her nose.

"Someone from the city has to get out here and find out what that smell is!" Clarinda said.

"We'll have Jamie call it in," Katie agreed.

They reached O'Hara's. As they started in, Katie felt the brush of Bartholomew's fingers on her shoulder.

She spun around.

And there was Danny Zigler. He was in the middle of the street, oblivious as cars and scooters and pedestrians passed him by, or walked right through him.

He lifted a beseeching hand to her.

Then faded into the crowd.

At the station, Liam told David that Mike Sanderson and Sam Barnard were being held at the detention center up in Stock Island.

"They'll be let out soon. They were just being held for drunk and disorderly, and, well, the place'll be filling up with pirates and vampires now," Liam said.

"Can you find out if they've already been released?" David asked.

"Sure."

Liam put through a call. The two would be released within the hour.

"I hope I can make it in time," David muttered.

"You can." Liam stood. "We'll take a patrol car."

"I thought you were holding down the fort, with Dryer prowling the streets," David said.

Liam shrugged. "We have more units. The lieutenant is good, but no one is on duty all the time. I'll just tell the chief that I'm leaving, working the case."

"Don't get in trouble here —"

"The chief is a cool guy. He put in his hours — bike patrol, night shift, day shift. And we're speaking with persons of interest in two murder cases, even if we haven't a shred of evidence."

Liam was gone less than a few minutes; a detective sergeant took over his place at the desk, which had apparently become the hot spot for the Stella Martin investigation.

The drive to Stock Island in the patrol car, even with mad traffic streaming into the city, took less than twenty minutes.

When they arrived, Sanderson and Barnard were already being released.

David and Liam stood at the exit, watching as the men procured their belongings and signed out. Sam saw them first, and stood still. Mike halted behind Sam.

"You came to pick us up?" Mike asked hopefully.

"Sure," Liam said. "I've got a car just outside."

"Look, it was a drunken bar brawl," Mike said. "That's all."

"Over what?" David asked.

The two looked at one another sheepishly. "My sister," Sam said at last.

Mike looked at David remorsefully. "I called her — a not nice name. I told him that if Tanya had ever been able to really make up her mind, she might still be alive."

"Let's take it outside," David suggested.

The two followed David and Liam to the patrol car. They looked suspiciously at Liam. "You're not under arrest — it's a ride," he said.

They crawled in. Liam took the wheel and

David sat in the front passenger's side. "What were you two doing together to begin with?" David asked.

"Well, first it was friendly," Mike said. "We started talking about Stella Martin — who was a whore, I mean, no doubt about it."

"Tanya wasn't a whore," Sam said.

"God, no," Mike said. "That was never what I meant. I was hung up on her, totally smitten. She was beautiful, man. So much spirit in her!"

David glanced over at Liam. The two had to be sober now, but it almost looked as if they were going to fall into a hug and sob together.

"So, let's work the whole thing out," David said.

Liam pulled the car over into the lot of a fishing-and-tackle store that had closed its doors for the weekend.

Mike and Sam looked at one another again.

"Mike, you were a liar. You told the cops you were up north the night that Tanya was murdered. You weren't up north," Sam said.

Mike looked out the window. "I was in Miami."

"Can you prove it? We've managed to dredge up the information that you were in St. Augustine twenty-four hours after she was killed, but the night of the murder . . ." Liam said.

"Lord, do you know how long ago that was?" Mike asked. "But I can tell you where I was."

"And what he was doing," Sam said bitterly.

"What were you doing?" Liam asked sharply.

Mike let out a sigh. "I was with a prostitute."

"A decade ago — that is going to be hard to prove," Liam noted.

"You know her name?" David asked.

"Yeah — Tiffany."

"You have a last name for her?" Liam asked.

"Tiffany — Number One?" Mike suggested. "Hell, that year, half the working girls in the country were named Tiffany." He stiffened suddenly. "Look, I'm not the asshole I sound like, really. I told you, I didn't believe that Tanya was going to come with me. She'd seen you again, David. I wasn't old, I wasn't mature — and I was lonely and hurt."

"You cheated on her — with a whore," Sam said morosely.

"I didn't cheat. She was leaving me, and I knew it," Mike said. He straightened suddenly. "Hey, maybe I can prove it! She was working for something called Elegant Escorts, and soon after, there was some kind of a sting operation on them. I did pay with a credit card." He looked out the window again, embarrassed. "I didn't help with the prosecution. I told them that I had just signed on for a massage and that nothing else happened. I was a kid. I lived at home. My mother would have killed me."

David looked at Liam. Liam shrugged. "We can track it," he said.

David stared at Mike.

Mike glared back at him. "Hey, you know what — you were the one in the hot seat, not me. I talked to her earlier. We know she was at O'Hara's. I was home all night after that."

"Something you can't prove," David pointed out. "Where were you that night, Sam?"

"She was my sister," Sam said angrily. "And, hey, I'm sorry, the people who could vouch for me — like the people who could vouch for you — are dead. You are a prick, Beckett. She was my sister. And no one ever looked at me with accusation before."

"There's another dead woman," David said.

"And you were suddenly back here, just

like the two of us," Sam pointed out.

"Actually, I've been back frequently," Mike said.

"Right. Dressing up as Robert the Doll and lying to your wife," David pointed out.

"Point is, I've been here before — and you and Sam have been gone forever," Mike said.

"I live in Key Largo. Two-hour drive. If I'd wanted to kill someone again and set them up in a Key West exhibit, I could have done it at any time," Sam pointed out.

Liam started the car up again. "I'll be checking on your whereabouts the night Tanya was murdered, Mike. Procedure, you know."

"Look, we believe one another," Sam said. "You bastards need to find out who did kill my sister."

Liam drove straight down Roosevelt to the police station. It was a long walk back to Old Town, but he made it evident that he was parking and going back into his office, and that was that.

Mike and Sam sat in the car for a minute, and then got out. "You heading back, Beckett?" Mike asked David.

"In a while."

The two walked off, muttering to one another.

"*That* Beckett isn't a cop — he's a film-maker or a cat photographer or whatever. And suspicious as hell, if anyone asks," Mike said.

"Yeah, but, hey, he's a Beckett. Damned Becketts still think they own the island," Sam complained.

Liam, watching them, grinned. "So?"

"So, let's see if we can check out Mike's alibi. Then I'll head on back in. I want to hang around O'Hara's tonight. I figure things will start getting wild."

David waited, mulling over the past, and the present, while Liam went through various conversations with Miami and Miami-Dade County law-enforcement groups.

Why did Danny have the Key West history books, and why had ten thousand dollars been slipped into one book?

Liam set his phone down, drawing David's attention. "Mike Sanderson was telling the truth. A vice guy in Miami remembers the sting. There was a Tiffany, and when it all went to court, she vouched for Mike Sanderson's statement — she had just given him a massage."

Scratch another one off the list.

"Thanks, Liam," he said.

"It's a walk — you want a ride?"

"I'll catch a cab," David told him.

■ ■ ■ ■

He called Katie on his way back and found out that she was at the house. He had himself dropped off at her address, and when he knocked, Sean let him in. "Good timing. We're about to head out again. Katie is in the parlor."

"Thanks," David said. He looked at Sean, who was wearing a pirate's bandana, a tricorn hat, striped pants and a black poet's shirt.

Sean grimaced. "Uncle Jamie wants to support the pirates."

"Great."

He went into the parlor. Katie was perched on the love seat, his family ledger book in her hands. She didn't even notice him as he entered.

He noticed her.

She wore pirate attire extremely well. It was definitely a look, and though she was completely covered, he thought that she'd rival any woman who was stark naked. Just the line of her throat and collarbone was visible, and the beautiful rise of rounded breasts. Her waist seemed minuscule, and her pirate boots added a touch of the wicked woman to her apparel.

He whistled.

She looked up, startled, nearly dropping the book.

"Hey," she said. She looked at him curiously.

"I visited the jailbirds. Mike Sanderson has an absolute alibi for the night Tanya was killed."

"Oh?"

"He was with an escort," David said.

She was startled. "But, I thought . . ."

"He says that he was certain that he'd already been ditched — for me," David told her.

She looked at him sympathetically, then rose, carefully putting the book down. "I need you to bring those books over tomorrow. It's important, I think."

"Why? I'm not arguing the point, but why are you so convinced?"

"I don't know how to explain it to you." She smiled. "The little ghost of an idea keeps coming to me. It keeps leading me back to the hanging tree."

"The hanging tree?" David said.

"Your ancestor avenged a pirate, did you know that?" Katie asked. She jerked forward suddenly, just as if she had been pushed. "Privateer!" she said firmly.

Frowning, he said, "I know the story, of

course. Some wretch named Smith managed to shift the blame for his own deed to another man. That man was hanged by a lynch mob. Later, the first Craig Beckett saw to it that Smith was hanged, as well. Katie, it was close to two hundred years ago. That's one hell of a long time to bear a grudge." He smiled. "You don't think that Smith's ghost is rising up to kill women and try to frame the Becketts, do you?"

"Ghosts don't really have that kind of strength," she said.

"What? Katie, these murders are being committed by someone who is flesh and blood, whatever may have gone on in the past."

"Of course," she said. "But I do think that the key lies in the past."

"Absolutely. I'll get the books tomorrow — we'll spend all the time before you have to go to work reading through them."

She smiled and nodded, and then her smile faded. "Any word on Danny Zigler?"

"I thought that you believed that he was dead."

"I know that he's dead. I was wondering if they had found him."

"How do you know for certain?" David asked her.

Sean came to the doorway. "She saw it in

a dream. Come on, Katie, you don't want to get started late tonight. The flaming temper of the Irish-American Jamie O'Hara is a terrible thing to behold."

"Yep, let's go," Katie agreed, anxious to be out.

When they walked in, David found himself instantly welcomed by Jamie O'Hara — who had shirt and frock coat waiting for him. "Arrrrr!" Jamie said. "Pirate night! They're closing the street off — there's going to be a parade happening in a few minutes. Katie, the place is hopping. Start them off with something pirate-y, will you?"

"Sure — can I boot up the computer and set the microphones and the amps?" Katie asked.

"Arrrr!" Jamie said in good humor.

"Hey!" Sean nudged David. "Head on back and change into that pirate garb, my good fellow."

David was about to protest; he didn't. Why not? He wanted to blend into the crowd. He wanted to watch. Years had gone by now, and he had no intention of leaving until the whole thing was solved. He couldn't explain it but he felt as if some pieces of the puzzle were coming together. He'd watch until, eventually, the killer made a mistake.

He headed back to the men's restroom to change. The acoustics and sound system in the place were good. He could hear Katie, welcoming everyone to Key West, Fantasy Fest and O'Hara's Pub. She pointed out her request slips and her songbooks, and said that anyone was welcome to ask her about a song not in the books, as well — some could be found on the computer. She opened the evening with a charming rendition of a Disney pirate song — one that every pirate in the place sang along with her.

He headed out, appropriately attired then in his huge blousy shirt, frock coat, swashbuckling hat — and Levi's jeans and Nike sneakers. As he headed around the bar to the stage area, he saw that Katie had stopped singing.

The pirates in the place assumed it was their job to keep going, and they were all certainly rowdy enough — and drunk enough — to do so.

Katie set down her microphone — and headed out the door.

"Katie!" He shouted her name and went running after her.

She was out in the middle of the street. The parade had begun, and chanting pirates, wenches, fire-eaters, flag wavers, small floats — even costumed dogs — were marching along, and sidestepping Katie. There was a figure running north down Duval.

Someone dressed as Robert the Doll!

Katie was chasing him.

David chased Katie.

Suddenly she stopped, and stared across the street at oversize Robert the Doll. Held in spot by a weight at the bottom by the feet, the figure seemed to move back and forth.

The huge effigy remained. The costumed Robert the Doll had disappeared.

"Katie!" David cried.

She seemed completely oblivious to him.

He rushed after her, but he was captured by a pirate wench, and spun around the street.

As politely and firmly as he could, he extricated himself.

He turned around, seeking Katie. She was across the street, wrenching at the effigy.

"Katie!"

Suddenly, he knew.

He knew the smell in the street.

And he knew what was going to happen.

Katie was tugging with a vengeance at the straw arms of the effigy. He reached her just in time to wrest her away as one of the arms came free.

As straw spilled out onto the street . . .

The thing crumbled, falling apart around the bottom weight.

Exposing the decomposing corpse of Danny Zigler.

15

It took forever for the sounds of sirens to cut through the revelry of the crowd, or so it seemed. It seemed forever that Katie stood there, staring at Danny.

The stench that rose from him was horrible. Even when the dead heat of summer ebbed and fall began to arrive in South Florida, the sun was viciously hot. Encased in the effigy, Danny had been held in something like an oven.

When she had ripped up the effigy and he was exposed, the odor had risen like a miasma.

Katie imagined that the odor was actually what had finally alerted the revelers to the fact that there was something very serious, horrid and tragic going on. At first, people thought it was all part of a Key West game.

A game . . .
Key West loved her pirates.
She loved her ghost stories.

Her eccentrics . . .

She was a city that loved equality and fairness, a party, a good time, history, water and more.

This wasn't customary.

Finally, though, the screams in the street became louder than the sounds of the sirens. The parade dispersed. Shopkeepers, innkeepers, costumed entertainers, bartenders — all came out to the streets, staring with horror. There was such a crowd that everyone had to whisper to everyone else, asking what had happened.

Uniformed officers on horseback were the first to arrive. The rescue vehicle was forced to park on a side road along with the detectives and crime-scene investigators.

Katie just stood, feeling it all, seeing all, sensing it all and feeling David's supporting arms around her, for what seemed like forever.

Then Liam was there, the one to officially question her while they awaited Lieutenant Dryer's arrival on the scene.

She heard snatches of conversation from the medical examiner and techs.

"Oh, Lord, he's ripe!"

"Been in there at least a few days."

"Must have been dead since he went missing."

"Cause of death?"

"No way to know — he's far too bloated. Got to get him to the morgue."

"Katie," Liam said. "What happened? Witnesses said that you just came to the effigy and started tearing at it. How did you know that Danny was in it?"

"What?" she asked, blinking.

"How did you know that Danny had been stuffed into the effigy?" Liam persisted.

"I — I, umm, well, I saw someone. Out the door — the doors at O'Hara's are open, of course, you know. And I saw someone dressed in a Robert the Doll costume, and then the giant Robert the Doll effigy was right behind him, and I remembered the — the odor — and it seemed as if it was coming right in the bar and I . . ." She let her voice trail away. "I guess that I freaked out a bit, Liam. I'm so sorry, I just couldn't take the smell and I suddenly realized it was coming from the effigy."

"What about the manufacturer — how did Danny wind up in the doll?" David asked.

"The doll was up before Danny disappeared," Liam said, glancing at his notes. "The manufacturer is local, just up on Stock Island. They've done these dozens of times. And the effigy was set up by the salsa club right there, and they're baffled and mystified — again, they said that the doll was in perfect shape from the manufacturer when they assembled it."

"So someone killed Danny Zigler and stuffed his body into a giant-size effigy of another Key West legend," David said.

"That's what it looks like so far," Liam said.

The medical examiner and police photographers gave the word and the corpse was lifted into a body bag — oozing liquids — to be taken to the M.E.'s office.

The owners of the salsa bar argued with the police; that area of the street would have to remain cordoned off until it had been thoroughly inspected and cleared by crime scene. It was Fantasy Fest. What was the city going to do about the amount of money they were going to lose?

Katie had felt ridiculously frozen and weak. Paralyzed. Horrified.

But she was suddenly angry. It wasn't a shock; she had seen Danny's ghost. When she had looked out the door and seen him, then the costumed Robert the Doll performer, she had known. Danny had been showing her where he could be found. Poor Danny. He would have been so horrified. He loved Key West.

Now, he was part of Key West. Part of the

stories and lore that would be told to generations from now until eternity.

"Am I free to go?" she asked Liam suddenly.

"Of course, Katie. But —" Liam began.

"Thank you," she told him.

She made her way through the gaping crowd on the street and back to O'Hara's. Her brother was there, looking aggravated, but managing to put up a stream of pirate songs with singers, music and words intact. He was startled when he saw her arrive.

"Katie, you just found the corpse of an old friend. Get David to take you home," Sean said. "Or leave David. I'll take you home. Hell, Jamie would close this place down and take you home."

"No," Katie said angrily. "No, everyone is acting like Danny is something disgusting in the street, as if he's an annoyance, ruining a pirate parade."

She took the microphone. "Folks, everyone knows that something terrible just happened. Everyone tried to get close, to find out what happened. Well, I'll tell you. A friend of ours disappeared a few days ago. People were mad at him — they thought that he'd sloughed off work. In fact, it was even suspected that he had killed a woman. But he didn't. He was murdered himself.

He wasn't an odor in the street — he was a good guy, a true conch, a real part of Key West. His name was Danny Zigler. He didn't need a lot of money. He loved Key West, and he loved the simple things in life. This is for him. Honor him with me, if you will."

She went to the computer and set "Danny Boy" to play. There was a dead silence at first.

"Danny Zigler was Irish?" Someone asked with confusion.

"Everyone's Irish on St. Patrick's day," a drunk sloshed out in reply.

"Sing along, a good fellow is gone and departed!" someone else said.

When it was over, she felt David at her side. "Katie, come on. We're going."

"We can't go," she said dully.

"We can. Sean and Clarinda can handle your system. And it will thin out early — even in the middle of Fantasy Fest, a dead man means something, Katie."

She let him drag her away. She had known that Danny was dead. He hadn't been her best friend, but he had been a fixture in her life. He had always been there.

David took her home. She wondered that he was with her, and she felt a little numb, and a little awed. He probably wanted to be haunting the police station. He'd want to know what happened to Danny Zigler. He had to be noting the fact that all the deaths were coupled with Key West legends.

At her house, she ran up and showered the minute they were inside. The smell of death had seemed to permeate her. She scrubbed her hair several times. At last she emerged and wrapped into her terry robe.

David had evidently decided to use her brother's shower — the scent of decay and death had been too much for him, too. He was out of his pirate garb and in Sean's clothing, something she was certain he would explain and Sean would understand. He had made her something hot.

"Tea — with a good dose of whiskey," he told her, handing her the cup.

"I'm all right. I'm really all right. I knew that Danny was dead. It was just that it was so horrible — seeing him, like that. I've seen the dead before, I've been to funerals . . . but that!"

"Death is seldom gentle," he told her.

She sipped the tea, and noted that it was very strongly laced with whiskey. She carried it out to the parlor and saw that Bartholomew was seated on the sofa, watching her with sorrowful eyes. "I wish I had realized, Katie. I can't really . . . I don't get scents and odors anymore. I would have stopped you. I tried to stop you, and you didn't even see me."

"It's all right," she murmured.

David had come behind her. He set his hands on her shoulders. "Go on up to bed, Katie. Try to sleep."

"I can't."

"You will. I'll be here."

She nodded after a moment, draining the tea. The whiskey washed through her, warm and soothing. "All right."

She gave him the cup and headed for the stairs. She heard him make a startled sound. On the first step, she turned back.

David was still standing in the middle of the parlor, holding her cup.

He was staring at the table.

The ledger, the Beckett family ledger was moving.

Bartholomew was pushing it toward him, of course. He didn't see Bartholomew.

But he had to see the ledger moving.

She went on up the stairs. As he had said, despite all that was haunting her mind — or perhaps because of it — she slept.

He'd had one beer. One damned beer.

And it seemed that the ledger on the table

was moving. It was open.

He was tired. So damned tired. And more disturbed than ever. When Katie had gone on into the pub, Liam had told him that the police had gone into Danny Zigler's house at last.

There had been no sign of books about the history of Key West.

There had been no money.

"You're sure it's what you saw, David?" Liam had asked him.

"Yes, I'm a photographer. I have pictures," David told him.

"Then someone else let themselves into Danny's apartment. Hell, David, I may have to let Pete know that you were in there."

"Liam, don't do anything just yet. Give me a little more time before I get arrested myself, thrown off the island, or until Pete decides he's not letting me move out the door."

"David, I'm feeling pretty damned slimy right now," Liam told him.

"Pretend I never trusted you. Just give me a little more time. I don't know why — I'm feeling that I can almost touch the last piece of the puzzle."

He hated what he was asking Liam to do. But he also knew that someone out there was wearing a facade of complete normalcy

— and killing people under that cover.

The ledger had been moving. In his mind's eye, anyway. It was subconsciously telling him that the answers were right in front of him — he had to find them.

He set Katie's empty teacup down and walked toward the ledger. It was open to a page filled with elaborate script that was somewhat difficult to read. But he knew the book; it had been in the family forever. Craig had told him that Alice and Esther had decided that their role in life was to preserve family history. They had recorded births and deaths, and events that had occurred in Key West during their lives.

Before Alice and Esther had recorded in the book, the task had been taken on by Josiah Beckett, his great-grandfather. Before that, it had been Helena, youngest daughter of the first Craig Beckett. And before that, it had been Beckett himself who had kept the records.

None of that mattered. The book was open to a page that recorded when the territory of Florida had become a state, and when David Porter had brought down his Mosquito Squadron, and piracy had been brought to an end.

He read over and over the part about the assault on the ship, the death of Victoria and the lynching of Bartholomew. He read about his ancestor's fury and insistence that an innocent man had been hanged, and that a guilty man must be brought to justice. And how he had watched at the hanging tree himself while Smith had met with his end. Craig Beckett had stood there while Smith had cursed his family, something that hadn't disturbed him in the least. He believed in men, in justice and in God — he did not believe in curses.

He definitely hadn't been cursed, David thought. The first Craig Beckett had lived out a long and prosperous life.

The key turned in the outside lock and Sean O'Hara came in. David glanced at his watch. It was nearly 5:00 a.m. He should have been sleeping himself.

Sean came into the parlor. "Katie?" he asked.

"She went to bed several hours ago," David said.

Sean nodded. "What a night, huh? Life is so — messed up, really. And then, maybe not. Maybe we all know that we're mortal, and we live just like Poe suggested in 'The Masque of the Red Death.' Dance until we drop ourselves. A man was found dead — even the most dense person has to assume murdered, since it would have been impos-

425

sible for him to stuff his own corpse in an effigy. The revelry continued though. Cities have lives of their own, I suppose. And since tourists didn't know Danny Zigler . . ."

Sean left off. "Did you wonder why I came home, David?" he asked then.

"Because you knew I was coming here," David answered.

Sean nodded. "Bizarre, really. I knew that you hadn't killed Tanya. Or, should I say, I believed that you hadn't killed Tanya. But there was just something about the fact that you were going to be here. I didn't know that you were seeing Katie, but I knew she wanted to open the museum. Maybe I knew that you would try to stop her. God knows, you're the only one not trying to make a buck off of tragedy! But something is going on. Something that started when we were kids just out of school and heading into college. It's still going on." He reached into his pocket. "I've made a list."

"Yeah?"

"You're on it, and I'm on it."

"Naturally."

Sean came in and sat down on the end of the sofa, spreading out his list, made on a cocktail napkin.

In a neat row Sean had lined up names.

Pete Dryer
Pete Dryer's family
David Beckett
Liam Beckett
Mike Sanderson
Sam Barnard
Sean O'Hara
Jamie O'Hara
Danny Zigler

"I've made a similar list a dozen times in my mind," David said. "We can scratch out Danny Zigler — Danny is dead. We can scratch out Dryer's family. I don't think they've ever come back, even though they don't live far away. Oh, you can scratch out Mike Sanderson — he proved that he had an alibi this afternoon."

"And I'm going to scratch out you and me."

"You can scratch out Jamie, your uncle, too. A dozen witnesses knew that he never left O'Hara's that night," David said.

"Okay, so that leaves Tanya's brother, Sam Barnard, my cousin and a cop, Liam Beckett, and Pete Dryer, a major-league cop," David said.

"That's right."

"My cousin was nowhere near the museum that night," David said. "Pete was."

"Pete's a police lieutenant. And who knows? Maybe Sam hated his sister. Maybe Liam has envied you his whole life. Hey, you were the apple of your grandfather's eye. You were the star football hero."

"Liam played football, Sean. I was a linebacker, he was a quarterback. He was never jealous of me. I have a hard time believing that Sam killed his sister. And Pete has risen like a meteor at the station. He was just a beat cop when the murder took place. He loves Key West. Maybe this list is bull. Maybe we should both be on it. Me more than you, of course. I found Tanya in the museum, and I was the one dating her. Odd, though. I've read the ledger over and over. Katie seems convinced it all has something to do with the first Craig Beckett, who had a man executed."

Sean looked around the parlor. He stared back at David.

He let out a sigh. "I'm thinking that we both need to pay more attention to my sister," he said.

"I always listen to your sister."

Sean gave him an awkward and crooked smile. "No, no, you're not really listening to her."

"What do you mean?"

He could have sworn that Sean was going

428

to say something — that he was about to break down and tell him something about Katie that was incredibly important.

But he didn't.

Sean shook his head, disturbed. "I can't," he said softly. "You have to speak to Katie. This is crazy. I've told Katie over and over . . . I love my sister. And people would think that she was crazy. You'd think that — never mind. I'm telling you, just pay attention to my sister. That's all."

David frowned, watching him.

Sean stood suddenly. "Hell, I'm exhausted. And there's tomorrow. Great idea for me, this coming home thing. Not a vacation at all. Two murders in a week, but for the living, life goes on. I guess that's the way that it always has been, and always will be."

David was tired, and wished that he could somehow shake Sean to find out what he meant. But Sean wasn't going to talk. He seemed really tired, disgusted and frightened for his sister.

"Some major cities have a murder rate of one a day, and they can't shut down, I suppose. Of course, statistically, our murder rate is two a *year,* not two a week. The investigative unit deals with drug deals, and cleaning up the street most of the time.

429

Drugs are dangerous, the officers are up against a lot, but . . . not usually like this," David said.

"You just said 'our,' " Sean told him.

"Our — as in Key West," David said.

"We both left," Sean said.

"Still, we're conchs," David said.

Sean was watching him thoughtfully. "So, once a conch, always a conch?" he asked.

"What are you talking about?" David asked, irritated. "We've been through history and statistics, so what are we on now?"

"My sister," Sean said softly.

"I don't think the city is safe right now, and I don't intend to let anything happen to her," David said.

"That's not exactly where I was going. She is my sister."

"Yes?"

"Well, this sounds odd as hell. Just what are your intentions with my sister?"

David stared back at him.

What the hell were his intentions.

"I —"

"Yes, yes, you're going to keep her safe. And I will, too. There's some kind of psycho out there, but a couple of fellows who work in video and print film are going to keep her safe."

David realized that Sean had made a good

point, and his defenses rose to the fore. "I served in the military, did my time in the desert, Sean."

"But what if you're the one putting her in danger?" Sean asked. "Say someone had been out to get you all those years ago — kill Tanya, frame you. So now that person has killed a prostitute — and Danny Zigler. And he still hasn't left clues, and he still hasn't been caught. It's not like you and Katie have this long-standing love affair. You could be putting her in serious danger," Sean said.

"Ten years ago, a killer got away with murder," David said. "But that was then, and this is now. Science has come a long way. They've just discovered Danny's body. The killer has to make a mistake. And it will be found," David said.

Katie suddenly appeared in the entrance to the parlor.

She walked into the room. She paused, giving her brother a kiss on the cheek, and then walking over to David. She looked up into his eyes and slipped an arm around him before she faced her brother. "Sean, I love you. I'm grateful that you came home, and I'm grateful that you care about me. I'll answer your earlier question. None of what's happening between us was intended, so no one can have intentions. I know that I'm not backing away from my life, and I don't want David backing away from me because of anything that's happening. No one knows what will come in the future, but I know that what's going on between us is honest, and that's the only intention I want."

"Maybe you two should just pretend then to step away from one another," Sean suggested.

"I think it would be too late for that," Katie said. She smiled and shrugged. "I think the damage is done, Sean, so please, don't go asking David to stay away from me."

"We've got to . . . I don't know. We've got to be careful with every move, that's all I have to say," Sean told her. "Well, that's not all I have to say, but we're all exhausted. I'm going to bed. After I make sure the doors and windows are locked." True to his word, he walked around the room, bolting the windows. With a nod, he left them there.

Katie turned in David's arms. "Sorry you got involved?" she asked him.

He held her close and shook his head. "Never, Katie."

He pulled her closer and lifted her chin. "Never," he said. "Katie, Sean said that you had a dream, that you believed Danny was dead."

She started to move away from him.

"Katie," he said, pulling her back.

She stared at him, and he thought that she was holding her breath, that like Sean she was about to say something.

But she didn't.

She stood on her toes and lightly kissed his lips. "We really do need some sleep," she said. She caught his hand, and she led him toward the stairs.

They slept. . . .

And they didn't sleep.

At first, they held one another.

He drifted to sleep. He woke, feeling the heat of her form against him, feeling her moving. He didn't move, not wanting to wake her.

But she was awake. Her fingers trailed down his chest, circled around his abdomen, moved lower. His breath caught as he felt her sudden, sure touch. He rolled, pulled her against him, taking her into his arms, meeting her lips and then using his own to create a slow trail of liquid fire along her collarbone and breasts.

For a moment, she was still, breath caught.

Then she moved. Fluid, easy, ridiculously graceful for the vital energy that suddenly poured through the two of them. Passionate, fierce . . . the ardent movement of her body escalated by the soft whisper of tenderness that came with the brush of her lips against his.

He became the aggressor, sweeping her beneath him.

The world went still, and there was nothing but the hunger and the need, the basic feel of flesh and cotton and sheets, and their words as they edged closer and closer to climax. Again, the world went still, and there were moments that were oddly as fulfilling as the instinctive need for sexual satiation, that could never be achieved unless more than just sex was involved.

He was becoming a philosopher, he thought.

No. Feelings were what they were. All the psychology and science in the world could never really answer the human question of why emotions raged where they did.

She lay beside him again, and slept, and he thought that again, maybe something as old as man was rising inside of him. He knew that he would die to protect her.

As the morning passed, he held her close, felt her flesh against his flesh, the rise and fall of her breathing.

What were his intentions?

He had never come home to stay. And then again, he had never felt this intimate with a woman, no matter how long they'd been together, no matter what the sexual appeal.

Not the time to think about it. There was a killer out there.

And they were no closer now than they had been ten years ago.

Or were they?

It seemed that the curtains suddenly flew, as if cool air whirled into the room. Katie sat up and looked around, and the ghost of Tanya Barnard was standing by her bed.

She reached out, and Katie took her hand.

"Please . . ." the ghost whispered.

She looked beyond Tanya. Danny was there, looking at her with prayerful eyes, and at his side, Stella Martin stood, watching her, waiting.

"You must help me," she told them. "You must help me. Please, think, what do you know? Who followed you, who was with you — who killed you? Show me."

They shook their heads, staring at her.

She looked to Danny. "The books, Danny — and the money. David saw them in your house. Who were you blackmailing — who gave you the money?"

She couldn't hear him. His lips were moving. She tried to come closer to him, to study the movement. She wanted to scream with frustration.

I took the books from the library. And then I got the call. Stop. Stop looking for the past, or I would join it. Leave it be, and there would be money. And there was money. I found it under my pirate-skull doormat. And I didn't know, but someone seemed to think I would find out what happened to Tanya, but I had no idea . . . that was the past. I kept the money. There was no way to give it back, no one to give it back to, because I really didn't know.

Katie looked at the three ghosts. "Can't you help me at all?"

Something, I saw something, someone thought I saw something. I saw Stella briefly. She came to the window, kept her back to the street. But then she was gone.

Stella stepped forward. *Now we're all gone, all gone, and there are impressions and things we see in our minds . . . Katie, help, you must help, you are the only one who can help.*

She had the oddest sensation of being approached by the ghosts of Christmas past, present and future, all in one. Air seemed to sweep around her in massive currents. She was suddenly standing with a group in back of La Concha Hotel. She could hear the ghost-tour guide speaking, talking about the tragic suicides from the roof, and telling the story of the young man who haunted the place, a young man who had perished in the not-too-distant past when he had been distracted by a pretty young woman and plunged to his death down an elevator shaft.

Danny was with her. So was Tanya. And Stella. They were grouped around her on the tour. The others in the group seemed to be faceless. The guide was wearing a Victorian frock coat and vest, and a top hat. She couldn't see his face. But then he turned. His face was Danny's face.

The tour group moved from tragic event to tragic event. All the while, the tour guide talked of the ghosts that still haunted these places. Behind him, like the chorus in a Greek tragedy, Tanya and Stella sobbed softly.

"She's still here," Danny said clearly. "She's still here. Go anywhere on the island, wax museum, oddities museum, history museum, you'll see our dear Elena, Elena Milagro de Hoyos. . . . You will see her. She is Key West. She is our most famous, and most bizarre, story."

Tanya let out a long, wailing cry, and the wind shifted and the earth moved beneath Katie's feet.

They were standing before the hanging tree.

By the tree, the building began to fade and disappear. Next door, where the main section of Captain Tony's stood, bar stools evaporated, and she might have been on a whirlwind tour through a time machine. Bar . . . telegraph office . . . morgue . . . the visions swept by. Then, the landscape was suddenly raw and overgrown, rocky, with patches around them that were barren. She could hear the sound of the water, coming from the south, coming from the north, and the west. It was all around her. . . .

A man was being dragged to the gallows. . . .

Cursing . . .

Cursing a man named Beckett who looked on with fierce and furious eyes, eyes that seemed so familiar. . . .

Again, the wind blew; it was as if she stood still while a hurricane raged. Time whipped by her. Fishermen, pirates, wreckers, smugglers and thieves . . . soldiers in blue, and soldiers in gray, and then sailors from a country united once again. She heard a cry on the wind. "Remember the *Maine!*"

And then, suddenly, the world was still. She was walking down a long hall in a building.

A strange-looking, skinny old man turned to her, arms before him, fingers flexing. "It is love, love for what is ours, love. Love — ah, yes, and family name. We are all that we create. And I have created love."

He moved aside. There was a bed, within the confines of an airplane cabin. There was a woman in a bridal gown, laid upon the bed.

It was just an exhibit. Count von Cosel, and his Elena.

But Elena rose from the bed and looked up. It wasn't Elena. Katie stared at her own countenance. *She* was there. *She* had taken Elena's place in the exhibit this time.

Her own arm raised and pointed.

She turned.

And once again, she was staring at the hanging tree, and the noose and the dead man who dangled and swung beneath the branches.

"Katie!" David said.

She had let out a cry; she was sitting up in bed, soaked with beads of perspiration, and yet shaking as if it had suddenly plunged to ten degrees in Key West.

He drew her to him. "Katie, I'm here, Katie, it's all right. You had a nightmare."

She stared at him. For a moment, her eyes

were unfocused. Then she seemed to really see his face.

"It was just a nightmare, Katie. And I'm here. I won't let anyone hurt you."

She relaxed in his arms. Then she pulled away. She stood, and she was naked and beautiful and natural, but somehow putting a distance between them, as well.

"Katie?"

She sighed, sat back down next to him and said, "David, even if we'd found Danny alive, he wouldn't have been able to help us. He wasn't blackmailing anyone, but someone did think that he'd seen something, or knew something. I think he had the books on Key West just because he wanted to make his stories better, but the killer knew that there was something in the books — in the history of Key West — that might give him away. He saw Stella the night before she died. The killer must have thought that Danny saw him then, because he'd seen Stella, and maybe the murderer. That's why Danny died."

"What?" David said blankly. Her words were so assured and natural. "Katie —"

"You're going to walk out on me, David. But you have to believe me."

"Katie, I don't understand you. Your words about Danny are making sense, but . . . you had a nightmare."

"No. It wasn't just a nightmare. I — I see things that other people don't, David."

It was late; she'd been through a lot.

"Katie, we all have nightmares and dreams. And sometimes, they're good and they help us. You have a lot on your mind. We're pretty damned sure that the truth is in the past. Your mind was working while you were sleeping, and what you're saying might be right."

She took his face between her hands. "David . . . I'm . . . I care about you so much. And that's why I have to say this. You can leave if you think I'm crazy. I see — I see the dead. When they remain. Not all the dead — some do pass on immediately. But I — I see ghosts. And I'm telling you because you have to listen to me and believe me now. *I see ghosts.*"

He was dismayed by the harshness in his voice, but he was worried about her. "Great. Ask them all who killed them."

She rose, stepping away from him. "They don't know. Sean has always warned me to keep my mouth shut. You don't believe me."

He couldn't bear the distance between them. He stood, walking to her. She backed away, but he caught her and pulled her close.

"Katie —"

"You don't believe me."

"Katie, that's a lot to take in suddenly. Please, you have to realize that."

"It's all right. I understand. You think I'm . . . not right."

"Katie, I think everything about you is right. Do I believe in ghosts? I don't know — that's asking a lot. But do I believe in you? My God, yes, Katie, please . . . Let me digest some of this, huh?"

She was tense. So tense, she was like a piano wire pulled taut.

"Let me just give it all to you then."

"What?"

"There's a fellow named Bartholomew. He was a pirate — no, no, a privateer. He's — he's been hanging around a long time. He was hanged for something that he didn't do. It was your ancestor who came back and indignantly saw to it that the real culprit, Eli Smith, was hanged, as well. That's when Smith cursed the Becketts. David, please, the killer really means to have his revenge on you. I can't really communicate with all ghosts, but Bartholomew has been around a very long time. He's very good at being a ghost."

He didn't reply. It was crazy.

He'd seen the pages of the ledger move.

442

He'd been drawn to it, as if a force was trying to make him understand, help him.

"Katie, I can't just . . . I can't just . . ."

"I understand." She was trying to slip away.

He really didn't understand, but he didn't give a damn. He would try.

"Katie . . ."

She must have heard something in his voice. The words he couldn't express. Suddenly, she eased, and she fell against him.

He held her with strength and warmth, smoothing her hair back.

"Don't patronize me?" she pleaded.

"I swear, I'm not. I don't know what I believe . . . but . . ."

She looked up at him.

"Katie, I believe in you," he whispered again.

16

Sean was awake, back out at Katie's desk, working at her computer, when David came downstairs in the morning. He had showered and dressed quietly, not wanting to wake her, although a glance at the bedside clock had informed him that they'd slept until well past two in the afternoon.

That happened, he decided, when you finally had some sleep when the light was coming up.

"Morning," Sean said, hearing David come down and head over to him. He looked up at David. "Or afternoon," he said dryly.

"Yeah, it's late. Have you been up long?"

"Only half an hour," Sean said. "Did you put the coffee on a timer last night?" he asked. "If you were the one who did it, your timing was perfect."

"No. Katie seems to have it rigged to start in the morning."

"Just to be brewed fresh when the first person makes it down the stairs. And I sure didn't wake up in the morning. Odd," Sean mused.

"She must have set it. Great plan, in my opinion," David said. He felt they had a great deal more to worry about than coffee. "I'm going to my place. Danny Zigler had three books on his table when — when I checked out his place. I had Katie get me the same books from the library. I'm going to my place to read. When Katie gets up, want to bring her over?"

Sean nodded at him, studying him. "Sure. I won't let her come alone. I promise you that!"

David thanked him. Sean locked him out of the house.

The newspaper lay on the front lawn. The headline blazed, Local Found Murdered and Decomposing in Festivity Decoration.

David read the article quickly. There was nothing there, except for the facts he already knew. Danny Zigler had been found, his body in a bad state of decomposition. The body had been removed to the Monroe County Medical Examiner's office for autopsy.

He started to leave with the newspaper, but then decided not to do so. Danny had been murdered; his body had been discovered. By Katie. Her seeing the story wasn't going to change what had taken place. They'd both see the bloated remains of Danny Zigler in their minds for years to come, he was certain.

He reached his house and opened the door right when he heard wheels in the drive. He turned around to see that Liam was pulling into the driveway.

David walked to the driver's side of the car. "Anything?" he asked.

"No answers," Liam told him. "But we're getting help. The streets will be filled with our own force tonight, and with officers down from Miami-Dade. The chief is considering canceling a lot of the events, the commissioners are going crazy and Pete has been nuts, prowling the streets."

"It's a good force. Your chief is a good guy — he's been up the ladder, he's local and he intends to make it the best force in the world, as he says," David said.

"He put through a call to the FBI. We're supposed to have a team of agents and profilers down here by the start of next week," Liam said. He winced. "Some folks aren't happy about that. We were the Conch Republic, briefly. Some of the guys are convinced we could have solved it all ourselves, but the chief says that pride isn't worth a life. Anyway, I was actually headed to Katie's place, looking for you. I'm going up to the M.E.'s office. Danny's autopsy is scheduled."

"Is that an invitation?"

"You hitchhiking?" Liam asked.

"Hell, yes."

He got into the car. "Thanks."

Katie woke with a start. She had been deeply asleep, but when she woke, she remembered the dream.

And that she had told David that — ghosts came to her.

He hadn't believed her. Neither had he walked away. She had told him about Bartholomew. He hadn't said that she was stark, raving mad.

She shivered, remembering herself as the corpse of Elena de Hoyos.

Maybe it meant nothing. No, it meant that two women had already been left that way!

They always came back to the hanging tree.

That was what was important, she thought.

When she came downstairs, she didn't see David, but Sean was at the computer. She thought that he was working. But he was looking up sites on the Internet. Sites that had to do with Key West.

"Hey. Where's David?" she asked.

"He went to his place. He wanted to read through the books that Danny Zigler had apparently been reading," Sean told her. He rose and stretched, pushing away from the computer chair. "You know, just a few years ago, they dug up seven bodies from the cemetery, trying to match them with DNA to missing persons cases."

"I remember, vaguely."

"And you know where most of our investigations into unnatural deaths are centered?"

"Accident victims? Drunk drivers?" Katie asked, pouring coffee.

Sean said, "No. Drowning and diving and snorkeling accidents."

"I suppose that makes sense," Katie said. "Sean, what are you trying to do?"

He shook his head with disgust. "Find anything that we don't know about Tanya's murder. Instead, I think I've just become a walking encyclopedia of trivia on my hometown."

"Nothing we learn can ever hurt," she told him.

Bartholomew took a seat at the computer. "Morning, Katie," he said.

She ignored him. He was purposely trying to annoy Sean, she thought. He hit a computer key, and pages started flashing by.

"You really have to replace that thing, Katie," Sean told her irritably. "Or is it the cable company? I think I had better service on the China Sea."

"The Internet is great — when it works," she said, staring at Bartholomew with a glare that meant, *Behave!*

"Sean," she said to her brother, "I'm going to go on over to David's."

"All right. I'll walk you."

"It is broad daylight, and the streets are busy."

"I'll walk you."

"All right, thank you."

"I'll walk you, too," Bartholomew said. He stood up and fluffed her brother's hair. Sean spun around, eyes narrowed.

"It's just Bartholomew," Katie said.

"What?" Sean demanded sharply.

She inhaled deeply. "Sean, for the love of God! You're not blind, you're not an idiot. I know you've spent your life afraid that people will think I'm crazy, and I get that! But you have to feel it, you have to have seen things move. Please, Sean, right now, it's important that you believe in me!"

He rose. He dragged his fingers through

his hair. "I don't want to believe!" he whispered.

"Admit that there's something!" she told him.

He held his breath; he let out a sigh. Bartholomew laughed, and tousled Sean's hair again. Sean jumped.

"It's Bartholomew, and —" Katie winced. "He's my friend. He wants to help us, and maybe he can. Please, Sean, for once, and now, believe in me!"

Sean was still for a long moment. "Yes, there's something in this house," he said.

"Someone. It's Bartholomew. He's real, Sean."

Her brother's face was hard. Then he grated his teeth, and let out a long breath. "Bartholomew. All right. Bartholomew the ghost. Tell him that I have to be in love — and that I am heterosexual — to enjoy anyone messing with my hair," Sean said.

"I've told you. He can hear you," Katie said.

Bartholomew proudly made a mess of Sean's hair again.

"Eh! Tell him to stop that," Sean said. His eyes narrowed. "If he's a damned ghost, why can't he help us solve the killings?"

"He doesn't know," Katie said.

"Why doesn't he just ask the other

450

ghosts?"

"Sean, I've tried to explain. They don't know." She turned away from him. "I'm just going to grab a cup of coffee quickly, all right?"

"Sure. Then I'll get you over there. I'm running up to my room for a minute. I'll be right back down."

She went to pour herself coffee. Bartholomew leaned against the counter casually. "So?"

"So what?"

"Danny Zigler has nothing?" he asked.

"Bartholomew, if I knew who the killer was, I'd be announcing it to the world."

Bartholomew was thoughtful. "So, Danny was taken by surprise, from the back, just like the others. Odd, though. I have a feeling that Danny knows something."

"He's not a talkative ghost. Except for . . ."

"For?"

"Last night, I had a dream, or a nightmare, whichever way you want to look at it. Danny was in it, and so were Tanya and Stella. First, I asked him about the books and the money. He received a threatening call — to drop looking into the books. Then, he found the money under his doormat. I don't think that the killer wanted to kill him, but finally felt that he had to. Oh! He saw Stella before

451

she died. Maybe the killer thought that he might have seen something."

"But he didn't."

"No."

"Then?"

"I begged them to help me."

"And?"

"We went on a ghost tour together."

"Danny did enjoy giving a ghost tour," Bartholomew said.

"The dream ended at the hanging tree. Bartholomew, you must know something more. Let's say that we're figuring this thing correctly. The killer is an islander. Someone with an old grudge, trying to relive a past they don't even really know. Can you think of anything?"

"Hey, it's not a descendant of mine!" Bartholomew said defensively. "I was avenged."

"By David Beckett's ancestor. But what about Smith?" she asked.

"Do you know a Smith?" he asked.

"No," she said with a sigh. "But decades — almost two centuries — have gone by."

"You don't think that the ghost of Eli Smith has come back, do you? I'm telling you, I'm a dammed good ghost, and I couldn't sneak up behind someone, smother them and then strangle them."

"There's no ghost. There's a human being

452

out there doing all this," Katie said.

Sean came quickly back down the stairs. His hair had been brushed. "Ready?" he asked his sister.

She nodded.

Bartholomew followed as they left the house, waiting patiently as Sean made sure that he locked the door. Katie picked up the newspaper and read the headline.

"Anything?" Bartholomew asked.

"No. Just the facts we already know."

"No what?" Sean asked.

"No, there's nothing new on Danny," Katie said.

"Bartholomew asked first, right?" Sean asked with a groan.

"Sean, he's real," she said softly.

Sean squeezed her arm. "I believe you. Well, I believe something, anyway. Let's get this straight then. You're there, Bartholomew? Quit being a horse's ass! Flipping my hair around is really beneath your dignity."

Bartholomew puffed himself up. Katie thought that he was going to explode with anger.

He didn't. He laughed. "Tell Sean that he's all right."

Katie did so.

Sean lowered his head, hiding a smile. "Let's go."

They walked the few blocks to David's house.

Sean knocked on the door, stepped back, frowned and rang the bell.

Katie did the same.

"He's not here," she said with dismay. "Or, he's not opening the door if he is!"

"Katie, there's this modern invention. It's called a cell phone," Sean reminded her.

"Funny," she told her brother. She pulled her phone out and dialed David's number. He answered before it seemed to ring.

"Katie," he said, sounding as if he were aggravated with himself.

"Hey. Where are you?" she asked him.

"With Liam," he said briefly. He groaned. "I should have gotten those books out and given them to you."

"I can go back to the library. They might have more copies," she said.

Sean nudged her, glaring at her. "Well? Where is he?" he asked.

"Indeed, where the hell is he?" Bartholomew asked.

She covered the phone. "With Liam."

"Great," Sean said.

"Katie, Danny had the books — and you found them for me at the library. I'm not sure how many more the library will have. They're research books. Look, I probably

454

won't be more than a few hours."

"I want to start reading now. It's worth a try. I'll go to the library."

"Wait. You don't need to do that. You still have keys to the family museum, right?"

"Yes."

"You know the desk where you buy tickets and go through the stiles?" he asked her.

"Yes."

"Third drawer down, under guidebooks with old prices. You'll find house keys there. I'm really sorry, Katie. And don't go anywhere alone."

"It's all right. Sean is with me," she said.

"Sure. Sean loves walking around town when the sun is beating down like a mother!" Sean said.

She nudged him with an elbow. "Stop!"

"All right," Sean told her. "Let's go get the keys. And walk around some more."

"We could have taken the car," Katie said.

"Wonderful. Take the car to drive three blocks here and there — and spend an hour looking for parking."

Katie laughed. "Bitch, bitch, bitch! David's house has a driveway. We wouldn't have had any trouble parking, but we're not going far! Anyway, walking is good. Let's go get the keys."

"Katie? Katie?" David's voice called to her

from the other end of the line.

"I'm here, and as I said, I'm with Sean, and we're going to go and get the keys to your house. What are you doing — exactly?" she asked.

There was silence for a minute.

Katie waited, but then she thought that she had lost him.

Then he answered.

"Autopsy," he said briefly. "Be careful, Katie."

"I'm with my brother. Everything will be fine," she assured him.

David knew that sometimes people thought of the Keys as being backwoods. Laid-back meant slow.

But the facilities in the Keys were state-of-the-art. The department was small, and like most other agencies in the world, when faced with an anthropological question, human remains might be sent out across the country. But the autopsy facilities were sterling.

David was offered a mask by an assistant.

"Take it," Liam advised him.

He wasn't a cop, and so David kept his place in the background and remained silent.

The mask didn't help much.

456

Danny's body had been washed and cooled, but he still barely resembled a human. Gases had exploded through bloated skin and crevices, and his flesh was horribly mottled and discolored.

The medical examiner had a good, clear voice, and he offered facts and figures of the body's appearance to Liam and two other officers who attended, and to the microphone above his head. He stated that due to lividity, the body was certainly left at an unknown location for some time; blood had pooled to the buttocks, shoulders, back, thighs and calves.

The room was cold, sterile. He could remember similar occasions, but in far less pristine conditions, when he had served in the military.

Land mine, a man's body all but blown to bits, picking up the pieces.

Unchecked syphilis.

Gunfire straight in the face.

Danny Zigler, more bloated, distorted and discolored than any horror he had seen before.

It wasn't right.

No, it wasn't right. And why Danny? He had been a suspect himself, a perfect patsy, just about.

"All right, he died somewhere else," Liam

said, suddenly impatient. "How did he die?"

There was silence. The medical examiner looked at him. "Liam, that's what I'm trying to determine."

Still, something about Liam's words made him change his intended direction. He turned to one of his assistants. "Let's slide him into X-ray."

Rearrangements were made. They stared at a computer screen.

"X-ray of the body shows a broken cervix. The neck was broken when he was strangled."

Sean stared up at the Beckett museum.

Katie looked at her brother, and then the old Victorian mansion.

There was something forlorn about it today. Craig had loved the place. He had believed that he had found a way to preserve a history he loved. He'd been such a good and decent man, and she had really loved him. What was the future for the museum? The oddities museum down the street was already back up and running.

"Hate the place. Hate it," Sean said, looking at her.

"It's a beautiful old house," Katie said.

"You don't remember everything that happened as clearly as I do," Sean said. "David had been my friend. Tanya and Sam . . . they'd been friends. Everything fell apart. Craig Beckett was never the same. David left, the Barnards left."

"People move on, no matter what," Katie said.

"Maybe I hate it most because David had been my friend. Did I back away from him?" Sean said.

"We were kids," she reminded him. She smiled, touching her brother's shoulder. "Maybe you actually learned from it, and became a stronger person?"

He laughed. "All righty, Katie-oke. Let's do this thing."

Katie tried the door, remembering how it had been unopened the night she had come to find David here. What a fool she had been, walking right in. Bartholomew had warned her. But she hadn't believed at the time that such a heinous crime could come back to haunt Key West again, in the way that it had. She had been worried about a commercial venture, which seemed silly and so long ago already!

Today, the door was securely locked; both bolts were secured. But her keys worked, and within seconds, they stepped into the entry.

Sunlight gleamed in. From the stairway,

Hemingway looked down at them both, as if they were intruders on a secret party that raged when the doors were closed.

"Where are the keys?" Sean asked.

"Desk. Third drawer."

He leapt over the turnstile and pulled open the third drawer. Katie leapt the stile and stood behind him, looking around. Sunlight couldn't penetrate the whole house. She was pretty sure that David still kept auxiliary lights in the floor, but they were on a timer.

Now, with the sun falling but not quite down, the place was cast in a strange shadow. It was somehow disturbing. Through the door to her left, she could see a number of the displays.

She had never been afraid or uneasy in the museum. Even knowing its history.

The figures were frozen in place.

And yet, in the ghost shadow of the house, it seemed that they might move at any minute.

And, if she were to move into the hallway, she knew what exhibit she would come to. That of the Otto family, Artist House and Robert the Doll.

She didn't want to look through the doorway that led to the exhibit. Danny had been found in an effigy of Robert the Doll.

She had to look. She had to make sure that the little robotic was standing right where he should have been.

He was.

Sean was oblivious to her.

"What's the matter with David? Sending us on a wild-goose chase. They're not here," Sean said.

"Of course they are. He wouldn't have told us to come if the keys weren't here," Katie said. "Oh, hell. It's already heading toward sunset. I'm not going to have any time to read anything if we don't hurry. I'm supposed to be at work soon."

"Okay, where did he say — exactly — that they were?" Sean said.

"The third drawer, under the old guide-books," Katie said. "He was certain of it."

"They're not here," Sean said.

Bartholomew had followed them in. "Impatient fellow, your brother."

Katie sighed. "You, chill," she said to Sean. "And, you! You just hush up," she said to Bartholomew.

"Great. Your ghost is still with us?" Sean asked.

"Tell him that I'm learning to work a razor. I'll shave his hair right off his head next time," Bartholomew said.

"Bartholomew is with us, yes," Katie said.

461

"And David might have been wrong, or mistaken. Try the second drawer. Never mind, move. I'll find the keys. I don't mind messing anything up here. I was already in here with Liam," Katie said.

She glanced up as she started rummaging through the drawers. Sunset was coming, and it was causing the light to play tricks.

It looked as if something was moving.

Something . . . a ghost shadow, in that first exhibit where Robert the Doll and the Otto family reigned supreme.

"Katie, you need to get out of here!" Bartholomew said.

"What the hell is that?" Sean demanded.

"Sean, let's just go," Katie said.

But Sean didn't heed her warning. "Katie, call the cops," he said. He started toward the exhibit.

"Sean, no, let's just get out of here!" Katie pleaded.

"Whoever the hell you are," Sean yelled angrily, his voice loud and deep, "show yourself. Come on out — you're breaking and entering and the cops are on the way."

Katie had dropped her purse when she'd started rifling through the drawers. She reached for it, couldn't find her cell phone and dumped the contents on the desk.

"Sean!" she called.

Bartholomew swore; she saw the ghost go striding after her brother.

Sean became shadow, walking through the doorway to the Otto family tableau.

She found her phone. Her fingers curled around it. She keyed in 911, and to her dismay, got a busy signal. "Fuck! Fuck, fuck, fuck!"

She searched her entries and found Pete Dryer's cell number and punched it in. There was no answer.

"Son of a bitch!" Sean roared.

"Pete, Pete, it's Katie O'Hara, I'm in the old Beckett museum, and there's someone in here. Please, please get this, and come quickly!"

Sean let out an oath, and then it seemed as if the world exploded. The sounds of breaking glass, thumping, crashes, came shrieking out at her.

"Sean!"

Katie grabbed a paperweight from the desk, and went tearing in after her brother.

They were in the car, driving back to town. David turned to Liam.

"The killer is playing with Key West legend. He's someone that history means a great deal to. He's fascinated by all the legends." He was quiet for a minute. "You don't know anyone named Smith, do you?"

Liam laughed. "Smith? In my life, I'm sure I've met a number of people named Smith. And Gonzalez, Rodriguez, Jones . . . and I even know a pack of O'Haras, none of them related."

"Okay, Liam. I believe that Tanya was murdered to hurt our family. So, there is someone out there who is carrying a grudge. And it seems to be a grudge that's hundreds of years old. Okay, first off, think about it. It couldn't be Sanderson to begin with — he was a tourist. He didn't know the Elena legend, he didn't know our family. He was an outsider."

"An outsider with an alibi," Liam reminded him.

"All right, as odd as it may sound then — Sam Barnard."

"Tanya's own brother?"

"He knew the island like the back of his hand. Knew all the legends. He admits that he saw Tanya the night that she was killed. He admits that they argued. He told me that he was angry with her for acting like a flirt — a tramp. And maybe it even went deeper. Damn it! If we'd just found Danny alive, he might have known something. He had the books, and the money. Lord, here's what it has to be — the killer read something sometime, during his life that ticked him off about the Becketts. Maybe he's like a functioning psycho. I believed from the time I came back here that the murder wasn't random. Think about it. Stella Martin winds up dead. The method of death didn't change. Danny winds up dead. Danny is small, but still, he might have put up a fight. Get him from behind. Smother him. Strangle him. And then here's the piece that makes it the same — he is found in a giant effigy of Robert the Doll. Who else knows these legends and stories better than anyone else? A local. And when violence happens, don't the police look at family members first?"

"All right, so what do I do? Well, I'll give your reasoning to the team, of course," Liam said. "But there's the thing — we still don't have a shred of physical evidence."

"I know. And I'm not certain. I think I will be — if I just get through those books," David said. "Maybe, by the time we get there, Katie will have found something. Maybe she's already found something," he said. He pulled out his phone and called Katie's cell. It went directly to voice mail. He swore softly.

"What?"

"She's either talking, or she never charged

her battery," David said.

He was already dialing again.

"Sean?" Liam asked.

David nodded. But Sean's phone rang and rang — and went to voice mail.

"Hurry," David told Liam.

"Hell, this isn't a sci-fi car, even if I have a siren!" Liam said. "I can't fly over those other cars."

"Put the siren on, do your best. Hey, have someone get over to Katie's house, and to my place, Liam. Please. Have them do it now."

There were figures tussling on the floor. Sean. And someone else. Someone else big and brawny, rolling with Sean. She heard a whack — a fist connecting with flesh. She heard another whack.

Robert the Doll stood in place, looking at her with his ugly face and beady eyes. She looked beyond him to the small-scale model of Artist House.

"Bastard! Asshole!" Sean raged. "The cops are on the way, you idiot!"

For a moment, one of the shadow figures rose high above the other. He turned blindly, heading toward the archway that lead to the next exhibit.

"Hey!" Sean roared, making it to his feet.

Ahead of him, as if he had hit a wall that wasn't there, the big shadow figure suddenly fell back to the ground.

"Sean, stop it, let him go!" Katie cried.

The figure crawled to its feet, then doubled over and came at Sean like a bull. Katie heard the sickening thud as they met. Her brother went down with the lug on top of him. Katie found a piece of wood that had been used to construct the miniature of Artist House.

She wrenched it free, and brought it down with all her strength on the back of the man on top of her brother.

He bellowed in pain, rose and staggered toward her.

She held the wood, and whacked him again, as hard as she could, across the shoulder.

Sean was up, hurrying toward her.

Light suddenly flickered in from a car passing by on the street.

It was Sam. Sam Barnard. And he was stumbling toward her now with the ceaseless drive of a zombie, his face frozen into a mask of anger.

"Stop!"

Sam lunged for her. She tried to back up; she crashed against the Artist House miniature and fell flat back on the floor.

467

Sam came down on her.

She screamed.

Robert the Doll looked down at her with malign eyes.

Sean was on top of Sam next, dragging him off her. He straddled over Sam, punched him, and punched him again.

"Stop!" Sam screamed. "Stop!"

"You murdering bastard!" Sean raged.

"No, no, no! I didn't murder anyone," Sam said. "I swear, I swear. I just came here . . . because I had to come here. Tanya was killed. That whore was killed. And now Danny!"

"Right. You were just sneaking around in here," Sean said.

"You're breaking my ribs, Sean, please, get up," Sam said.

"No. The cops are coming, right, Katie?"

"Yes," she said. She didn't really know if they were coming or not. She was struggling up from the broken pieces of the Artist House.

Pete would come. For the moment, though, they were in the house, alone, with Sam. And she didn't know for the life of her if he was telling the truth or not!

"I'll help you up," Bartholomew said. "Hey, did you like that stop? Did you see it? Don't tell me you didn't see it. I stopped him like a brick wall."

"I saw it," she assured Bartholomew. He had extended his hand. She took it, not expecting much real help. But she could feel him — she could actually *feel* him, as she got to her feet.

"What's she doing, who's she talking to?" Sam cried out, as if he were in mortal terror.

"My sister talks to ghosts," Sean said, eyes widening, waving his arms in the air. "And guess what, asshole? The ghosts aren't saying good things about you."

"What?" Sam cried.

"The spirits are assembling!" Sean said.

"Sean!" Katie protested, stunned. But Sam was scared. It was the place, it was her brother's fury. Maybe it was a combination.

"I didn't do anything wrong!" Sam swore. "Yeah, all right, I broke in here, but I just needed to see the place. I needed to see the place again where my sister died."

There was something forming in the shadows behind Sam and her brother. The two were still talking, but Katie didn't hear them.

It was Danny. Danny Zigler. And once again, just as in her dream, the girls were with him. Tanya and Stella. They flanked him, looking over at her with sorrowful expressions.

Danny pointed upward. She frowned, and realized that he was referring to the exhibits above them. She thought briefly, and she knew which tableau stood right above them, on the second floor.

The hanging tree.

They heard the door open.

"What the hell is going on in here?" Pete Dryer demanded in his husky, authoritative voice.

"Thank God!" Sean breathed. "Pete, we found this bastard lurking around in here," Sean said.

"Is that a fact?" Pete demanded. "What are you, some kind of a sicko? You killed your own sister, and now you're back at the scene of the crime?"

"No!" Sam cried out. "Get this jerk off me, for God's sake."

Sean stood. Pete pulled out his cuffs. "Time to pay the piper, you little snot-nose creep!" Pete said.

Pete was here. It was all under control.

"Whether he killed anyone or not, Pete, he was breaking and entering here," Katie said.

"Oh, what, it's your place because you're sleeping with Beckett?" Sam demanded. "That asshole — my sister dies over him and he's still out there poking everything in a skirt!"

Katie ignored him. "I have to run upstairs for just a minute. It's important. Pete, you've got Sam, right? Sean, you can fill Pete in? I'll be right back."

She didn't give them a chance to answer. Danny was beckoning, and he looked worried, as if speed might be of the essence.

"I'm calling it in," Pete said, "but I'll drag the little goon in myself. Tell me exactly what happened, Sean."

"Katie, what the hell . . . ?" Sean demanded angrily.

"I'll be right back down!" she swore.

She wasn't afraid. Her brother was there, and Pete had Sam Barnard — he'd be cuffed any minute, and safe.

She came out upstairs. The auxiliary lights had come on, giving her a footpath to follow. In the very strange orange-and-purple light that filtered in from the sky of the dying day, figures rose all around her. Pirates, smugglers, scalawags. Navy men and soldiers, Union soldiers, Confederate soldiers. They posed, ready to speak, ready to move.

She made her way to the hanging tree.

The figure there was posed with its back to her as it dangled from the tree. She stepped up. There was a large plaque on the floor, noting the tree, telling its present location, stating its grim utility as a means of execution.

On the wall, closer to the exhibit, was a small handwritten explanation. Craig Beckett had lovingly written up small wall plaques when the place had been younger, when no velvet ropes had barred visitors from getting too close.

"The hanging of Eli Smith," the plaque read. "Justice was hard; another man hanged for his crimes, lynched by a mob. But truth caught up with a reckless killer."

Underneath it Craig Beckett had noted that Smith still had descendants living in the city today. He had left behind a daughter.

The cursive handwriting was difficult to read. Katie leaned closer.

As she did so, there was a tremendous thud from down below.

The auxiliary lights went out.

As they did so, her mind comprehended Craig's cursive handwriting, and she gasped as the room fell into a shadow land of darkness.

She knew the killer.

And she knew he was in the museum with her.

He already had Sean.

17

"Everything is fine," Liam assured David, snapping his phone shut.

"What the hell do you mean, fine?"

"I guess there was some trouble — and that you might have been right."

"What?"

"Sam Barnard was at the museum. Sean and Katie heard him, and there was a major tussle, I guess between Sam and Sean. But Katie had gotten through to Pete Dryer and he arrested Sam. Katie might have lost her phone, what with everything going on. Anyway, she's supposed to be at work now. Should I leave you there?"

"Yeah. You're sure everything is all right?"

"The lieutenant called it in. He had it under control," Liam said. "Look, I'll leave you at the bar, and I'll head to Katie's house, and then, if she's not working or at her place, I'll meet up with you at Craig's place. Your place. Whatever."

"All right, thanks," David said.

He didn't know why. He'd been the one pointing out all the reasons that it had to have been Sam Barnard. But was it?

Liam let him off before reaching the insanity of Duval Street. David turned the corner and headed into O'Hara's. Katie had not set up.

He found Clarinda and caught her by the arm. "Katie, where's Katie?" he demanded.

"She hasn't come in yet." Clarinda's eyes widened. "She isn't with you?"

"She's with Sean. She was with Sean."

"Jamie just sent Jonas to the house. She hasn't answered her phone, and neither has Sean. Jamie is breathing fire," Clarinda said. "Oh, my God! Has something happened?"

"I'm heading to my house. If she shows up here, call me immediately. Screw Jamie and every customer in this place, Clarinda, and call me!"

"Oh, my God, David, you're scaring the hell out of me!" Clarinda said.

"Just call me!"

He didn't have time to reassure Clarinda, not when suddenly he was so convinced that he didn't have time. He left the bar, and ran down the backstreets. A drunken party of six swaggered by him, almost knocking him over. A woman, in ridiculously high heels, staggered and caught his arm.

"Cool, thanks . . . Hey, help us along there, shoulders, will ya?" she asked.

He pressed her onto the nearest man; if they all fell flat on their faces, so be it.

He hopped a hedge to race across the lawn and up the porch steps of his house. He inserted the key in the lock, and twisted it. He reached inside to flick on the lights.

The electricity was out.

Her heard movement in the bushes and swung around. Liam.

"What's going on?" Liam asked.

"Electric."

Liam swore. He reached for his phone. David stopped him. "If he has them, they might still be alive. No alarms."

Liam nodded. He drew his service revolver and they went into the house. "Fuse box?" Liam asked.

David nodded. "I can see — I can see enough."

He went up the stairs and made a hurried sweep of the house. He came back down the stairs and went into the dining room.

The books lay on the table, undisturbed.

He turned to go back and look for his cousin.

But he was shoved. Shoved, back toward the table.

He swung around, ready to fight, ready to survive. There was no one there.

He was shoved toward the table again.

The top book flew open.

He drew out a penlight and threw the glow onto the page. He looked at it, puzzled. It was a family tree. He turned the page.

The paper nearly ripped as the page turned back.

"What? What?" he demanded aloud. The book offered a host of pages of old names, the kind of names the streets had taken on in honor of early residents, and names of those who had gone before and not been honored.

He studied the page again that the unseen entity wanted him to read. The headline read, Smith.

He ran his fingers down the page, following the descendants through the ages, births, marriages and deaths.

He swore aloud as Liam came back into the house. "Search this place, top to bottom!" he told him. "Get someone here, Liam, quickly, for the love of God!"

David burst out into the night and started running.

Katie was stunned as she heard movement — real movement — behind her. She blinked, trying to adjust to the slim filter of outside light that made its way in.

She longed to cry out; she was terrified for Sean. Tears stung her eyes.

She couldn't cry out. She had to find Sean in silence.

A noise startled her.

She swung around. It was as if the museum had been activated. Next to the hanging tree, military ruler Porter waved a broadside that promised death to all pirates. His arms were jerking spasmodically. His jaw jerked and there was an awful moment when he talked without sound.

Then a bad recording came on. Rasping and hollow. "Death . . . death . . . death . . . to . . . to . . . all . . . all . . . all . . . pirates!"

She moved quickly by Porter, only to crash into a tall robotic of a wrecker.

"Storm! Storrrrm . . . warning. First ta' reach her, salvage is mine . . . mine . . . mine . . . mine."

She had to stay calm. She couldn't heed the jerky movements or the eerie voices of the robotics. When she moved again, a sailor with the insignia for the *Maine* seemed to leap ahead of her in her path. He hadn't moved. She was terrified, and she knew that someone had hit the mechanization that Craig Beckett made.

They were just robotics. Just robotics coming to mechanical life. She had to ignore them.

She had to get downstairs to Sean.

She started to walk again, and then she heard stealthy movement. Not a robotic.

Someone was stalking her in the darkness. She made her way carefully then, letting the robotics talk and move, and using them for cover.

She came to the robotic of Ernest Hemingway. He jerked and spoke, complaining about his wife, Pauline. He said, in grating and broken words, that he'd set a penny into his patio — because his wife had certainly taken his very last penny. Katie slipped by him, glad of the noise he was making, and headed down the servants' stairs to the exhibits below.

She paused, having reached the first floor. She was going to have to sneak across the open entryway to get to the left bank of rooms if she didn't go through the pantry corridor in the back.

She didn't want to go through the pantry corridor; it was too narrow. If there was someone there, that someone could too easily nail her.

As she hesitated, she heard a strange whooshing noise, and, at first, she thought one of the robotics was speaking in a rusty voice once again.

"You . . . you . . . you . . . you . . . you. You are going to die. Come out, come out, wherever you are! We're locked in, and your poor brother! Paying for the fact that you had to sleep with a Beckett!"

She froze. The voice was near. But from which direction?

She streaked out from the passage beneath the stairway and raced over to the left hall of exhibits where she had left her brother. She burst in on Robert the Doll. In silence, he was jerking back and forth on his stand.

She nearly tripped over a body. She hunched down. It was Sam Barnard. He was wearing handcuffs, and when she gingerly touched him, she discovered a plastic bag wound tightly around his head. With trembling fingers, she ripped it away from him.

"Katie!"

The whisper was Bartholomew's. His hands were on her shoulders. He motioned her to silence, but beckoned her to follow him.

Her brother was stretched out in the facsimile of the cemetery, where the servicemen from the *Maine* were buried and honored. A bag was on his head; it wasn't tightened. She ripped it away from him, and lay against him, desperate to hear his breathing.

He had a pulse. There was a gash on his head; she knew from the stickiness beneath her fingers when she touched him.

"Oh, God!" she prayed in a breath.

"Katie!" Bartholomew warned her again.

"You . . . you . . . you . . . you . . . you . . . are dead!" The words were followed by laughter. She tried to rise carefully, to start to move.

"Katie, the other way!" Bartholomew urged her.

Too late. She ducked to avoid a nineteen-twenties flapper, and crashed right into the wall of a big man's chest.

He reached for her. He was wearing gloves. The gloves he had always known to wear. Diver's gloves, so plentiful in the Keys!

His hands wound around her neck. She struggled.

He winced and jerked suddenly, as if he'd been hit from behind.

Katie took the moment. She pushed against him and bit his arm, bit as hard as she could. She clawed at his flesh.

If she died, which well she might, the bastard wasn't getting away with it again.

Nor would he blame David Beckett.

"Bitch!" he roared.

His huge hand came flying across her cheek. The blow was stunning; she felt it with her jaw and head, stars sprung up before her eyes.

And then a darkness deeper than any she had ever imagined.

David slowed when he reached the lawn of the museum. Any alarm now would cost Katie her life, and he knew it. He had to believe that he had a chance. That the killer was determined to tease and taunt her before ending it. He wondered if she was meant to be his finest work. Katie O'Hara, so well-known and beloved in Key West. Beautiful, and a songstress. With a family as old and renowned as his own.

And Sean was in there, somewhere.

The door hadn't been locked. It remained open. He couldn't be sure how the killer would act and react, and he was certain that Liam would turn the house upside down. But he had to hurry — if sirens suddenly riddled the streets, if he knew that time was nearly up, the killer would work faster.

The killer had made a mistake. He wouldn't be able to cast suspicion on David or anyone else. But David thought that he was so overconfident now in his quest for some kind of belated family vengeance that he wouldn't believe that. He would still believe himself invincible.

And he would have taken care.

David didn't enter right away. He stared at the floor behind the doorway. It took him a moment, and then he saw it. A trip wire. Somehow it would alert the killer that he was here.

His eyes had attuned well to darkness. He paused for just a moment at the entry, then leapt the turnstile as silently as he could. He hurried toward the left hall.

There was a body on the floor. Heart in his throat, he hurried to it.

Sam Barnard. David checked for a pulse. The man was breathing.

"Ch-cha-cha-Charleston!" A flapper warbled out in a gritty voice.

David jerked around. There was movement. He hadn't intended to ever have these robotics work; he'd have brought in some experts and gotten them off to good homes elsewhere.

But tonight, they had a life of their own.

They'd been activated to hide other noises in the museum. They had been turned on to scare and frighten, and distract.

He wouldn't be distracted. But he had to be very careful. He knew where the killer was. And he knew that the killer would be waiting for him.

Hurriedly, he searched the room, but he could only find Sam Barnard. He silently swore to the unconscious man that he would arrange for an ambulance the second he could. Once he had found Sean. And Katie. Katie . . .

Alive. She had to be alive!

He thanked God that he was good in darkness, and silence. He started through the museum. The killer would be waiting. He prayed that there was a way to surprise him.

Katie felt a stunning pain in her head. She blinked, and the world was still a realm of murky darkness — with odd, milky shapes blurring her vision.

She tried to move, and she could not. She tried to twist around, and she realized that she was strapped to a table.

She was covered in . . .

White. White. A white wedding dress.

She was wearing a wedding dress and veil, and she was strapped down on the slab that was a bed in the Elena de Hoyos exhibit in the museum.

Terror streaked through her, filling her with horror and panic. She almost squirmed; she would have screamed in hysteria if it hadn't been for the gag in her mouth and the tape over it.

"Katie, Katie O'Hara!"

She was more horrified as she heard the crooning voice. For a moment, things seemed to jiggle above her, and then come into focus.

Pete. Lieutenant Peter Dryer. Of course. They'd been so stupid.

Who knew the families? Who could get keys to houses and museums? Who could be at any crime scene, and be expected?

Who had been the great-great-great-grandson of a man named Smith, Smith who had left behind a daughter who had married an immigrant named Dryer?

"Oh, Katie, I've saved the best for you. There's a trip cord there, by the door. When David Beckett comes to save you, he'll pull the wire. So cleverly planned. See — well, you can't really see, so I'll explain. I have your brother all trussed up and dressed like Carl Tanzler. All right, all right, so you saved your brother once! But I'm very good, and I can change my plans, and I really like this. I like this so much. Tanzler! Ha-ha. Sure, sure, Sean is young and much, much better looking, but . . . He's got himself a syringe full of embalming fluid and other toxins, and if I've got this right, he'll plunge them right into your heart when David enters. Then, of course, I'll shoot the bastard for what he's done to you. At first, I thought about letting him squirm in prison, but there are so many appeals, and hell, this is Key West, and the State of Florida considers us their wacky tailpiece to begin with. He might not get the death penalty. So! Old Key West justice. He dies here on the spot."

She shook her head, unable to speak.

He fixed that for her, ripping off the gauze, jerking out the gag. It was horrible. She thought that she would choke.

She opened her mouth to scream, "David! It's a trap!"

"Ah, loverboy isn't here yet," Pete said. "You can scream for a moment. Oh, yes, and it's so good, so damned good! See what I did for your brother? He is a fine, strapping lad! Had that Sam Barnard down for me, and in a lock. Held him while I handcuffed him. And didn't blink until I crushed his skull with the butt of my gun! There you go. Even the big and powerful fall to knowledge and careful planning. Remember that. Ah, well, you won't really need to remember it long."

"You're a cop!" she told him.

"A good one. But you have to understand,

Katie. I thought that maybe you did. My ancestor cursed the Becketts. He was hanged — because of a Beckett."

"He was guilty!"

Pete shook his head. "Katie! You don't understand. Some vile pirate had already been hanged, and there was no reason that *my* ancestor should have died."

"He killed people."

"He had a right! We were meant for great things. Don't you understand anything? I had to get revenge on the Becketts for my family. For honor! I am the curse!"

"No! You're a cop!"

"Yes, yes, and such a good one. Katie, time has gone by — time has waited. For me! Don't go thinking I'm crazy, young lady. I have been on a mission. And David Beckett will finally pay the piper for his vile family. He should have been arrested and sent to the electric chair for Tanya — now that didn't really hurt much. She was a little tramp. I was only a patrolman at the time, but she was so tipsy. And it was so easy. She was walking on one of the side streets, pacing. I stopped to give her a ride. She got right in the car, and I said I'd take her to the museum, to see David. She looked out the window, and I was ready. I didn't even really know what I was doing then, but it was easy. I'd been prepared for the right moment, so I slipped that clean plastic over her head, and she had so much alcohol in her system . . . well, she went easy. Laid her out in back of the car . . . used the key to the museum I'd copied at least two or three months earlier, just waiting on ol' David to get back, Mr. Hero Serviceman! Then, after midnight, I had lots of time to set her up. Now, that Stella, she was just at the right place at the right time, and I was at the right place at the right time, and good ol' David was back in the city, thinking he could tear the case apart."

"Why did you let him?" Katie asked.

"Because I'm so damned good. With Stella, the city was rising. I just walked right up behind her while she was peeking through the bushes — afraid of the cops! Killed her — and left her there for hours. Who knows? Maybe folks even saw her and thought she was a drunk, sleeping it off. I went back for her, and hell, yes, missy, I had a copy of the key to that place, too — that shoddy new museum where I left Stella. Of course, I took the tapes from the surveillance cameras." He paused to chuckle. "I even called David Beckett to come see the crime scene."

"Danny," Katie whispered. At least he was

talking, at least she was playing for time.

"Danny, well, that saddened me," Pete said regretfully. "I thought I could bribe him to just stop playing around. He got interested in old curses and figured out that I was descended from Eli Smith. He thought that it was funny that the police lieutenant's ancestor was hanged for murder — funny! I tried to bribe him anonymously — couldn't work up enough anger to kill the guy and thought that a little money might satisfy him. It would have worked, too — Danny was never exactly what you'd call ambitious! But then he saw me with Stella and I knew that he would start to put the pieces together. Danny wasn't ambitious, but he wasn't stupid."

"He left the money and the books — that's why you took your time getting a search warrant for his apartment, right?"

"I knew I had to get in there first," Pete said.

"Why me?" she asked softly.

"Oh, Katie! Such a pretty, sweet thing! But he loves you, so . . . this is really the revenge I wanted. With Tanya, it was perfect — he had motive, he was young, he was big, he should have been angry. There's motive for you! And . . . he cared about her, but not the way he cares about you. That's too perfect. That's real revenge!"

"Pete, Pete, think, you're a cop, they'll know it was you now!"

He laughed. "I'm a cop, yes. And that's the point. We've come full circle from the hanging tree, and now it can all rest. The past will really be avenged. And as to my position, it's perfect. And I am the best! I've served this city. I've been firm, and I've been fair. I've taken down some of the biggest drug lords to darken our door. And now, my life will be purged. Now, once Beckett is dead and he's history — a vicious killer brought down by the descendant of the man he wronged — I'll make history myself. I'll take the chief's place in a few years. And, in time, I'll run for office. I'll be governor, you'll see. My life is bigger than this small island. It's my destiny to carry out the curse. That's how powerful I really am!"

He was serious. Dead serious. That was perhaps the most terrifying aspect of it all. He believed that he had been wronged. He probably had been a good cop — other than being a psycho murderer.

"Why are you hurting my brother?" she asked.

"Katie O'Hara! You don't know your history. Your brother's death adds so much to all this. Don't you know? Oh, please, you might have guessed. An O'Hara was on the jury that denounced my ancestor, did you know that? An O'Hara helped deliver a death sentence. So, well, I just hadn't expected quite this much justice, but it's all fallen in nicely." He lifted her head for her, twisting it so that she could see clearly.

She winced, trying not to cry out.

Sean looked like an oversize doll. He'd been set up in a stand. He was lolled against it, still unconscious. He was wearing Tanzler's hat. Sean was tall and broad-shouldered. It must have irritated Pete that he couldn't possibly shove Sean into Carl Tanzler's much smaller clothing.

"Katie!"

She heard the soft whisper. Bartholomew was standing by her side. Behind him she could see Danny, Stella and Tanya.

"We're trying, Katie. Work your left wrist. We're trying . . . we're trying."

She smiled. Her head was killing her.

She wondered if she was going to join them soon.

Suddenly, something flew across the room and crashed against the wall. Pete Dryer spun around, his gun out. He fired shots into the wall, then he turned to face the dark corridor that led to the room.

"Beckett! I know that you're out there!"

Dryer warned. "Show yourself — or I'll shoot her in the kneecaps long before I put her out of her misery!"

"Oh, that will go unnoticed by law enforcement," David's voice called from the darkness beyond.

"You ass! I'll do it!" Pete said.

David moved into view. He didn't look at Katie. She was certain that he didn't dare.

She felt movement at her wrist. She twisted it. The tie was loosening.

"Shoot me, Pete — isn't that your plan?" David asked.

Pete raised his gun. "Yes, it is."

He fired.

But David wasn't there. There was a sound of exploding glass. Katie dimly realized that he had taken a mirror from one of the exhibits. Pete had shot at his reflection.

Something came flying into the room. It was a headstone from the *Maine* exhibit.

It caught Pete right in the chest, slamming him backward. She heard his gun fly — and crash into the floor.

Somewhere.

"Get up, Katie, get up!" Bartholomew urged her.

She wrenched her wrist free. Halfway up, she started tearing at the other tie herself.

"Don't! David, there's another —"

"Trip wire, I know!" he shouted back to her.

Pete Dryer made a dive for the gun. David leapt the wire, and went flying down for it himself. Pete was closer.

He almost reached it.

But someone else was there. Not Bartholomew. Not Tanya, or Stella.

She was Bartholomew's lady in white, the broken hearted Lucinda, and she used a foot that was clad in a delicate white slipper to send the gun sliding farther back in the room. Katie freed her hand and leapt from the table.

Pete staggered up, ready to fly for the gun again.

But David was in a fury. He tackled Pete, bringing him facedown on the floor, sending his nose, chin and forehead into a hard thud against the wood. He slammed the man's head down again, and again, then jerked up to his feet, and slid back down to reach the gun.

He caught it.

Pete staggered up. David had the gun on him.

Pete started to lunge, but wavered.

"Don't make me shoot you, Pete. Don't," David said.

Pete's nose was bleeding profusely. He was bleeding from a gash on his forehead. He smiled.

He didn't go for David, and he didn't go for the gun.

He made a dive for the trip wire.

"No!" David raged, flying after him.

"Get up, all the way!" Bartholomew screamed to Katie.

And she did so.

Just as her brother's trussed and propped-up arm came crashing down on the bed where she had lain. The sad marital bed of the long-dead Elena de Hoyos.

But it was empty.

And this time, David laid a punch into Pete Dryer with such a fierce anger that the man went down like a limp rag.

It would be a long while before he gained consciousness again.

Katie ran over to David, and threw herself into his arms. He held her against him as if she were as fragile as blown glass for a moment, then he crushed her to him and buried his head against her shoulder, trembling.

"Ambulances, we have to get ambulances out here!" Katie said.

David worked his mouth. "Liam," was all that he said. And then managed, "I'm sure they're on their way by now."

He was right. The night came alive with the sound of sirens.

Then a shout. "David! David, where the hell are you?" his cousin shouted.

"Up here!" David yelled in return. There was a clatter in the entry below as Pete Dryer's trip-wire sound alarm went off. There were footsteps hurrying up the stairs.

David was staring in the shadows over Katie's shoulder.

She spun around.

"Thank you," David said. "Thank you, all of you."

They were all there. Bartholomew, Danny, Stella and Tanya.

Bartholomew swept off his hat and bowed elegantly. "Ah, yes, well, I owed a debt of gratitude to the Becketts, you know. And the O'Haras."

Tanya's spirit stepped nimbly past Bartholomew. She came to David, and Katie. She touched their cheeks.

She faded as she did so.

Then Stella was gone.

Then Danny.

"Bartholomew!" Katie whispered.

He smiled. "Oh, I'm not going anywhere," he told her.

He stepped past them all, and Katie saw

that his lady in white, Lucinda, was waiting for him on the other side of the room. He took her hands in his own.

"Dear lady, what a lovely, feisty creature you've proven to be! Lucinda, I'm Bartholomew."

"David, Katie!" Liam was there, with officers behind him. The room became flooded with light. "Medics, get the medics up here!" he roared.

The worst of it all, to Sean, since they had all survived, was the humiliation.

Katie was released from the hospital in the early hours of the following morning.

Sean was not.

But Katie wasn't going to leave him.

He was bandaged in a massive turban, and though his skull hadn't been crushed, he had stitches that ranged over a large mass of it.

"I beat Sam practically to a pulp — did that bastard's work for him, and sat there like a sitting duck while he creamed me!" he told Katie and David from his hospital bed. Then he mused, "How the hell could he have been so damned crazy, and none of us known it?" he demanded, bewildered.

"I wonder how we didn't see so many of the clues staring us straight in the face,"

David told him. "And you did what you thought you had to do — you defended your sister. Sam appeared to be the real enemy. Who the hell could know?"

Sean nodded bleakly, and looked at his sister. "You saved our lives, Katie. We'd have died for sure if you hadn't kept us from suffocating in those bags."

Bartholomew was seated in the one big chair in the room while David stood and Katie perched on the end of her brother's bed.

He sniffed loudly. "Excuse me, but I do believe I get a little of the credit!"

"I'd hug you if I could," Katie told him.

"Almost — I'm getting there," Bartholomew said. "Look, you can all talk this out until you turn blue in the face. No one will ever be able to understand the human mind." He waved a hand in the air. "Liam is down at the station now, where he will be for hours on end, filling out paperwork, and filling in the gaps from all the statements that were taken last night." He pointed a finger at Katie. "You two — go home. Get rest. I'll be looking after Sean. Have you seen your brother's notes? He wants to get David in with him and start filming the shipwrecks of the Keys."

"That's marvelous! He'll stay home,"

Katie said.

"She's talking to herself again," Sean said.

"No, she's talking to Bartholomew," David corrected.

Sean's jaw dropped. He stared at his sister. Katie shrugged.

"You mean, you can see him, too?" Sean asked David.

David shook his head regretfully. "No — but I did see him, for a brief minute last night. He's real, and he's looking out for you."

Katie grinned, patting his leg. "Sean, cool. You're staying home!" she said.

Sean groaned. "My plans aren't really solidified yet," he said.

"You're going to ask David to work with you," Katie told him.

"Hey!" Sean protested.

"It's all right. I think it's a great plan," David said. He lifted a hand toward Katie. "We really do have to get some sleep." She stood to join him, glancing at Bartholomew.

"Get along now, you cute little kiddies," Bartholomew told her. "I'll be here, I swear."

Katie kissed her brother's cheek carefully. "We're a short drive away. Call if you need anything! I'll be back in the morning," she promised.

David shook Sean's hand. "Jamie is on his way up to spend some time with you. He'll be here soon."

"I'm all right. I'm really all right. I want to come home."

"They'll release you soon," David told him.

"Hey, David," Sean said.

"Yes?"

"You're really interested?"

"I'm really interested. My *intentions* are not to leave home for quite a while now," he said.

He took Katie's hand and they left the hospital room. Katie peeked in on Sam, but his nurse said that he was resting comfortably, so they tiptoed away.

In the car, Katie was silent for a while.

"I heard you talking in the kitchen when I woke up," she told him.

He glanced her way. "Yes, you did."

"You were talking to?"

"Bartholomew, of course."

"But —"

"I don't see him. I can hear him."

"Oh. What was he saying to you?"

"Ah. Well, they've gone on. Tanya, Stella and Danny."

"I'm so sorry for all of them."

"Well, Stella and Danny were together."

"Poor Tanya."

"I don't know. Some people believe that we forget about the ones that were most important to us in this life. I don't believe that. We don't forget those who mean everything to us here."

"You sound sure."

"I am," he told her.

"Why?"

He looked over at her, a slanted smile cutting his features.

"Because love is our finest human emotion," he said. "And losing it is the true depths of hell."

"That's lovely," she said.

He pulled off the road suddenly, turned to her and took her hands. "Katie, I know that I've barely had time to really get to know you, for you to have time to know the real me. Your brother asked me my intentions. Well, my intentions are to stay here. To be with you. And, I'm thinking, when the time is right, when you're sure . . . well, then, my intentions become absolutely old-fashioned and honorable. I want to marry you. I want to raise a family — and live happily ever after, of course."

"Ah!" she said.

"Ah?"

She leaned over and kissed him.

"I do know you," she said softly. "And I already know that my life without you would be hell. So — ah! I love you. And yes."

"Yes?"

"Yes, I'll marry you!"

He smiled.

They drove on home.

And that day, as they turned onto Katie's street, it seemed only right that the angel parade was going on, and that fireworks went off as well, down at Mallory Square, just as they pulled into the drive.

They stood by the car, watching the lights in the sky.

David pulled her close.

"Home," he said.

And so they were.

KEY LIME PIE

Key lime pie is extremely popular in Key West and the Keys because — well, of course, it's made with Key limes! Floridians can be extremely picky about the dish, and they can even feel a bit haughty over knowing what a real Key lime pie should taste like. This pie should pass anyone's test.

Ingredients

The pie shell
16 graham crackers, crushed
3 tablespoons sugar
1 cube (1/4 lb) margarine or butter

Pie
4 large or extra-large egg yolks
1 14-ounce can sweetened condensed milk
1/2 cup fresh Key lime juice (ten to twelve limes)

No meringue!

But if you want a topping, go for real whipped cream.

Whipped cream for garnish
1/2 cup whipping cream
2 teaspoons granulated sugar
1/4 teaspoon vanilla

Start with your crust
Mix the ingredients and press them into a 9″ pie plate. Preheat the oven to 350°F, and then bake the crust until it is just lightly browned — about 15–20 minutes. Let it cool.

Pie filling
With an electric mixer, beat the egg yolks until they are a pale yellow and thick. Slowly add the condensed milk, adding it in bit by bit. Again, on a low speed and slowly, add the lime juice. When it's all blended, fill the pie crust, and bake for about 12 minutes — at 350°F. Don't under-cook (salmonella!) but don't overcook. Make sure oven temperature is right.

Whip up the whipped cream! Dollop on top! A cherry is always lovely on top of the whipped cream, or a curl of the Key lime!

Some people add shredded pieces of the lime skin to the filling mix, but I prefer an even texture. Either way, that's a "real" Key lime pie!

ABOUT THE AUTHOR

Heather Graham is a *New York Times* bestselling author of over 100 titles, including anthologies and short stories. She has been published in more than 15 languages and has over 20 million copies of her books in print.

The employees of Thorndike Press hope you have enjoyed this Large Print book. All our Thorndike, Wheeler, and Kennebec Large Print titles are designed for easy reading, and all our books are made to last. Other Thorndike Press Large Print books are available at your library, through selected bookstores, or directly from us.

For information about titles, please call:
  (800) 223-1244

or visit our Web site at:
  http://gale.cengage.com/thorndike

To share your comments, please write:
  Publisher
  Thorndike Press
  295 Kennedy Memorial Drive
  Waterville, ME 04901